That Night in Paris

Sandy Barker

OneMoreChapter

One More Chapter
a division of HarperCollins*Publishers*
The News Building
1 London Bridge Street
London SE1 9GF

www.harpercollins.co.uk

This paperback edition 2020

First published in Great Britain in ebook format by
HarperCollins*Publishers* 2020

A catalogue record for this book
is available from the British Library

ISBN: 9780008362843

Set in Birka by Palimpsest Book Production Ltd, Falkirk
Stirlingshire

Printed and bound in Great Britain by
CPI Group (UK) Ltd, Croydon CR0 4YY

For my dear darling adorable little sister, Vic.

Chapter 1

"I have completely cocked things up."

"Hello to you, too." My sister, Sarah, peered out from my iPad, her nose bigger than it was in real life.

"Sorry, *hello*," I retorted. We were sisters and best friends—couldn't we skip niceties in a crisis? And this *was* a crisis.

"So, how have you cocked things up?" she asked as the screen turned white.

"Sez, have you put me down?"

"Oh, yes." Her face hovered over the screen. "I'm folding the washing." She'd put her iPad face up on the bed, giving me a lovely view of her ceiling. "Sorry," she added, her face moving out of frame again.

"It's fine. Don't worry."

"So, you, cocking things up—go," she prompted again.

"I slept with Alex."

Her face reappeared as she righted the iPad and stared at me, a questioning crease between her brows. "Sorry, what? Alex?"

"My flatmate," I answered flatly.

"Oooh, Alex. So, he does exist." She grinned, obviously pleased with herself.

1

"Ha ha, very funny." Sarah had stayed with me after her trip to Greece a couple of months before. She'd met my flatmate, Jane, but Alex hadn't been around that week, so Sarah thought it was hilarious to joke that he wasn't real. Believe me—and my lady parts—he was real.

"So, what happened?" She abandoned her washing and propped herself up against her bedhead, settling in for the duration.

I snuggled amongst the throw pillows on the sofa, also settling in. It had been two days and fourteen hours since The Incident (note the capital letters), but it was the first time I'd been alone in the flat and my first opportunity for a proper sister debrief. Until that moment, I'd been lying low in what I'd like to think was an impressive display of both restraint and stealth.

"Well, it's nothing you haven't heard before—the usual stuff really. Jane went out. Alex and I stayed in. We ordered Indian takeaway and opened a bottle or two of wine, *aaand* we ended up having drunken sex on the sofa." She made a face. "What?"

"The one I slept on?" She looked like she'd smelled someone else's fart.

"Yes, Sarah, *that* one. The sofa I am currently sitting on. It's not like we had sex and *then* you had to sleep on it. You were here *ages* ago. Besides, we cleaned up afterwards." Her grimace intensified. "Look, you're focusing on the wrong thing."

"Sorry," she said. I waved off the apology. "Well, how was it?"

"What?"

2

"The sex."

"It was *drunken sofa sex*. How do you *think* it was?"

"Oh-*kay*. So, what now?"

It was a good question. What I had wanted to happen was absolutely nothing. I'd wanted to wake up the next day, make our usual pleasantries over tea and coffee and get on with my life. What I *didn't* want was Alex making goo-goo eyes at me over the toaster, then professing his long-held and undying love for me.

Yes, that really happened.

"Well, we each went back to our rooms and I fell into a wine-induced coma. When I woke up, he was waiting for me in the kitchen with a cup of tea and a weird look on his face. I took the tea and he launched into a monologue about being in love with me—how he's always hoped something would happen between us, and that he wants me to meet his mum."

Sarah's eyes widened and her mouth hung open a little. It was the exact same reaction I'd had in the kitchen two days before. Her face contorted. "Fuuuuuck," she said slowly. I hadn't realised how much you could drag that word out.

"That's what *I* thought—*think*. Yes, I still think that."

"So, I'm guessing you don't feel the same way?"

I snorted in reply. I couldn't help it—totally involuntary. "*Alex?*" I asked, as though his name alone was enough to convey how ridiculous her question was. Of course, my audience of one had never met Alex, so how was she to know? The left side of her mouth pulled taut. Bollocks, that had definitely come out snarky. "Sorry," I muttered. She shrugged, instantly forgiving me—one of the things I loved about my sister.

"It's just that, yes, I mean, he's cute in a British sort-of podgy, floppy-haired, Andrew Garfield kind of way, but I don't really *fancy* him. Plus, he's nice enough, but he's *so* dull. He only ever talks about his work—boring as anything—and his latest obsession—get this, virtual reality. He's even kitted out his room with a whole set-up since you were here."

"Oh, wow. That sounds cool."

"Are you paying attention? It's not. Besides, I tried it. It made me sick."

"Oh."

"Anyway, I've been hiding from him."

"So, how's *that* going?"

"So far, so good. Although I had a near miss with him last night when I got up to go to the loo." I could see the smirk tugging at the corners of her mouth and watched her succumb to laughter. My giggles followed soon after.

"You're a dork," she said, her laugh subsiding.

"Yes, thank you, I know."

"So, what's your long-term plan? You going to keep skulking about your flat, hoping you don't cross paths on the way to brush your teeth?" I could tell she was enjoying herself.

"Actually, no. I've booked a tour."

She looked intrigued. "A tour?"

"Yep. For half-term. I leave on Saturday. It's, uh, well, it's a Ventureseek tour."

I let my reveal hang in the air.

Sarah had worked for Ventureseek ten years ago as a Tour

Manager. She'd shared all the glorious—and gory—details, and I had a pretty good idea what I was in for. What I didn't know was how she'd react.

Apparently, it would be blinking at me, her mouth opening and closing like a goldfish out of water. "I'm sorry, what? You're going on a Ventureseek?" She used the tour company's name like a common noun.

"Yes," I replied, sticking to my guns. I've never really understood that expression, by the way, and I'm an English teacher, but whatever metaphorical guns were, I was sticking to them. Besides, I'd just forked out eleven hundred non-refundable pounds.

Her brows furrowed. "But you said you'd never go on one of those tours. You specifically said, and I remember this clearly, they were for drunken hooligans and idiots who couldn't find their way around Europe by themselves. You said you'd never *ever* go on one—*ever*. You were quite clear about the 'ever' part."

"Yes, I know."

"So? What happened?"

"I panicked," I answered, half-resolute, half-defensive.

She was quiet for several moments, then shrugged. "Huh. Well, okay. So, you leave Saturday?"

"Yes."

"And which tour is it? I mean, how long?"

"Two weeks, fifteen countries, or something like that." She nodded, and I could see her mind at work.

"So, Paris, the *château*, Antibes, Florence, Rome, Venice, Lauterbrunnen, Koblenz, and Amsterdam. Right?" Damn, she was good. Ten years on and she still knew the itinerary of a two-week tour looping around Europe.

"Uh, yes, I think so. That sounds right." She nodded again. "Cool. You're gonna want to pack a few things that won't be on your list." Big Sister Sarah kicked in and I retrieved a pen and paper to take notes as she dictated. Insider info is the best.

Two days later, at a ridiculous hour of the morning—7:00am— I was standing on the footpath outside a large inner-London hotel amid the bustle of travellers lugging their luggage. Peering at my phone, I re-read the confirmation email for the tour, which included the tour code. I looked along the line of identical buses—I counted eight—and back at the tour code. How was I supposed to know which one was mine?

"Hi. Can I help?" said a friendly Australian voice to my left. I looked up to see a guy in his mid-twenties wearing a shirt with the Ventureseek logo embroidered on the pocket.

"Uh, yes, please. I'm not sure which bus I'm on. Here's my tour code." I showed him the screen of my phone and he read it, his head at an awkward angle.

He lifted his eyes to meet mine. "You're in luck. That's my tour. I'm the driver—Tom—and this is our coach." He indicated the closest bus and I made a mental note to call it a 'coach'. "Here, let me take that," he said, indicating my case. I passed over the handle and he expertly retracted it and slid the case into the hold under the bus—sorry, *coach*. When he turned around, he pointed to the leather messenger bag slung across my body. "That one stays with you."

"Oh, lovely. Thank you." The coach thing sorted, my mind leapt to caffeination—I am next-door-to-useless without my morning tea and it was excruciatingly early for a Saturday. "Uh, do you know where I can get a cup of tea?" I also needed a wee, but I wasn't about to tell him that.

"There's a café in there. It has decent tea." He pointed towards the hotel lobby, then checked his watch. "You've got about twenty-five minutes."

I had a sudden thought. "Oh, can I bring tea on the coach?" I said, prouder than I should have been for calling it by the right name.

"Of course! But if you spill, you'll be on coach-washing duties," he deadpanned. I wasn't sure if he was serious until the smile broke across his face. "Kidding, mate."

Several other people were now waiting for him to take their cases, so I skedaddled. I found the toilets, then got myself some tea and a giant gooey brownie. I am not usually a cake-for-breakfast person, but my only other choices were a ham and tomato sandwich, which had seen better days, or a floppy croissant. I was going to be in Paris that afternoon; I could wait for a decent croissant.

When I left the lobby, the coach was filling up and I climbed aboard, holding my tea steady. I walked down the aisle and a few faces looked up and smiled. I smiled back and kept going, passing up several empty aisle seats.

You might not guess this about me—even if we met in person—but I don't like people very much. I don't mind my friends or my family or a small portion of the people I work with, but strangers and crowds, and most people in general, irk me. So, I avoid them. It's a flaw, I know, but it keeps the extroverted introvert in me sane.

When I got to two empty seats about a third of the way along the coach, I scooted in next to the window, tucking my bag under the seat in front of me.

I sipped my tea and regarded the brownie. I didn't want it, and I wished I'd said yes when Jane offered to make me some toast for the ride into the city. She'd been an absolute gem and had driven me. Granted, it was in my car and I was letting her drive it while I was away, but we'd had to leave home at the ungodly hour of 6:00am—on a *Saturday*.

I wrapped the brownie up and put it in my bag just as a tall woman stopped in the aisle next to me.

"Hi, is this seat taken?" she asked in an American accent, or it could have been Canadian.

She had a pretty, approachable face which made me like her instantly—a rare occurrence—and knowing I'd have to share my row with someone, I replied, "No, go ahead." She pushed a large floppy bag onto the parcel shelf above us and sat down heavily with a sigh.

"Gosh, I'm so glad I made it. I came straight from the airport."

"This morning?"

She nodded and tucked her short blonde bob behind both ears. Her hair was the kind of naturally sun-kissed blonde that screams of good genes and makes you turn an ugly shade of green.

"Yep. Just arrived from Vancouver." She'd flown internationally and was getting straight on a bus tour—sorry, *coach* tour?

I figured she wouldn't want to hear me moan about waking up at 5:00am.

"I'm Catherine—Cat," I said instead.

"Louise—Lou," she replied.

"Well, we're clearly destined to be friends, Lou, because your name is my middle name."

"No way." She chuckled.

"Way. Catherine Louise Parsons."

"Louise Eva Janssen."

We shook hands to formalise our budding friendship, then sat in easy silence as we watched the coach load up with pairs and singles and a four-pack of Kiwi guys who made their way noisily to the back of the coach.

We exchanged a look as they passed by us, only Lou's look said something quite different to mine. "They seem fun," she said brightly.

They seem like trouble to me. My teacher senses tingled.

Or perhaps it was being a thirty-five-year-old on an 18-35s tour that had my hackles up. What the hell was I doing? I should have booked a Trafalgar tour where I'd be the youngest person on the coach. I'd get to spend two weeks travelling across Europe with people my grandparents' age, being fawned over and called "love" and "dear".

I shook the ridiculous thought from my mind. This tour was going to be a blast and by the time I got back to London, Alex would have realised his feelings were nothing more than a silly crush. Then we'd go back to being normal flatmates, who barely saw each other and squabbled over whose turn it was to take out the recycling.

The large red numbers at the front of the coach showed 7:26am when an attractive woman with shoulder-length brown hair stepped on board and called out above the hubbub of chatter, "Good morning, everyone." The whole coach quietened down immediately, which impressed me. I wondered if she'd ever been a teacher—she had that air about her.

"I'm Georgina, your Tour Manager, and this is our driver, Tom." Tom turned around in his seat and waved to us. We waved back like a bus full of schoolchildren on our way to an excursion. "If you do *not* have a British or an EU passport and haven't checked in with me yet, come up to the front now so we can get away on time."

I did have a British passport—*thank you, Dad, for being born a Brit*—so I stayed seated as two people moved along the aisle, passports in hand. Lou answered my unasked question with, "I saw her when I got here."

"Oh, good. You know," I said, changing tack, "I only just booked this tour three days ago—the last seat, apparently." I figured if Lou was going to be my bus bestie, I might as well fill her in on why I was there.

"Oh yeah? Me too! Well, not the last seat, obviously, and it was Monday when I booked—Monday West Coast time—so what's that? Five days ago."

"Huh. We're probably the only ones, don't you think? Booking last minute, I mean. It hardly seems like the sort of tour most people would book on a whim."

"Yeah, you're probably right. So, why did you?" she asked, emphasising "you".

"I slept with my flatmate and he's decided he's in love with me."

"Ahh. And you're not in love with him?"

"Correct. And you?"

"I think I left my husband. He's an alcoholic."

I had not expected that. Rendered verbally impotent, all I managed was, "Oh." She clenched her jaw, drew her mouth into a tight line and nodded, all while blinking back tears. Instinctively, I laid a hand on her knee and she let me. Heavy stuff for first thing in the morning.

Georgina appeared in front of us again, lifting a microphone to her mouth as the bus—sorry, *coach*—pulled away from the kerb. Not having to project this time, she spoke quietly into the mike with a deep, throaty voice. "Good morning, everyone."

Again, like schoolchildren, we replied en masse with a sing-songish, "Good morning."

"As you can see, we're underway. Our drive to Dover will take around two hours, then we'll catch the ferry to Calais—with the coach—then on to Paris. We should arrive around 5:00pm. We'll get you situated at the campsite and then we'll get back on the coach for the Paris night tour, which I know you'll just love."

A panicked voice from the seat in front of me spoke in a not-so-subtle whisper to the woman next to her. "Campsite? She said campsite. Are we on a *camping* trip?" I peeked between the seats to see her frantically searching her phone, probably for the confirmation email. "Oh, my God. Is that why they made us pack sleeping bags?" she hissed. I tapped her on the shoulder. Her head swivelled and two chocolatey-brown eyes fixed on mine.

"Hi," I whispered.

"Hi." Her seatmate turned around and joined the between-the-seats huddle.

"It's not a camping trip," I said, hoping to reassure her with the confident tone of my whisper. She looked dubious, so I explained. "We're staying in cabins at a campsite. We're not camping." I saw her visibly relax, then turn around and rest her head against the seat.

Her seatmate introduced herself. "I'm Danielle."

"Hi. Cat." I pointed to Louise, "Lou."

She pointed at the woman next to her, "Jaelee." Jaelee swung her head back around and offered a relieved smile.

Although we were being quiet, I suddenly realised that the rest of the coach was silent. When I lifted my head, I saw Georgina staring at us with a look that could turn someone to stone. Yep, definitely a former schoolteacher. I had to stop myself from saying, "Sorry, miss."

Jaelee and Danielle turned towards the front and Lou and I threw each other a look, then ducked behind the seats, stifling giggles. Maybe *we* were going to be the naughty ones, rather than the four Kiwi guys up the back.

Georgina continued her first-day spiel. I knew all about these from Sarah, because I'd helped her perfect hers when she was touring. It took nearly the whole drive to Dover and was all about the logistics of life on the road with fifty-five people. I tuned out of a lot of it as I watched the London traffic and busy streets evolve into green hilly countryside, with pastoral scenes of sheep and cows lazily wandering around paddocks.

When I heard, "Let's talk about the difference between tourists and travellers ..." I tuned back in. This is a philosophy the Parsons girls subscribe to—although Sarah more so than me, because she's more intrepid and I tend to consider travel a means to finding good food and drink.

The theory says that the traveller embraces the differences of each new location and the tourist bitches and moans about them, often incessantly. I was very much an appreciator of different places, particularly the wine, the beer, the cheese, the bread—well, you get the drift. But unlike me and my fellow travellers, tourists should just stay home and watch Netflix.

My phone vibrated inside my bag and I retrieved it without thinking. Alex—for the third time that day. I felt a twinge of guilt, which vanished as soon as I read the text.

I'll miss you.

I sighed heavily. How had he *not* got the message? I was *leaving the country* to get away from this mess—from *him*—so things could blow over. I put my phone away without replying.

So, yes, I may have been a traveller, but first and foremost I was an escapee, a runaway, a fugitive from love.

I was ridiculous.

Ten Years Ago

"Catey? Are you okay?"

I want to punch that concerned look right off Scott's face. Instead, I glare at the offending screen.

"Do I look okay?"

"What's going on?"

"You're still logged into your email."

"What?" He leans over my shoulder.

"On my laptop." I point at the email. "You're still logged in."

"Oh, fuck." I snap the lid shut and stare at the inverted Dell logo.

"You said you ended it."

"I didn't say that."

I leap up, my fury making it impossible to sit. "Bullshit. Why—*why*—would I have agreed to this stupid trip if I knew you'd just rush home to her afterwards?"

"I ..."

"'I hate being here with Catey,'" I sing-songed. "*Do* you? Do you *really*, Scott?"

"Sometimes, yes."

I feel like I've been slapped. "Wow. That's ... you said you loved me—*yesterday*. *Yesterday* you said that. Was it a lie?"

"No. Yes. I—"

"Which is it, Scott? Oh, my God." My hand flies to my mouth. "Do you love *her*?"

"I ... yes."

"But ... but why did you say you love me, then?"

"Because I do."

"That doesn't make any frigging sense! You can't love both of us."

"I know! But I do, and I'm all fucked up."

"Oh, poor you. Poor Scott!"

I collapse on the end of the bed, the weight of his revelation sucking me down.

"You did this, you know," he says quietly.

My head snaps up. "What?! It's *my* fault? You stuck your dick into someone else, and you're blaming *me*?"

"That's crass, Catey. And you *left*! *You* did. You moved to London without me."

"For a year! Just a year—*and* I asked you to come with me."

"I came."

"Not to stay."

"I never wanted to live in London. That was your thing. There's nothing for me in London."

"There's *me*."

"That's not what I mean, Catey, and you know it."

"Well, what *do* you mean, Scott?"

"You have your sister, your friends, but ..."

I can no longer look at his contorted face; I don't want to

feel any empathy towards him. "I stupidly hoped you'd want to come with me, but when you said you didn't want to, I thought we'd be all right, that we could make it work. It was just a *year*, Scott."

"We should have broken up in Sydney."

I lift my eyes to his. "What? No, don't say that."

"We should have. We want totally different things."

"Then why did you come?"

"Jesus! I came to see you. I can't win! For fuck's sake, I came!"

"Yes, yes, you did, even though you screwed someone else the moment I left and now you supposedly love her."

"I hate this." He's on the verge of tears and all I can think is, *good.*

"We shouldn't have come here. I can't believe you talked me into this frigging trip after everything that happened," I say, almost spitting the words.

"We've had some good times." *What?*

"You've got to be kidding. It's been the week from hell, Scott. I never know from one day to the next who I'm going to wake up next to—whether you're going to love me that day or not. And apparently you have been miserable the *whole frigging time*."

"Catey ..."

"What?" I snap.

"Can I come sit by you?" I concentrate on the pattern of the tiled floor, the fight ebbing out of me.

"Fine."

"Catey, I am *so* sorry. I know I hurt you. I don't know what to do. I am so confused. I do love you."

"No—"

17

"I *do*! I'm ... I'm really messed up."

"Wonderful." The sarcasm feels good on my tongue.

"No, it's horrible. I didn't mean for this to happen. I thought you'd have your year away and I'd come to visit, then you'd come home, and we'd be together. And then when I met Helen ..."

"Do *not* say her name to me."

"I'm sorry. I thought ..."

"No! Don't talk about her." I rise from the bed and take my suitcase out of the tall wooden wardrobe, plonk it on the bed and start flinging my clothes in, not caring that I'm mixing dirty and clean clothes together. I even don't bother folding them.

"Wait, what are you doing?"

"Packing," I answer as though it's not completely obvious.

"You don't have to do that. We still have a week left. What about Italy?"

"You can't *possibly* think I can stay."

"Why not? Everything's paid for."

"Scott, *you sent a love letter to another woman*." I let the statement hang in the air, pinning him with a scrutinising stare. There's a moment of stillness before he speaks.

"Yes." It's almost a whisper.

"But you want to keep going on our trip?" He can't possibly mean it.

"I know it sounds crazy—"

"Um, yes. It does."

"But I *do* love you. And I know how important this trip is to you. I don't want you to miss out."

18

"Because if I do, it will be your fault." I realise the truth of it as the words come out of my mouth. "*That's* why we're here. That's why we're in *frigging Paris.*"

"No, that's—"

I cut him off, unwilling to hear another word. "You need to come with me to the train station. I have to change my ticket and it's on your credit card." I go into the bathroom to retrieve my toiletries.

"Catey Cat, please—"

"*Don't,*" I shout from the bathroom. I return to the room, the fury rising. "*Don't* call me that—ever again."

"*Please* don't leave me."

"I can't stay, Scott. How do you not get that?" My tone rises with incredulity. I stuff the toiletries bag into my case.

"*Please!*"

I stop and turn and watch him with a detached fascination. I'm stunned by his tears and I can't decide if he's heartbroken or just feeling sorry for himself.

I don't care.

"You know what? You don't get to be upset," I reply, oddly calm. "I'm not interested in how awful you feel."

His face hardens in an instant and I have my answer—crocodile tears. "Fine." He shoves his feet into his shoes.

"Yes, exactly—*fine.*" I zip up the suitcase and scan the room with my eyes. If I forget anything, I'll never see it again. Because I'll never see *him* again.

"Let's go, then," he mumbles as he opens the door.

I lift the suitcase from the bed and follow him, now numb.

Chapter 2

"Well, that's not a cabin," said Jaelee.

The four of us stood facing a row of wooden structures at the Paris campsite. Jaelee dropped her case to the ground with a thud, and I waited for a foot stamp that didn't come. I was still deciding about her. Danielle's face scrunched up like she smelled something bad. I was still deciding about her too.

Bus bestie Lou shrugged her shoulders and forged ahead, boldly stepping inside the cabin assigned to us. She promptly came back out again.

"I don't think we're going to fit," she said, a smile twitching at the corner of her mouth. Danielle's grimace intensified and Jaelee stayed rooted to the spot, scowling.

I leant in and surveyed the entire cabin in approximately half a second.

Jaelee was right—these were decidedly *not* cabins. I'd seen cabins before. I'd even slept in a few—mountain cabins, lakeside cabins. Cabins were cosy and had fireplaces and handmade quilts to snuggle up with. Sometimes, they had dead animal heads hanging on the walls (as opposed to live ones). Cabins had room for people to gather in, to sit on overstuffed furniture and drink mulled wine and hot chocolate, or even do tequila shots.

What we were looking at was the opposite of a cabin. It was essentially a gardening shed with bunks—bunks with plastic-covered mattresses. *In case we wet the bed?* I wondered.

I straightened up and turned to Lou. "Where are we supposed to put our cases?"

"Pretty sure we leave them outside when we go to bed." We grinned at each other. My affection for her was growing with each minute, our wromance well underway. She pulled Danielle into a side hug, cajoling her with, "Hey, neighbour—" an eye roll in response "—it's not *that* bad. And it's only for two nights."

"This isn't even Paris," Jaelee scoffed, holding up her phone for the rest of us to see. "We're *miles* out of Paris." Jaelee— possibly Danielle too—was most definitely a *tourist*. I kicked into teacher mode, easy for me since I'd been in the classroom the day before.

"Right, you two, that's your cabin. Take your cases inside, freshen up, change clothes if you like, and meet us out here in ten." Their eyes widened, then they did as they were told. Yes, there were grumblings I could only just make out, but I'd heard far worse from the mouths of teenagers.

Lou murmured, "Nice work," as we entered our cabin, swung our cases onto our respective beds and sat down. Our knees didn't quite touch.

"So, we're definitely going to be friends with them, right?" she asked quietly. I pursed my lips, trying not to laugh. "I

22

mean, I'm just checking, 'cause I don't think they're gonna be easy."

Giggles exploded out of me and I grabbed the pillow off my bed to cover my mouth. Lou did the same and we laughed long and hard. Hopefully, they didn't hear us—they *were* right next door.

Half an hour later, the whole tour group gathered outside what I had dubbed "the circus tent", a giant yellow and white striped tent where we'd eat dinner that night and both Parisian breakfasts. My dreams of *café au lait* and *pain au chocolat* had vanished. I seriously doubted there was an espresso machine in there—clowns and a trapeze, more likely.

Ventureseek reps sped amongst us with stacks of plastic cups pouring scant measures of what was likely cheap bubbles. I took one from an Aussie girl and gave her a smile. It wasn't her fault my mattress had a plastic cover.

Cup in hand, I turned to my three new friends—Lou and I had decided to keep the other two after all. "A toast—to new friends and to Paris's finest garden sheds."

To their credit, even Danielle and Jaelee smiled at that, tapping their cups against mine and Lou's. I took a sip and grimaced—make that *extremely* cheap bubbles. *Traveller, traveller, traveller.*

"What do you think they're going to serve us for dinner?" asked Danielle.

A sardonic look passed over Jaelee's face as she murmured, "From the look of the place, hotdogs and tater tots." Her American accent hit the "r" hard.

"Summer camp?" I asked.

"Ages seven to sixteen."

"Is it like in the movies?"

"Exactly." She proffered a snarky smile and I thought how nice it was being eye to eye with someone. As a shortish woman—five-foot-one-and-three-quarters—I look up to most people. I mean this literally, not figuratively. It is my experience that most people suck.

Danielle pestered one of the reps for more bubbles, so we each got a top-up. I was glad we'd decided to keep her.

"So, Dani ..." She cocked her head at me, a furrow between her brows. "Sorry, I probably sound English, but I'm actually Australian and it's a bit of an Aussie habit, shortening names." I pointed around our quartet. "Jae, Lou, Cat ..."

She appeared to be considering whether she wanted to spend the rest of the tour being called "Dani". From her expression, she didn't. "So, 'Danielle', then?"

"Actually, I don't mind it. You can call me Dani."

I was surprised, but pleased. "So, *Dani*. You're travelling alone too?"

"Yes," she said pointedly. "My best friend, Nathalie—well, we were supposed to be on this trip together, but she eloped instead."

Three pairs of wide eyes stared at her, unblinking.

"She got *married*?" asked Jaelee.

"Yeah, well, not yet. Tomorrow, actually. In Mexico. I ... I wasn't invited." I thought leaving an alcoholic husband was having a hard time. Well, it was, but so was this. Dani chewed on the rim of her cup.

"Well, that sucks. I'm sorry, Dani." I could already tell that Lou was a terrific commiserator.

"Okay. We're clearly going to be a foursome, so let's get the preliminaries out of the way." Jaelee took charge. Pointing to Dani she said, "Crappy best friend." Dani seemed to take the label in her stride and sipped her bubbles.

Then to Lou, "You. Go."

"Alcoholic husband, probably separating, taking some time by myself—to decide, so, yeah ..." We all nodded solemnly.

"Now you." Jaelee pointed a perfectly manicured finger at me.

"Well, it's nothing like any—"

"No rationalising. Just go."

"Apparently my flatmate's in love with me, but I don't feel the same way and I'm on the run."

She nodded with approval. "Good." *Good?* "So, me ..." She paused—for effect, I was sure.

"The love of my life just married someone else."

Frigging hell. Somehow, I'd managed to gravitate towards three women who'd had the shittiest of shitty things happen to them, and there *I* was, just a lowly love fugitive.

Still, any lingering doubts about booking the tour on a whim had vanished. As I drained the last of my cheap bubbles, I took a moment to appreciate my new gal pals. We'd have the next two weeks together, and no doubt we'd spend a good chunk of the time talking about all the shit going down.

In the absence of Sarah, I'd hit the jackpot.

"And if you look to the right ..."

There was a collective gasp as fifty-three people got their first glimpse of the Eiffel Tower from the Champ de Mars, silhouetted against a darkening orange and pink sky.

Georgina was right—I was loving the Paris night tour.

I'd been to Paris before—lots of times. It was the sort of place I could get to for next to nothing and it had been the destination for several last-minute girls' weekends away. Discounted flights on easyJet—carry-on only—then staying in a cheap hotel or an Airbnb in one of the not-so-nice parts of the city, sharing a bedroom and sometimes even a bed.

My London-based bestie, Mich, taught at the same school as me and was my usual partner in crime—or enabler, whichever one corresponds with me spending an indecent amount of my disposable income on last-minute travel.

In Paris, we'd shop in the mornings—mostly looking in windows and salivating—then find a little hole-in-the-wall bistro where we could eat chunks of baguettes slathered in cheese and drink cheap red wine.

We'd hang out for a few hours and halfway-to-sloshed, we'd step out into the late afternoon to wander the streets and "ooh" and "ahh" over how *French* everything was. Maybe we'd fit in a gallery visit—*Oh my God, I'm standing in front of an actual Monet. Wow, the Mona Lisa!*—or a quick excursion to see some iconic landmark, before finding another hole-in-the-wall bistro for a late dinner of cassoulet and more red wine.

For day two, rinse and repeat.

Then, still tipsy, we'd catch the train to the airport late Sunday evening and fly home, dragging ourselves to work the next day—utterly shattered and swearing we'd never eat another piece of cheese as long as we lived.

And there was the trip to Paris with my ex, Scott. It was where we broke up—well, not right away. I think we knew we were breaking up when we arrived, but instead of being adults and ending it, we hobbled along for another few days until we'd flogged that poor dead horse into the dust.

Actually, *that* trip to Paris had been nothing more than a blur, a string of emotionally wrought snapshots that I rarely let see the light of day.

But I could tell, even on the first day, that this tour would be vastly different from my previous trips—and not just the trips to Paris—*all* of them.

For a start, I saw more of Paris that night than I'd seen in all my previous trips put together. The tour route took us to some of the most famous—and infamous—sights in Paris, and Georgina's commentary was impressive, peppered with fun facts and historical titbits, making it all come to life.

No, Georgina, I did not know millions of people were buried in the catacombs, or that the Académie française voted every year on which words to add to the French language.

Occasionally, the coach stopped so we could get out and take photos. And at each of those stops, Jaelee handed someone her phone and requested, or rather *commanded*, "Take a photo of me." We would come to know it as her catchphrase for the tour—maybe they hadn't heard of selfies in Miami.

As we explored the nooks and crannies of Paris, I started questioning my typical travel style—maybe I *was* a tourist. Wouldn't a traveller, especially one who'd been to Paris so many times before, already know all the history and facts I was only just learning?

And I know I'd exaggerated how much of a whirlwind tour it was—fifteen countries in fourteen days, I'd joked to Sarah—but I'd never travelled like that before. Most of my travel was like the Paris trips—quick jaunts to somewhere in Europe with lots of eating and drinking. I also wasn't much of a culture vulture and, yes, I probably should have visited the Brandenburg Gate, but there was beer to drink and bratwurst to eat.

I'd booked the tour to put some distance between me and Alex and to drown my sorrows. Actually, "sorrows" was hardly the right word. Exasperation? Drown my exasperation? Irritation? Self-flagellation? Why, oh why, had I slept with Alex? As annoying as he'd become since The Incident, I was more ticked off with myself for being a love fugitive. I was hardly setting myself up to be a proper traveller.

Just as we flew into the Arc de Triomphe roundabout—did you know the traffic on the roundabout stops for the incoming traffic? And that *twelve roads* converge there?—I made a pact with myself. I was not going to fritter away my time in Europe. I was going to see all the things and do all the stuff. Starting with Paris, where we'd have the next day to ourselves.

"Hey." I nudged Lou gently in the ribs.

Lou's eyes were fixed on the giant arch, which was so beautifully lit it looked like it was sculpted out of butter. I'd never really noticed before how beautiful it was.

"Hey," she replied without breaking her gaze.

"You up for exploring tomorrow? I mean, like squeezing the hell out of the day and seeing as much as possible?"

That got her attention; her eyes whipped to meet mine.

"Oh, for sure. I want to see everything."

"Brilliant."

"It may be the only time I'm here. Also, Paris is the main reason I booked this trip."

"We're coming back to that—" I took out my phone "—but first I'm going to get us tickets to go up the Eiffel Tower—to the top."

A grin broke out across her face. "Cool." The coach careened off onto a side street and there was a collective sigh from its occupants. It really was a busy roundabout; traffic was manic.

A quick check with Jaelee and Dani, who were sitting just in front of us, confirmed what I already thought—it would only be me and Lou for the Eiffel Tower. Over dinner, they'd made it clear they were all about the shopping, and not the window variety. They'd both come with spending money—*lots* of it.

"Actually, it's what I've been looking forward to the most," Jaelee said as she speared a soggy piece of broccoli, eyeing it with distaste.

I wasn't really one to judge considering my typical travel style, but *shopping* was what she was looking forward to the most?

"Really?" asked Lou. I wasn't the only one then.

"Totally," replied Jaelee, matter-of-factly.

"Oh, yeah, me too," added Dani. She had already pushed her plate away and was twirling a paper serviette between her fingers.

I could see how someone into designer clothes and shoes

and bags would want to shop in Paris. I loved all those things too—bags especially—only I'm a teacher and I shop at TK Maxx for my designer wares. Still, we were in one of the world's most beautiful cities; there were famous landmarks and spectacular artworks to see.

"You mean in *Paris*, right?" Lou pursued her line of questioning. "What you're looking forward to most in *Paris*?"

"No," said Jae, "I mean on the whole trip. The shopping in Europe is supposed to be insane—here, Florence, Rome. I can't wait for Rome." Jae gave up on the broccoli and put it back on her plate. Dani nodded in agreement, and Lou and I shrugged our shoulders at each other.

A couple of hours later, as I booked two tickets to the top of the Eiffel Tower, I was secretly pleased it would just be me and Lou.

Not surprisingly, sleeping in the garden sheds was less than optimal. Even in early October, when the leaves had started turning gorgeous shades and the night itself was quite chilly, the shed was stuffy. It was also extremely difficult to get comfortable inside a sleeping bag.

I couldn't remember the last time I'd been in a sleeping bag—I hate camping as much as the next sane person—but sleeping bags were required for the places with cabins, like Paris—or to be more precise, somewhere in the outer outskirts of Paris.

As I rubbed sleep from my eyes and cracked my sore back, I reminded myself of two things. *I am a traveller* and *I am going up the Eiffel Tower today.*

"Lou," I whispered, which was a silly thing to do, because I was trying to wake her up.

"Yes," she whispered back facetiously.

I had set my phone to vibrate at the ungodly hour of 6:00am with the sole purpose of getting us into a shower before the hordes showed up and we had to A) wait in a queue and B) stand in someone else's shower water. *Blech!* Apparently, the bathrooms at the Paris campsite were the worst we'd encounter on the tour and I silently thanked my sister for the insider info.

"Showers," I reminded her.

I heard a slight groan and then, "Yep. I'm up."

By 7:00am we were showered, dressed, made up, coiffed, and caffeinated. Danielle frowned sleepily at us when she made her way into the circus tent.

"Where's Jae?" I asked.

"She's blow-drying her hair. Is there coffee?" she drawled in her eastern Canadian accent as the frown intensified. Clearly, Dani was not a morning person. Lou pointed to the giant urn with a sign on top saying "coffee" and Dani ambled off.

I finished the rest of my scrambled eggs. That was breakfast, by the way—eggs and as much toasted commercial white bread as we could stand. In *France*, where decent baked goods are a basic human right.

Traveller, traveller, traveller. My plan was to adopt it as my mantra until I stopped thinking negative thoughts.

"Morning," called a cheery male voice. Craig sat down opposite us and placed a plate brimming with eggs and toast

31

on the table. The previous night, we'd added a fifth to our little group. Craig was eighteen—yes, really—from Oregon, and was travelling alone.

That last part is why we'd decided to adopt him. Also, I was nearly twice his age *and* a secondary teacher. I believed it was my moral obligation to make sure Craig had *people* on the tour. We would be his people.

"Good morning, Craig. Hungry?" asked Lou, semi-mocking his enormous breakfast.

He missed the jibe and nodded while shovelling a massive forkful into his mouth. Lou turned my way. "I have three brothers. They're all like this at eighteen. Insatiable." She watched him with a bemused smile, or was it a smirk? And she meant insatiable *appetites*, right? I didn't want Lou getting ideas about our boy.

"*Three* brothers?" asked Craig through a mouthful. If he did it again, I would have to say something. I can't abide that.

"Uh huh. I'm the baby, so three *big* brothers. My dad had to shop every other day." I caught the lilt of affection in her voice—and that she hadn't mentioned her mum.

I couldn't imagine growing up with brothers. It was just me and Sarah, and we'd always been close—except for the year she started uni and became an insufferable cow. That year sucked. Don't tell her I said that.

Craig smiled at Lou, then swallowed. "My mom always says that about me—that I'll eat her out of house and home. It's only me and her," he added without a trace of self-pity.

Only me and her. I wondered if it was why he'd gravitated

towards us the previous night, rather than the four Kiwis, or any of the other guys.

He took another bite. "How did you end up on a Ventureseek tour?" I asked. Part of me wanted to scream, "Why are you here all alone? You're practically a baby!" I didn't though.

He finished his mouthful before replying—maybe he'd caught my earlier frown. "I kinda crashed and burned towards the end of my senior year. I put a lot of pressure on myself to get into the school I wanted." I knew he meant university. "I did get in, but I've deferred a year. My grandfather bought me this trip for helping out at his store when I can, just with stocking after hours, that sort of thing. He can't carry as much as he used to." Craig smiled again, affectionate thoughts of his grandfather evident on his face.

Dani returned to the table with her coffee and sat down next to Craig.

"Good morning, Danielle."

"Well, good morning to you too, Craig." Wow, the coffee had kicked in fast. "You remind me of my baby brother," she said, cocking her head appraisingly. "Did I tell you that?" I guessed we all had our reasons for bringing him into the fold.

"No, but that's cool," he said, sounding like he meant it.

I was glad we were his people. He was a good kid.

Jaelee made her entrance five minutes before we were due to get on the coach. She wore a pair of white skinny jeans, a bright pink silk blouse and a pair of matching pink stilettos. Her hair was a sleek sheet of black down her back, and she carried a bright green Michael Kors bag.

I wondered how in the hell she was going to walk the

cobbled streets of Paris all day in those shoes, but she looked incredible.

Jae and Dani—with her gamine haircut, slim figure, eyeliner flicks, and Audrey Hepburnesque outfit of a black turtleneck T-shirt, cigarette pants, and ballet flats—were exactly the types of women Parisian sales assistants would fawn over.

"Okay," Jae said, as though she was addressing the whole tent and not just the four of us. "Let's do this." Then she looked at us expectantly and we all got to our feet and followed her out of the tent—even Craig, who grabbed two more pieces of toast for the road.

It seemed I wasn't the only one who liked bossing people around.

As we climbed on board, I heard my phone beep inside my bag. I pulled it out as soon as I sat down next to Lou, and my face must have said it all. "Is it the guy?" Lou peeked over my shoulder and I angled the phone so she could see it.

How's Paris? x

She nodded solemnly. "It's the guy."

"Yes."

"You may need to spell it out."

"Yes."

Later, I thought. Love fugitives are cowards.

Lou and I saw the hell out of Paris that day.

Armed with Sarah's insider info and a to-do list as long as a baguette, we started the morning with the rest of the group at Sainte-Chapelle. If it had been two years before, our day would have started at Notre-Dame, and I tried not to think about the great loss—besides, they were rebuilding and no doubt it would be spectacular when they were done.

After Georgina gave a short spiel about the church, she had us open the maps on our phones so we could mark the pick-up point for 5:00pm. Then we were on our own.

Lou had entrusted me with the mammoth task of curating the perfect day out in Paris. There were some bucket-list must-sees, which would only take a few minutes, but I was planning for the truly amazing stuff, like Musée d'Orsay, to take some proper time. I'd also never seen the Arc de Triomphe up close, so that was on the list too.

I planned for us to have a quick look inside Sainte-Chapelle, then we'd have just over two hours to get from Île de la Cité to the Eiffel Tower in time for our 11:00am tickets to the top, with one important stop in between.

"So, the church—how about we pop our heads in, then make our way over to the Louvre for nine. Good?"

"Yep," She replied.

And when I said "pop our heads in" I meant we'd elbow our way through the crowd, gawp at the incredible gothic ceiling and wonder at the vast array of stained-glass tableaux in fifteen minutes flat. When our whirlwind visit was over, I was filled with the kind of relief I felt after a Marks & Spencer season sale—glad I went, but even gladder to be out of the melee.

Sainte-Chapelle ✓

With Sarah's tip to use the side entrance of the Louvre, we'd avoided the massive queue in the main courtyard, and were inside at five past nine. I had the floor plan open on my phone and led the way to the *Mona Lisa*, hopscotching around tour groups and art lovers. Sure, it was a touristy thing to do, but would you go to the Louvre and skip the world's most famous painting?

By the time we arrived at 9:15am, the crowd was only three-deep. "Right, similar approach to Sainte-Chapelle—get in there, elbows out, and I'll see you back here when you're done."

"Wait, you're not coming?"

"I've seen it—the first time I came." That was mostly true. I'd seen *glimpses* of it—from the back of a hot and bothered horde, who took turns to stand on my toes and elbow me unapologetically in the ribs and head. I'd left with sore calves from being on tiptoe for twenty minutes, a multitude of bruises, and an odd sense of accomplishment. I hardly needed to go through all that again to see a painting I knew by heart.

"Got it. So, should we synchronise our watches?" Lou deadpanned. She took off without waiting for a reply and I chuckled to myself. I had chosen my bus bestie well.

At around five-ten—my best guesstimate—Lou was easy to follow in the crowd. She made some impressive early manoeuvres, and I decided to add her to my crew should I ever form one for a caper or a heist. She came back to me within minutes, a little out of breath.

"It was touch and go there for a moment—encountered a Chinese tour group—but I pushed them out of the way. I think one of them may need an ambulance."

"Hah!" The laugh escaped and echoed around the cavernous room. No one seemed to notice.

"So, what did you think?" She shrugged. "Yeah, me too."

Mona Lisa ✓

"Now, is there anything else you wanted to see here? I mean, there are literally thousands of pieces," I asked.

"Nothing in particular—most of the art I want to see is at Musée D'Orsay." Our tickets were for 2:00pm.

"All right, then there's something I want to show you. I think you'll love it."

Ten minutes later—the Louvre is huge, if you've never been—we emerged into the atrium where the *Marly Horses* reside.

"Oh my gosh," said Lou, her mouth slightly open as she took in the vastness. Yes, I'd been before, but I had to agree.

Glass diamonds, almost as tall as a person, had been pieced together to form the impressive roof, and marble was ubiquitous. It formed the archways, window casements, stairs, walls, and floors. With slats of morning sunlight beaming down on the smooth, milky surfaces, the whole atrium looked like the inside of a vanilla cupcake. It was accented with topiary trees, which were dotted about for pops of green, and then there were the statues.

The *Marly Horses* are my favourite pieces in the Louvre, but really, any marble statue with that much detail impresses me. How does a person start with an enormous block of stone and work their way in to something like that? I can't even carve a pre-roasted chicken from Sainsbury's without hacking it to pieces.

We found an unoccupied bench and sat for a moment, taking it all in.

"It's just so beautiful," said Lou after a few minutes.

"I completely agree."

"And I don't just mean this—I mean, yeah, this is gorgeous—but the whole city. You know how you see a place in photos or in movies and you've wanted to go there for so long you can't remember a time when you didn't, and then you go and it's way more ... well, just *more* than you could ever have imagined? It's that."

"You said Paris was the main reason you booked the tour."

She looked down at her sneakers and rubbed the toes together, then sighed. "Yeah. Jackson—my husband, well, maybe he's my *ex*-husband now—he never really wanted to travel. And I mean, *anywhere*. Even for our honeymoon we just went to Whistler and *that* was a big deal for him, an hour's drive from Vancouver. And all he did the whole time was complain about missing home."

Her gaze shifted to the glass panes above us, then fixed on the wall across from us. "And I knew, even then, I'd made a mistake, that for all the things I loved about him—and he's not a bad guy when he's not drinking, which at the moment is almost never—him *not* drinking, I mean ... sorry, I'm getting off-track.

"Anyway, I used to say all the time how I wanted to go to Paris. It was number one on my list, you know? And he'd always make out like we would go for our tenth anniversary—Paris, Venice, maybe even Florence, 'cause they were on the list too. But I guess, for him, ten years was so far into the future, he didn't think he'd ever have to make good on his promise.

"And then when the drinking started to get really bad and he lost his job—when he kept refusing my help, or *anyone's* help—I knew we weren't going to make it to ten years. And I made the decision to leave ..." Her voice cracked, and I didn't have to look at her to know she was tearing up. I reached out for her hand, not turning my head in case she was embarrassed by her tears. She grasped mine tightly.

"After that, I thought, 'Screw it.'" She started laughing through her tears. I looked at her, and she smiled as she said, "'I'm taking *myself* to Europe—I'm gonna see Paris and Venice and Florence.' And then I booked this trip." I smiled back at her. "Now here I am sitting in an incredible place, and I've met you and the girls and Craig. And ..." She trailed off.

I let go of her hand to pull her in for a side hug, letting her know she didn't have to finish the thought.

Sometimes you meet people not only because of what they will mean to you, but because of what you will mean to them.

Louvre ✓

We moved on with time for a leisurely walk through the Jardin de Tuileries, the rough stones crunching under our feet. Then we crossed the vast and scarily busy Place de la Concorde and strolled up the Champs-Elysées.

"Do you think we'll run into Dani and Jaelee?" Lou asked after we passed the fiftieth designer shop.

"Unlikely. They were going straight to the Marais. It's supposed to be better for serious shoppers." A perfectly timed group of American retirees filed out of Chanel babbling at each other in their thick accents, nary a Chanel shopping bag in sight.

"Rather than for window shopping?" asked Lou as we detoured around them.

"Exactly."

Champs-Elysées ✓

"Close your eyes," I commanded. Lou did as she was told, which was trusting, because people were milling all around us. I led the way, keeping her close to me, until we were standing with a perfect view of the Eiffel Tower—straight through the middle of the Trocadero Fountains and along Pont d'Iéna. I positioned her in front of me and said, "Now."

"Oh my gosh!" Giddy with glee, she jumped up and down on the spot, her hands waving as she made a sound something like, "Eeoieooeio."

I fell in line beside her. I'd seen that exact view once before. Scott had planned it just like I had for Lou, only *I'd* been a little distracted by our impending break-up. But being there with Lou, being able to give her that moment, swept the ghost of boyfriend past back where he belonged.

"I just can't believe I'm really here. And it's gold! How did I not know it was gold? I always thought it was grey, but it's not! I mean, when we saw it last night, all lit up, it *looked* golden, but I thought it was just the lights. Oh my gosh, Cat!" She was giggling as she dug her phone out of her bag. "Here." She thrust it at me. "I need proof—proper proof."

I took the photo, then tucked in close to her so we could

take a selfie. "And how cool, you lining it up like that? Thank you. Thank you so much. I mean it."

Her enthusiasm was infectious, and I replied with a lilting laugh. "You're welcome. Now let's go, so we don't miss our window."

By luck, we'd landed a perfectly blue sky and visibility for miles, and one of the incredible things about seeing Paris from that high up was the city's symmetry. Looking south-east down the Champ de Mars to the military school, or back towards Palais de Chaillot, across to the Arc de Triomphe and down the Champs-Elysées to the Louvre—every view was remarkable.

It's also the one place in the city that's higher than Sacré-Cœur, which sat perched on Montmartre hill across the way. What a stunning city. I already knew I needed to return—and *not* for one of those boozy girls' weekends that would pass in a blur, but for a proper holiday where I could take my time to savour the city.

Eiffel Tower ✓

Several hours and some incredibly sore feet later, Lou and I perched on the edge of a fountain at Place de la Concorde waiting for the coach with some others from our group. The plan—well, *Georgina's* plan—was to go back to the campsite, shower and change, then return to the city for a group dinner and free time to explore. Lou and I had already decided to skip the dinner.

"I can't believe how much we saw today," said Lou, inspecting the beginnings of a blister on the back of her left foot.

We'd left the Eiffel Tower and caught the Metro over to Musée d'Orsay, grabbing a couple of ham and cheese baguettes from a street vendor and eating them on the forecourt of the museum. I'd even used my terrible French to buy them, which—to my amusement—had impressed Lou.

Once inside, we paused side by side, taking in the incredible architecture of the one-time train station. "Well, this doesn't suck," said Lou, eloquent as ever.

I *love* the Orsay Museum. I think it looks like the set of a steampunk gothic murder mystery film. If I lived in Paris, I'd go all the time.

Because Lou had particular pieces she wanted to see, we decided to go our separate ways and meet up at 3:30pm near the entrance. My sister's like that too—someone who loves art enough to have favourite pieces. She'll sit in front of a single painting for an hour, just taking it in—*Sunflowers* by Van Gogh is her fave.

I prefer to wander. I'll stop for a minute or two if I see something that captures my attention, and though I'd be hard-pressed to name a favourite piece, or even artist, I do like the Impressionists. It's like the whole movement stemmed from wanting to capture the stuff of dreams—and not the weird, distorted dreams the Surrealists had—seriously, what were they smoking?—but the kind of dreaminess the Impressionists depicted by choosing the right colour and applying it just so.

Maybe I *do* like art. And, of course, I love a marble sculpture.

From the museum, we had walked to the Arc de Triomphe, where we watched a handful of idiots try to cross the road *at the busiest intersection in the world*, then took the underpass. We wandered around all four columns, through the smaller arches, and stood under the largest arch looking up.

"Can you believe the detail, especially in the murals?" asked Lou, as we craned our necks.

"It's ridiculous. I mean—" The beeping of my phone interrupted me. "Hang on." I took the phone out of my bag and read the text from the home screen. "Oh, for fuck's sake."

"The roommate?"

"Alex, yes."

"Are you going to reply this time?" She gave me a look. It said, "Reply already," and I exhaled heavily. "Look, if you don't, he's just going to keep texting you—every day for the whole trip." She said the last part *really slowly*, so I would get it. I knew she was right, but I was in *Paris*. Couldn't I put Alex off until we were somewhere boring, like on a motorway or something? "Look, send him a quick text. You don't even have to talk to him. Here," she signalled for me to show her the phone. "What did he say?"

I showed her the screen.

I really want to talk to you. Is now a good time?

"Okay, so, maybe it's not just a text message then."

"Oh, bollocks. Just give me a couple of minutes." I searched for a quiet place under the most iconic arch in the world and settled for a spot in the shade where I could face a wall. I tapped the "call" button and Alex's phone started to ring.

"Hi! Hello!!" He sounded surprised.

"Hi, Alex, what was it you wanted?" I asked with feigned politeness.

I don't think I pulled it off, though, because he stammered his reply. "Oh, I … I just … uh, wanted to say hello, to hear how it's going." I sighed, not thrilled that I was becoming a frequent sigher, but I realised I wasn't frustrated with Alex. I was frustrated with myself.

The whole "love fugitive" thing was already tiring, and it was only day two. Yes, I was having a good time. Yes, I'd met some interesting people, but I could not spend the next twelve days dodging Alex's texts because I'd end up back in London with exactly the same problem I'd had when I left.

"Cat, are you there?"

"Sorry, yes, I'm here." Deep breath. "Alex, I have to tell you something, all right?" I carried on without waiting for a reply. "I know you think us sleeping together was the start of something, and you have all these feelings for me. But, I'm sorry. I don't feel the same way. For me, you're just my flatmate— friend—my *friend*, and that's all." I wished I hadn't made the "flatmate/friend" blunder, but at least I'd been clear.

Silence.

"Alex? Can you hear me?" I hoped my mobile signal hadn't dropped out, or I'd have to say it all again—obviously without the "flatmate" part.

"Uh, yeah, I heard you. Wow, I uh … I didn't realise. I feel really stupid."

What? No!

"You're not, Alex. I should have said something before I came away. I'm so sorry. That's my fault."

"God, I am a right idiot." I couldn't tell if he was talking to me or thinking aloud. Either way, the call was going horribly.

"No, Alex. This is all on me." Great, I had resorted to, "It's not you, it's me."

"All good, Cat. Not to worry. I'll, um, I'll see you when you get back, I s'pose. Bye."

He hung up and I found myself, phone to my ear, frowning at a giant slab of marble. I tucked the phone into my bag and turned to look for Lou. She was standing at the ropes surrounding the Tomb of the Unknown Soldier, staring down at it.

I joined her, the conversation with Alex pressing on me. "Hey."

"Hey. How'd it go?"

"Not well."

"You were clear, though?"

"Yes, crystal."

"But?"

"He called himself a 'right idiot'."

"Ouch."

"Yes."

"Poor guy," she added.

"Mmm."

"Doesn't this make you sad?" For half a second I didn't realise we were talking about something else. I looked down at the flickering flame.

"It does, yes." It also put things into perspective. So, things with my flatmate were a little awkward. So what? There were far worse problems in the world.

The small group of fellow tour-trippers soon turned into a larger group, and at 4:50pm Dani and Jaelee showed up, each laden with shopping bags.

"Hey, girls!" chirped Jaelee. She dumped her treasures at our feet with a loud, "Phew! What a day!"

Dani was close behind her, but less ebullient. She dropped her shopping bags and joined me and Lou on the edge of the fountain. I noticed red marks on her wrists from where the bags had hung.

"Did you have a good day, Dani?" I didn't know her particularly well—was the look on her face fatigue or something else? Apparently, it was something else, because my question triggered a barrage of tears, the kind accompanied by boo-hoos. Even Jaelee seemed shocked, and they'd spent the day together.

Jaelee sat next to her and patted her on the shoulder. "Hey, what's wrong?"

Dani snuffled and wiped her nose with her hand. "I've tried to hold it together, but it's today—Nathalie's wedding day." *Oh, right.* I'd completely forgotten—what an insensitive cow.

Dani took the tissues Lou offered her and blew her nose. "My best friend is getting married today and I'm not there." She dissolved into tears again. The three of us shared helpless looks. I tried to think of anything I could say to make it all right and I guessed the others were doing the same.

I was not fond of this Nathalie person. How could she elope without her best friend? If Sarah went off and got married without me there, I'd bloody kill her!

46

After a few minutes of soothing back pats and a wad of wet tissues, Dani's tears started to subside.

"Dani, we're all so sorry." Jaelee and Lou nodded in camaraderie. "Look, Lou and I were going to skip the group dinner tonight. Why don't you and Jae come out with us? We'll find a nice little bistro, have some delicious food and some wine, and you can bitch about Nathalie all you want."

She snuffled and wiped her nose again. She nodded. "Okay." Not quite over the moon, but it was a start.

"So, is there a reason for skipping the group dinner?" Jae looked at me over Dani's head.

"Tip from my sis. We'll have a better meal if we find our own place." I'd already told her about Sarah's insider info and Jae nodded in quick agreement.

"Well, why don't we just go out from here?"

"Jaelee's got a point," said Lou. "We can wait for the coach, tell Georgina what we're doing, and find out where they're picking us up tonight."

Part of me loved the idea of an extra couple of hours in Paris. The other part of me scrutinised my outfit. Did I really want to go out in boyfriend jeans, a long-sleeved T-shirt, and a pair of sneakers—in *Paris*? Uh, no. I did not.

Dani spoke up. "Uh, guys? Would you mind if we did go back to the campsite? I really want to clean up and I need to deal with this." She waved her hand in front of her tear-stained and blotchy face. "And we have all our shopping bags."

"Actually," said Jaelee, "I really should change my shoes. I don't know how much longer I can walk around in these."

Dani gave us a diluted, but somewhat hopeful, smile. It

was settled. We'd freshen up at the campsite, catch a ride back to the city, then head out to dinner, just the four of us.

Or five of us. On the ride back to our sheds, Lou invited Craig to join us and he accepted. He was probably in for a night of girl talk, but hopefully he wouldn't mind.

As the coach pulled into late-afternoon traffic, I leant my head against the window and yawned, helpless to stop it. For a fleeting moment, I wished we were back in London and our girls' night out was a girls' night in at my place—pyjamas, no makeup, home-made cocktails, takeaway pizza and ice cream for dessert.

But I was in Paris and I could rally.

48

Ten Years Ago

"Hello?"

"Sez, it's me."

"Hello?"

"Sarah, it's me, Cat. Can you hear me?"

"Oh, I can now. Hey. What's up? How's the trip?"

"Well ... we broke up."

"What? Sorry, I can't hear you. You're breaking up."

"Yes. We broke up. Me and Scott."

"Hang on. I'm going somewhere quieter. Okay, say that again."

"It's Scott—we broke up—I'm leaving him!"

"Oh, Cat. Shit, I'm so sorry. What happened? Are you still in Paris?"

"Yes. I'm trying to get back to London—today. I'm at Gare du Nord."

"And where's Scott?"

"He's at the ticket counter. He's trying to get me on the last train back to London."

"But what happened?"

"He cheated, Sez."

"What?!"

"He cheated on me. He told me before we came away."

"Oh, my God! Why didn't you tell me?"

"I didn't ... I don't know."

"But why'd you go away with him?" She was only asking me the same question I'd asked myself a thousand times this week.

I sigh. "Because I thought it would be all right. I thought we'd work it out."

"Oh, darling."

"But he lied. He said he'd ended it, but he lied. I read his email to her."

"His email? Hang on, how?"

"He used my laptop and forgot to log out, the dickhead."

"Oh, I'm so sorry. I wish I was with you right now." I wish she was here too. Her voice quietens. "But who is she?"

My throat tightens, but I answer. "Her name's Helen. He works with her. It started right after I left Sydney." Saying the words aloud somehow makes it even more real, and the lump in my throat sends snaking poison into my gut.

"Oh, Cat. You poor love. This sucks."

I flick a glance at Scott. He seems to be arguing with the ticket agent.

"He keeps saying he's sorry. He's been crying and everything, but Sez, I ... I hate him so much right now." I glare at him, even though he can't see me.

"Of course you do, darling. I hate him too. I'm *so* sorry. I wish I could be there—I'd smack him in his *stupid* head."

"Hah!" The thought of my affectionate, funny, sweet sister thumping my soon-to-be-ex-boyfriend gives me a moment's reprieve from the pain. "So, where are you?"

"Rome."

"Oh."

"It's bad luck, the timing. I was in Paris last week. I could have come and got you ... Cat, you poor thing. Are you going to be okay?"

"I just really wish you were here right now." I let the self-pity settle on my shoulders and feel the sting of tears. Scott suddenly appears at my side, interrupting my self-pity party. "Hang on, Sez."

"There are no more seats on the Eurostar, not 'til tomorrow. And they won't swap the ticket. We have to buy a new one." A double whammy.

The poison from my gut rises and turns into words. "That can't be right," I spit.

"I even told them there'd been a death in the family—but no luck."

The irony of him lying to get my ticket changed smacks my senses. I wonder if infidelity is a good enough reason to change my ticket, then remember we're in France where infidelity is practically a given.

"Well, if a practised liar like you can't convince them ..." I let the thought trail off, feeling the hollow victory as his face crumples. "What are we going to do, then?" I remember my sister on the other end of the call. "Hang on, Sez." I don't wait for her response—even knowing this call will cost us both a mint.

"I could drive you back, to Calais at least." His eyes don't meet mine.

"I'm not getting in a car with you, Scott—not to drive through the night. Just give me a minute, will you? I'm talking to Sarah." He skulks away and flops onto a chair. "Hi, you there?"

"Yes."

"Sorry." I sigh heavily. "So, there are no seats left on the Eurostar tonight. I can't get back to London until tomorrow. I guess I have to stay here."

"What? With Scott?"

"I don't have much choice. I'm going to have to buy a new train ticket—fuck, that's so much money—and we have a room. It's already paid for."

"Make him sleep on the floor."

"Absolutely."

"Call me as soon as you get back to London."

"I will."

"I'm so sorry, Cat."

"Five *years*, Sez. *Five!* If he didn't want to do long-distance, he bloody well should have said so. He didn't even last a month before he started screwing someone else." The tears threaten again.

"Cat, you have every right to be furious with him. Are you sure it's okay to stay with him tonight?"

"I have to. I can't really afford my own hotel room."

"Sure, okay, that makes sense."

"I'm gonna go, now."

"Okay, darling."

52

"Sez?"

"Yep."

"Paris is a shitty place to break up."

"I know, Cat. I'm so sorry."

"Bye."

"Bye."

Chapter 3

The ablution block was a nightmare.

Although we hustled over as soon as the coach arrived at the campsite, the line for a shower was already thirty-deep and there were only six shower stalls.

"I don't need a shower," I declared. I mean, I did, but I could make do with a wipe down with a wet washcloth—good thing I'd brought one.

"Well, I stink," said Lou. "I'm gonna wait it out."

"Meet you back at the shed?"

"Yup."

For the umpteenth time that day, I finessed my way through a crowd. I positioned myself in front of a sink, wet the washcloth, and got to work on the important bits, ignoring the screwed-up noses I could see reflected in the mirror. I brushed my teeth, washed my face, and ran wet fingers through my wavy hair. It would have to do. By the time I walked past Lou on my way out, she'd progressed two places in the line.

"Good luck." She rolled her eyes.

Back in the shed, I reapplied my makeup and added some product to my hair to up the shine factor. From my case came a blue jersey wrap-around dress which accentuated my waist. I slipped it on along with a pair of silver flats. They weren't great for walking long distances, but I am not the type of woman who can pull off a pretty dress and sneakers. I added my midnight blue motorcycle jacket—another TK Maxx special—spritzed on some of my favourite perfume, L'eau d'Issey, and sat ready on my bunk scrolling through my Twitter feed—all before Lou returned.

Finally, the cabin door swung open and Lou, wrapped in a towel, barrelled through.

"You walked across the campsite like that?"

"I know! I forgot to bring my clean clothes."

"Well, I'm sure there were many appreciative onlookers." Her mouth pulled taut. She seemed dubious.

"How long do I have?"

I checked my watch. "Seventeen minutes."

"Darn!"

"And phooey!"

She cracked a smile. "I don't swear much."

"I gathered. I'll leave you to it," I said as she frantically rummaged through her suitcase.

I stepped out into the cool, but still, evening and made my way over to a picnic table. Craig was reading something on his phone, and I sat down next to him.

"Hey."

"Hey," he replied, seeming distracted.

"Want some privacy?"

"What? Oh, no." He put his phone face-down on the table. "Everything all right?"

56

"It's my mom."

"And ...?"

He sighed. "Things aren't good with her boyfriend."

"Oh. Sorry to hear that."

"He's kind of a dick."

"Oh."

"Yeah—I'm trying to be supportive, but really, I hope they break up. He's not good enough for her."

"Doesn't sound like it." *Heavy load for a young guy.* He picked up the phone and spun it in his hand. "How was your day in Paris?" I asked brightly.

To his credit, he didn't wallow, and his grimace gave way to a smile. "It was intense."

"Really?"

"I'm from Oregon," he said, as though it was the backwater of the earth. "I've been to Washington and California, but that's it. So, yeah, Paris kind of blew my mind. I mean, this place is *old*, and everything—the buildings, the bridges, *everything* here is like, really beautiful. In a way, it doesn't feel quite real."

"I know what you mean."

"But I thought you'd been here before."

"I have, but it feels different this time. Being with Lou has helped. She's so wide-eyed about everything, it's like I'm seeing it for the first time too."

He nodded as though he understood, and I wondered at how mature he was. Not that I'd tell him. I didn't want to come off as condescending. "So, you ready for a girls' night out?" I teased.

"For sure."

"Do you have any idea what you're in for?" I raised my eyebrows at him.

"Not a clue. But I'm game. Hopefully, it'll keep my mind off my mom."

"I made it," said an out-of-breath Lou from behind us. We turned around in sync.

"Looouuu. You look hot," I said, taking in her maxi dress, cropped denim jacket, silver hoop earrings, and barely-there-but-very-pretty makeup. She grinned and did a couple of curtsies.

"Not bad for fifteen minutes, huh?"

"Oh bollocks." I checked my watch. "The coach!"

We made it—just. Georgina threw us her signature school-marm look, her mouth twisted like a pretzel. It would have ticked me off if I wasn't so impressed. I had no idea a mouth could do that. Telling her we wouldn't be joining the group for dinner made it worse. I hurried down the aisle before she could give us detention.

Dinner was sublime. The conversation got a little heavy when Dani lamented the wedding she was missing, but the food was fantastic. And all we'd done was step off the coach, head in the opposite direction from the tour group, and follow our noses.

We'd been dropped off on the Left Bank, and within minutes came across a street lined with cafés and bistros. With Dani being French-Canadian, we let her take the lead and she selected a smaller bistro in the middle of the block which had room for the five of us.

In rapid-fire French, her tone slightly officious, she requested a table. Our waiter nodded curtly and showed us to a cramped table, which, by the time we worked out the seating arrangement, bore bread, a large bottle of sparkling water, and five small glasses.

The smells coming from the tiny kitchen were incredible and my mouth watered at the thought of proper French food. I certainly didn't count the lunchtime baguette.

The menu was written on a chalkboard which hovered precariously above Craig's head. I had enough French to make out most of the dishes, but Dani translated the whole thing for us. It didn't take long, as it was the kind of place where there were only three choices per course. I figured that with such a limited menu, every dish would most likely be delicious.

They were. I had onion soup to start, then *cassoulet de lapin*—rabbit casserole—and I finished with *tarte aux poires*—pear tart. After my first bite of the tart, I groaned with pleasure and Jaelee asked if I wanted to be alone with it. I had no idea what the others ate; I was in my own little culinary heaven.

As the dessert plates were cleared away, Dani lifted her glass. "I'd like to propose a toast. To my new friends—if it wasn't for you, this day would totally suck. So, thank you for being here with me, thank you for the endless supply of tissues, and thank you for being such awesome company. *Salut.*"

A chorus of "*Salut*" erupted as we clinked together cheap glasses filled with cheap house wine—drinkable, but hardly memorable.

"You've handled it really well, Dani," said Lou as she

scooped up some breadcrumbs from the table and deposited them in the breadbasket. "If my best friend pulled a stunt like that, I'd probably have flown down there anyway."

"I definitely would have," I added.

"Yep. Me too." Jaelee rounded out our supportive indignation. Craig stayed quiet.

Dani's eye revealed instant panic. "What? You would have? Should I have? Oh, no! I should have gone to Mexico!" She was half out of her seat when Jaelee grabbed her hand and pulled her back down.

"No, that's not what we meant. Right?" she looked to us for support.

"Right," said Lou.

"Of course," I added.

"*That* would have been wrong," Jaelee clarified.

"Terrible."

"A disaster," I agreed.

"You did the right thing. You respected her wishes, no matter how hard it was to do," said Lou. We watched as Dani slowly nodded, her brow uncreasing. "Okay?"

"Okay."

"I mean, I would totally tell Nathalie *exactly* where to stick her elopement if I ever—" I threw Jae a silencing look, cutting her off, even though I agreed with her. Nathalie could fuck right off.

"Oh, my God, I'm stuffed." Dani seemed to be in finer spirits when we rolled out onto the street a little while later.

"Did you enjoy dinner?" I asked Craig, falling in step alongside him. He'd been rather quiet, and I wondered if he was overwhelmed by us, or maybe his mum was still on his mind.

"Oh, for sure. That was incredible. I've got to make that French-style casserole for my mom when I get home."

"You cook?" I asked incredulously. *Could I be any more sexist? Or ageist?* "Sorry."

He laughed it off. "It's fine. I know most guys my age don't cook. But it's just the two of us and my mom works long hours, so I've been responsible for dinner since I was fifteen. I got sick of frozen pizza and Lean Cuisine pretty quick, so I started reading recipe books and trying out stuff."

"Wow."

"Yeah. At first, I got a bit of ribbing from my buddies. But then I made brisket for them this one weekend—they shut up about it after that. Of course, now they bug me to cook for them all the time."

"So, you're good at it."

"No, I'm great at it." He grinned down at me. "I was even thinking of maybe skipping college and going to culinary school." I caught a look of consternation.

"Is that a possibility?"

He shrugged. "Not sure. How do you tell your mom you want to be a chef when you got into Stanford?"

"Wait," I stopped and tugged at his arm. He stopped walking, a sheepish look on his face. "Stanford?"

"Yep." He started walking again, and I hurried to catch up with him.

"Studying what?"

"Biochemical engineering."

"Oh, wow."

"Yeah."

"That's ... congratulations. I mean, it's good, right?"

He smiled. "It's good. It's not like I don't love that too—I do. I've been interested in bio-hacking for a while now—it's essentially knowing exactly how to get your body working optimally—diet, supplements, hormone balancing, activity—that sort of thing."

This explained why he was so fit. I mean, not that I'd been perving on our baby brother, but Craig was obviously into health and fitness. Whereas my approach to the whole "optimal body" thing was to eat what I liked, drag myself to the gym a couple of times a week, and send frequent silent thanks to my paternal grandmother for the "naturally slim" genes. *Thanks, Grandma.*

I didn't want to burden Craig with my miscreant ways, however, so I omitted the gory details and replied, "Sounds interesting."

"Yeah, I mean, it totally is—but *food*." His fists pumped his chest over his heart. "I *love* cooking. So, you see? Conundrum."

"Hah! Good word. So, you *haven't* told your mum?"

"Uh, no. I haven't."

"Look, I know I don't know you very well, but it seems like you're close to your mum. Can't you tell her just like you told me? I mean, your passion is *obvious*. She might surprise you."

"I got a full ride."

"Well, bollocks."

"Yeah. And we're not poor or anything, but there's no way she could afford Stanford. How do I turn it down? I'd be an idiot to turn it down."

"Mmm." My brain went into noodling mode; it was chewing on something. "Hey! What if you studied both and became the world's first bio-hacking chef?"

He laughed. Out loud. At my brilliant idea.

I backhanded him in the chest, which for a short gal like me was literally a stretch. "I'm *serious*. Anyway—maybe think about it."

"C'mon. The others are way ahead." I hadn't noticed we'd got so far behind. I also had no idea where we were going. We caught up as Dani pulled out her phone.

"Where are we heading?" I asked.

"Good question," replied Lou.

"I was following you guys," said Jae.

Dani threw her hands up in the air. "I have no idea where we even are. We all just started walking."

"Seriously?" I asked. We shared a round of looks and burst out laughing.

"Now, we all agree that we must never speak of this again, right?" asked Lou, which was followed by smirks, head-shaking and heart-crossing.

When all that died down, Jae looked around as though she was searching for something. "There," she said, pointing to a man walking towards us. I'd barely clocked he was there, let alone how attractive he was, when Jae stood directly in his path, stuck her hand on his chest—*What the actual fuck?*—and said, "Excuse me, do you speak English?"

I never knew it was possible to die from embarrassment until that moment.

The man stopped, smiled, and replied, "Yes, of course," right as Dani started protesting that *she* spoke French. Jae silenced her with a curt "Shh" thrown over her shoulder.

I removed my hand from my mortified face and looked at him properly, taking in his outfit in a matter of seconds—a white T-shirt under a battered denim jacket, and slim-fit—but not too tight—tan trousers rolled up at the ankle, and suede sneakers in navy blue. The whole look sat easily on his six-foot-something, trim-but-not-skinny frame. If I'd been a modelling scout, I would have signed him on the spot. Even his hands were beautiful.

My eyes returned to his face, which was framed by longish medium-brown hair falling over one eye. His smile—full lips, which were far redder than a man's lips had a right to be—stretched across white teeth, a front one ever-so-slightly crooked. His nose would have been too big on someone else, but fit his wide face and high cheekbones perfectly, and his large eyes twinkled with amusement at Jaelee, crinkling at the edges. *Oh, I love an eye crinkle.*

He was immensely fuckable—and I mean that in the nicest possible way. A tug of familiarity niggled at me; he reminded of someone.

Jaelee continued her verbal assault, undaunted by basic manners. "So, we're here in this gorgeous city, just for tonight, and we want to go somewhere cool, somewhere fun, somewhere we can meet more men as gorgeous as you ..." I'm pretty sure I heard Lou groan at the last part. At least there was solidarity—we were *all* being humiliated in front of the spectacular-looking man.

I was tempted to walk away until the whole embarrassing exchange was done but, for some reason, I was rooted to the spot. *Who does he remind me of?*

"... So, can you help us out?" Jae's head tipped up to the Frenchman, her chin jutting out expectantly.

He laughed then and ran a hand through his hair. *Oh, my God, I want to do that.* "For sure. I know a place. I'm going there now to meet some friends. I would walk with you, but I have this." He pointed to a powder blue Vespa parked at the kerb.

Dani said something to him in French—maybe she was apologising. I *hoped* she was apologising, but whatever it was, he waved it away, smiling. Then he said something back in French and she typed into her phone. "What's happening?" asked Lou in a low voice.

"She's getting directions?" I replied, just as quietly.

"Got it," Dani said, smiling at the Frenchman as he climbed onto his scooter. "Are you sure you don't mind us crashing your party?" she asked. *Please don't mind. Please don't mind.*

His reply was another laugh. "Not at all. It will be fun, *non?*" I found myself nodding a response even though he wasn't even looking at me. Then he did look at me and there was a flicker of something across his face as his eyes held mine for a moment. His mouth pulled up at one corner and I felt a sharp intake of breath.

"So, you will definitely come, *non?*" he asked. My mind went somewhere crass, but in my defence, he *was* spectacularly sexy. Four women and one guy gave affirmative responses in varying degrees of enthusiasm, and by then it was really starting to bug me—*who* did he look like?

Before I could figure it out, he started the scooter, rolled it off its kickstand, and waved a goodbye before scooting— scootering?—away and leaving the five of us slightly dumbfounded by the whole exchange, even Jaelee.

"Dani, let me see that." Jae pointed to Dani's phone and she handed it over. Jae's face scrunched up.

"What?" asked Lou.

"It's an Irish pub."

"Hah!" My laugh released some of the tension I'd been holding in. "Well, I don't care. We're going."

"Oh yeah," said Dani. "That guy was, like, *uber* hot. We are totally going. Especially if there are more like him at the pub."

"Um, Craig," said Lou. "Are you okay with this?"

He shrugged good-naturedly. "Sure. I mean, it's a pub and I can drink here, so ..."

"Oh, that's right—you can't drink in the US." I only just realised we'd given him illicit wine with dinner. We were corrupting the man-child. I'd worry about that later—there were more important matters at hand. "Jae, we are going."

"But—"

"Nope. We're going. Dani, lead the way."

Dani needed no coaxing—I guessed she was as intrigued by the handsome stranger as I was. She struck off at a decent pace. I had no idea if he would be there when we arrived—*or* if he'd want to hang out with us—but we were going to that pub.

Dani led the way, her phone held like a divining rod. "It should be right up here." Music and light spilled out onto the footpath in front of what was, unmistakably, the right place. The awning was bright green, a fluttering Irish flag was visible from half a block away, and the sound of Ronan Keating's voice pumped out of the outdoor speakers. If a leprechaun had jumped out and waved us in, I wouldn't have been surprised.

Most importantly, though, there was a powder blue Vespa parked out front.

I felt a tingle in my nethers and a pep in my step, then I glanced at the rest of my party. Jaelee, Dani and Lou were all very attractive women. Even if we did end up talking to the Frenchman—*and* he was single, *and* interested—there was every likelihood he would be into one of my friends.

For all I knew, he might have been into Craig.

Dani had navigated, but Jaelee led us into the pub. As expected—I'd travelled to Ireland and had frequented more than a few Irish pubs—it was loud, poorly lit, and smelled like beer. It made me want a Guinness very badly—actually, I preferred Caffrey's, if they had it. I spied the tap on the bar and got a little excited.

A hand rested on my shoulder and I turned around to meet a chest clad in a denim jacket and a white T-shirt. *Oh, my God, he smells like happiness and sex.* I tilted my head to meet his eyes—his Kelly-green eyes framed by thick brown brows.

And that was when it hit me.

"Jean-Luc." It came out as barely a whisper.

"Catherine." He said it the French way, "Cat-er-in". He'd

always said it that way, even as the precocious teenager who'd refused to call me Catey. Only this time, it made me melt into a puddle of molten woman.

If it was possible to swoon in the twenty-first century, that was what I did—and thankfully, Jean-Luc was there to catch me. As my knees buckled beneath me—traitors—he grasped my elbow and guided me to a chair where he gently helped me to sit down.

"What's happening?" asked an annoyed Jaelee as she peered down at me.

There was a rushing in my brain, a flood of memories, as I tried to grasp the reality of Jean-Luc Caron standing in front of me, his hand on my shoulder and a concerned look on his face.

I watched as he turned to Jaelee and said, "Catherine and I, we are old friends. To meet like this, it is, how would you say? Kismet." To me, he said, "Are you okay?" His brows knitted over those gorgeous green eyes and I felt myself nodding like one of those bobble-head thingies.

"I'll get you some water."

"Caffrey's," I managed to squeak out. Then he was gone. *Please come back*. "He's coming back, right?" I asked Lou. Panic asserted itself in my gut.

She looked unsure. "I think so. Cat, seriously? You know him?"

Did I know him? It was the most rhetorical question ever asked. Yes, I knew him. I knew him very well. Well, not *that* well, but close. Jean-Luc had been my best friend when I was—sorry, when *we* were—fifteen.

I managed a slight head nod as a pint of Caffrey's and a pint of water appeared on the table next to me. I went for the Caffrey's first. I downed about a third of the pint before I realised that five sets of eyes were peering at me, all with the same expression.

I put down the glass and, with what I am guessing was a scowl, told my new friends—including Lou—to bugger off. Of course, I'd lived in England long enough for it to come out as, "Can you please give us a moment?"

Lou squeezed my hand and offered a weak smile before following the others to a nearby table.

A different hand rested on top of mine and I looked at it. His hand—Jean-Luc's. *God, he has beautiful hands. Had they always been like that?*

I shook my head to orient myself in the present. It didn't work. Finally, I got up the courage to meet his eyes. "Hi," I whispered. I wondered if my voice would ever come back—and if he could hear me over Damien Rice.

"Hi," he replied. The crinkles were back.

We stared at each other, him looking confident and slightly amused, and me squirming. A wave of nostalgia swept through me. "I ... I've missed you," I said. It was a massive understatement. He squeezed my hand and gave me a sweet but sad smile, and I swear I nearly burst into tears. When he leant back in his chair, pulling his hand away with him, I was left wanting—what exactly, I wasn't sure.

Jean-Luc Caron.

I tried to dredge an image of him, younger, from my dusty memories. I couldn't manage a full picture—only glimpses.

69

He was my age—thirty-five—so we hadn't seen each other for twenty years. And I couldn't remember the last time we'd been in touch.

Actually, yes, I could.

It was when I started seeing Scott, when I'd pinned a photo of Jean-Luc to my mirror. Scott hadn't liked that, and nineteen-year-old Cat—Catey—was a coward. She'd acquiesced to her new boyfriend and cut ties with the French exchange student who'd returned to Lyon years before, but who had written her every week since.

She'd cut ties with her best friend.

He was watching me. Perhaps he saw what played behind my eyes—a zillion feelings at once, with regret, guilt and yearning duking it out for first place.

"You look great," I blurted, my libido driving my tongue. At least it was better than, "You turned out so ridiculously hot that I want us to get a room *maintenant.*"

He laughed, clearly at ease with himself, and ran his hand through his hair again. The ensemble of moves brought me back to the present.

"So do you, Catherine." I never wanted anyone to ever call me Cat again. I'd have to teach everyone I knew, including my parents, to say my name the right way, *his* way.

A moment later, his compliment registered, and I was beyond glad we'd gone back to the campsite before dinner and that I didn't look like a hag in slouchy jeans and sneakers.

I returned his smile. "So, what do we do now?"

"I think we reacquaint ourselves, yes?" His smile was charming, the boy I once knew peeking out. How had I not seen it when we met him on the street?

But hang on. I looked around the pub. "Here?"

"No. Here it is too noisy. But I have a thought—if you will come with me."

He wanted me to leave with him and my mind went in a dozen different directions at once—unfortunately, they all tumbled out of my mouth in a highly ineloquent soliloquy. "Come with you? I ... my friends—we're staying ... Oh, God, where's the campsite? Hang on ... I think I have the name in my phone. Or you could take me back—or to the meeting place ... And what about *your* friends?"

The look on his face was pure amusement.

"Sorry," I added. He cocked his head indicating it was fine. "Let me go talk to my friends, all right? I'll be right back. *Don't. Go. Anywhere.*" I wasn't chancing him disappearing again until I at least had his phone number.

I sped over to the other table where the four of them had been watching everything—well, three. Jaelee was turned around in her chair speaking Spanish to a cute guy at the next table. Of *course* she'd met a Spaniard in an Irish pub in Paris.

"Hi," I said to my friends. Jaelee stopped talking and spun around mid-sentence. "So, I know tonight was our night out, but Jean-Luc wants to catch up and I'm going with him." No one said anything, so I leapt ahead with, "All right?"

Jaelee's eyes narrowed as she looked past me and threw

Jean-Luc a look. *Geez, woman.* After a beat, the three women spoke at once.

"Are you sure? I mean ..." said Lou.

"Go for it! I would," said Dani.

"No way. You're not ditching us," said Jae.

Right, that settled it. I was going. "Thanks, Dan." I grinned down at them. "So, I'll see you guys later?"

Lou spoke up. "Cat, I'm not sure about this. You haven't seen him in a long time. You don't really know him anymore."

"I've got his phone number," Dani offered, helpfully.

"So, you *are* ditching us?" Jae talked right over Dani; she looked properly ticked off.

"Lou, like Dani said, she has his phone number ..." Dani nodded, her chin perched casually on her hand. "And his name is Jean-Luc Caron, like Leslie Caron, the actress. And, I have my phone." On the five-hour journey to Paris the day before, we'd all friended each other on Facebook and Lou had saved my number in her contacts. I had more than one lifeline to my friends in case I needed them—which I was sure I wouldn't. "So, it's all good, right?"

Lou shrugged, clearly still uncomfortable about me leaving with someone she considered a stranger. I flicked my eyes to Jaelee, who was glaring at me.

"*What?* You'd do the same thing." The left side of her mouth tugged. "You *would*."

"I would not ditch my new girlfriends—and Craig—on our one night out in Paris." I seriously doubted that, but I didn't have time to argue. I glanced at Craig, who'd been silent throughout the whole exchange.

72

"Craig?"

He smiled, good-naturedly. "Look, if I ran into my high school sweetheart in Paris, I'd totally go hang with her."

"Craig, for you high school was a few months ago," Dani pointed out.

He shrugged, "Still, though, what are the chances Cat was going to run into him? Or that Jaelee was going to accost Cat's ex-boyfriend on the street?" Craig had a cheeky side—I loved it. Jaelee, not so much. She backhanded him in the chest with a "Hey!" And I almost corrected the "ex-boyfriend" part, but by then it was moot.

"So, I'm going …"

"But how will you get back? Are you meeting us at the coach at eleven?" Mama Bear Lou again.

"Hang on."

I dashed back over to Jean-Luc. "Hi."

"Hi."

"So, we're staying at a campsite. It's about thirty minutes out of the city and—"

"I'll take you there."

"You will?"

"*Mais oui.*"

"Excellent. Hold on." I went back to my friends and took in the tableau of facial expressions. Lou still wasn't entirely on board, Dani seemed wistful, and Jae looked like she'd sucked on a lemon. I told them I had a way back to the campsite and before I had to field any more protests, I returned to Jean-Luc and collected my bag from the back of my chair.

Jean-Luc unfolded from his chair and ran his hand through his hair. "*Tout va bien?*"

I nodded, grinning. It was impossible to play it cool with those eyes looking down at me, especially with the lovely crinkles.

Seeing Paris at night from a luxury coach with giant windows was fabulous. Seeing it from the back of a scooter, with my arms wrapped around a very taut torso, was even more so.

We stuck mostly to side streets, weaving through Paris's inner *arrondissements*, a labyrinth of cobblestones and asphalt. We passed Musée d'Orsay, crossed the Seine at Pont Royal, and to our right was the Louvre. I pinched myself. I was in Paris.

More notably, I was in Paris with Jean-Luc.

Our route took us past the Opera House, which I'd seen on Georgina's tour the night before, but could never tire of. It was a stunning building—especially at night. It looked a bit like someone had dipped a carousel in gold—only without the horses. I hummed the title song from Lloyd Webber's *Phantom* as we flew by.

We wound our way through the ninth *arrondissement*, climbing higher, and I guessed we were heading towards Sacré-Cœur in Montmartre. It would be my first time seeing it up close, but I wouldn't admit that to Jean-Luc. He didn't need to know I was a travelling neophyte.

As we rode, I pressed myself against him and took his lead to lean into the corners. The few times we had to stop and wait for traffic, I loosened my grip on his waist, not wanting to appear too eager to lay my hands on him—although I was.

My mind scrolled back through dozens, hundreds of memories, while my lady parts champed at the bit. He was the most spectacular man I'd had between my legs since, well, ever. I wondered if there was a way we could sleep together *and* reacquaint ourselves as friends.

So, Jean-Luc, how about we head to yours and you can ravish me until the sun comes up. Then we can grab a croissant and a coffee and catch up.

Perfect. I was sure he'd go for it.

He leant forward as we headed up a particularly steep street and I clung to him. Above the rooftops I could see the domes of the church, all beautifully lit. *Paris must have a whole lighting department*, I thought—a lightbulb brigade traversing the city bringing light to one and all, no bulb left behind.

We pulled over on the street in front of the church, and Jean-Luc rocked the scooter onto its stand. I dropped my hands from around his waist, missing the feel of him immediately. I climbed off the scooter as modestly as I could, then I took off my helmet, the spare. I hadn't asked him why he rode around with an extra helmet, mostly because I didn't want to know who usually wore it, whatever her name was.

I handed it to him and he hung it on the handlebars on the opposite side to his. "This will be okay. We are not going far, and no one will take them." It was the first time he'd spoken since we got on the scooter and he'd asked if I was comfortable. I hadn't minded the lack of conversation throughout the ride. It had given me time to plan what I wanted to say to him.

Besides, "Let's go to bed," it was something like, "I'm sorry for being a crappy friend all those years ago."

"Come," he said, reaching for my hand. He held it loosely in his without entwining our fingers—like a friend would. *Just friends*, I thought. We'd always been "just friends" when we were at school together, which baffled my girlfriends and was fodder for teasing by everyone else—hardly anyone seemed to believe it.

He *was* cute back then, sort of. He hadn't grown into his nose then and had been only a little taller than me, but he'd had those incredible green eyes and a cheeky grin. What had drawn me to him most, though, were his wit and his mind. He'd been hands-down the smartest kid in our year, and when the Aussie boys had teased him, his retorts had been so clever, they hadn't even known they'd been insulted. And all of that was in his *second* language. Actually, his third. He also spoke German. He'd taught me a bit, but I'd lost it soon after he'd returned to France.

Twenty years. How on earth did you catch up on twenty years in one night?

We climbed the stairs in front of Sacré-Cœur and Jean-Luc stopped. There were some small congregations on the steps, and a few people were solo. Almost everyone was looking at their phone. In *Paris*. I hadn't really looked at mine much since we'd arrived—there was too much else to see.

Jean-Luc dropped my hand, which I should have expected, but all the touching, then not touching was wreaking havoc with my lady parts. I looked up at the church. It was beautiful, but the word felt banal. I knew if Sarah was there, she'd have something clever or even poetic to say about it. She has a gift for that sort of thing.

I saw five pointy domes, one of them big, and a bunch of ornate archways and statues. It kind of looked like a giant pavlova—a fancy one, granted, although saying it looked like a meringue hardly encompassed the majesty of it. Majesty! I had a word.

"It's majestic," I said, far too impressed with my synonym for "beautiful".

When I looked at him, he was smiling down at me. "If you like the basilica, look." He placed a hand on my shoulder and turned me around.

Oh, my. Now, that's a view.

Unlike the view from the Eiffel Tower, the view from Montmartre seemed more real, more *Paris*. The city sat below us as though cupped by giant hands, thousands of points of light punctuating the dark. I glanced at my watch—it was getting late, 10:00pm. I wished we'd met up with Jean-Luc earlier. We were leaving Paris in the morning, and a few hours together didn't feel like enough.

I sighed, suddenly feeling the weight of our reunion.

"Catherine, *ça va?*"

I nodded. "Yes. I'm all right. I just—" How did I say all the things I wanted to say? How did I make up for what I'd done, then catch him up on my life, and catch up on his? It would be impossible to do all that in only one night.

"It's been a long time. Is that it?" My gaze left the city.

"Exactly. I don't know where to begin."

His mouth pulled into a straight line. "I know. *Moi aussi*." Me too. We were quiet for a moment. "Let's get a drink," he suggested, cutting through our shared melancholy.

"Hah! That's an excellent idea."

"Come. I know somewhere close. We can walk." He took my hand again and I almost pulled it away. It was confusing enough just being with him without adding touching to the mix, especially as he smelled incredible. But I didn't pull my hand away. Instead, I let him lead me to a bar down the block from the church.

The wooden and glass door opened into a small room with a handful of tables, each lit with its own lamp. Lena Horne played softly, and it sounded like the music was coming from an actual record player. Couples sat at two of the five tables and there was an ornate wooden bar along one wall. Jean-Luc pointed to an empty table near the window before heading to the bar.

I took the seat facing the bar, so I could watch him. He chatted easily with the bartender, who poured two glasses of white wine. He reached into his pocket and unfurled some notes, peeling one away and putting it on the bar. He then waved away the change and carried the glasses to the table.

Oh my, he's gorgeous.

I told my lady parts to please shut the hell up and smiled as he sat down, his stature making the short-backed chair seem inadequate. He took off his jacket and turned around to lay it across the back of his chair while I watched his T-shirt pull taut across his back. When he turned around, I lifted my gaze and he lifted his glass in a toast. "To old friends. *Salut*."

I picked up my glass and tapped it against his. He watched me as we both took a sip. It was delicious and I must have seemed surprised, because he laughed. "It's good, *non?*"

"*Oui. C'est très bon.*" I only had about ten words of French—enough to order a baguette and for a casual chat with a handsome Frenchman.

"So, Catherine. Twenty years to explain. You should go first." His eyes challenged mine, a playful smile on his lips. I took another sip—all right, it was a gulp—and breathed deeply.

Right—a succinct summary of my adult life. Go.

"Well, I finished uni—I became a teacher, like I'd planned, like my sister, Sarah. You remember Sarah, yes?" A quick nod signalled for me to keep going. "So, I started teaching, obviously ..." *Why am I nervous? Damned gorgeous Frenchman.* "Then ten years ago we moved to London—me and Sarah."

"This explains your accent."

"Mine?"

"Yes, it is, ah, mostly English, but still some Australian, *n'est-ce pas?*" he teased. He was right. I'd never really shaken some of my Aussie-accented words. It was a dead giveaway to anyone who paid attention to that sort of thing.

"*C'est vrai*—guilty." He smiled. "Anyway, Sarah went back to Australia after a couple of years, and I stayed in London. Teaching. And that's about it," I lied, ignoring the glaring omission of Scott from my tale.

"Now you."

His lingering look told me he had questions, but he didn't

pry. Instead, he said, "I also finished university and moved to Paris. Then I started working for a magazine—"

I interjected. "Writing?"

"*Oui*, yes, writing articles." He'd been a terrific writer when we were kids. I was glad he'd stuck with it.

"There, I met my wife ..." *Whoa. What???*

"Hold on, you're married?"

He licked his lips and took a sip of wine. It took far too long for him to answer and my stomach plunged into my shoes as the moments ticked by.

"I was. For a short time, a few years. We were very young."

"So ...?"

"We divorced, uh, eight years ago. We remain friends." *Oh.* "Vanessa." Great, so she had a name. Vanessa. Certain Jean-Luc's wife would have been stunning, my mind immediately produced Vanessa Paradis stealing languidly between rose bushes, like in a perfume ad.

I tried not to be jealous of the woman he had married—mostly because I had no right to be. I abruptly changed the subject. "So, do you still work for the magazine?"

He shook his head and drank more wine. "*Non*, I stayed there for a few years, then I went freelance. A little bit of a risk, but it was good in the end."

"And now?"

"Now it is the same. I write for some magazines and some blogs—they are less money, but often more interesting—and sometimes the newspaper. Current affairs, important issues, political matters at times."

"Wow, that's impressive, Jean-Luc." I meant it.

"*Merci*. I think it is interesting—at least for now. I travel a lot, though, and that is, ah, you know, *comme ci comme ça*." Like this, like that, the equivalent of "so-so". I'd never regularly travelled for work, so I could only guess how quickly the shine would wear off. Sarah said the two years she worked for Ventureseek were the best *and* the worst she'd ever had.

"And what about the guy?" His question shook me from my thoughts. *The guy? Oh, you mean Scott, the cheating bastard!*

"We broke up. Ten years ago. Here, actually."

"Here?"

"Paris." The surprise on his face was nearly comical. "Yes, I know."

"What happened?" I looked at him and oscillated between telling the whole truth, telling an abridged version, or quipping his question away. I went with the short explanation.

"When Sarah and I moved to London, it was only for a year. Scott ... well—we were still together, and I thought we could make it work long-distance. Apparently, he didn't. He started cheating with a colleague soon after I left—which sucked because he came to visit, and we had a whole trip planned—Paris, Nice, Florence, Rome. He confessed about the affair right before we left on the trip and *foolishly*, I decided to come anyway, thinking we could fix it—fix us. The whole thing unravelled from there." So *not* such a short explanation.

"I'm sorry, Catherine."

"It was a long time ago."

"And now? You have someone?"

I did not.

I had not had someone since Scott. I'd had dates and lovers

and a couple of fuckbuddies. And I'd stupidly slept with my flatmate a week ago, but no, I did not have someone. I didn't want someone. I was good without having a someone.

"No," I said as lightly as I could. "No one."

It was natural I would then ask the same question of him, but a hard lump formed in my throat. I thought of the extra helmet and barely choked out, "And what about you?"

Again, he took an annoyingly long time to respond. At least, it felt like it. It was probably no more than a second, but time halted while I waited. He shook his head and smiled. "No, no one at the moment." *At the moment.* My mind leapt back to Vanessa in her rose garden, a trail of lovely women following her in flowing dresses. Surely, there was a line-up of beauties waiting their turn with this scrumptious man.

His fingers played with the stem of his wine glass, and I noticed that his sipping had slowed down—probably because he had to drive me back to the campsite soon—*too* soon.

"I missed our letters ..."

Guilt engulfed me, followed closely by anger—at Scott.

"Me too." Deep breath. "Jean-Luc, I *so* regret ending our friendship like that. I thought it was the right thing to do ... Scott, he was just so jealous of you. But still, I felt terrible about it—*feel* terrible about it. And I've missed you—not only the letters, but *you*, our friendship."

He was staring at his wine glass, his brow creased. "I'm really sorry," I added for good measure. He wouldn't meet my eyes, and I reached across the table for his free hand.

If I'm honest, before that night in Paris, I hadn't thought

about him in a long time. But it didn't mean the feelings weren't there. I'd stuffed them into a little box that I'd tucked away deep inside me. From time to time, I'd open the box and remember what it was like having a clever French boy as my bestie. On trips back to Australia, I'd pull an actual box down from the top of the wardrobe in the guest room and spend an hour or two flicking through photos and reading back over the dozens of letters.

But in my everyday life, Jean-Luc Caron was a spectre of a long-ago friend. Even watching him across the table, I had a hard time remembering his exact face at the age of fifteen. He looked up and I saw a gloss of tears in his eyes. *I am an utter cow.*

He blinked them away. "And right when email became a thing, too," he replied, a smile tugging at the corner of his lips.

"Sorry?"

"We could have kept writing and saved all that money on stamps." His smile was gentle, but it didn't reach his eyes. He squeezed my hand, then let it go. It seemed I wasn't quite forgiven and all I wanted was to make it right between us.

"Do you remember when we stole your parents' brandy?" he asked, taking the conversation off on a much-welcomed tangent.

"Hah! Oh, yes, I remember that clearly. It was my first taste of a hangover. You, I recall, were fine the next day."

"The French, we train our children how to carry their liquor," he teased.

"It's *hold* their liquor." He shrugged at my correction. "And yes, you were quite the sophisticated teenager." He grinned. "And such a charmer. I think my mum was smitten with you."

"We also like older women in France."

"Oh, that's … just, no. That's awful." He laughed and his eyes lit up.

"Everyone thought we were boyfriend and girlfriend," he said lightly.

"Even my mum."

"Really?"

"Sure. There was this one time I asked if you could sleep over—do you remember? We were going to watch *Deep Impact* and *Armageddon*? Anyway, she decided it was time to give me *the talk*." His eyebrows lifted a centimetre. "Exactly. I had to explain to her that A) I already knew all that stuff, and B) you were just my *friend*, and C) Ewww, gross, how could she think *I* was thinking about having sex? 'Mum, I'm only fourteen!'"

"And she responded how?"

"I think she was as embarrassed as I was. And she let you stay over."

"I remember. I slept in the guest room."

"Well, yes, I mean, we were friends—just kids really, but still, we were fourteen … even if one of us fancied the other—"

"I did."

"You did what?"

"I *liked* you." It was my turn to laugh.

"You did not." His lips rolled in until they disappeared. "You *didn't*. You never said."

He ran his hand through his hair—my new favourite thing

in the whole world. "I was a long way from home, and you were my closest friend, and we spent a *lot* of time together—every day. And you were very cute ..."

He let the thought hang in the air, and I scoured my brain for any evidence of his twenty-year-old feelings, coming up short. I'd leave the scouring for later. Instead, I latched onto his depiction of teenaged me. "Cute?"

He shrugged. "You were. Let's just say it's a good thing your family *had* a guest room."

"Oh really? You would have made a move?"

"As you said, I was sophisticated for my age." I rolled my eyes. He held his hands out, mock offended.

"And now?" I asked.

"Now what?"

"Am I still cute?" *Oh bollocks. I did not say that.* I glanced at my glass—nearly empty. *Bloody wine.*

"Oh, no. Definitely not cute." *Oh.* "Sexy, yes. Beautiful, yes." *Ohhh.*

My eyes widened. I did not give them permission, but they were going rogue. I opened my mouth to speak and the words wouldn't come.

"I have shocked you?"

"No, you've, well, yes, a little, but ... thank you, for the compliment." He tilted his head and lifted one shoulder, as though my beauty was a given and there was nothing to thank him for. My eyes flicked to the clock above the bar. Coming up on midnight.

"You need to go soon, yes?"

I sighed. I didn't want to go back to the garden shed and

sleep in a sleeping bag. I wanted to go to Jean-Luc's bed and crawl under the duvet and snuggle up with him and reminisce about how much he'd fancied me and never told me.

"Yes. I should. We leave early tomorrow—at seven." He sucked air through his teeth in horror. "I know. It's barely civilised."

"And you go where?"

"Uh, next is the *château*—it's in the Beaujolais region, so that should be nice—then Antibes, Florence, Rome ... we go to a lot of places."

"Over what time? How long?"

"It's only two weeks."

"Two weeks for all those places?" he scoffed.

"I know, and that's not even all of them. We only got into Paris yesterday."

He shook his head and tutted, and I suddenly felt very foolish for having booked myself onto a rapid-fire touristy tour.

"But still, there is something very good in all this."

"What's that?"

"The Eurostar," he said, grinning. "When you get home to London, we're only a few hours apart."

Bollocks, I was going to swoon again.

Chapter 4

I didn't want to leave the nameless bar in Montmartre.

I wanted to stay there all night and drink scrummy wine and talk to the handsome man who had once been my best friend.

After his remark about the Eurostar, it was impossible not to project into the future where we shared an apartment on the Left Bank, him writing the great French novel, and me lying about on beautiful linens, sexily mussed up from all our lovemaking and eating grapes and cheese from a wooden board. Perhaps our future was in the nineteenth century.

He was talking about his next writing assignment. I should have been paying attention instead of fixating on his long fingers as they tapped on the table.

"When are you in Roma?" At his question, my eyes lifted to his.

"Oh, um ... Thursday." He smiled.

"*Parfait.*" Perfect.

"Sorry?"

"Well, as I said, the interview is on Wednesday."

"Oh, right." Why wasn't I listening?

"It's not so far, Naples to Roma. I could catch the train and see you there."

"In Rome?" I must have sounded like a moron.

"*Oui*. You arrive on Thursday. Perhaps I can steal you away from your group. For dinner."

Ohhh.

"You know, I've never actually been to Rome," I confessed.

He looked confused. "Never?"

"No. I'm really looking forward to it."

"Of course. You must. It is extraordinary."

"High praise from someone who lives in Paris."

"*Peut-être*." Perhaps. "So, we have a date, *oui*, Catherine?"

It took approximately two-point-four seconds for me to decide. "That should work," I replied, as though we'd just scheduled a business meeting. What a romantic, huh?

One of the couples said goodnight to the bartender and left. It really was getting late, and I was trying to eke out the last sips of my wine, but Jean-Luc took the couple's departure as our prompt to go.

"We should ..." he said, standing.

"Yes, of course." I couldn't remember the last time I'd been so disappointed. Bugger the stupid bus tour to hell. I wondered what he'd say if I abandoned it and invited myself to stay in Paris. Probably something like, "Uh, *non*, *merci*, crazy Australian-British woman."

Jean-Luc didn't take my hand when we left the bar. More disappointment, but seriously, what did I expect to happen, that he would declare his undying love for me? He'd thought I was cute twenty years ago, and even though I was head-over-heels in lust, it wasn't like we'd be sending out the wedding invitations any time soon.

I had a firm chat with myself on the way back to the scooter. It had been a minor miracle I'd found Jean-Luc again—or rather, that *Jaelee* had. I'd thank her properly as soon as she was speaking to me again. But I needed to take the whole situation for what it was—a wonderful, remarkable, one-in-a-million fluke—and stop indulging my lustful thoughts.

The ride to the campsite was far longer than was comfortable, especially as the night's chill had set in and my bare legs were freezing. It was also shorter than I wanted it to be. Even when we stopped at traffic lights, I held onto Jean-Luc's waist. We pulled up outside the campsite just after one, and Jean-Luc rocked the scooter onto its stand.

I had to be up in five hours.

I didn't care.

This hadn't been a date and I'd never been in this exact situation before, so I wasn't sure what the protocol was for saying goodnight. I wanted to kiss him, but no doubt that was just my lusty lady parts talking. I slipped off my helmet and started to climb off the scooter, but his hand landed firmly on my thigh, stopping me. *Breathe.*

"*Attends.*" Wait. I waited. He took his helmet off and hung it on the handlebars. He got off the scooter, reached for my helmet and hung it in its spot. Then he climbed back on the scooter facing me.

There's something you need to know—scooter seats are not particularly long. We were very close together, our knees touching, crotch facing crotch. I self-consciously adjusted my dress over the seat so I wasn't flashing my knickers.

"Hi," he said, a smile playing on his ridiculously luscious lips.

"Hi."

He shook his head, his eyes locked on mine, and sighed— not a sad sigh, or a hopeless or frustrated one, but a contented sigh. It was very sexy. *Is he going to kiss me? He's definitely going to kiss me.*

"I still cannot believe it. You. Here. It is ... I don't know the best word in English. I've thought about you many times over the years, do you know?"

I did and I didn't. It was rhetorical anyway, so I said nothing, my lips pulling into a taut line. There was a flash of sadness in his eyes, which sent another shockwave of guilt through me.

Then he did something so sweet, so intimate, it brought tears to my eyes. He placed his forehead against mind and rested it there a moment. I closed my eyes and when he lifted his head to press a soft kiss on my forehead, I had to stifle a gasp. *Zut alors!* The French expressions were coming back thick and fast.

He sat back abruptly, and I missed the feel of him, the night chill asserting itself between us.

"I should go," he said unnecessarily. It was so late, and he had at least another thirty minutes' ride before he got home. If I'd had more than half a plastic-wrapped mattress to offer him, I would have invited him to stay.

He climbed off the scooter and helped me off. "Thanks for the ride," I said, the lightness of my voice a farce.

Smiling eyes peered at me. "So, Thursday in Roma, yes?" I nodded. "Oh, your number." He pulled out his phone, tapped out my name, and handed it to me. I added my number and tapped *save*, then sent myself a text message so I'd have his number. Sure, Dani had it, but what if her phone had fallen in the Seine or something? I wasn't taking that chance.

"Here."

"*Merci*." He leant down, and I nearly cocked up the French-style double cheek kiss. Hopefully, he couldn't tell how much I wanted a proper kiss. And I did—badly.

"*Bonne nuit, ma chérie*."

"Goodnight. Ride safely." I gave him a half-wave, then turned and walked briskly through the gates of the campsite, my arms wrapped around me.

I'd started the night exploring Paris with my friends, and I'd ended it with a serious crush on a super-hot French guy who'd once taught me how to swear in German. *Scheisse*.

And French. *Merde*.

I couldn't remember if the door to our shed creaked or not, so I opened it as slowly as I could. "Hi," said a whispered voice from the dark.

"Oh, my God, Lou, you scared the crap out of me," I replied far too loudly. I pulled the door shut behind me and plonked onto my bunk, dropping my bag on the floor. "Please don't tell me you've been waiting up."

"No. But I mean, the door's *right there*. And this cabin is so tiny—you were never going to sneak in."

"True. Sorry."

"Hey, no problem." Lou was such a darling. "So, how was it?"

"Oh, Lou, so much to tell, but first I need a wee."

"Oh-kay."

"Sorry, TMI." I contemplated the long walk to the ablution block. If I *hadn't* needed a wee, I would have forgone teeth brushing and face washing—I'd be showering in a few hours anyway. With a sigh, I foraged for my toiletries bag.

"I'll wait for you. I want to hear about your night."

I abluted quickly and returned to the shed less than ten minutes later, opening the door to a loud yawn from Lou's side.

"We can talk in the morning if you like. We have to be up in ... bollocks, four and a half hours." I slipped off my shoes and jacket and shimmied out of my dress.

"Yeah, good idea. I don't think I can keep my eyes open much longer."

I dug my PJs out from under my pillow and was pulling the top over my head when Lou whispered alarmingly, "Oh my heck, what is *that*?"

I pulled the PJ top all the way on and sat on my bunk, looking around frantically for the offending item. Nothing.

"What?"

"The thing on the wall."

My eyes flew to all four of the cabin walls. Still nothing.

"Which wall? Where?"

"*There*, next to the door."

"What is it?"

"*I don't know.*" The whole whispered exchange was becoming a poor rendition of *Who's on First?*

"But what do you see?"

"A big *white* thing." I scoured the darkness for the invasive white thing. A moth? A glowing white spider? Some kind of French iridescent slug?

"All right, Lou, I'm turning on the light."

"Okay."

In one deft movement, I leapt out of bed and flicked on the light switch, my head swivelling as I took in every flat surface in the cabin in search of the scary white thing. Then I realised Lou was laughing.

I spun towards her. She was laughing so hard there were tears in her eyes and she was fanning herself with her hand. "Oh, my goodness," she gulped between barking laughs.

"Lou, what?" My tone must have permeated the hilarity, because she met my eyes. The hand fanning became flapping and she started pointing, still gulp-laughing.

"The thing ... the thing ..." She flapped her hand in the general direction of the door. I scowled at her. This was too much for one-thirty in the morning. "It was ... it was the *light*." Then she dissolved into a fresh bout of laughter and I finally understood.

I sat on my bunk. "The white thing?" She nodded. "The terrifying white thing on the wall was the light?"

"Yes," she panted.

The giggles bubbled up and consumed me. Soon we were both doubled over on our respective bunks. Eventually, I had the presence of mind to get up and turn off the terrifying light.

As our laughter subsided, I said, "Night, Lou."

"Night, Cat."

Despite the time, it was a while before I could fall asleep. It had been a big night.

I woke with a start to Lou calling my name. Her voice was barely above a whisper, but after that little sleep it felt like she was screaming in my ear.

Why the hell had I booked a bus tour when I could have spent two weeks on the beach in the Canary Islands?

"Ugghhh." I threw my arm over my eyes to block out the weak morning light. "What time is it?"

"You don't want to know, but we should get to the showers."

"I hate you."

"I love you too, now get your little butt out of bed."

I did as I was told, and we made the coach two minutes before the 7:00am departure. I held two pieces of cold toast wrapped in a thin paper napkin and longed for a cup of tea I wouldn't get.

Lou and I handed our cases over to Tom with an apology for being so late. He took them with a smile and squashed them into the hold under the coach. I had a sudden memory of Sarah telling me that she, the driver and the cook slept under there when they were on a camping tour—more comfortable than tents apparently, but the thought made me shiver. I'm claustrophobic.

When I climbed onto the coach, Craig was sitting in the seat next to Lou—*my* seat. I looked about for Dani and Jaelee. Jae was on her own and gave me a wave. I plopped down next to her, gratefully. I wasn't in the mood to make new friends.

"Hi," I said through a mouthful of toast, my hand over my mouth.

"Hi. You look terrible."

I threw her a look and swallowed. "So, are you still ticked off with me?"

"About last night?" I nodded. She shrugged.

I changed tacks. "Where's Dani?"

"She's back there."

I turned in my seat and saw Dani—sweet, adorable Dani— seated in the middle of the back seat surrounded by Kiwi guys. My brows nearly met my hairline. I swivelled back to Jaelee waiting for the explanation.

"I really don't know how or when, but she and the tall one—Jason—have a thing."

"A thing?"

"He thinks she's cute."

"He's right." I turned back around right as Dani threw her head back and laughed. "Hmm. Good for her." Jaelee sulked beside me. "Hey. What's up?"

"Everyone's pairing up."

"Uh, no."

"*You* are." I rolled my eyes—it was involuntary, but I was not in the mood for a sulky seatmate either. I ate my toast as the coach pulled out of the campsite and Georgina stood up and turned on the microphone.

"*Bonjour* everyone," she said with an appalling French accent. I knew mine wasn't particularly good either, but I think my lack of sleep had got the better of my goodwill towards (wo)men.

She told us the ride to the *château* would take nearly five hours, including a stop for morning tea. Tea! I latched onto the word as the life-preserver it was. I finished the cold toast and did my best to wipe the melted butter—actually, it was probably margarine—from my fingers with the near-useless napkin. I rested my head on the seat and closed my eyes.

"So, how was last night?" Jaelee was not going to let me snooze.

"It was ..." The thought fizzled, because I didn't know. I hadn't had time to process everything we'd said, and all the feelings Jean-Luc had aroused in me. Aroused. I wondered how Jaelee would react if I told her it was arousing. A small bark of a laugh escaped me. Oh, God, I needed sleep.

Jae looked at me expectantly. "It was lovely." An insipid response, but it was all I had.

"And?" *Geez, Jaelee.*

"And ... well, it was completely out of the blue. I mean, when you stopped him in the street, I thought he looked familiar, but I couldn't place him. And I mean, he's just so ..." My hands left my lap to gesture exactly how gorgeous Jean-Luc was.

"He is. He's definitely 'just so'..." My annoyance dissolved and we shared a smile. "*Yes*, and then when we were at the pub and I realised who he was ... I mean, it was the most surreal moment of my life. And the whole night I kept looking at him trying to see the fifteen-year-old, you know? There were glimpses, but they were eclipsed by *him*—the man. He's so, well ... *manly*."

"Mmm."

I was on a roll, my tiredness forgotten. "We were close, though, when we were teenagers—closer than I was with any of my girlfriends—nearly as close as I was with Sarah—she's my sister. It was kind of like having this super cool French guy as my brother. In the year he was in Sydney, he spent more time at our house than with his host family. It sucked royally when he went home."

"Did you keep in touch?"

"We did, yes, absolutely. He was a great letter writer—me too. I mean this was, what, ninety-eight? No, ninety-nine, so email was a thing, but back then, we didn't have the internet at home. And even when we got it, Jean-Luc and I kept writing letters. Some weeks I'd write a little every day, almost like a journal. Then I'd mail it before it got too big to fold."

"Huh. So, what are we talking, every month?"

"Every week."

"Seriously? For how long?"

I thought about Scott's horrible ultimatum and felt the familiar sting of guilt. "Around four years. We stopped writing when we were nineteen." I omitted the part about me being a giant cow.

"I don't think I've ever written to anyone like that, letters *or* emails. It would be cool to read back over your letters to him, don't you think?"

"I guess."

"But, hang on. You must have tried to find him on Facebook or Insta or something?"

"Of course, but do you know how many Jean-Luc Carons there are online? And I could only guess what he looked like as a man—and I obviously had no clue anyway, or I would have recognised him right away."

"True. So, did anything *happen*?" She loaded "happen" with all the meaning it could possibly hold.

"Last night?" She nodded, a conspiratorial smile on her face. "No." The smile dissolved. "We talked, caught each other up. He's been married." I wasn't sure why I added the last part.

"Oh. But divorced now?"

"Yes. They're still friends, apparently. Vanessa." I *really* wasn't sure why I'd shared that.

"Mmm. That 'still friends with the ex-wife' thing."

"Right?" So *that's* why I'd brought it up—to validate my feelings about Vanessa, even though I had no claim on Jean-Luc, or any reason to be jealous that his ex-wife was still on the scene.

"So, no kiss goodnight?"

"Do you count kisses on both cheeks?"

"Uh, in France? No."

Then I remembered the forehead kiss. "What about him touching his forehead to mine and then kissing it?"

Her eyes widened. "He did that?"

"He did that."

"Like a quick smack?" her eyes narrowed, questioningly.

"No, like softly pressing his lips to my forehead."

She fanned herself with her hand. "Well, darlin'" she said with a pretty good Southern accent, "that *is* something."

"Hmm. I thought so. Oh! I almost forgot! He's coming to Rome. I'm seeing him on Thursday night for dinner."

"Way to bury the lead, Cat."

"Sorry." I laughed. "I've had four hours of sleep. My brain is a little … you know."

"So, again, you're *not* pairing up?"

"Oh, well, maybe. I mean, at the very least I have a date."

"With a hot French guy who, apparently, has your heart."

"No, he doesn't …" I stopped myself. Did he? Sure, we'd had a childhood friendship a million years before, but I was madly in lust, that's all.

"Hi, Mum, it's me."

"Who?"

"Me, Cat."

"Oh, Catherine. Hello, love."

"Why did you have to ask who I was? There are only two people in the world who call you 'Mum'."

"You and Sarah sound so alike, love."

"I'm the one with an English accent."

"If you say so." I was regretting the decision to call my mother during the stop for morning tea, but curiosity is a powerful motivator and talking to Jaelee had got me thinking.

"All right, Mum, I need a favour."

"Where are you calling from?"

I looked around. I had no idea where we were. It was just some random highway rest stop. Besides, it didn't matter and I needed to hurry things along—the call was costing me an absolute fortune. I would have used FaceTime, but Mum *still* didn't know how.

"I'm in France, Mum. I told you I was going on a tour. Anyway, I need a favour."

"Of course, darling. Do you need money?" *Oh, for fuck's sake.*

"No, Mum. I'm ... I have a job. I make money. I just need you to get something from the box in the guest room."

"Which box?"

"The *only* box I have stored in the wardrobe in the guest room—*that* box."

"Oh, yes, I'll have a look." I realised she was about to go and look. "Mum. Wait."

"Yes?"

"Sorry, you don't need to go look now. Or, you can, but take the phone with you."

"Okay." I could hear her on the move, then a door opened. "Oh yes—the one with all the packing tape on it."

"Yes, that's it. So, in there are some shoeboxes—they've got dates on them—and I need you to get the 2004 box out—"

"Well, your father's going to have to get the box down, love. *I* can't do it."

"I know, Mum. I'm just telling you what I need, all right?"

"Okay, so the box inside the box that has 2004 written on it. What do you want me to do with it?"

"Inside the 2004 box are letters—they're in order. I want you to get out the last one."

"Okay. Only that one?"

"Yes. Then send it to me."

"Mail it to you?

"No, sorry, can you scan it and then email it?"

"Scan it?"

"Yes, with the scanner in the study."

"I think your dad will have to help with that too, Catherine."

"All right, Mum. That's a good idea. And one more thing."

"Yes?"

"There's also a smaller box of photos in there—they're photos of me and Jean-Luc, do you remember him?"

"Of course, darling. He was like part of the family."

"Yes, well, if you could scan one of those too? The one of us at my fifteenth birthday party, if you can find it. If not, any of the others will do."

"Sure, darling. Uh, Catherine? Why do you need these? I mean, now. Didn't you say you're on a tour?"

"Yes, yes, I am. But it's important. I uh ..." I was about to tell her I'd seen him, but Lou appeared at my side with two giant takeaway cups of tea. I took mine from her and whispered, "Thanks," as she tapped her watch at me. It was nearly time to get back on the coach. I held up a finger and she nodded.

"Mum? I have to go. We're getting back on the coach. You'll get Dad to help, right?"

"Okay, darling. Will do."

"Love you."

"I love you too, bye."

"Bye." I pocketed my phone. "Thanks for the tea."

"No problem." We started walking back to the coach. "So, you're fine with me sitting next to Craig for the next leg, yeah?"

"Of course. Jae's good company. And, I mean, we're not Bert and Ernie ..."

"Nice one. Chandler and Joey." I loved that she got my FRIENDS reference right away. "Anyway, Craig's got some stuff going on, and I think I may be helping him sort through it." Louise was a counsellor for troubled teens. Craig was more of a young man than a teenager, and certainly wise beyond his years in many ways, but if anyone on the tour was going to help him, it was Lou.

"No, no, it's totally fine. I get it. As long as we still get to sleep together."

"Did you just hear yourself?"

"I did, yes." She laughed and nudged me with her shoulder, almost toppling me. She was quite a bit taller than me. "Yes, yes, leave me alone. I barely slept, you know." She climbed on the coach ahead of me, just as Georgina caught my arm.

"Um, Catherine, can I talk to you for a moment?"

"Sure."

She walked a few steps away from the coach door and I followed. She turned towards me and in a hushed voice said, "It's about last night."

"Oh. Yes?"

"It really is best for you to ride back with the group at the end of the night." Was she kidding? I searched her face for any signs of mirth. She wasn't kidding.

"Did the girls tell you I had a ride?" I was sure they had, but I didn't know what else to say.

"Yes, they did, but still ..." Still, *what*? Resentment bubbled up in my veins. I was a paying customer and a grown-up, and I was at *least* five years older than her—maybe more—but she was telling me off like I was a naughty schoolgirl. My

102

mind flashed to the first day of the tour when she'd shushed us with her teacher look.

She was clearly waiting for me to say something. I had a choice: tick off the tour manager or get her back onside. "Well, good to know. I will keep that in mind. Thank you, Georgina. If that's all?" Without waiting for her reply, I turned sharply, stomped to the coach and climbed aboard.

I never was one to take the easier path.

I sat down heavily next to Jaelee. "Do I want to know?" she asked in a low voice.

"We don't like Georgina," I replied.

I got the sense that Jae could—and would—turn "mean girl" with me, no questions asked.

"Got it," she replied. See?

"So, did you talk to Dani?" The coach pulled away from the rest stop and I sipped my tea. Calm and happiness spread through me along with the warmth of the liquid—yes, really. Tea is magic like that.

"Briefly. I think it's on with Jason."

I leant into the aisle to peek at the Kiwi four-pack, singling out the tallest one. "He is cute."

"He seems okay."

At that exact moment, Dani laughed at something he'd said, touched his arm, and batted her eyelashes at him. Flirting 101.

"Dani seems to think he's more than 'okay'."

"Mmm."

"So, let's do you now," I said, settling back into my seat.

"Me?"

"Yes. The 'love of your life married someone else' story." I must have been all fired up from my encounter with Georgina, launching myself carelessly into what was bound to be a difficult conversation. Jaelee sighed beside me. "Come on." I jostled her with my shoulder. "We still have two hours 'til we get to the *chateau*."

It *was* a difficult conversation.

Jaelee had refused Paco's marriage proposal, breaking his heart, and then when he found someone else, realised she did love him, and she did want to marry him. And she only realised all of this when she received an invitation to the wedding.

"He *invited* you?"

"Yep."

I thought about inviting Scott to my wedding—if I ever had one—and couldn't even imagine it. "And that's when you realised?" A nod. "Oh Jae, that's horrific." Another nod. "Did you ever tell him?"

"No, of course not. Why would I? Oh no, do you think I should have told him?" She was second-guessing one of the biggest decisions she'd ever made. I needed to dial it back.

"Nooo. No, you did the right thing. You respected his wishes. It's like what we told Dani about Nathalie's wedding, right?" A third nod. "So, did you go to the wedding?" I asked gently.

"I couldn't. I just ..." She sighed again. "I made up some work excuse. I even booked a conference in LA on the same weekend so I'd legitimately be out of town and wouldn't be tempted to go, you know?" I did not—we were way beyond any experience I'd ever had.

"Oh, yes, totally. You did the right thing." Poor Jaelee. No wonder she was tetchy about Dani and Jason—*and* about me and Jean-Luc. Not that Jean-Luc and I were *together*. Just old friends catching up for dinner in Rome. I knew I was deluding myself. Old friends indeed. New lovers, I hoped.

"*Cat!*" Apparently, I had wandered off into the wonderful land of Jean-Luc.

"Sorry, what?"

"Look." Jae was looking out the window and I leant forward so I could see past her.

"Oh my …"

"Right?"

We were travelling along a narrow, undulating road. On our right was a low stone wall, crumbling in places, and beyond that were dozens, maybe hundreds, of rows of grape vines, climbing and falling over rolling hills. It must have been close to harvest time, because the vines were heavy with bunches of dark, dusty-skinned grapes.

"That's a lot of grapes," said Jaelee.

"That means a lot of wine," I replied. We shared a look and a grin. "Definitely wine o'clock, don't you think?" I knew it was only just noon, but when in France …

"Oh, definitely," She replied. I loved any friend who was willing to day-drink with me. Jae was a keeper.

Chapter 5

There was a chorus of "Oooh" as we rounded a bend, and Jae and I both craned our necks to see what it was about.

"Ohhh, wow," I added to the sounds around me.

"Holy crap," Jae uttered breathlessly.

We were staying in an eighteenth-century *château* owned by Ventureseek and it was perched on the highest hill for miles. The midday sun bounced off its façade of marble and windows, casting a kind of golden aura around it. There were two towers, I guess you'd call them, with capped slate roofs, and a pair of symmetrical stairs which led left and right from the *château* to the grounds. It was frigging gorgeous.

"Oh, this is gonna be good," said my seatmate.

Georgina picked up the microphone. "So, everyone, as you can see, the *château* is something really special. We're going to head through the gates soon and when we arrive, please meet on the front lawn—the top level, not the lower level with the pool—so the reps can give you your room assignments."

Earlier in the drive, when Georgina had passed around the rooming sheet, Lou, who was closest to the front of the coach, had claimed the only room at the *château* that slept four. When the sheet got back to me and Jae, I could have leapt up and kissed her. I had my bus besties and I wasn't interested in rooming with strangers or making new friends. Sometimes, I am a cliquey teenager.

The coach stopped just outside the *château* gates and I leant into the aisle. "He's not driving us through that gate, is he?" I asked. Jae half-stood in her seat to see what I was talking about. The gate was narrow—very narrow—almost as if it was designed before giant touring coaches existed.

"Well, this will be impressive." Jae sat down as Tom got out of the coach and tucked the mirrors in on both sides. Back in his seat, he edged the coach through the gates inch by inch, and I held my breath until we came to a stop. Then the whole coach exploded into spontaneous applause. I added, "Woohoo!" and there were some whistles from behind me.

"Yeah, yeah," we heard from the driver's seat.

Standing in the aisle, I took our day bags off the parcel shelf and handed Jaelee hers before we shuffled off the coach. It was kind of like getting off a plane, only we did it several times a day and, believe me, it was *not* fun.

When I finally stepped off the coach, a warm and fragrant breeze hit me, earthy with a strong scent of jasmine and just a hint of happiness. I closed my eyes and tipped my head to the sun. I'd lived in England for a decade, but deep down I was an Australian who thrived on warm weather and sunshine.

"I can't believe how good this weather is—in *fall*," said Jaelee. She was right. It must have been in the mid-twenties.

"I want to stay here for the rest of the tour," I said.

"Me too," replied Jae. "Look." I opened my eyes and followed the line of her finger. There was a long table covered in huge globe wine glasses, each brimming with ruby red wine. I'd had wine from Beaujolais enough to know that I loved its bright fruity flavours, and these were seriously generous pours.

"Hi, everyone!" called a heavily Kiwi-accented voice. A tall redheaded guy stood on what was essentially the doorstep, although this one was twelve feet wide and made of marble. We gathered around. "I'm Keith, and I'm the senior rep here. *Bienvenue au château!*" It was a good attempt, but with an accent that bad it was also a little grating. I tried not to hold it against him.

"Kayla here—" a short curvy blonde girl waved and a few in the group waved back "—has your room keys. I'll call out the room number, then the names of the people in the room. The first name on the list, come get your room key. The rest of the team is waiting inside the foyer to direct you to your rooms. As I'm sure you can appreciate, this is a big place and we have another tour arriving in an hour or so, so we want to get you settled as quickly as possible."

If that was the case, he needed to stop talking. People were getting antsy. All right, maybe it was just me.

"And when you've dropped your bags in your rooms, come back down for your welcome drink." My eyes fixed on the perfect rows of glasses, shaded from the midday sun by an awning.

Less than ten minutes later, we arrived at our room. "Oh, my heck, this is incredible." Ah, Lou—even "hell" was too salty for her. She was right, though, the room was incredible.

It had the highest ceilings I'd ever seen, and everything was white—the marble floors, the plaster walls, the windowsills, the bedding. It was like walking into a giant marshmallow.

Lou dropped her case and went straight to the window. "Look at this!" I left my case next to hers and crossed the cavernous room to stand beside her. We were on the second floor and had an uninterrupted view of the *château*'s grounds. Beyond its borders was a landscape of valleys, hills, and vines—vibrant greens punctuated with flecks of gold and brown. There was only one tiny cloud in the sky, puffy and snow white.

"Frigging hell. I'm so glad we're here." Unlike Lou, I liked salty language.

"That's amazing," drawled Dani, joining us.

"Bunk beds?!" said Jaelee from the door. We turned in unison and stared at her. "I'm not sleeping on the top." She challenged Dani with an unpleasant look. I'd been certain Jaelee could do a mean "mean girl", but I never thought she'd turn on one of our own.

"I'll sleep up there. I don't care," said Dani with a shrug. After only three days, she'd mellowed considerably. I thought of her taut face when she'd seen the garden shed in Paris.

"Good." Jaelee stomped over and sat down heavily on the bottom bunk. Lou and I shared a look, and I could see she was about to go all mama bear. I literally stood back as she crossed the room and looked down at Jaelee, her hands on her hips.

"You owe Danielle an apology." I saw Dani start to protest, then stop—maybe she wanted that apology.

110

Jae suddenly became very interested in her cuticles. Her mouth squirmed. "I'm sorry, Dani."

"And us."

Jae looked up at Lou, then me. "Sorry." Lou's whole manner changed in a heartbeat and she sat down next to Jae and wrapped her in a huge side hug.

"I'm sorry you're having a hard time." I saw a sheen of tears in Jae's eyes and watched her blink them away.

"It's no excuse. We all are. Well, maybe not Cat," she teased. She caught my eye and I pretended to be insulted. "Anyway ... you girls, you're just so ... sorry. I'll behave, I promise."

"Good, 'cause I want me some of that wine," said Dani. It broke the tension and I was grateful for her graciousness. If Lou was mama bear, then Dani was the peacemaker. Jae was probably the closest we had to a troublemaker. I wondered what that made me.

"So, what's our game plan then? Welcome wine, then buy a couple of bottles and find somewhere nice to sit? Maybe the vineyard?" I asked. Ah, right, I was the enabler.

"Welcome wine, then a swim," replied Lou. *What?*

"Yeah, I'd like a swim," said Dani. "I wasn't sure if it would be warm enough, but I'm not wasting this gorgeous weather." *Oh, bollocks.*

"I'm definitely busting out one of the bikinis," said Jae.

"Hang on, did you say, 'one of'? You brought more than one swimsuit?" I asked, distracted by Jaelee's excessive bikini packing.

"Yes. I'm from Miami," she replied, as though that explained it.

My three roommates erupted into action, unzipping their cases and pulling out swimsuits and wraps. I stood motionless, watching, until Lou realised I wasn't getting ready. "What's up?" she asked, as she stood.

"Uh, I don't really want to go swimming."

Three blank faces met mine.

"Yeah, you're probably gonna have lots of chances to go swimming at a *château* in the middle of a French vineyard." Jae's point was undeniable.

"I didn't bring a swimsuit," I lied. Of *course* I'd packed one—it was on the list.

Lou looked at me confused. "I thought I saw one in your bag. It's red, right?"

I sighed heavily, caught out. "All right, yes, I have a swimsuit, but I am not fit for human consumption in *this*—" I circled my hand in front of my crotch "—area. I didn't have a chance to get waxed. This tour was very last-minute. *All right?*"

"Ohhh," said Lou and Dani at the same time.

"'Oh', nothing. I'm still stuck on the 'human consumption' part," said Jae, dryly.

"You know what I mean. I wouldn't want to scare anyone."

"Hey, it's all good. I've got some wax strips with me." Jaelee was full of surprises.

"What?"

She pulled out her toiletries bag, which was huge by the way, and took out some of those ready-to-go all-in-one wax strips. "Here."

"I don't DIY." That wasn't a lie. I'd had some very bad experiences DIY-ing a bikini wax.

"Extenuating circumstances." She raised a single eyebrow at me. *I wish I could do that.* I needed to focus. I did not want to apply sticky wax on my lady parts, no matter how inviting the pool was.

"C'mon!" Dani was practically jumping up and down. "It'll be fun."

"C'mon, Cat." Even Lou was betraying me.

"Fine!" I said as I snatched the strips from Jaelee's hand. "I'll meet you downstairs after—well, once everything is under control." I went into the Jack-n-Jill bathroom which connected our room to the next, loud laughter following me. I didn't care.

An hour later, I was glad I'd confessed my body hair dilemma. Not only did something like that cement a friendship, but I'd forgotten how lovely it was to take a dip in a pool, then dry myself in the sun.

And the afternoon was *definitely* enhanced by the endlessly flowing wine.

After we finished our welcome drinks, in what was very likely record time, Jaelee made a beeline for the *chateau*'s bar and brought back two bottles of the locally produced wine. One of them was still unopened on the grass beside us, but we made short work of the first. A bottle *is* only five glasses of wine—four if you pour like Jaelee.

"So, did we want to do the wine tasting later?" asked Lou.

"Pass," said Jaelee. "Besides, we're tasting the wine. I like it. What more is there to know?"

"We'd probably get to see the barrels and where they make it," said Lou.

"I'm with Jae," I said. "Plus, Sarah said the winemaker is this leering old guy."

"Ewww." Dani, who had her feet in the water and was watching a sort-of water polo match between the Kiwi boys, threw a grimace over her shoulder.

In a moment of perfect timing, a rep—I hadn't caught his name—stood at the top of the double staircase and called out to get everyone's attention. "Hey, everyone. If you want to do the wine tasting, meet us up here in ten minutes." The other half of "us" was a young Italian guy who made old jeans, dusty work boots, and a flannel shirt look good.

"Who's that?" asked Jaelee, shading her eyes against the sun.

The rep and the flannel guy were having a lively conversation and we could hear snatches of their laughter from our spot on the lawn. "Do you think it's the winemaker?" asked Lou.

"Could be. Maybe he's the leering old guy's son," I added.

"Well, whoever he is, he's hot." Jae was succinct, I'd give her that. "I'm doing the wine tasting." And decisive. "Anyone else coming?" she asked, standing and brushing grass off her legs.

"I'm good," replied Dani, her attention firmly on Jason's bare torso.

"I'm good too," I answered. I had a nice buzz going and wanted to enjoy the sunshine, not wander around a cold dank wine cellar.

"Me too," said Lou. It was decided. Jaelee was scoping out the hot wine guy and we were staying put to drink her wine.

"I'm going for a swim," said Dani as she slipped into the pool. So maybe it was just me and Lou drinking Jae's wine.

Just then, my phone beeped. I squinted at the screen, then shaded it with my hand. A Facebook friend request. I punched in my pin and drew a sharp intake of breath—Jean-Luc.

"What? It's not Alex again, is it?" asked Lou.

"Jean-Luc friended me on Facebook."

"Let me see." I handed her the phone. "Huh." She tapped "accept".

"Hey!" She giggled. "Gimme." I held out my hand for the phone and she gave it back. I tapped on Jean-Luc's profile and immediately saw why, even though I'd looked for him on Facebook before, I'd never found him. His profile pic was a cartoon, a line drawing of him in profile. It looked like him, only highly stylised.

I scrolled through his feed. A few political posts—he was pro-Macron and anti-Brexit, some links to his own articles—mostly in French and a few in English. I could read those later. What I was looking for was evidence of his *life*—who were his *people*?

I finally got to a photo of a group of friends in a bar, Jean-Luc in the middle looking away from the camera. He'd been tagged by someone called Claudine. I went to her profile, but I couldn't see anything other than her name and her profile pic. She was pretty and I tried not to be jealous of someone who was probably just a friend.

The group photo was more than three months old; it was obvious that Jean-Luc wasn't one of those people who filled his feed with inane details of his life or silly memes—like I did. Just quietly, I love silly memes.

I held my breath, then tapped on his friends list and typed "Vanessa" into the search field. There were three Vanessas, but only one of them was around our age, so I guessed it was her. I navigated to her profile and I nearly dropped the phone. She hadn't restricted her privacy settings and I could see everything. Her Facebook life was there for the scrolling—if I wanted to.

I looked at Lou, who was lying on her back, her eyes closed. "Lou?"

"Mmm."

"Jean-Luc's ex-wife's Facebook page ..."

Her eyes flew open and she flipped onto her front. "Wait, what? He was *married*?"

"Yes. Sorry, I should have said." I'd given her the abridged version of the previous night, but I'd forgotten to mention Vanessa. "So?" I held up the phone and showed her the open feed. She made a face and sucked air through her teeth. "So, that's a no, isn't it?"

"I think so. I wouldn't."

I bit my lower lip. "She's beautiful," I said, simply.

"So are you." *Maybe to some people, but not like she is.*

I wasn't just being modest. I am attractive—when I make an effort. I'm short, but in proportion and I have nice boobs. I also got the good hair, if you ask my sister. It's medium brown and shoulder length—nothing special there—but it's not curly and not straight. I have "natural beachy waves", as they're called. A hairdresser will charge fifty quid to blow-dry someone's hair to look like mine, so maybe Sarah's right.

Most days, I can look in the mirror and think, "Not bad." I know what to do with makeup, and don't shy away from a smoky eye or a pouty red lip for a night out. Sometimes, I'd even call myself "hot". But even all dolled up and hot I would fall woefully short of the French supermodel staring up from my phone.

"Has she kept his name?" Lou's question dragged me away from my masochistic comparison.

"No. But maybe she never took it in the first place."

"Mmm, true."

The phone beeped again, and I dropped it onto my towel like a hot potato. Lou laughed at me. When I picked it up, I flicked through the alerts at the top of the screen. "It's him." I stared at the phone. Why on earth hadn't I left it in the room?

"What does he say?" Lou said every word slowly, like she was talking to a child. It was apt, because I was behaving like one.

I opened the message.

Bonjour Catherine. We are now connected on the book of faces. ;) I imagine you are drinking some wonderful wine and enjoying the sunshine. Nice to think of you just a short distance from my family home. I always wanted you to visit. Have a good day and I will see you soon. J-L

Oh, that's right. I remembered how he used to sign off his letters with an invitation to visit. Of course, back then we were just kids with no money, so I never took it seriously.

But being in that beautiful place on a warm October day, it was easy to imagine a giant family gathering in Lyon, relatives of all ages milling around a long table laden with trays of food and carafes of wine.

Jean-Luc would hold my hand as he introduced me to everyone, and they would call out hellos in French and broken English. I would charm everyone with my bad French, because at least I'd made an effort.

I would play chasey with the children after lunch, then help the women clear the table—very old school in this fantasy—and afterwards, play *pétanque* with the menfolk. From time to time, Jean-Luc would seek me out to share a smile and ask how I was enjoying the visit. Late in the day, he'd pull me under the rose trellis and kiss me.

"Wow, that must have been some text." Lou's voice broke my reverie.

"Hmm?"

"You were in your own little world."

"Oh, yes. Here. You can read it."

She did, then handed back the phone. I pressed the "off" button and put the phone down next to me. I didn't want to be tempted to go back on Facebook or re-read his message a hundred times.

"I have no clue how he feels about me, Lou."

"Mmm. He didn't really give anything away in that text, did he?"

"No."

"I guess you'll find out on Thursday."

"I hope so." The thought of seeing him again washed away

my confusion and replaced it with giddiness. Yes, indeed, I was deeply, utterly in lust.

By the time Jaelee returned from the wine tasting, Lou and I were a little sunburned and a lot drunk. Dani had stayed in the pool the whole time, first frolicking—really, it is the best description of what she was doing—and then bobbing about with her legs wrapped around Jason. Apparently, they were happy to boldly publicise their "thing".

Good for her, I thought. If my bestie had run off and got herself married without me, I'd probably do something similar.

"Hey, guys," said Jae as she plopped down next to us on the lawn. She was grinning and lifted her very dark sunglasses to reveal that, like us, she was more than half-cut.

"So, how was it?"

"Oh, the wine was good, really good. We even got to taste some other varietals, but I think the gamay is their best—that's what we've been drinking today. And Marc—the wine guy—he's the grandson of the previous winemaker—he's been experimenting with different grapes. Of course, in this region, everything is all gamay all the time, you know?" She was rambling; it was highly entertaining.

"Sure," Lou said, an amused smile on her lips.

I adjusted my cover-up, so it was actually covering me. I'd had more than enough sun, but I *really* didn't want to go inside. "So, how many people were on the tour?"

"Oh, for the first part, there were probably ten of us?" She posed it as a question, her inflection going up at the end of the sentence. She sounded like a Sydneysider.

"And was there a second part?" prompted Lou.

"Um, yes, there was." She picked at some blades of grass.

"Jaelee, seriously," groaned Lou, "you're killing us. Spill already."

"Well, Marc—that's the—"

"We *know*," we both said at the same time.

"Well, *Marc* offered to show us the room where he's been experimenting with some blends."

"How nice of him." She flashed me a pointed look which I ignored. "And I'm guessing you were the only one who took him up on it."

"Well, me and this guy from the other tour group—Phillip or something. He's into wine."

"Something tells me there's more," I said to Lou, as though Jaelee couldn't hear me.

"He asked me to dinner." Then she grinned like an idiot and squeaked out a little squeal. It was the most un-Jaelee-like thing I'd seen her do.

"Wow, you move *fast*." I was honestly impressed. We'd been there less than four hours and she'd teed up a date.

Like I was one to talk.

"It's like Noah's ark around here," Lou added. Jae had said almost the same thing on the coach. I scoured Lou's face for any sign of self-pity—none that I could see.

"Are you all right with that, Lou?" I asked, just to make sure.

She replied matter-of-factly, "Oh, totally. Romance is the last thing on my mind. Right now, I'm about scenery and sunshine and wine ..." She picked up the now empty second bottle. "Speaking of which—" she cocked her head to the side "—I'm pretty sure it's my buy." And with that, she was off across the lawn, up the stairs and into the *château*.

"That was insensitive of me." Jaelee seemed to have suddenly sobered up.

"No, I think she's legitimately steering clear of romance right now. Remember on the first day when she said the thing about having time by herself to think things through?" She nodded solemnly. "Hey. You deserve a little fun. We all do. And I mean, look at Dani."

Dani shrieked on cue as Jason hoisted her in the air. She landed with a splash and emerged smiling. She tried to splash him as retribution, but it was like watching a mouse take on a bear. Jason was a big guy.

"I think you might be right."

"I almost always am." She rolled her eyes, then pulled out her phone to check the time. "One more swim before I need to get ready."

"What time is dinner?"

"Seven." She got up and performed a perfect dive into the deep end.

I watched her, doubting it could take someone as put-together as Jaelee nearly three hours to get ready, but then again, maybe that was *why* she was also so put-together. I suddenly realised the reason she was travelling with her own bikini waxing kit and dismissed the thought immediately. TMI.

"I got us food." Lou took up Jae's vacated spot.

"Oh, thank God." We were supposed to have bought our

lunch when we'd stopped for morning tea, but Lou and I had been too focused on hot beverages to get anything else. Dinner wouldn't be for hours, and two pieces of cold toast at breakfast didn't sop up much wine at four in the afternoon.

She started pulling things out of a paper carrier bag. "You're supposed to buy this big picnic basket to go have lunch down in the vines or something, but that sucker was huge. So I convinced the rep to just sell me just the cheese, the olives and these." She took out a small packet of crispbread. I saw the flakes of sea salt crusting them and started salivating.

"Lou, as soon as your divorce comes through, I'm proposing."

She grinned at me. She was certainly holding it together way better than I would if my marriage was ending. I added it to the long list of things I already loved about her.

She laid out the food and pulled the last thing out of the bag—a bottle of wine. "I also got us this." I actually groaned. Maybe there was such a thing as too much wine.

There is such a thing as too much wine.

Even though Lou and I had snuck into the kitchen around 1:00am to steal big bottles of water, and even though we'd each drunk nearly a litre before bed, I was decidedly hungover when my eyes creaked open the next morning. I peeked around the room, not daring to open them all the way.

Dani had snuck in around three—well, she'd stumbled in, attempting to be quiet, and had woken us when she called out in pain from stubbing her toe on the bed frame. She was sprawled across the top bunk on her stomach, her head under a pillow and snoring softly.

I looked at my wrist and my watch taunted me with 7:18am. We were leaving at eight. Breakfast, for those who could stomach it, had started at seven. By the time I dragged myself out of bed and made myself presentable, it would be over. I groaned.

"Morning, sunshine," croaked a voice from above.

"Lou, I hate you. Do not speak to me." This was followed by a low rumbling chuckle. If I didn't know better, I would have sworn she had a smoker's hack. "I'm serious. I *never* get hangovers. *Never.*" This was (mostly) true, because my method was (mostly) fool-proof. Water after every drink, a pint of water and two paracetamols before bed. On a particularly big night, add two ibuprofens and two slices of buttered Marmite toast to the mix—and *voilà!*

The thing is, the method only works if you actually drink water in between drinks *and* take the pills. I had not done either of those things and I cursed myself as much as I cursed Lou. I'd been wrong—*she* was the enabler.

"How do *you* feel?" I asked.

"Meh, I'm okay. I haven't let loose like that in a long time— since before ..." She trailed off, but I knew what she meant. Once Jackson had started drinking, she'd become a teetotaller, the responsible one.

"I get it." I did. No matter how disgusting I felt, I wasn't going to begrudge Lou letting her hair down. "Hey, Lou, you haven't heard anything—"

She cut me off. "Nope. I told him not to."

We were both quiet, and I contemplated the heft of Lou's situation. A *divorce*. Just awful.

I realised that the ripe smell stinging my nostrils was me. "Uh, Lou? Why do I stink?" I tried to remember what had happened after dinner, which was a stir-fry so dense with capsicum, that by the time I picked all the capsicum out, there was barely anything left on my plate. I came up empty.

"The dancing." There was dancing? A series of snapshots of a dark, musty bar and a throng of sweaty bodies flickered through my brain. Dancing + red wine − water = massively huge bugger of a hangover. Whose brilliant idea was that?

"Oh, right. That was your idea?"

"Nope. Yours."

"I suck," I proclaimed.

"Yes." Lou paused then said, "Hey, Cat? Where's Jaelee?"

My head turned abruptly to see a perfectly made-up bottom bunk across the room. How had I missed *that*?

"Huh. Well, would you look at that?"

Lou started giggling and I joined in. "This trip is way cooler than I thought it would be," she said.

Dani's head emerged from under her pillow as she made a loud snuffling sound, which made us giggle even louder. "What? Oh, uh, what time is it?"

"Morning, Danielle," replied Lou in a sing-songy voice.

"It's twenty past seven, Dan," I said.

"I'm dying." She flipped onto her back and shielded her eyes from sunlight streaming in the window.

"Get in line," I replied, throwing back the duvet. I needed

to shower to get the stench off me, and to pack. And somehow, I needed to scrounge up some tea for me and Lou.

Anyone who thinks a coach tour is "going on holiday" needs their head read. We had a five-hour coach ride to the south coast of France ahead of us and if my seatmate didn't let me sleep, I would have to start murdering people.

Chapter 6

There was a chill in the air that morning at the *château*. The tour group milled about in the shady driveway as a few of the guys helped Tom pack the luggage under the coach.

Jaelee had shown up by the time I was out of the shower. She was wearing the previous night's clothes and a contented smile. She changed clothes and packed quickly, then freshened up at the sink in the bathroom, giving me, Dani and Lou the chance to have a quick and very quiet conversation.

"Ask her," whispered Lou.

"No." Dani looked like we'd asked her to step into the lion's den.

"She's your roommate," I added, ganging up on her.

"She's yours too," Dani retorted. Technically, she was right.

"I'll ask her later," I said. "Or she'll tell us. All right?"

Breakfast was well and truly over by the time we got downstairs, so ten minutes before we were due to leave, Lou and I bribed one of the reps to rustle up some takeaway cups for tea. And by "bribed", I mean we showed up with half a Toblerone and she humoured us.

Georgina made her way noisily through the group wishing everyone a good morning before she climbed onto the coach. "I didn't see her yesterday," I said, blowing on the too-hot tea.

"What's that?" asked Lou.

"Sorry—thinking aloud. I was saying I didn't see Georgina yesterday. Did you?"

She thought for a moment then scrunched her nose. "No, I don't think so. Huh. I wonder what she got up to."

"Sarah told me that on days off all she did was sleep."

"All I want to do *now* is sleep."

"Actually, I'm hoping I can nap on the coach. Do you mind if I have the window today?"

"Go for it. It's super annoying, but I can't sleep sitting up."

Tom slammed the three doors to the luggage compartments in quick succession, the unofficial signal to board the coach, and I started making my way over with the rest of the group.

A whispered exclamation from Lou stopped me short. "Oh, wow!"

"What?"

"Look."

She pointed towards the entrance of the *château* where Craig was hugging one of the reps, the curvy blonde Aussie girl, Kayla. They shared a quick kiss and then he walked towards us, throwing a smile over his shoulder. She waved and smiled back, then disappeared inside.

Craig saw us watching him and walked over, grinning.

"You sly dog," teased Lou.

He went beet red, which made him even more adorable. "Morning," he said, rubbing the back of his neck. "I, uh ...

I'm getting on the coach now." He trotted off and I burst out laughing.

Lou started singing, "The Love Bus, soon will be making another run ..." to the tune of *The Love Boat* theme song, which made me laugh even more.

"Owww. Don't make me laugh. The drugs haven't kicked in yet." I'd taken two ibuprofen and a paracetamol after my shower. I'd also eaten a squashed muesli bar I found in my messenger bag. I desperately hoped I would feel better soon.

"Time to board the Luuuv Buuus," sang Lou. She really needed to stop that. I didn't want to have to find a new bus bestie.

I did manage to nap. I finished my tea, half-listened to Georgina explaining the day's itinerary—I was finding it hard to concentrate—then took my beach cover-up out of my bag and scrunched it up to use as a pillow against the window. Even hungover I'd managed to plan ahead, and I was a little proud of myself. Not for the hangover—that was gross stupidity and never to be repeated—said every hungover person ever, right?

I slept until right before we stopped for morning tea and a wee, which was terrific timing, because I needed both.

"I'm starving," said Lou as we shuffled off the bus.

"Where are we?" I yawned, looking out the window. So far, all French rest stops looked the same—an acre of concrete and a building that looked like it was built in the 70s.

"I don't know—halfway between the *château* and Antibes, I guess."

Inside I ordered, "*Deux grands thés, s'il vous plaît.*" I emphasised "*grands*" and was pleasantly surprised when two one-litre hot drinks were handed over the counter. I felt like someone from an American television show.

"This is the best tea I've ever had," said Lou.

"Hangover tea. It always tastes better than regular tea." She nodded in solemn agreement.

Back on the coach, I let Lou have the window seat and sat down heavily beside her, hoping the tea would kick in soon. The Love Bus pulled out of the rest stop and onto the motorway. I saw signs for Avignon and promised myself to stay awake and pay attention to the scenery for the rest of the drive. We were heading into Provence and though I'd never been, I hadn't been living under a rock. Provence was bound to be as beautiful as promised.

"Hey," I said.

"What's up?" Lou was looking out the window too.

"So, all this Love Bus stuff ..."

"Yeah?"

"How are *you* about all of it?" She let the question hang in the air a moment, still watching the view.

"I'm okay." She turned her head and gave me a less than convincing smile.

"Does that mean *just* okay or *totally* okay?"

"Just, heading towards totally." She leant her head back against her seat. "Oh Cat," she sighed. "Sometimes, when I think about being single again after all this time, I feel sick. I mean, I'm thirty-one and I know that's not old, but it's old enough that just the *idea* of starting again—and I mean *everything*, new apartment, new commute, new couch, new *towels*—*maybe* down the line, a new relationship ... all that change, all at once ... it's overwhelming, you know?"

I did know, yes, even though my first and only serious break-up was ten years before.

I would never forget those few months after Scott and I broke up—they were the hardest of my life. Every day I rode out a maelstrom of feelings that eventually dulled into something else, but never truly went away.

Once I'd decided that there was nothing for me in Sydney and I wasn't going back, I exchanged one life for another. I made dozens of changes all at once and when I finally settled into my London life, I made sure that very little changed from then on. On purpose. I'd been a happy creature of habit ever since, so considering the tsunami of changes Lou was facing when she got home, I felt for her.

"I know I told you he hasn't contacted me, but I lied." *Oh*.

"That's all right, Lou. This is hefty stuff. You don't have to talk about it if you don't want to."

"No, I do—want to, I mean. I didn't tell you this before, but I actually left Jackson a few weeks ago. I've been staying with my parents. It's all very messy, because our parents are close with each other. They actually *socialise* together. We've been one big happy family for years, until now. Until I broke it." The sarcasm dripped from "happy family".

"Lou, you didn't—"

"I mean, I know this isn't my fault. It's not even Jackson's fault; it's a disease. He's sick, but after years of watching him descend into some sort of private hell, denying the whole time that he even needed help, I just couldn't do it anymore." I put my hand on her leg and she grasped it. "I tried, Cat. I'm a *counsellor*, for crying out loud, and *I* couldn't help him."

"I'm sure you did everything you could." She nodded and dropped my hand to get a tissue out of her pocket. "Lou, I'm serious. No one can ask any more of you, not your parents, or his, not even Jackson. At some point, you have to focus on looking after yourself."

She dabbed under her eyes and wiped her nose. "I know. That's what I've been telling myself. It's why I came here." She signalled the coach with her hands. "Honestly, the whole Love Bus thing is a welcome distraction. I'm kinda getting a kick out of it."

"I'm glad." I could have left it there, but one thing was niggling at me. "So, Jackson *has* contacted you since you've been here?" She nodded and looked out the window. "Do you want to tell me about it?"

"He's going into treatment." She nibbled on her lip, her face set in a grimace.

"That's good, right?"

"It is. It's what I've hoped for ... for ... well, for years now."

"So ..."

"So, even if he's sober, I'm not in love with him anymore. I know that now. I can't ever go back to him."

"Oh."

"I want a divorce. I mean, I know I've been saying that—maybe it was so I could get used to the idea, you know, hearing it out loud—but in the last few days, since I heard from him,

I've decided. I'll tell him when I get back. I just hope it doesn't push him back into the hole, you know?"

"I'm so sorry, Lou."

"Eh, what are you going to do?" She closed the heavy topic with faux ease.

I patted her leg, hoping she knew I was there for her. I didn't want to say it out loud, because I sensed she was a millimetre away from bursting into full-on tears. *Poor Lou*. It really put my "love fugitive" status into perspective.

We were quiet for some time after that.

"Tom and I have a surprise for you, everyone." Georgina sounded more than a little pleased with herself. "We've made good time this morning, which means we're going to stop in Aix-en-Provence in a little while. We'll only have ninety minutes there, but that should be long enough to have a look around and get some lunch. And I think you'll love it. It's really beautiful—the quintessential French provincial town. I'm so glad we've been able to squeeze it in today."

I knew from Sarah that squeezing in so-called "unscheduled stops" was part of managing a tour, but I had to admit that Aix-en-Provence sounded nice.

But it wasn't nice. It was stunning.

Tom stopped somewhere near the centre of town—or as close to it as he could get—and I dropped a pin on Google maps. The town was replete with narrow, several-storey terraced houses, many of them painted in bright colours, with wrought-iron Juliet balconies spanning tall shutter-framed windows, and accents in contrasting colours. In every direction, the elegance and beauty of the town were undeniable.

I grabbed Craig's arm as he walked past the four of us. "Hey, do you want to have lunch with us?"

"Oh, yeah. That'd be great."

"Dani's in charge."

"I am?"

"You speak French. We're in the countryside. Not as many people are going to speak English here."

"Good point." She scanned the small square. "Let's try one of the side streets—that's where the locals will go." She struck off and we followed behind like ducklings. She made a left into a narrow street and we hugged the edges as cars squeezed past us.

The sun couldn't penetrate this part of town and I felt a chill after the sunny warmth of the square. We seemed to be chasing the sun the further south we went, and after leaving the typically damp autumn of the UK, I was loving this extra stretch of summery weather.

"Oooh, that looks promising," Dani said, pointing to a striped awning ahead. Several tables, all with squares of white paper clipped to them, sat out front. There were no customers yet—it was barely noon and the French don't typically eat until later—but a waiter, or maybe he was the proprietor, was standing in the doorway, a clean white apron wrapped around his formidable waist.

"*Bonjour*," called Dani with a smile. She rattled off some French and he smiled, then gestured to two of the outside tables. He gestured again, asking for help to move them together, which he and Craig managed quickly. Before long we were seated, each with a glass of sparkling water. A giant basket of bread and a small ramekin of pale butter appeared in the middle of the table, and the man handed around one-page menus written entirely in French.

Like the café we'd gone to a couple of nights before, there were three choices for each course, and Dani translated them all for the group. It was a *prix fixe* menu, which meant we got three courses for only fifteen euros, including a glass of wine. Even if the food was only mediocre, it was a bargain, and after a squashed muesli bar and three headache tablets for breakfast, my stomach was doing gymnastics in anticipation.

I decided on *soupe au pistou*, *salade Niçoise*, and *tarte aux poires*. I'd loved the pear tart in Paris, and I wanted another fix before we left France the next day.

The man arrived with the wine, holding two carafes by the neck in one hand, and five inverted wine glasses threaded between the fingers of his other hand—impressive and probably impossible if he didn't have such giant hands. I poured wine for my friends and when we all had a glass in hand, proposed a toast. "To unexpected stops and to unexpected friends."

Dani gave me a head tilt and an "Aww" before she clinked glasses. The others settled on "Cheers" or *"Salut"*. The wine was good—light, aromatic, dry. I am not one for cloyingly sweet wines—why does *anyone* like Moscato?—so it was perfect. I picked up a piece of bread and slathered it with the butter.

"Oh, my God," I said through my mouthful, ignoring my own table etiquette. I pointed repeatedly at the bread, indicating the urgent need for everyone to try some.

"That good, huh?" asked Jae, dryly. I nodded, but she didn't take any. I'd noticed Jaelee wasn't into bread and baked goods as much as most people were. The others had some, though, and there was a refrain of "Mmm"s accompanied by nodding heads.

"So, I'm not sure *which* of you great dirty stop-outs I should start with," I said after swallowing my bread. I raised my eyebrows and looked at Jaelee, Craig and Dani.

"What in God's name is a great dirty stop-out?" Jaelee asked, narrowing her eyes at me.

I had forgotten I was the only (sort of) English person amongst a group of North Americans, so I explained.

"It is a person who stays out all night—or *most* of it," I added, pinning Dani with a look—*she* wasn't getting off the hook. She responded with her own raised eyebrows and defiantly popped a piece of bread in her mouth. I continued, "*and*, got some."

There was a beat, then loud laughter from the group. Craig shook his head and brought his fingertips to his forehead. I would have bet a million pounds he was wishing he'd turned down the lunch invitation. I zeroed in on him.

"Craig?"

When he lifted his head, his face was red again. I was having so much fun.

"C'mon, Craig, spill," said Dani, dodging the first bullet. We'd get back to her later. "Where did *you* sleep last night?"

136

"Well, there wasn't much sleeping ..." That brought another round of laughter as he grinned at us. It was clearly a mix of embarrassment and pride. "I slept in Kayla's room."

"Good for you," said Lou.

The first course arrived, another reprieve for Dani, and we all settled down like schoolchildren who'd been misbehaving while the teacher was out of the room.

The *soupe au pistou* was a clear vegetable and white bean broth served with a quenelle of pesto. It was a vibrant-looking dish and smelled divine. It tasted better than it looked, and I realised it was the most delicious food I'd had in days. I could taste every ingredient, all the fresh vegetables. Dani was having it too and when I lifted my eyes to hers, she nodded her agreement.

When we'd all finished the course, the man cleared the table with a practised efficiency I couldn't master in a million lifetimes.

"So, Jae, what about you?" asked Lou, her chin propped on her hand.

"Okay! I obviously didn't sleep at the *château*. I was at Marc's cottage, just down past the vines, near the property line. It was really cute, actually, hundreds of years old. But unlike Craig, I actually slept. It was all very chaste."

"Really?" My eyes narrowed. I wasn't buying it.

"Really." She gave me a pointed look, then addressed the rest of the table. "He cooked us a nice dinner and we drank wine and talked. Then, somehow it was nearly two, and rather than stumble back in the dark, I stayed there. He gave me his bed and he slept on the couch. *In a different room. Okay?*"

"Sounds delightful," said Dani, but I still wasn't buying it.

"So, how come you looked so happy this morning, like, you know ... something happened?" I asked.

"Because, it was the nicest date I've had in ... well, I don't know how long, and I *needed* that."

"So, it *was* a date?" asked Lou. Jae sighed impatiently. "What? I'm living vicariously here. Throw me a bone."

"That's what she said," joked Dani under her breath.

"Hah! Dani, you crack me up." She threw me a crinkle-nosed wink.

"Are we done with my interrogation yet?" asked Jae. It was crystal clear that *she* was done.

"Did you at least get a goodnight kiss?" asked Lou.

"I did."

"*And?* Geez, girl. *Details*."

"Geez, *Louise*. A lady doesn't kiss and tell."

Lou rolled her eyes and shook her head, and Jaelee took a sip of wine, remaining tight-lipped.

"We're getting nowhere," I cut in. "Dani, you go."

"What? There's nothing to tell. Jason and I danced until I practically fell over, then I went up to bed. The end." Well, I bought *that*. No subterfuge with Dani—what you saw was what you got.

"Huh. All right, Craig. It looks like you win this round of *Great Dirty Stop-out*. Thanks for playing, everybody. See you next time." I can be quite the comedian sometimes. My friends laughed, but it was probably *at* me.

Saved by the salad!

Niçoise is a favourite of mine and this one didn't disappoint.

138

The tuna was fresh, the outside seared and the inside rare and pink, and the tiny potatoes and the green beans were cooked to perfection. The Dijon and vinegar dressing was tangy, *and* a little spicy. I was in foodie heaven. Although I worried my body wouldn't know what to do with all the vegetables after three days of baked goods, cheese, and more wine than I needed.

Speaking of which ...

"We need more wine." I looked around for the lovely man in the apron and he magically appeared. "*Encore du vin blanc s'il vous plaît, monsieur.*" He nodded and disappeared back inside. Dani caught my eye, her eyebrows raised at my near-perfect French. "The more I drink, the better my French gets."

"Impressive."

"Thanks, Dan."

The wine arrived and the table was cleared. This time, Lou poured. "I don't know if I can fit in dessert," groaned Dani.

"Of *course* you can. Don't be ridiculous," I rebuked playfully, as five desserts landed on the table. Jaelee and I had ordered the tart, Craig had gone for the chocolate mousse, and Lou and Dani for the *clafoutis*, a kind of light cakey flan filled with cherries. Dani eyed hers with a pout.

"I'll eat it if you don't want it," offered Craig. At about six-foot-three and a voracious eighteen-year-old, as Lou had described him, it was likely that lunch hadn't filled him up—even with the generous portions.

"You can have mine," said Jaelee, pushing her plate over to Craig. I wondered if that had been her intention all along. Dani took one bite of her clafoutis, closed her eyes as she savoured it, then handed the plate to Craig. He finished all three desserts before I'd finished one. Boys.

"Hey, guys," said Lou, "I hate to be that person, but we need to be back at the coach in less than ten minutes."

How had that happened? I guess time flies when you're having a delicious meal in a beautiful location with lovely friends. The day had definitely turned around from its horrendous beginnings.

We finished up, settled up—lunch *had* been a bargain—and followed Dani back to the square where our coach was waiting. We were the last group to arrive and even though it was before the departure time, Georgina gave us a look that said otherwise.

I breezed past her, ignoring her schoolmarmish scowl. Jae did the same, but Lou hadn't got my memo and started chatting with Georgina about where we went for lunch. I left Lou to it, climbed on to the coach, and nestled into the window seat. We'd be in Antibes soon. The French Riviera! Huzzah!

My phone beeped inside my bag and I dug it out. One new message and three that had arrived during lunch. I was suddenly very popular.

Mum:

Dad helped me with the box. I've got the last postmarked letter and the birthday photo. Sending you a photo of the photo. I took it with my phone! You look so cute together. Will scan the letter tomorrow, because we're playing golf with Lisa and Ciaron today. Mum xxoo

What did she mean, we look so cute together? I looked at the photo, a wave of happy memories crashing over me, before moving onto the next message.

Sarah:

I have news! Call me asap!! ps It's good. I think. Squee! S x

Well, that was intriguing. I'd have to FaceTime her when we got to the campsite in Antibes.

And Jean-Luc:

How early can you meet me on Thursday? J-L xx

Well, Jean-Luc, I can meet you as soon as I step foot on Roman soil. I was fairly certain we were supposed to go on a walking tour with a guide, and it was *Rome*, so that would probably be amazing, but I wanted to see Jean-Luc more than I wanted to see ancient piles of rocks. I made a mental note to ask Lou to ask Georgina what time we were getting into the city on Thursday.

And Alex:

Hey Cat. Just letting you know I've given Jane notice and I will be moving out at the end of the month.

No sign-off. No other information.

On the phone he'd called himself a "right idiot", and now he'd decided to move out. Both were my fault, and I couldn't help feeling awful about the whole thing. Because he didn't need to move out. Sure, it would be a little awkward for a while, but we were adults, right? We could still live together.

Even I didn't believe myself.

I also couldn't ignore that my stomach was churning at the thought of finding another flatmate with only two and a half weeks' notice. And beneath the guilt and the worry was something else, something I wasn't proud of—relief. I shot Jane a quick text just as Lou sat down next to me.

"Georgina's so nice," she said.

"Yes, she's lovely." Who was I to burst her bubble? Besides, I had bigger worries than Georg-bloody-ina.

Chapter 7

"Hey!" It was so good to see Sarah's face. It had only been a few days since we'd chatted but so much had happened.

"Hi! How are you? Where are you?"

"We're in Antibes now." I said it the proper French way, *Onh-teeb*.

She laughed. "Oh, yeah, that place is ... uh ... pretty crappy."

"That is an accurate description."

"Not quite the garden sheds, though. A bit of a step up." She was right. The campsite was nothing special, but we were in actual cabins and the four of us got to room together again. We still had to walk across the campsite to have a wee or to shower, but at least there was room for our luggage, and there were windows on opposite sides of the cabin, so we had a cross breeze.

"Want to meet my lovelies?"

"Yes!" she clapped her hands together a few times. The girls were in various stages of settling in. Jaelee was sorting through her bikinis—I'd lost count at four. Lou was scrolling her phone, and Dani was lying prone on her bed.

I started with my bus bestie. "This is Lou," I said, sitting down next to her so Sarah could see us both.

"Hi, Sarah. Your sister's awesome."

Sarah laughed. "I completely agree." I beamed, enjoying the adoration from two of my favourite people. "How are you enjoying the tour so far?"

"It's awesome. Sorry, I need another word, but it is. Mostly because of the girls." Dani interjected with her signature, "Aww." "Your tips have been good too."

"Oh yeah? That's great. It's been a while—about a decade, now—but a lot of it will still apply."

"Hey, Sez? What about the excursion to Monaco? It's tonight."

"That's a must. Definitely. It's just beautiful there."

"We're supposed to go to a casino?" added Lou.

"Uh, yeah, if it's the same one we used to go to, you could probably skip it. It's not like it's super nice or anything. Then again, it is kind of cool to say you've gambled in Monaco. The walking tour should be good, though. How's your TM?"

Lou looked at me quizzically. "She means Georgina."

"Oh, she's great," Lou said at the same time I said, "She's a bit schoolmarmish."

Lou's brow furrowed. "You don't like Georgina?"

"I'll tell you later." It was a good time to introduce the others, so I switched to the back camera. "This is Jaelee." Jae was kneeling next to her case and lifted her hand. "She's from Miami. And this is Dani from Montreal."

"Hi, Sarah," drawled Dani, as she waved with a slight flick of her fingers.

144

"Hiya."

I switched back to the front camera and headed outside. "I'm just going to catch up on Sarah's news. I'll be outside."

"Don't forget to catch her up on *your* news, Cat," called Jaelee to my back.

Thanks, Jae. I wasn't going to tell Sarah about Jean-Luc until after our date. Maybe by then I'd have something more interesting to say than, "He grew up ridiculously hot."

"What news?" asked Sarah as I perched on the wooden step outside our cabin.

"Nope, you first." I could see she was bursting with whatever it was.

"Okay. But although it's kind of great, I'm also really confused about everything."

"Oh, my God, Sarah. Just say it."

"I'm going to Hawaii with Josh—for New Year's."

"Right." Why did she think this was news? She'd told me all about Josh, the American guy she met in Greece, when she got back to London—including their plan to meet up in Hawaii.

"As in, I've booked the flights and he's got us accommodation, and it's *happening*."

"*Ohhh.*" The penny dropped. It had been tentative—and now it was official. "Well, that's amazing, Sarah." I was happy for my sis. After Neil the dickhead, Josh sounded like a much better match for her—even though I was only going from what Sarah had said about him.

"Yeah, I think so too. But there's more." She bit her lip and a frown scuttered across her face. "Um, James is coming to Sydney in January."

"*Ohhh*," I said, the second penny dropping. James was the other man she'd met in Greece—the one she'd seen in London while she was staying with me, the one I'd met, the rich, handsome silver fox.

"So, you're seeing *both* of them again? And *soon*."

Her head bobbed up and down. "Yep."

"And how do you feel about that?"

"That's what I was saying. I'm all over the place—excited—confused—nervous. Mostly excited—I think."

"Good!" God, she really got stuck in her head sometimes. "Um, Cat?

"Yes."

"Do you think ...?" She trailed off.

"What?" I asked gently. I could tell she was really stewing on something.

"Am I a bad person?"

"What? No, why? Because you're seeing two men?" A nod. "No, I don't think that. Have you committed to either of them?" A shaken head. "No, you haven't. You have to *see*, Sarah. How else will you know which one is right for you?" She nodded along with my brilliant logic.

"And maybe neither of them is." I am not sure why I added that last part, but I immediately regretted it. My sister would be a terrible poker player and I could tell my remark had stung. "Sorry."

"It's okay. You're right. I need to be honest with myself—especially after the Neil debacle, the fuckhead. And, you know, maybe I *will* end up alone—"

"On your own. Not *alone*."

146

"Right. On my own." She shrugged. "Anyway, for now I just want to be excited."

"And you should be. I'm happy for you."

"Thanks." She grinned. "So, now, *your* news. Jaelee, is it? She said you had news."

"I do, sort of." She looked at me, her large eyes unblinking. "Do you remember that French exchange student——"

"Jean-Luc? Of course. He practically lived at our house. He walked in on me on the toilet once. It was mortifying." Of *course* she remembered that. Sarah's life could easily be defined as a series of embarrassing moments. "Although I think he was more embarrassed than I was. Anyway, sorry. It's him, right, Jean-Luc?"

"Yes, it's Jean-Luc. *Anyway* ..." I gave her a look to tell her to let me finish uninterrupted. She pressed her lips together, then mumbled, "Sorry," making me laugh. I do adore my sister.

"*Anyway*, so, the other night when we were in Paris, Jaelee literally stopped some random man in the street to ask him something, *aaand* it turned out to be Jean-Luc." Her eyes widened. "You can say something now."

"So, wow. Oh, my God. Did he recognise you? What does he look like? Did you get to talk to him?"

I answered each question in turn, "Yes, gorgeous—like, ridiculously gorgeous—and yes. He invited us to this pub, and we talked, and then he took me up to Sacré-Cœur, and we went to this bar, and we talked some more, and we're meeting up in Rome on Thursday. For dinner."

"That's. Wow—it's like something out of a movie."

147

"Hah! Coming from you, that's hilarious. But yes, it *was* kind of surreal. And, I forgot to tell you. I didn't recognise him at first, on the street. He was just this random hot guy. I mean, Sez, he's so incredibly handsome. He's like six-one or six-two and has this sort of longish hair and his smile is so sexy, and his *eyes*!

"You probably don't remember, but his eyes are this intense green and anyway, I didn't even know it was him until we got to the bar—an Irish pub of all places—in Paris, mad. So, we get there—me and the girls and this guy, Craig. I'll tell you about him later, and Jean-Luc is already there, and he walks over and looks at me and says, 'Hello, Cat-er-in.' Just like that, all sexy and French. I nearly died. In fact, I nearly fainted. Oh, I just remembered that. He caught me. I mean, literally. So ..."

"Wow. You are a smitten kitten."

I sighed. "Yes, rather." It was my sister. I had no need to play coy. "I'm desperate to go to bed with him."

"Right." She cleared her throat—was that her being prudish? She with the two international lovers? "So," she continued, "did anything happen that night?"

"No—nothing happened in Paris. We just talked. I mean, he held my hand a couple of times, but not like fingers laced, more like you'd hold Mum's hand. But he did kiss my forehead, really soft and slow."

"He kissed you on your forehead?"

"Yes."

"Wow, that's ..."

"I know, right. That's like ...?"

"Yeah, that's definitely ..." Sister shorthand is the best. "So, you're seeing him in Rome?"

"Right. He's got this interview thing down in Naples tomorrow—he's a writer, for magazines—and he's going to meet me in Rome on Thursday for dinner."

"Sounds divine. Oh, Cat, you're gonna love Rome. It's ... you know, some people get all mushy about Paris, but I preferred Rome. It's just so chic, and it's this incredible combination of modern and ancient. I mean, people are on their way to work and there are these ruins, like, *right there*. The whole city is steeped in this incredible history. It'll be amazing."

"Well, we're supposed to have this tour when we first get there, but I was going to skip it to meet up with Jean-Luc. But maybe I should go?"

"On the tour? Yeah, you should *definitely* do that. It's only a couple of hours and you'll get to see the Roman Forum and the Colosseum. I'd say go."

"Thanks for that. I'll think about it."

"Cat?" Lou was standing on the other side of the screen door looking down at me.

"Oh, did you want to come out?" I said, standing.

"Yeah, in a minute. Sorry to interrupt, but we're going down to the beach soon. Did you want to come?"

"Go!" said Sarah. "It's the Côte d'Azur!"

"Yes, definitely," I said to both of them. Lou disappeared. "So, I'll let you know how Thursday goes."

"You better. Okay, I love you."

"Love you, too. And I'm really happy for you, Sez."

"Thanks." The grin was back, but I knew my sister. She'd be beating herself up for the next few months over the whole "love triangle" thing. "Bye."

"Bye." I ended the call, then went inside to dig out my bikini. It was time to go swimming on the French Riviera!

"Huh," said Dani, summing up what I was thinking.

We'd changed into our swimsuits and cover-ups, packed up beachy things—towels, sunscreen, hats, reading materials—and had left the campsite for the one-mile walk to the beach. It was completely unremarkable, a straight road with nothing of interest on either side, meeting the coastal highway perpendicularly. We crossed the highway, then a train track and when we got to the beach, we stood stock-still side by side, somewhat in shock.

What we'd expected—what *I'd* expected—was rows of sun loungers, white sand, blue water, and beautiful people milling about drinking cocktails and laughing at witty repartee.

What we got was grey stones all the way down to grey water and not a person in sight.

"Where are the people?" asked Dani.

"Where's the *beach*?" asked Jaelee.

"Didn't Georgina say we should catch the train to either Nice or Cannes, because the beaches are better than Antibes?" asked Lou. I had no idea. I'd been dead asleep, drooling on the coach window.

"I vaguely remember her saying something like that," said Dani.

"I'm not swimming in that," said Jae. "I'm from Miami—"

150

"We *know*," replied Dani, cutting her off.

"Okay. So, this isn't what we'd hoped for. I say we get on the next train to Cannes and go to the beach there. What do you think?" Thank God for Lou taking charge—*and* for listening to our tour manager.

"I'm up for it," I said.

"Me too," added Dani. "Jaelee?"

"Well, I'm not staying here," she scoffed.

It was decided, and less than an hour later we approached a completely different kind of beach, Plage Zamenhoff. It was the kind with soft white sand and sun loungers you could rent for ten euros a pop. Dani found it online while we were on the train. It was a public beach, so about half the price of the more exclusive beach clubs, and for four tourists (let's be honest, we were far from travellers that day), it was ideal.

We paid a short French guy and he led the way through rows of sun loungers to four sitting side by side. "Merci," said Dani, giving her approval. We could see the sea from our vantage point and there were a few empty loungers between us and the nearest people.

I was settling onto mine when I turned around and was met by the surprising sight of Jaelee's breasts. "Oh, wow ..." I didn't *really* care—there were bare breasts everywhere on the beach. I'd thought of going topless myself. I just hadn't expected to get a face full of boob.

"Jaelee," said Dani. "Do we need to see your boobs?" Apparently, Dani *did* care.

"We've shared a room since we started this trip. You've seen

151

my boobs before." Jaelee lay down on her lounger and placed a large straw sunhat on her head.

"That's different."

"How?"

"It just is."

I noticed that Lou was silent. She didn't swear, so maybe public nudity wasn't her thing either. Jae ignored Dani, who tutted loudly as she set up on her own lounger.

I got out my sunhat, put it on and pulled the brim low over my face, then made sure my cover-up covered my arms and chest. I'd slathered on sunscreen before we left the campsite, but I was feeling the slight sting of the previous day's sunburn and I didn't want to take any chances.

"I'm going for a swim," said Lou. And if I hadn't seen it myself, I would never have believed what she did next. She whipped off her bikini top, dropped it on her lounger, and marched towards the water.

"Woo hoo, go Louise!" called out Jaelee.

"Oh, brother," said Dani, nestling further into her lounger.

I sat upright and watched as Lou walked into the water. She waved to us and called, "Come in. It's great!"

"What the hell," said Jae, standing. She headed off.

"Dani? Are you going in?" I asked.

"Not if I have to go topless."

"You don't."

Dani didn't look convinced. "What if I just stay here and watch our stuff?" She had a point. It probably wasn't a good idea to leave everything unattended.

"If you're sure."

"Go!" she ordered.

I stood and slipped off my cover-up, then looked out at Jae and Lou, both standing waist-deep in the blue water, boobs out, no qualms. *The hell with it*, I thought. I undid my bikini top and put it on my lounger. I heard another, "Oh brother," from Dani but I ignored her. I held my head high and, for the first time in my thirty-five years, walked half-naked through a throng of strangers. No one stared. No one cared.

I got to the water's edge and walked in. Then walked straight back out again. *Holy crap, that's cold.*

"You coming in?" asked Lou.

"It's freezing." My teeth started to chatter despite the sunny afternoon.

"Like hell, it's great," chided Jaelee.

"I thought you were from Miami, Jae. Isn't the ocean hot there?"

"You're a lightweight, Cat."

Jaelee had found my weakness—I, bold, gutsy, do-not-mess-with-me Cat Parsons, was absolutely *not* a lightweight. I lifted my chin, stuck out my boobs, and strode purposefully into the water, the iciness biting into my legs, then my lady parts. That was the most shocking part. The poor things nearly crawled up inside me as I waded over to Lou and Jae.

"Isn't this awesome?" asked Lou.

It most definitely was *not* awesome. I may have been an Aussie girl deep down, but I'd also acclimated to the land after ten years in England. I tried to remember the last time I'd been in the sea. I couldn't.

Lou submerged herself up to her shoulders, then swam off

with a few strokes of breaststroke. Jae followed, and I was left standing by myself in the gently undulating swell. *Bollocks*, I thought before taking off after them. Maybe swimming would warm me up.

I'm doing it. I am a wild, sexy, sophisticated woman and I'm swimming on the Riviera. I'm … Let's be honest, I'm freezing my tits off.

I tried to touch the bottom, but I was in over my head, so I swam a few strong strokes towards the shore. Jae and Lou were treading water a little way off, and Lou called to me, but I was single-minded. I wanted to be on dry land, *tout de suite*.

When I could finally touch the sandy bottom, I did that weird "walk out of the sea" thing where it's like walking through quicksand and the water's pulling against you and you're leaning forward struggling to get to shore while still looking cool. I got to the shallows and straightened up then, boobs out, walked back towards Dani and our stuff.

French Riviera ✓

"How was it?" She peered at me above her sunglasses.

"Amazing. You should go in." Sometimes I am a sadist.

"Meh, maybe later." She rolled over and let the sun hit her back. I dried off and was just shimmying into my bikini top (note: this is very difficult when you're wet and it's dry) when I heard a man's voice say, "Oh, hey, guys."

Before I could register whose voice it was, I clutched the bikini top to my chest.

"Oh, hi, Craig," said Dani. *What?! Bollocks, bollocks, bollocks.* Wonderful. It was Craig, his man-boy mountain frame towering over us as I tried to retain my dignity. It was all well and good sharing my breastage with hundreds of beach strangers, but Craig? Little bro' Craig? Just, no.

"Hey, Dani. I thought it was you coming out of the water, Cat." Great. So, he'd seen me without my top on. "I'm here with some of the guys." He pointed in the opposite direction from the water—bollocks, maybe the other guys had too. "Oh, Dani. Jason's here. Should I go get him?"

"Sure. Yeah."

"Be right back." The whole time I was standing there with my bikini top in hand and covering my boobs as best I could considering I have C-cup boobs and A-cup hands. It was one thing for Craig to have seen me half-naked from a distance, I didn't need to scare the poor boy. As soon as he left, I turned towards the sea and put the top on as quickly as I could before he came back with Jason in tow.

I stretched out on my lounger and waited for the sun to warm me up, and Lou and Jae arrived shortly after. "God, I love swimming in saltwater," said Lou as she grabbed her towel to dry off.

"Reminds me of Cabo," said Jae. "Without all the trash in the water." *Yuk.* I'd never been to Mexico and if it *had* been on my travel list, that one comment would have made it plummet to the bottom.

"You may want to cover up, you two. Craig's here and he's just gone to get Jason." They shared a panicked look and hustled to get fully dressed—well, as fully dressed as both halves of a bikini.

"Shit," said Jae and she fumbled with one of her clasps.

"Here." I signalled I would help, and she turned her back

to me and perched on the edge of my lounger. I did up the fastener.

Just as Lou pulled on a T-shirt over her swimsuit, the guys showed up. Jason made a beeline for Dani, who perked right up, smiling at him as he leant down to give her a quick kiss. The Dani-Jason thing seemed to be progressing rather nicely. Craig gestured to ask if he could sit with me and I pulled my knees up to my chest, so he could sit down.

"So, what have you guys been up to?" asked Jae.

"Same as you. Hanging out here," said Jason. "I wish we'd found you sooner."

"Yeah, 'cause we should probably head back soon," said Mama Lou. "We've got Monaco tonight and I'll be darned if I'm going looking like this." Sorry, make that, *Glamma Lou.*

"There's a train back to Antibes at five-twenty," said Craig, reading from his phone. "It's five now." He looked at the group.

Jason stood. "I'll go get the boys. Meet you at the train station," he said to Dani, giving her another quick kiss. Craig had to get his stuff and left with him.

"That was fun," said Dani, as we picked our way through the streets of sun loungers.

"You're only saying that because Craig showed up," teased Jaelee.

"Hey! Not true."

"You didn't even go in the water."

"Hey, in my mind beaches are for looking at, not swimming in. He is cute, though, don't you think?" she cooed.

We cleared the loungers and emerged onto the boardwalk.

Lou put her arm around Dani's shoulder. "He's *adorable*. You're both adorable." Dani beamed.

"Yeah, yeah, adorable," said Jaelee, a bite in her tone.

"Hey! Glass houses, Jaelee. Remember where *you* spent last night?" *Dani's not takin' any yo' crap, Jaelee.* I liked seeing Dani stand up for herself.

"... And it's said that Prince Rainier placed a rose on her tomb every day until his death in 2005."

"Pretty hard to do *after* he died," said Jaelee in a low voice. I stifled a giggle and Lou dug an elbow into my side.

"Hey," I whispered at her.

"Shh," she whispered back, her attention focused on Georgina.

I had to admit, it had been a pretty good tour. Georgina knew her stuff and Monaco was, as Sarah had promised, beautiful. I don't think I've ever been anywhere as perfect and pristine, before or since.

It was like one of the worlds in Disneyland—Monacoland, where every streetlamp, every building, every staircase and footpath was designed to bring the greatest joy to adult children everywhere—and the views! If Paris was the city of lights, then Monaco was the principality of lights. And with it perched on—or it was clinging to?—a mountainside, that meant spectacular views and very sore calf muscles by the end of the tour.

"I'm dying," said Dani as we crested another hill. Georgina was fit, that was for sure. Her walking tour could have been rescheduled, relabelled and added to the itinerary as a fitness excursion.

"Wanna piggyback?" Jason asked. I figured he was kidding. Dani didn't.

"Yes. Please!" He stopped, crouched down, and she climbed on.

I decided they needed a couple name. "I'm calling you two "Jasni'" from now," I said, a little out of breath myself.

"Ewww, that's awful," laughed Dani.

"Danson?"

"Worse," replied Jason.

"How about—"

"How about nothing?" Dani cut me off playfully, then giggled as he trotted ahead with her bouncing on his back.

"The Love Bus ..." sang Lou beside me, quietly.

"... Soon will be making another run ..." I joined in.

My phone beeped in my clutch. "Oh, hang on." I stopped walking and took it out, tapping the screen until I could see the message from Jean-Luc. I'd texted earlier to say I could meet him at 5:00pm on Thursday. I was taking Sarah's advice about the Roman city tour.

"Is it *him*?" Lou peered over my shoulder.

"Yep."

"And?"

I grinned at her. "He's sent the name of a bar so we can meet for drinks. He says it's near Piazza Navona." I had no idea what that meant, but I'd look it up.

"Just remember to invite me to the wedding," she joked.

I looked up at her through my lashes. "Hilarious."

She shrugged. "You never know."

But I did know—I didn't *do* marriage. I sent a quick reply.

Sounds good. See you there. Can't wait. Cat x

I'd tapped "send" before I could rethink the "can't wait" part. I showed Lou and she nodded with approval. "C'mon, we need to catch up."

Georgina released us around ten, dropping us at the entrance of a casino. She made sure we had the pick-up location pinned in our phones and told us to meet her and Tom there at 12:30am. I stifled a yawn and Lou nudged me again with her elbow.

"Stop doing that," I chided.

"Sorry."

"You must know you have at least eight inches on me. I'm going to have a permanent bruise on my shoulder."

"I'm *sorry*." Her Canadian accent asserted itself as she dragged out "sawwreee".

"I forgive you, but remember, I'm just little." It's what I'd always said to Sarah when we were growing up. She's around five inches taller and, though I am not proud, I definitely played the "little sister" card more than a few times—being younger and smaller. A shout of, "Muuu-uuummm," and she'd get told to leave me alone. I was cheeky like that sometimes— I still am.

Somehow, we ended up at the Grand Casino.

And by "we" I mean, the four of us, Craig and the Kiwi four-pack. And by "ended up" I mean we completely ditched our tour group and made our way to the Grand Casino on purpose.

It was both sublime and surreal.

The architecture was incredible, keeping right in with the adult Disneyland theme. It looked like the palace Belle and the Beast moved into right after he transformed back into the prince—lots of ornate flourishes—and for some reason, there were palm trees in the forecourt.

But the real attraction was the cars parked out front. Name a super car and it was there. My dad loves cars, and Sarah and I were brought up to love them too. Consequently, we are total rev-heads. I've watched *Top Gear* since it began and when it became *Grand Tour*, I switched allegiance and followed Clarkson and the boys. I still have a mad crush on Richard Hammond, and my dream car is a Bugatti Chiron. You can Google it. It's *gorgeous*. Lego even made one—that *drives*! Sorry, I digress ...

That night, the boys and I did walk-arounds of all the cars. We weren't the only ones, and I suspect if you park your car out front of the Grand Casino, you're fine with people gawking. We did this under the watchful eyes of two security guards—looking, but not touching, guys. No Chirons, but still ...

"So, are we going in?" asked Jae, loudly. Her impatience was obvious, but *I* could have happily spent the whole evening in the parking lot.

"In there?" asked Dani. She looked dubious.

I made my way over to the girls. "Uh, Jae, we can't get in there."

She looked confused. "What do you mean?"

"I mean, there's no way we meet the dress code." We were all dressed in the nicest things we had in our luggage, but

160

dress jeans and wrinkled button-down shirts and equally wrinkled dresses weren't going to cut it.

Jae looked down at her outfit. She looked great in her tiny black skin-tight sheath, but that wouldn't cut it either. The Grand Casino was strictly black-tie. "But—"

"Jae, *look*." Mama Lou pointed to the men and women who were ascending the staircase. Tuxes and gowns abounded.

"Oh. I ... in Miami ..." She stopped before she finished the thought.

"You look great, Jae, really," I said. "*Beautiful*, but this isn't Miami."

She nodded, clearly baffled. I doubted Jaelee had ever been refused entry anywhere. With her looks and her wardrobe, she'd probably never paid a cover charge either.

"It's cool," she said, shrugging it off. "But I'll be damned if I'm not placing a bet at a table in Monte Carlo," she added.

And that is how we ended right back where we'd started in a lesser-known and kinda-seedy casino well off the main drag. Right back with our tour group.

"Hi, guys!" Georgina locked onto us as soon as we walked in, far more effusive than usual. My eyes zeroed in on the glass in her hand. Ahh, that explained it.

"Georgina!" Oh, darling Lou.

"Where have you guys been?"

Walk away. Walk away.

Lou started in on a newsy report of where we'd been and what we'd seen. Jae sidled up to me and nodded towards a blackjack table. It seemed far more interesting than a tipsy Georgina. The rest of our little group had dispersed, Dani

161

tucked under Jason's arm as they both watched one of the Kiwi guys—Paul?—throw dice onto a craps table.

I followed Jae. We took side-by-side seats and she laid a fifty-euro note on the table. The dealer took it and signalled a guy who replaced it with a stack of chips. She halved the stack and gave me twenty-five euros worth of chips. I started to protest and she shushed me.

I'd played pontoon when I was at uni in Australia, but I'd never played blackjack and I'd certainly never sat at a casino table. Excitement revved inside me. I threw Jae a smile and she shut it down with a look that said, "Cool it." I cooled it.

On the dealer's signal, she placed a five-euro chip on the table; I did the same. He dealt and when I peeked at my cards, I saw two tens. *Holy crap!* I'd seen enough films to know I needed to split the pair *and* up the ante. I did both. My next cards were a seven and a nine. I sat on those. The dealer was on fifteen, so he had to turn over another card. It was another seven. He was bust, and I won both hands. On my first ever time playing blackjack. In a casino. In Monte Carlo. I won!

My mouth formed an O and when I looked at Jae, she was smiling at me, her cool façade gone. "Nicely done. First time?" Was it that obvious? I nodded. "Nicely done, *rookie*."

I pushed twenty-five euros in chips over to Jae. "No—"

"*Yes*. I'll play with my winnings."

"Okay," she acquiesced.

We stayed at the same table—my lucky table—until Georgina rounded us all up. Beginner's luck accounted for an extra one hundred and twenty euros of spending money.

Hello, Italy!

Chapter 8

There is scenery and there is *scenery*.

We'd been riding in the coach for days and we'd seen some beautiful landscapes, especially on the approach to the *château*, but the drive from Antibes to Florence was something else.

After another late night and another early departure, Lou and I were both content with minimal conversation and looking out the window. Nice was stunning and as we drove through it, I wished we'd gone there the day before instead of Cannes.

Tom took us right along the seaside boulevard—palm trees and neat pastel-coloured buildings on our left and wide stretches of sand on our right. There were a few private beach clubs with their standard rows of coloured sun loungers, but most beaches were open and there were quite a few morning beachgoers, strolling and swimming.

I could see the similarities to Cannes, but it seemed a little more welcoming, less harried, less "French Riviera". Our excursion to the beach had mostly been about checking off a bucket-list item, but I got the sense that Nice would have been nicer.

We skirted around Monaco, not dipping into the principality like we'd done the night before, but looking down on it—high-rises and terracotta roofs in equal measure encircling a brilliant blue marina, with dozens, maybe hundreds, of luxury boats moored in neat rows.

Leaving France, we stuck mostly to the coast and I was glad Lou and I had purposely chosen seats on the right side of the coach. We were welcomed across the invisible border with a perfectly blue sky, which reflected off the Mediterranean in a million points of light.

But despite the views, a knot of nerves was starting to grow in my stomach. I was seeing Jean-Luc the next day, and I couldn't stop thinking about how I'd ended our friendship. I'd been an utter coward. Yes, it all happened fifteen years ago, but even so ...

And what if he thought dinner was the start of something? An actual relationship? I hadn't been in one since Scott, and I certainly wasn't looking for one. A lover, definitely. A friend, absolutely. But a boyfriend, a partner—or, like Lou had alluded to the day before—a *husband*? What a horrendous thought.

There was a very good reason I owned a permanent site in "Camp Single".

For a decade, I'd avoided meeting the parents or the best friends, had never been a "plus one" at a wedding, and I'd managed to avoid being introduced as someone's girlfriend. I'd never been anything more than a casual fling, a fuckbuddy, or a lover.

And I was completely fine with that. Fuckbuddies did not get fucked over.

I realised, as I stared out at the incredible Apennine Mountains, I was a big fat hypocrite. I *was* a champion of love—*if* it was for other people. Sarah and her boyfriends—I had huge hopes that it would work out with one of them. And I often bragged about my parents' forty years of marriage. I even wanted Dani and Jason to work out, although I suspected it was just a holiday fling.

"I think I'm in love with Italy already," said Lou, leaning past me to get a better look at the mountains. *Speaking of love.*

"It is kind of ridiculous, isn't it? Makes France look like a poor cousin."

"I won't tell the entire country of France you said that."

"You know what I mean."

"I do, yes. You've been before, right?"

"To Italy? No. I am ashamed to say I've lived this close to Europe for a decade and I've never been." I omitted that Scott and I were supposed to have gone to Italy after France.

"I'm so excited about Florence."

"Oh, right, it's on your list."

"Uh huh. Although I can't believe we only get a night there."

"Mmm." I'd thought the same thing.

"Remember when you asked me if I wanted to see the heck out of Paris?" she asked, swapping "hell" for "heck".

"Of course, Lou. It was only three days ago."

"Well, how about we do the same in Florence?" My snark-iness had flown right over her head, and I softened. "Sure, Lou. I'd be up for that. I mean, other than the Duomo, I don't really know what's there. I saw *A Room with a View* about a million years ago. I loved it, but I don't remember much about the city."

"Yeah, so the Duomo—" she was ticking destinations off on her fingers "—then the Uffizi, the gallery where *The Birth of Venus* is."

"Yep."

"Ponte Vecchio, for sure."

"Sure, yes, Ponte Vecchio." I had no idea what she was talking about.

Lou must have been onto me. "It's the old bridge that crosses the Arno," she explained. "You know, with all the tiny different-coloured stores on it?"

"I think I know the one you mean." I did not. I was an utter fraud.

"And I definitely want to go to Piazza della Signoria. They have all these incredible statues there, including a replica of David—we could *try* to fit in going to Accademia, where the original is, but that could be cutting it close, timewise."

"Wow, this is going to be quite the afternoon."

"I'm going to set up a map for us." She pulled out her phone and I returned to gazing out the window.

Can you fall in love with an entire country?

"Okay, so this is a really quick stop—just fifty minutes. And this is our pick-up point. We'll have to move the coach while you go and see the tower, but we will meet you as close to here as possible at—" Georgina checked her watch "—twelve-fifteen. Please be on time—today especially. We need to get

166

you to the campsite, then into Florence for the walking tour. Have fun everyone!"

I was eager to see the Leaning Tower of Pisa, but to get to it we had to dodge dozens of hawkers selling everything from knock-off handbags to cheap bracelets and nylon scarves, all arrayed on giant blankets on the ground. Add a huge milling crowd of tourists, who clearly had *all the time in the world*, it earned its place as my least favourite attraction in Europe before I even saw it.

"Oh, my heck!" exclaimed Lou when we made it through the gates. "It really is *leaning*."

"Really? And you expected what exactly?" I may have been a little tetchy. I hate crowds—most short people do.

She made a face and softly backhanded my arm.

"Here," she said, fishing out her phone, "take a picture of me."

"You sound like Jaelee." If I'd been given a euro every time Jaelee had said that, it would have paid for the tour.

"Just—here." She thrust her phone at me, and I nearly dropped it. Her eyes widened.

"Sorry. All good, I've got it."

She found a spot amongst a hundred other people all doing the same thing and adopted the pose that every person who has ever been to the Leaning Tower of Pisa does. I took the photo.

"Now you."

"No, that's fine."

"Catherine. You will absolutely take a stupid touristy photo. Now stand over there." Sometimes Lou didn't take any of my crap and I kind of loved her for it. I did as I was told and was rewarded for my efforts with one of her infectious smiles.

"Come on. Let's go walk around it." We did. I had to admit, it was cool being there, even with the masses and the fake Gucci handbags.

"Is it time for gelato yet?" I whined.

Lou tutted, then acquiesced. "Okay. You can have a gelato—for being good." She looked at her phone and tapped away on Google Maps. "Come on." She led the way out of the giant stone walls that surrounded the tower grounds, and down the street to a gelato shop with a queue out the door.

"Oh," I said, eyeing the queue.

"It's got four-point-eight on Google Maps," she said.

"What about the second-ranked place?"

"This *is* the second-ranked place. I thought the lines would be better here."

I looked at the time. "I think we'll make it. Plus, it's lunch-time and I'm starving." Gelato is a perfectly acceptable lunch food—please don't judge us. We took our place at the end of the queue.

"Hey, that's Dani and Jason," said Lou.

Dani turned around at the sound of her name and waved at us frantically. "Hey, you guys, come up here."

"Should we?" I asked Lou.

"Yeah, why not?"

"It's just ... I'm British. The queue is sacrosanct."

"Well, today be an Australian and cut the line with me."

We cut the line. I didn't feel good about it, but the people behind Dani and Jason didn't seem to mind. Also, we only just made it back to the coach in time, laden with giant cones of gelato we wouldn't have had if we'd played by British rules.

Georgina eyed the melting cones of gelato and asked the four of us to be careful with them on the coach, like we were children. Of *course* she did. I wondered if she knew she was a tour manager and not a primary schoolteacher. I slipped past her, licking drips of molten chocolatey goodness from the cone. At this rate, I was going to put on a dress size before I got back to London.

Leaning Tower of Pisa ✓

"So," said Lou as she licked her cone. How did she still have so much left? I'd already finished mine. "Tomorrow's your date with Jean-Luc. You excited?"

"Of course." She stopped the licking and looked at me. "What?" I wiped my sticky hands on my shorts.

"What's up?" she asked.

"Uh, nothing. I just said I'm excited."

She eyed me dubiously, then went back to her gelato. I realised it was a total counsellor move—being quiet—but it worked. "I'm a little nervous about it." She nodded silently—another pro move. "Ever since the other night, I keep thinking about how awful I was to him."

"You mean when you stopped writing?" I nodded. "You were kids. I'm sure he's forgiven you."

"Maybe. I hope so." I was quiet for a moment. "It's not only that, though. What if he wants ... well, *more*?"

"You mean sex?" Had I still been eating, I would have spat gelato all over the seat in front of me. Lou seemed like butter wouldn't melt in her mouth, but then she'd blurt out something like that.

"No. I mean, yes to sex, but I mean, what if he wants *more*, a relationship."

"And that's a bad thing?"

"Well, yes. It would be. I don't want anything like that. I just miss my friend, that's all."

"Your extremely hot friend who you want to have sex with?"

"Yes, that one," I replied. "Oh, I want to show you something. I can't believe I forgot."

I took out my phone and scrolled to the photo Mum had sent. "Here. This was at my fifteenth birthday party." I handed Lou the phone and looked at the photo from side-on—for about the fifth time that day.

Jean-Luc and I were standing with our arms around each other's shoulders, grinning at the camera. He'd had a growth spurt the month before and was a couple of inches taller than me, and he had the same longish hair he had as a man—only back then it had overwhelmed his face and only one of his green eyes peeked out from under his fringe. He was wearing a boxy dress shirt and jeans—the height of 90s fashion. He was adorable.

My hairstyle back then was "the Rachel" like millions of other females around the world who loved FRIENDS. I was wearing a strappy floral dress, not dissimilar to what I'd wear today, with a white baby T-shirt underneath, something I would *never* wear today. Why did we do that? My lips were a matte burnt orange—and why did we love matte lipstick so much? Although my look was quintessential late-90s and rather dated from my current vantage point, I was adorable too.

We were both adorable.

"Oh my gosh, you two are adorable."

I chuckled. "I was just thinking the same thing."

"But you don't want a relationship with him?"

"With *anyone*."

"Why?"

I trotted out my stock response. "Because, I'm happily single." It was mostly true. The whole truth was that there was no way I would *ever* put myself through another devastating break-up like the one with Scott. And the best way to avoid a break-up was to steer clear of relationships.

Lou's eyes narrowed, just slightly, but I forged ahead on my previous trajectory, hoping to distract her from probing further. "Lou, I cannot *tell* you how hot I am for him. I mean, the other night when we were at the bar in Montmartre, sometimes I didn't hear what he said, because I couldn't stop thinking about sleeping with him. I *really* want to sleep with him."

"Yes, you've mentioned that."

"So, I'm torn. Is this just two old friends reconnecting, or should I sleep with him and have what I am guessing will be the best sex of my life, then call it good?"

"Why would you want to have the best sex of your life and call it good?"

"Well, you know what I mean."

"Nope. I don't. I don't get the whole thing. You're going to

171

have to explain it to me." Bollocks, she'd stomped right into my (literal) no-man's land. I was going to have to say it out loud.

"I don't do relationships."

"Ever?"

"Ever. I do friendship and I do sex, but not the middle."

"The middle?"

"Yes. *Love*. Well, I did—once—but that was aeons ago."

"Like, how long? When were you last in a relationship?"

The ghost of boyfriend past did a fly-by and I felt my stomach tighten. Ten years on and just *thinking* about the break-up could still blindside me. "Ten years ago," I replied, my voice tight. Lou didn't seem to notice.

"Oh, wow. And how old are you? Thirty-five?"

"Yes." *Why won't she stop asking me about this?*

"That's ... well, you *were* young back then."

I decided to give her the truth; maybe it would appease her, and we could talk about something else—*anything* else. "I *was* young, yes—we both were—but it was also a long relationship. Five years, actually. Then he cheated. We also wanted different things, which is probably *why* he cheated. Not an excuse, just the reason." I omitted the truly gory details, like how I had wanted to live across the world, and how Scott had wanted life to be staid and normal and *boring*.

"It hit you hard," she said, simply, and I suddenly found it difficult to swallow.

I'd thought I could just give her an abridged version of the truth and she'd be satisfied, but I had forgotten who I was talking to.

"Oh, Lou ..." My voice cracked, and I let the rest of my words dissolve into the air. *Do not cry, do not cry.*

I blinked back the tears and swallowed. When I finally spoke, my voice was steady, resolved. "I lost myself. I was a shell, a human shell. *Maybe*, if we'd just broken up like normal couples do sometimes, it would have been all right, but he *cheated*. He didn't love me enough not to do that. I wasn't enough." She reached over and squeezed my hand. I hadn't expressed it quite like that before—to anyone, not even Sarah. I was proud of myself.

"Even so, you survived it and you're a whole woman now. You're no longer that girl riddled with self-doubt. But, you're also still *you*. The teenager who was best friends with Jean-Luc is still in there. That's why you two connected so quickly the other night."

I nodded as I chewed on my bottom lip.

"Hey, did your mum send the letter?" she asked.

I felt the weight of her scrutiny lift from my shoulders as she shifted conversational gears. "Not yet. I hope I get it before tomorrow night, though. I just want that glimpse, you know, of the younger Jean-Luc."

"Sure."

I stared down at the photo. We *were* adorable, but were we adorable *together*?

The rest of the drive was quiet, Lou leaving me to my contemplative funk. She was a wise woman—I'd decided that about her almost as soon as I met her—and she was right. I was still me.

But I wasn't going to fall in love with Jean-Luc. Or anyone.

An hour later, we arrived at the Florence campsite—well, a campsite in the hills outside Florence; I was seeing a pattern—Ventureseek tended to fudge the location of their campsites a little.

Dani and Jaelee had filled in the rooming sheet, and we were all pleasantly surprised to discover that the cabins were a huge step up from Paris and a big step up from Antibes. Each pair got a room and there was a shared bathroom in the middle. I could barely contain my excitement at not having to traverse the campsite to go for a wee!

The excitement was short-lived, however. We only had fifteen minutes to get changed and get back on the coach for our drive into Florence. "Right, it's supposed to be quite warm this evening, so I'm going with a dress," I said.

"Remember, shoulders and knees," said Lou as she pulled clothes out of her case with the abandon of a traveller in a time crunch.

"Oh, that's right." We wanted to observe church dress for the Duomo—and any other church we might want to visit.

"I need to brush my teeth too. The gelato was incredible, but they're furry," I said.

"Yeah, that's *way* too much information."

"Sorry."

On the way back to the coach, we told Dani and Jaelee our plan for the whirlwind tour of Florence and invited them along. Neither seemed enthused.

"I think I'll do the tour with the group," said Dani.

"You mean with Jason," said Jae.

"Well, yeah, he's in the group. *Hello.*"

"I'm going shopping," said Jae.

"You can go shopping anywhere," said Dani.

"Um, it's Italy. *Hellooo*," mimicked Jae.

Lou and I threw each other a look. *Trouble in paradise?* Maybe the two of them spending some time apart was a good thing.

"Are you guys going to the group dinner?" asked Lou. She was braver than I was—I was steering clear of the firing line.

Surprisingly, they both answered in the affirmative. "Sure, that sounds good," from Dani and, "Yeah, why not?" from Jaelee.

"Lou? Should we go too?" I asked.

"I don't mind."

"Great!" I said with far more enthusiasm than I felt. Maybe these were mid-tour blues and we all just needed a break from each other. Maybe dinner together was a bad idea. *Oh well, too late now.* I decided I'd find Craig and Jason and the boys and make sure they joined us. Buffers.

"Oh, my heck. Three hours? Three hours?!" Lou did not react well to the sign posted at the end of the massive queue for the Duomo.

"Wait here." I wanted to make sure it was the correct queue and walked to the head of it. Fortunately, it was the queue to go to the top of the dome, and there was no way in hell I was doing that.

Sarah had told me what it entailed: hundreds of steps up a narrow spiral staircase, then going *inside* the outer and inner domes up a narrower staircase to get to the roof, *while people were coming down the same stairs!* It was a claustrophobe's nightmare. Even Sarah said she'd felt a little faint and she's usually fine with things like that.

I needed to find the queue for the church itself. I saw a small group of people crowded around a young Italian woman and could hear the jabbering American accents from fifteen feet away. I surreptitiously made my way over and eavesdropped. It was exactly what I needed to know.

"Right," I said, a little breathless from my jog back to Lou. "We don't need to line up."

"Really?'

"Really. This is to go up inside the cupola to the roof. We go into the church over there." I led her away from the queue and spilled the other nugget from my eavesdropping. "It's even free—they can't charge to go inside a church. It will probably be crowded, but at least we'll get to see it."

I grabbed Lou's hand and led her through the multitude of people to the other side of the immense structure. When we got to the correct entrance, I stopped still and dropped her hand.

"What's wrong?" asked Lou, impatience clear on her face.

"*Look*, Lou. It's incredible." I peered up at the cathedral, at its intricate marbled façade and the enormous terracotta-tiled dome.

"We're in Florence, Cat," she said after a few moments.

"Yep. We're in Florence. I can't believe how massive this is." She grinned at me. "C'mon, let's go in."

When we emerged about half an hour later, my neck was

sore from staring at the ceiling. I hadn't known about the incredible fresco under the dome. I heard a nearby guide say it was called *The Last Judgement*. It was extraordinary, with six tiers and hundreds of figures depicting heaven and hell and everything in between. Most of the time I was looking up, I was wondering how they'd built scaffolding that high five hundred years ago.

"Oh, my heck. That was incredible. I can't believe I've been to the Duomo." Lou was flushed, and I wasn't sure if it was the excitement or that the cathedral had been crowded and quite warm.

"Are you Catholic?" I asked. I hadn't seen her wear a cross, but that didn't mean anything.

"No, Christian, yes, but not Catholic. Still, it is one of the greatest churches in the world, and I'm just ... wow ... this *trip*. Sainte-Chapelle, now this. And on Friday, St. Peter's!"

I'm not religious, but I was also enjoying the landmark churches. They impressed me in a multitude of ways—architecturally, historically, and especially artistically.

Duomo ✓

"Hey, thanks for figuring out that we didn't need tickets."

"Of course."

"I feel like an idiot for not knowing. I mean, I've wanted to come here for so long, you'd think I'd do some research. You know, like logistics! Geez, *Louise*."

"Hey, it's no problem. Don't be so hard on yourself. We got to see inside—that *ceiling!*"

"I know, right?"

"Now, you said Piazza della Signora?"

177

"Signoria."

"Right. Lead the way."

She pulled out her phone and frowned a little as she searched the pins on her Google map. She lifted her head to get her bearings, then declared, "This way." She sounded confident and this time it was me following Lou through the crowd. I'd had no idea Florence would be so overrun with tourists—in October. It seemed busier than Paris.

The afternoon and early evening flew by in a whirlwind of piazzas and statues and more untenable queues. There was no way we'd get inside the Uffizi that afternoon. We'd have to settle for a postcard of *The Birth of Venus*, and Lou looked a little deflated. "It just means you have to come back. I mean, this tour is ridiculous—less than a day to explore *Florence?*"

"*You* booked it." She cocked her head at me.

"So did you."

"Well, I'm glad I did, because I got to meet you and Dani and Jaelee. It's corny, but it's true."

"It's not corny, it's sweet. Right, we've got about forty-five minutes before dinner and we still haven't walked across the fancy bridge."

She laughed—it was *at* me, I could tell. "Ponte Vecchio. Old Bridge. How can you not know that? It's, like, as famous as the Eiffel Tower."

"Bollocks it is. I bet you every adult in England would know the Eiffel Tower from a photo, but would have no idea where Old Bridge was, or even *what* it was."

178

She sighed in exasperation. "Can you spout lies and walk at the same time?" She walked away and I ran to catch up—her stride was much longer than mine.

"Hey!"

"Hey nothing. Hurry up." Mama Bear Lou was turning on her cub.

"And this!" said Jaelee. She pulled a red leather handbag out of a carry bag—six others were shoved under her chair at the restaurant.

"Well, that's gorgeous," I admitted. "Let me see it." I reached across the table and took the bag from her. I smelled it. "Ahh, divine. What is it about leather?"

"I don't like that smell. It just smells like dead animal to me," said Dani, her nose scrunching up.

"You ordered the veal," Jaelee retorted.

"So?"

"Well, isn't that a little hypocritical?"

"How so? I mean, I *wear* leather. I just don't like the smell."

"Here you go, Jae," I said handing the bag back across the table. I wished I hadn't said anything.

"So, how was the walking tour, Dani?" asked Lou, brightly. I sensed she was tiring of our bickering bus-mates too.

"Yeah, it was okay. I mean, Jason and the guys didn't end up going, but there was this old church, Santa Croce, and that was cool. And we saw Ponte Vecchio, like you did, and we went past the warthog at the markets ..."

"Wait, what warthog?" Lou seemed concerned she'd missed an attraction.

"It's this statue of a warthog. It's made of brass and if you rub its snout, you're supposed to return to Florence." Lou's frown hadn't budged. "You know, it's not far from here," added Dani. "Maybe we can go see it after we finish dinner."

Lou perked up. "Really?"

"Sure, yeah, it's, like, five minutes away."

Craig arrived with Jason and the other Kiwi boys. I'd long given up trying to remember their names. As a teacher, I kept the names of hundreds of pupils in my head. I didn't have room for many more.

"Hey, guys," I said as they found their places on the table. Who needed names? "Guys" was fine, right? Craig sat next to me.

"Hey, Cat."

"What did you guys get up to this afternoon? Dani says you weren't on the walking tour."

"Yeah, the All Blacks were playing, and I went with the guys to a bar so we could watch." He meant the New Zealand rugby team.

"Who were they playing?"

"South Africa."

"Did they win?"

"Too bloody right we did," said Jason from across the table. Dani beamed at him as though he'd just won the Nobel Prize or something.

"Oh, well, good." I picked up my cheap wine glass, which was brimming with cheap wine, and raised it in a toast to a team I didn't support for winning a game I hadn't known was on, in a sport I didn't follow. Being on tour with strangers was sometimes like entering the staffroom at a new school for the first time—banal small talk abounded.

Dinner was fine—not great, but the food was abundant. Family-sized platters of pasta arrived for the first course, a red sauce and a cream sauce. For *secondi*, we'd had a choice of veal, chicken or fish. I'd gone with fish to offset the gelato for lunch, but it was so bland, there wasn't enough salt on the table to turn it around. I also ate a reasonably sized portion of the overcooked boiled vegetables—again, gelato for lunch! I was eating my penance.

Dessert was *tiramisù*, which I think is disgusting. Why would anyone take a perfectly good biscuit, make it soggy, then pile it up with other soggy biscuits and call it dessert? I nibbled on some of the *biscotti* that came with the coffee.

The food was mediocre, but the company turned out to be great. I quickly discovered that the Kiwi boys were hilarious, and that Jason was a very good sport about bearing the brunt of nearly all their stories—maybe "escapades" is a better term. One of the guys, Chris, was about to launch into what promised to be another excruciating retell for Jason, when my phone beeped.

Jean-Luc:

Can I call you?

My stomach plummeted. Was he going to cancel?

Yes. Give me two minutes. I need to step outside.

181

I pushed my chair back and wound my way through the loud and crowded restaurant. I stepped out into the evening, which was cooling down—refreshing after the stuffy atmosphere inside. Even though I was expecting the call, my ringtone made me jump.

"Hi," I answered, a little breathless.

"*Bonsoir*, Catherine. How are you?"

"Good. We're just out for dinner. In Florence."

"Oh, Firenze is magnificent. Did you see the Duomo?"

"Of course. You can't miss it—giant orange dome in the middle of the city." He laughed. I waited, sure he was going to cancel dinner. "So, you wanted to ask me something?"

"Uh, no. Nothing. I just wanted to hear your voice." *Squee.* "I know I will see you tomorrow, but I'm already in Roma and I called to say hello."

"Hello."

"Hello." He let out a heavy sigh and without being able to see him, I couldn't tell if it was a good sigh or a bad one. My stomach did a somersault. "Oh, Catherine. I am so glad we saw each other in Paris. Every time I think about how close I was to missing you, it makes me a little sick. You know?"

I did know. As excited (and nervous) as I was about seeing him the next day, I *had* also entertained the thought of Jaelee approaching someone else in the street. It was like when you bite the inside of your mouth and can't stop touching it with your tongue. It hurts, but you can't help it. But on the flipside of our kismet meeting was a void where no magic existed and where Jean-Luc remained a long-lost friend. So, yes, I completely understood feeling sick about it.

182

"I do. I feel that way too. It's why I got your phone number even though Dani already had it. I didn't want to chance you disappearing into the world again."

"*Exactement.* So, I shall have to keep myself very busy tomorrow—working, writing, so the day goes quickly and I will see you sooner, *n'est-ce pas?*"

"*Oui, bonne idée.*" Good idea. More of my stale French was coming back to me. "And your interview, it went well?"

"Ah, *oui*, yes, I am pleased."

"That's good."

He sighed. "It is. So ... *à bientôt, ma chérie.* I will see you tomorrow. I cannot wait, but I will. I have to!"

"Yes! Me too. See you then. *Ciao, bello!*" The call ended over his chuckle on the other end of the phone.

I held the phone to my chest. Even hearing his voice gave me squidgy feelings. I was definitely head-over-heels in lust.

Fifteen Years Ago

"S o, who's this?"

"Sorry?"

"This photo. On your mirror. It wasn't there before." Scott is peering intently at the photo tucked into the corner of my mirror.

"Oh, that's Jean-Luc."

He turns to me. "But who *is* he?"

"I don't know what you mean."

"I want to know why you've got a photo of another guy on your mirror, Catey." I catch the edge in his voice, but I refuse to bite.

"He's my friend. I told you about him," I reply breezily.

"No, you didn't." The edge sharpens, and his handsome features twist into something ugly.

"Yes, I did." The breeziness dissipates. "He's the French guy. He was here on exchange in Year Ten."

"He doesn't look like he's in Year Ten."

"Well, no. That's him now."

"So, you're still in contact."

"Yeah, so? We were really good friends. He even knew my family. He was over all the time."

"So, does he have a photo of you on his mirror?"

This is getting ridiculous. "How should I know? And, what's the big deal, anyway?"

"Well, I don't know, Catey. Don't you think it's weird that you're *my* girlfriend and there's some other bloke's photo taped to your mirror?"

"No, actually, *Scott*. I don't. We're just friends. I've known him a long time. A lot longer than I've know *you*."

"Oh, that's nice, that is."

"Well? You're being silly."

"Well, you're being defensive. If there was nothing to be defensive about—"

"There's nothing going on!"

"But you're still in contact? What, do you write letters?"

"Yes."

"So, how often? Like, once in a while?"

"No."

"No, what?"

"Like, once a week, or so."

"Once a *week?*"

"Or, once a fortnight, maybe."

"What do you even write about?"

"I don't know, nothing really. Just *life*, stuff I'm thinking about."

"Me? Do you write about me?"

"Sometimes."

"So, he knows about me?"

"Of *course*. You're a part of my life."

"Then why don't you share those things with me instead?"

"I *do*. For fuck's sake, you're not making any sense. There's no competition between you and Jean-Luc. You're my boyfriend and he's my *friend*. That's it. Get it?"

"How would you feel if I had a female friend I hung out with once a week?"

"*Do you*? Do you have a mysterious female friend you hang out with once a week?"

"No! I'm saying, imagine if I did."

"But that's not the same thing—if you're seeing someone in person, then that's—"

"*It's the same thing*—if we were just friends—you know, like you and whatshisname."

"It's Jean-Luc."

"Yeah, well, whatever. So, when were you going to tell me about your very best friend, Jean-Luc?"

"He's not—never mind. And I *did* tell you about him."

"No, no, you didn't. You might have said something about an exchange student once, but *this* is all news to me."

"You're being ridiculous."

"I don't want you writing him anymore."

"What?"

"You heard me."

"Scott, this isn't the 1950s. You can't just tell me to stop writing letters to my friend."

"I'm not telling you, Catey. I'm saying that if you love me, you'll stop."

"I ... you're not serious."

187

"I am totally serious. If we're going to be in a relationship, then I should be your priority."

"You *are*—being friends with Jean-Luc ... it's—"

"I mean it, Catey. Look, I don't feel like going to the movies anymore. I'm gonna go. I—just decide, will you?"

"Decide? Decide what—*between* you? That's—wait, Scott!"

Sarah pokes her head around my bedroom door. "Hey, what's going on?"

"Everything's fucked, Sez." I can tell she didn't expect me to say that.

"What do you mean? What happened?" She sits next to me on the bed, a concerned look on her face.

"Scott saw Jean-Luc's photo and he just started going off on me about how if I love him, I won't write to Jean-Luc anymore—like I'm a bad girlfriend or something."

"You're not a—Cat, that's ridiculous."

"That's what I said, but what if he breaks up with me?"

"Then good riddance."

"Don't you like him?"

"Uh, sure. But, Cat, he can't tell you who to be friends with. That's not okay."

"I know."

"And don't bite your nails."

"Sorry."

"No, it's ... look, maybe he'll calm down and realise he's being a massive dick about it."

"Maybe."

"Jean-Luc—he's a great guy. It was almost like having a

little brother around, you know. That kind of friendship, you gotta hold onto those. Okay?"

"Yeah, I guess."

"It'll all work out. Here—wipe your nose."

"Thanks."

"I've got to go. I've got a uni thing, but hang in there, okay? No doubt Scott will realise he's being unreasonable, and he'll be back to say he's sorry, okay?"

"Yep."

"Love you."

"Yep. Love you too."

Chapter 9

Darting off after dinner to see a brass warthog turned out to be a terrible idea.

While most of the tour group headed to a seedy bar with Georgina for karaoke and overpriced drinks—Sarah's advice was to avoid it at all costs—our little band of merry men and women went in search of a warthog.

The searching part wasn't difficult, because, well, *Google*. Her phone in hand, Dani led the way through a maze of deserted cobbled streets. I wondered where the throngs had disappeared to, but I realised it was 10:30pm on a Wednesday. The tourists were likely asleep in their hotel rooms and the locals were probably still eating dinner. They ate late in Italy; the restaurant where we'd eaten was only just starting to fill up with locals when we left.

"There it is," she said, pointing up ahead to a row of shuttered markets. The statue guarded the marketplace from its stone plinth, its weird little spikey penis the second ugliest thing about it.

"That is seriously ugly," said Lou, saying what I was thinking. Its *face* was the ugliest part of the warthog—tiny beady close-together eyes, a long snout, and giant fangs protruding from its almost comical smile. I'd never seen a live one, and I was certain I could live the rest of my life quite happily without rectifying that.

Lou rubbed its snout and I did the same. As unappealing as the warthog was, I wanted to return to Florence. And yes, I knew it was a stupid superstition, but what if I never went back—and it was because I didn't rub the warthog's nose?

Jaelee rolled her eyes, then took out her phone and handed it to Lachie—damn those boys, I was learning their names. She asked him to take a photo of her and rubbed the statue, her smile disappearing as soon as he took it. He handed back the phone and kept hold of it a little longer than he needed to, teasing her with it. Her smile came back, only this time it was a flirty one.

It was my turn to roll my eyes and Lou caught me. She shrugged. The Love Bus indeed.

The other guys, Jason, Paul and Rob—see? actual names—did not care about ugly statues or superstitions, so we managed to wrap up the whole excursion in about six minutes.

"Okay, so now what?" asked Jaelee, peering at us expectantly. She looked weighed down carrying all those shopping bags. I would have offered to help carry them, but I didn't want to.

Craig spoke up in a rare moment of leadership and I was a little proud of him, our baby bro. "So, we've got almost two hours 'til we need to meet the coach. Cat, you said that the bar is a no-go?"

"The one where everyone else went?" He nodded. "Yes, definitely. My sister, Sarah, used to run these tours. She said

192

if it was the same bar—and it is—to stay away. Quite nasty, apparently."

Jae breathed out heavily from her nose, her impatience obvious. Lachie, whom I was starting to like more as the night went on, reached for her shopping bags. She feigned fobbing him off, but he insisted and she finally "let" him take them. She perked right up after that.

Dani had her phone out again. "Well, if we cross Ponte Vecchio and walk a few blocks, there's a wine bar that looks good." A chorus of agreement, ranging from, "Sounds great," to, "Yeah, why not?" rang in the cool night air. Dani, once again, led the way.

As we walked, I glanced around at our motley crew. The man-child from Oregon, the Kiwi four-pack, who were sporting buddies, and the four of us. *How will we go in a wine bar*, I wondered?

It turns out, rather brilliantly. Stupid Cat, where are two of the best wine regions in the world? Oregon and New Zealand.

Being only eighteen, Craig didn't have *vast* experience drinking wine, but it turned out that his grandfather was a specialty wine merchant so Craig grew up having sips of this and that at the dinner table. And from the way Craig talked about him, I thought I would love his grandfather—wine or no wine.

And yes, the Kiwi boys had spent the night in a pub drinking beer and watching rugby, but they also knew quite a bit about wine. Paul, especially, had an impressive understanding of the differences between Old World and New

World wines. I mentally slapped myself for being such a snob. Me! The woman who was happy with a five-pound bottle of whatever was on sale at Sainsbury's.

The bartender had enough English to be helpful with the Italian menu and after some conferring, the menfolk selected a Chianti and a Barbera. The bartender nodded at the order, giving us a quick smile. We moved from the bar to two small tables and the guys took no time to push them together and find two extra chairs. We squished around the tables, Jaelee's shopping tucked away in the nearest corner of the room.

The bar's décor was rather modern, with stainless steel and blonde wood dominating, but it was also cosy. The bartender arrived with the glasses, two bottles and a bottle opener. The anticipation was palpable as he neatly cut the foil on the first bottle, expertly removed the cork, poured a splash into a glass, and waited for Paul to give him the nod.

Paul explained the difference between the wines, while the bartender repeated his ritual with the second bottle. "So, the Chianti's going to be brighter, fruitier. You'll see when the Barbera's open that it has a darker, richer colour. It will have more tannins and will be more of a sipper than the Chianti." When there was wine in the second glass, he held them both up to the light above us. "See? So, you should try both, but it's likely you'll prefer one over the other." His patter came off as helpful rather than condescending.

We all tried both wines, and although I'm usually partial to a Chianti, I asked for a top-up of the Barbera. Paul happily obliged, and when we all had a glass of our chosen wine, he raised his. "A toast. Here's to travelling halfway around the world with your best mates and making new friends." That cemented it. I liked Paul. In fact, I liked all the Kiwi boys.

As I sipped my wine and listened to the several conversations going on around me, I chided myself again—this time for not being more open to meeting new people. Instead, I'd done exactly what I usually did. I'd found my tribe at the beginning of the tour and had stuck with them. Granted, they were a good tribe. I was confident I'd stay in touch with Lou—and maybe Dani and Jae, perhaps Craig. We were all connected on Facebook, so at least there was that.

But I'd forgotten how much fun it was to hang out with a large group of men and women. I thought about the last time I'd done that, and remembered it was when I'd been with Scott. That was so long ago.

My relationship with Scott hadn't been all bad. We'd had lots of couple friends back then and I'd felt very grown up having dinner parties for ten, even when it meant borrowing folding chairs from Mum and Dad's and all of us chipping in for a couple of casks of wine. It had been fun.

This was fun.

Well, bollocks. Had I forgotten how to have fun?

I dismissed the thought almost immediately. I was Cat Parsons, teacher extraordinaire and fuckbuddy supreme. I took mini-breaks with my girlfriends—well, with Mich. I went to the *theatre*—once a year with discounted tickets counts, right? And I was on a bloody bus tour of frigging Europe, out late on a Wednesday, drinking wine in a Florentine wine bar with my new best friends.

I was fun, damn it!

I was biting on the edge of my wine glass and realising, I stopped. Craig caught my eye from across the table and mouthed, "Are you okay?"

I assured him with a nod and a carefree wave of my free hand. *Good grief, get out of your head, Parsons. Pay attention. Be fun.*

Twenty-minutes before we were due to meet Tom and Georgina near Ponte Vecchio, we each dug out some euros. Paul counted them up, ensuring we had enough to cover the bill and a little extra for a tip. We gathered our things and Lachie picked up Jae's shopping bags—really, it was a ridiculous amount of stuff. I could only wonder how she was going to fit it all into her case.

"Okay, so there's actually a shortcut if we go this way—" Dani lifted her head in the direction she meant. "It's around the corner, down the street, then across a little piazza."

Again, there was a round of verbal agreement and we struck off with Dani in the lead, a straggling single-file line. We turned right and were halfway along the street, the piazza in sight ahead, when two police cars flew past us, sirens blaring.

In the narrow streets of Florence, after midnight when everything else was silent, it was quite alarming. Dani stopped, so we all stopped. Looking behind us, I saw something more disturbing. A third police car was setting up a barricade to close off the street.

The two cars ahead of us pulled into the square with screeching tires, and the piazza lit up with spotlights. There was a lot of shouting, which sounded like commands, and the two police officers from the car blocking the street ran up to us. They spoke in rapid Italian, but the gist was clear. Bunch together, and don't move or speak. They left us, completely unprotected, to join their colleagues in the piazza.

We were trapped. In a police raid. In Florence. After midnight.

Georgina was going to kill us.

Georg-bloody-ina did not kill us. But she did leave us.

Apparently, she did not receive Dani's text, which explained our dilemma and that we would be late to the coach, until *after* they'd left us in the middle of Florence.

We only found this out the next morning, however. Once the raid was over—the culprits cuffed and stuffed into the waiting police cars—and we were free to go, it was sixteen minutes past the 12:30am pick-up time. But we'd sent a very clear text asking them to wait for us and why, so we had every reason to expect the coach to be there waiting when we ran— yes, we all ran—to the meeting place.

It wasn't.

"Well, fuck," said Lou and I nearly keeled over from shock. All right, maybe it was from the running. I am *not*, by any stretch of the imagination, what one might call a "runner".

"Well, what do we do now?" whined Jae. "Did you send the text?" she asked Dani accusingly.

"Yes, I sent the text. I even told her who was with me." She checked her phone. "It definitely sent."

I decided to say it out loud. "Georg-bloody-ina!" There were some mumbled agreements.

Lou piped up with, "But she's been so lovely." Jae and I locked eyes and engaged in some synchronised eye rolling.

"Okay, it's going to be fine. We just need to get a taxi." Craig, the eighteen-year-old voice of reason, stepping up again. The nine of us looked around at the completely deserted streets. There wasn't a car, a scooter, or even a bicycle in sight.

"There." Paul took off at a sprint before the rest of us could react. He'd spotted a taxi turning onto our road, but it was going in the wrong direction. He was a fast runner, I had to give him that. The taxi slowed—*Hallelujah!*—and Paul caught up and leant down to talk to the driver through the window. Then he got in.

"Is he ditching us?" Jae asked. She always seemed to see the worst in people. I knew this about her because I tended to do the same thing and recognised the signs.

"Naaah," said Rob. "He wouldn't do that." The taxi made a U-turn and pulled up next to us. Paul got out. "See?" Rob said to no one in particular.

"He's calling his friend to come get the rest of us. It'll be squishy in one of the cars, but better than nothing, right?" said Paul.

We all wholeheartedly agreed.

"Well, why don't you girls take this one. Maybe Craig, you go with 'em—you sit up front."

It sounded like a plan to me. I didn't care if I had to sit on someone's lap. I'm small; it wouldn't be the first time. Dani seemed unsure, but Jason reassured her, and Craig got in the front seat while the four of us figured out how to share three seatbelts in the back. I hoped we wouldn't get pulled over—

198

although if we did and I recognised any of the coppers from the raid, I'd give them a piece of my mind.

Twenty-five minutes and eighty euros later, two taxis pulled up at the gate of the campsite. It was nearly one, but we didn't leave the next morning—sorry, *that* morning—until nine.

We walked up the hill and bid each other whispered "goodnight"s before the girls and I disappeared into our cabin.

As I lay in my bed, the adrenalin still coursing through my veins, I couldn't shake the thought of that stupid ugly warthog.

"Hey." Jaelee popped her head into our room as I was zipping up my case. We still had half-an-hour before we were due to leave, but I wanted to find Georgina and ask her why the bloody hell she'd left us behind in the middle of the night. I was almost looking forward to the conversation.

"Hey," I called back over my shoulder. "What's up?"

"I was just wondering what you're planning on wearing for your date with Jean-Luc tonight."

"Actually, it's this afternoon. I'm meeting him at five, right after the walking tour."

"Oh, so, something day-to-night then?"

"I guess. I mean, I was going to wear this." I looked down at my jersey wrap-around dress in a black-and-pink floral pattern, which I was wearing with a pair of black flats.

"Oh."

Uh oh. "But this is all right, isn't it?" It was last season, but it was pretty and I thought I looked good in it. And really, there was no better option in my luggage. I mentally scanned my wardrobe at home where several day-to-night date dresses were hanging. *Bollocks*.

"It's nice." *Nice?* "But wait here."

She disappeared, and a knot of nerves started twisting in my stomach. How was I supposed to know when I packed that I'd run into my one-time best friend who had grown into a super-hot guy who set my loins on fire? I'd packed for warmish weather and walking around a lot. *Bollocks, bollocks, bollocks*.

"Here." Jae came back into the room holding one of her paper shopping bags from the day before. "We're about the same size and I think this would look gorgeous on you." She put the bag on my bed and pulled out a silk shift dress in that brilliant blue you see in photos of Santorini.

"Oh, Jae. It's *beautiful*, but I can't borrow it."

"Don't be ridiculous. Of course you can. Put it on." I'd been topless on a beach with Jae two days before, so there was no need to be modest. I unwrapped my dress, then slid hers on over my head. It settled onto my body and she reached around me to grab the ends of the waist tie, then tied a bow in the front. She smoothed the dress over my hips. "You look amazing. That's a great colour for you."

"Really?"

"Yes, really. And it'll look awesome with your motorcycle jacket."

Lou walked into the room wrapped in a towel. "Oh, wow. Nice dress."

"You think? I wish there was a full-length mirror in here."

"You're going to have to take our word for it," said Jae, "because you're wearing it. Oh, hang on."

She disappeared again. I shrugged at Lou.

"You really do look good. Jaelee's?" she asked.

"Yep. She bought it yesterday."

Jae came back into the room with a silver leather handbag. "Here. Better than your messenger bag." She was right, but it was tiny compared to the bag I'd been carrying every day. "And you should wear your silver ballerina flats." Jae seemed to have an excellent working knowledge of the contents of my case—thank goodness.

"Oh, yes, excellent," I said, unzipping my case. I pulled out the silver flats, then slipped off my black ones and packed them. "Oh!" I remembered I'd packed a silver cuff bracelet and I produced it from my case with a flourish.

"Yep. Great." Jaelee nodded approvingly.

"You look beautiful, Cat," said Mama Lou. Both women seemed to understand what this date meant to me—perhaps even more than I did—and I was overcome with a surge of affection for my new friends.

"Hey, what's going on?" Dani poked her head in. "Oh, you look *nice*," she said.

I grinned. "Thanks, girls." I blew out a long breath. "Now I just have to get through the next eight and a half hours without *freaking out!*"

"And without spilling anything on my dress."

My mouth formed an O and Dani and Lou produced synchronised cries of "Jaelee!" She backpedalled immediately with, "Kidding. *Kidding!* Sorry!" Even so, I would try very hard not to spill anything on the dress. I'm not usually a klutz—that's more my sister's department—but I'd be extra careful.

For the drive to Rome, I'd asked Jaelee to sit with me under the guise of getting her advice about Jean-Luc, but it was really to see what was up with her and Dani. She'd unwittingly agreed, and Lou said she was happy to share the ride with Dani, because she was Lou and possibly the nicest person I'd ever met.

"So," I said as we got on the road, "are things all right between you and Dani?"

"Yeah, why?"

"Well, yesterday you both seemed a bit snippy."

"Oh, that. Yeah, I'm not used to such close quarters. I live alone and I guess the whole 'summer camp, twenty-four-seven' thing is getting to me. That's why I went off by myself yesterday. I needed a breather."

"And you booked a group tour *because* ...?"

"Same as you. Running away." I laughed at us both. "Seriously, though, it was last minute and easier than planning the whole thing by myself. Oh, was I *ever* kicking myself that first day when I thought I'd booked a camping trip. Thank you for setting me straight, by the way. I nearly asked to get off the bus. But it's been good. Mostly. Yesterday was just, you know ..." I did, yes.

She sighed. "It's also ... I've been Facebook stalking my ex. His fucking honeymoon."

"Oh, Jae."

She shook her head. "It's like the most masochistic thing ever. Stupid. Just, like ... totally stupid."

"Yes, you should probably stop doing that."

She nodded. "Yep."

"Listen, if you feel the urge, come find me, all right? I'll talk you out of it, or distract you with pastries, or slap you across the face—whatever is needed, I'm your woman."

She threw me a half-smile. "Okay, sure." After a few seconds she added, "Thanks."

"Of course! You'd do the same for me. Oh, I meant to show you and Dani." I dug out my phone and showed her the photo my mum had sent.

She burst out laughing, and I wasn't sure how to take it. "Look at you, like a mini Jen Aniston." Perhaps that was a compliment, Jaelee style. I mean, Jennifer Aniston was still one of the most gorgeous women on the planet.

"And no wonder you didn't recognise Jean-Luc in the street. Look at him. What a dork." Well, that was definitely an insult. I snatched the phone from her and threw her a teacher look.

"Sorry. Not like a total dork, but you know, like a puppy who hasn't grown into his feet yet." I gave her a sideways glance. "I've put my foot in my mouth," she said.

"Yes."

"Sorry."

"It's all right. I still love you."

"You two look really good together, you know."

"You don't have to say that. We were awkward teenagers."

"No, I mean now."

My head swivelled so fast I nearly got motion sickness. "What do you mean?"

"I mean, he's so tall and hunky and you're like this petite little cutie. You should have seen the way he was looking at you after you nearly fainted. It was adorable." There was that word again.

And neither of these descriptions played into my "seduce the hell out of the hot guy" fantasy, *or* the "old friends reuniting" scenario. They meant couple stuff—that giant black void in the middle of my two comfort zones—the one manifesting itself as an ever-increasing knot in my stomach.

Why was I doing this to myself? Life was perfectly fine when Jean-Luc was a distant memory locked safely away in a box. I was happy in my life—ecstatic even. I had a great life. *Great!*

But Jae had said all that stuff about me and Jean-Luc as though it was a universal truth or something, like it was undeniable. So, maybe Jean-Luc and I *were* cute together. *Bollocks, merde, and scheisse.*

"Hey," Jae said quietly. I was staring at the back of the seat in front of me, revisiting my nineteenth-century fantasy about the Parisian apartment I shared with Jean-Luc.

"Hmmm?" I replied, somewhat reluctant to leave my imaginary bed.

"So, I haven't even told Dani this. Actually, I don't think I will, but I wasn't exactly truthful about Marc."

"Marc?" I grasped for the name in my memory. "Oh! *Marc*," I said a little too loudly. She shushed me and I looked around us. No one had heard me, or they had and didn't care. "Sorry, so what do you mean? Oh! You *did* sleep with him?" I whispered. She nodded and a sly smile crept over her face. "Well? What happened?"

"It was like I said, we talked—a lot. For *hours*. It was amazing and, you know, his English wasn't great, but we managed. It was good enough and if we got stuck, I tried Spanish, which he has a little of, and we made it work. He's just coming out of a relationship too, so we talked a lot about that. And, there wasn't even any big moment where I had to decide. It just felt right—like we'd shared something ..."

"And?"

"And, it was nice. Not earth-shattering, but kind of sweet. Then we fell asleep all wrapped up in each other, which I can *never* do. That part surprised me."

"And how did you leave things? In the morning?"

"He walked me to the *château*—well, close but not the whole way. People were up by then. And he kissed me goodbye and that's it."

"You're not going to stay in touch?"

"No," she replied simply. "It wasn't like that. It was just, you know, that night. We both understood."

"Wow."

"Yeah."

"That's so lovely. And you've kept it to yourself."

"You can say it, Cat. I lied."

"Well, yes, that."

"I just ... I'm usually a very private person, and I wanted to keep it just for me, you know?"

"So, why tell me, and why now?"

"Because, I think you're putting a lot of pressure on

meeting up with Jean-Luc today—and part of that's probably my fault."

"Ya think?" I teased.

"Yeah, well, maybe you should let it be what it's going to be." She shrugged. "It could be nothing. It could be everything. But most likely, it will be something in between. I just don't want you to set yourself up to be disappointed."

I chewed on the thought. Jae was right. I was coming at the date from completely the wrong perspective. I was putting too much pressure on myself—*and* on Jean-Luc. It would be what it would be. I just needed to chill the hell out.

Easier said than done.

The Colosseum was far more impressive in real life than I could ever have imagined. Yes, it's a relic, yes, half of it is missing, but it was easy to visualise being in the crowd while gladiators fought it out for their lives. I was certain my impression was as much to do with our guide, Gabriella—who was *fantastic*—as it was to do with the Colosseum itself.

She was a tiny human. I say this knowing that by most people's standards, *I* am a tiny human. Yet I towered over Gabriella, who was four-foot-eleven at most and couldn't have weighed more than seven stone. And although she must have been in her seventies, she had a huge presence and was able to project her voice so well, I wondered if she'd ever been a stage actress.

She finished her spiel and gave us some time to explore and take photos. I obliged Jaelee's request for a photo of her—solo—then asked Craig to take one of the four of us girls. "And let's do a selfie," he said, leaning in and sticking out his enormously long arm to capture the five of us together. When I got my phone back and saw the photo, I immediately posted it to Facebook with the caption, "tour group besties", tagging them all.

I loved these people and we were nearly halfway through the tour. I knew I would miss them when I got back to London, back to real life. Yes, it would be nice to have my own space and not cart my toiletries around in a bag and have access to the perfect outfit from my own wardrobe, but there was something kind of lovely about discovering new places and sharing experiences with people who'd become so special to me.

It was one of the things Sarah had loved most about touring—watching the friendships take shape between the travellers. She'd even made some friends herself, people she was still in touch with. I was starting to understand what she meant by how intense those relationships could be, and how they form in such a short time. When you're with people twenty-four-seven, they become like *family*. I looked at the photo on my phone. My bus besties.

We left the Colosseum and trailed behind Gabriella as she led the way to the Roman Forum, across a wide and very busy street. She spoke rapid-fire Italian to the man at the gates, handed over a piece of paper, and counted us in as she shooed us past her. "*Sbrigati,*" she said repeatedly—hurry. She was little, but she was mighty. We hurried.

The Roman Forum was just as impressive as our previous stop. So much of it was intact, and even when only a skeleton of a structure remained, or a partial one, it was easy enough to see what it had been. On the last part of the tour, we walked along a cobbled street rutted by the wheels of chariots. *Chariots!* Gabriella explained that the width between them became the standard gauge for train tracks. I wasn't sure how true it was, but it was a fun factoid.

As we followed Gabriella, stopping at various places of interest, I let my mind wander to Shakespeare's *Julius Caesar*. It was the shortest Shakespearean play, but by no means the simplest, thematically speaking. I'd studied it at uni and had taught it several times, and I'd grown to love it. The political manoeuvrings were so *human*. I could see it in my mind's eye, playing out on the historical landscape around me. I couldn't believe I was *right there*.

Oh, I was falling in love with Roma.

At the end of the tour, Gabriella led us out the exit to where Georgina and Tom were waiting for us with the coach. When she wrapped up her tour and bade us, *"Arrivederci,"* I had an overwhelming urge to hug her. I didn't though. She didn't seem the hugging type with her pantyhose, red lipstick and tight bun. She shooed us onto the coach and she and Georgina exchanged a few words and an envelope.

Colosseum ✓

Roman Forum ✓

On the coach, I realised I still hadn't talked to Georgina about ditching us in Florence. She'd been MIA that morning, only stepping onto the coach a minute before nine, and there hadn't been time when we got to Rome. I leant into the aisle and whispered to Dani, who was two seats up. "Hey, Dan?"

She turned around. "Yeah?"

"Did Georgina say anything to you about last night?"

"Oh, yeah. Sorry, I forgot to tell you. She said she didn't get the text until they were nearly back at the campsite."

"But you texted her at, what, twelve-fifteen?"

"I know." She shrugged.

"Well, that's total bollocks. How—"

I stopped talking and looked down the aisle past Dani, who turned around to see what I was looking at. Georgina had stepped onto the coach. Dani spun back to me. "Talk later," she said.

I nodded and sat back in my seat. "She's lying," I said quietly to Jae.

"Dani? Oh, you mean Georgina?"

"Mm-hmm. She said she didn't get Dani's text 'til it was too late."

"Yeah, Dani told me that this morning."

"Seriously, though? That's bollocks!" I hissed.

"Hey," she held her hands up. "I'm on your side. I was stranded too, you know."

"Sorry."

"So, how about this? Instead of grinding your teeth over Georgina—seriously, you need to stop that—" I hadn't realised I was and stopped. "Think about Jean-Luc. T-minus thirty minutes." She waggled her eyebrows and me and I quickly forgot all about Georg-bloody-ina, my stomach playing host to a kaleidoscope of butterflies.

While Tom drove the coach through peak-hour traffic, I pulled out a lipstick and a mirror from Jae's silver handbag and slicked Mango Madness across my lips. As I rubbed them together, Jae told me I looked great. "Thanks." I took a deep breath and had to stop myself from biting my lip and ruining the lipstick.

I watched the streets of Rome out the window, suddenly remembering that Mum still hadn't sent the letter. I pulled out my phone and checked my email. Nothing. *That's a long round of golf, Mum.*

Tom stopped the coach next to the Tiber across from Castel Sant'Angelo. "Okay, everyone," said Georgina. "You've got free time to explore, and we're meeting for dinner at seven-thirty at Ristoranti Prati. If you don't have the address yet, see me before you head off. And if you're not coming to the group dinner, then this is the pick-up point for 10:00pm." I dropped a pin on my Google map. "That's ten *sharp*. We don't want a repeat of last night."

Jae and I turned to each other and locked eyes. "Oh, she's a ..." Jae shook her head, leaving the thought unfinished. My mind filled in the end of it with "total cow".

"Told you," I replied smugly. Jaelee replied with an actual growl.

I stood and smoothed Jae's dress down my thighs and draped my jacket over my arm, then slung the handbag strap over my shoulder. Jaelee joined me in the aisle, shuffling along behind me, and when we got off the coach, Dani and Lou were waiting for us.

Lou wrapped me up in a big hug. "Have a great time!"

"I will."

Dani gave me a much less effusive back-patting hug. "Say hi from us." *Uh, sure, Dani.* Jae hugged me next, which surprised me a little. She wasn't usually the huggy-kissy type.

"Just remember, no expectations," she whispered.

"Right." I stood back and looked at my three friends, noting the pride on their faces. It was like they were seeing me off to the prom or something. "See you all later!" I said cheerily.

Then I turned and walked away—in completely the wrong direction.

Chapter 10

I had a destination and Google Maps. How on earth had I managed to get lost?

I was supposed to meet Jean-Luc at the bar at 5pm, and I *thought* I was following Google's very specific instructions to arrive at the address exactly on time, ignoring that her British accent was murdering the Italian street names.

Except it wasn't a bar. It was a trattoria, and it was completely devoid of Jean-Lucs.

At 5:08pm I texted him.

So sorry. I'm lost! I thought I had the right place, but you're not here.

Standing underneath the trattoria's awning, I chewed my lip while I waited for a response. The *signora* behind the counter eyed me suspiciously, and I moved away from the entrance as my phone beeped.

Pas de problème chérie. Meet me at Piazza Navona near the fountain of the four rivers. I will see you soon. J-L x

Now I needed to find Piazza Navona. What if it was on the other side of the city, or it was enormous and I couldn't find the fountain with four rivers? I was whipping myself into quite a tizzy, but I hated being late and I hated being lost in a city I didn't know. *Traveller, traveller, traveller.*

I pulled up the map on my phone again and tapped out "Piazza Navona". *Phew.* I was practically on top of it, about a three-minute walk away. I oriented myself and headed off, my phone leading the way. Her English instructions were far too loud and raised a few eyebrows as people passed, but I didn't care. I needed to get to that damned fountain—*pronto*!

I emerged into the piazza to discover two things: it was bloody huge—*bollocks*—and there were only three fountains—*thank God*.

I scanned the people around each fountain, and my breath caught as I saw him leaning against the giant fountain in the middle of the piazza—I didn't notice, or care, if it had four rivers.

He was wearing dark-wash jeans and a green button-down shirt with the sleeves rolled up. I just knew that green would match his eyes perfectly. I took a moment to marvel at how beautiful he was, then skipped off towards him. It was not the most elegant way to approach a man I fancied, but I was so happy to see him, the giddy schoolgirl in me took over.

"Hi," I said, arriving a little breathless. I grinned up at him and he grinned down at me. Then, as though we'd done it a hundred times before, he swept me up in a hug, his arms around my waist and my feet leaving the ground for a second.

I held him close, my arms around his neck, as nostalgia and lust mingled and washed over me.

God, he smelled good—like cotton sheets dried in the sunshine amongst citrus blossoms.

"*Bonjour, chérie*. Welcome to Roma. You look wonderful," he said, putting me down and sweeping his eyes over me. They crinkled at the corners and he bit his bottom lip through a smile. When it emerged from between his teeth, I wanted to lick it badly.

Momentarily struck dumb by his handsomeness, I eventually replied, "So do you." And he did. As I'd guessed, the green of his shirt did incredible things to his eyes, and up close his forearms were tanned and muscular.

I suddenly remembered my manners. "I'm so sorry I got lost and you had to wait. I hate being late. It's so rude."

"*Ne t'inquiète pas*, it's no problem. I'm just glad you are here." As much as I would been perfectly happy to stand there and smile at him until it was time to say goodbye, it was hardly an action-packed itinerary. And it definitely didn't factor in my plans for that bottom lip.

"So, what have you seen so far? Do you want to explore, get a drink?"

"Well, yes to both. I've just come from a tour and we saw the Colosseum—wow—and the Roman Forum—also wow. But that's about it, really. I mean we have tomorrow to explore on our own, but if you know of some places I should see ... you've been here before, right?"

"Yes, many times." It didn't come out as arrogant, just matter of fact, but I still felt idiotic for asking.

I replied with an insipid, "Oh, right."

"Which means I do have some favourite places to show you," he responded enthusiastically.

"I'd love that."

"Well, this, right here, is one of them." He took my hand in his and for a gesture so chaste, it pushed lust to the fore-front of my competing emotions. I forced myself to concentrate as he led me around the fountain, explaining it to me.

"This was designed by Bernini. You might know some of his works." I did not. "He was a sculptor mostly, and these figures represent the four great rivers of the world—each from a different continent. You see here, the Ganges from Asia, the Danube—Europe, of course—the Rio de la Plata from the Americas, and the Nile from Africa—his face is covered, you see? It is because when this was sculpted in the 1600s, the source of the Nile had not been discovered yet."

I peered at the details of the sculptures as we circumnavigated the fountain. Again, it was awe-inspiring that a human could start with a block of marble and work inwards to *that*. "It's incredible," I said, almost to myself.

Piazza Navona ✓

"Oh, I do want to see the Trevi Fountain, if that's all right?

"But, of course. It is magnificent."

"It's a little touristy, though, isn't it?"

He laughed. "I think when we get there, you will see it is *very* touristy, but it is a must, I think, e*specially* your first time in Rome."

"And I've got some coins."

"Ah, yes, for the three wishes, *non*?"

216

"*Oui.*"

He gestured towards one of the roads leading off the piazza and we walked side by side.

"And what will you wish for, Catherine?"

"Hah! I'm not telling you my wishes. They won't come true."

He shot me an amused smile. "I think if you tell me *before* you make them, they will come true."

"Oh, is that right?"

"*Oui.* I believe so." When I looked up at him, I was met with an amused smile. Was he fishing? Was he supposing my wishes would be about him?

"I think I'll play it safe." I honestly had no idea what I'd wish for. And, of course, it didn't really matter. It was a silly thing, like rubbing the brass warthog's nose. But as we walked, I realised I *did* have a wish in mind and it had to do with Jean-Luc's very kissable lips.

Our first stop after leaving Piazza Navona was not the Trevi Fountain, but it did leave an indelible mark on me. The Pantheon.

After spending much of the afternoon exploring ruins, it was incredible to see a structure *that* ancient—built around two millennia ago—and *that* intact. From the sentries of wide pillars which guarded the entrance to the elaborate designs of the porticos and walls, from the geometric marble floor to the vast dome with its oculus, an eye open to the elements, I couldn't stop gawking. My jaw started to ache with all the open-mouthed wonder.

"Spectacular, *non*?" said Jean-Luc leaning over my shoulder.

"Yes, just spectacular. It seems even bigger inside than it does from the outside. It makes me feel ... so small."

"Perhaps this was the intention of the Romans, to make people feel insignificant when they came to honour the gods."

"If that's the case, it's effective." I took another long look at the blue sky visible through the top of the dome before wandering back towards the door.

Pantheon ✓

We stepped into sunshine and I marvelled at how, all around us, Romans were going about their day ignoring this impressive structure right in their midst. They bustled by, dressed impeccably, as though they were collectively late for something important—most likely to meet someone for coffee or an after-work vino. If they weren't on the move, they were sitting around tiny tables drinking from tiny coffee cups.

And I had scrubbed up well that day, but the Roman women were next level. For one thing, through some sort of break with the laws of physics, they were able to traverse a city where cobblestones reigned supreme while wearing stilettos. Most women were either pencil slim or curvy in all the right ways, and most had long hair, even the middle-aged and older women.

Like Gabriella, they wore full faces of makeup despite the warmth of the weather, and I ended up with a roving girl crush as it transferred from woman to woman on our journey across town. I wished I could pull off a perfect red lip, especially at the end of a workday. I usually chewed off my muted beige lipstick by recess, and I never bothered to reapply it.

I was giving myself whiplash admiring the Roman women,

when out of the corner of my eye I spotted a familiar face. I stopped short and stared as I realised that Isabella Rossellini was crossing the street towards us. Her signature gamine haircut framed one of the most beautiful faces the world has ever seen—that *I've* ever seen—and she wore black capri pants and a high-neck short-sleeved black top. *Dani would rock that look,* I thought.

"What is it, Catherine?" He must have followed my line of vision, which was a good thing, because I'd lost the ability to speak. "That's Isabella Rossellini," he whispered and I nodded mechanically.

She breezed past us with a brisk gait and I involuntarily smiled at her. She flashed a smile back and when I looked at Jean-Luc, we had the same round mouths and wide eyes. I burst out laughing and a beat later, so did he.

"Oh, my God! I can't believe I saw her—that *we* saw her—and she smiled at me. She did, right? I wasn't imagining that?"

"No, she definitely did." He blinked his eyes a couple of times and shook his head. "She is beautiful, don't you think?"

"Uh, hello! Yes! She's like, Isabella Frigging Rossellini. I can only hope I look *half* that good in my sixties."

"Oh, I am sure you will, *chérie*." I suddenly knew what my second wish would be.

As we got closer to the Trevi Fountain, the crowd of tourists thickened, until we were in the midst of a human stew, shoulder to shoulder with hundreds of people shouting, "Take the photo!"

It was awful—*and* amazing.

The fountain itself was magnificent. Sure, I'd seen it in

films, but there was little that could prepare me for the grand scale of it. It was enormous and ornate and impressive and just *beautiful*.

With my hand in his, Jean-Luc pulled me towards the centre of the fountain, into the fray, with a series of *"Scusi"*s. Men deferred to him, probably because of his height, and women gawked at him—his gorgeousness undeniable. Both worked to our advantage and when we got to the centre, he stood behind me with his hands on my shoulders and positioned me so I could see the whole fountain.

He leant down and spoke into my ear. "What do you think?"

"It's magnificent," I said over the crowd. I knew we wouldn't want to stay there long, so my eyes hungrily roamed over the details of the statues, especially Neptune and those incredible horses.

"You will make your wishes?" I was so taken aback by the grandeur, I'd forgotten. I fished in my handbag for my purse and pulled out three brass-coloured coins. No use in spending more than I needed to. Eighty cents would do.

I turned my back on the fountain and under Jean-Luc's amused gaze, tossed the coins one at a time into the fountain.

I wish to kiss Jean-Luc—maybe more, but kissing is the bare minimum. That one was quite specific. *I wish to be a beautiful sixty-something someday, like Isabella Rossellini.* I paused for a moment before I tossed the third coin, because I really didn't know what else to wish for, and "world peace" seemed a bit twee. Then it came to me. *I wish to make it up to Jean-Luc for being such a terrible friend all those years ago.*

I took a deep breath and exhaled, then turned back around

to take a final look at the fountain. "You made good wishes?" I heard from behind me.

I faced him, smiling. "I think so, yes."

"Well, then I hope they come true." He tipped his head and kissed my forehead again.

I should have wished I was four inches taller so he would have made it all the way down to my lips. And what was with all this forehead kissing? The first time back in Paris had been sweet, somewhat melancholic, perhaps—even intimate. But standing next to the world's most famous fountain, I wondered if he saw me as an old childhood friend and nothing more. Unfortunately, I was not fluent in forehead kissing. I knew my way around all sorts of other kissing, but not that one.

"Everything is all right? You are frowning." *No, Jean-Luc. Everything is not all right. You are super hot and super confusing.*

"Of course," I replied, my English manners speaking for me.

"I think it is time for a drink, yes?" He'd read my mind, even before I'd formed the thought.

"*Oui.* Lead on, McDuff." Confusion flickered across his face before it settled into a smile. Maybe he wasn't au fait with his bastardised Shakespearean expressions.

Trevi Fountain ✓

I felt myself relax as we extricated ourselves from the masses of fountain-goers and stepped into a quiet side street. The late sun no longer visible, we walked along in shadows and I shivered, then slipped my jacket on.

"You are cold. It's not much further. Then we can warm up with some wine." He was so attentive, so acutely aware of me and how I was feeling. I couldn't remember the last time a man had made me feel like that—that I *mattered*.

As we walked, I sifted through memories of me and Scott together. Once in a while, he'd make me a cup of tea without me asking him to, but he didn't really notice when I was cold or needed something. Instead, I'd make a show of it, then he would say something unhelpful like, "You should've brought a cardy."

And I wasn't sure how I felt about being with someone so *nice*, especially as I was particularly keen to shag him senseless. Reminisce and shag—that's it. Old friends and (hopefully) lovers. Nothing in between. I was glad our destination wasn't much further. I was having quite the chat with myself and it was just making me more confused.

"This place has almost any wine you can think of." We had arrived at a wine bar called Cavour 313. Its narrow entrance was recessed into a giant stone wall and I would have missed it if he hadn't led me straight to it. Inside, it was busy. A casually dressed man held court from behind the bar and when he saw us, he pointed to two free barstools. Jean-Luc signalled that we wanted to sit in the back and he nodded at us.

I followed Jean-Luc into another room where it was obvious that someone had a love of dark red wood. Wood panelling up the walls, wooden booths with wooden tables *and* seats, and a grid of wooden beams above for wine storage. It was like being inside a giant wine barrel—maybe that was what they were going for.

There was an empty booth for two against the wall and

Jean-Luc slid in on the far side. I sat opposite him and we smiled at each other. I wondered if, like me, he was still trying to marry this new person with the one he knew twenty years ago.

"Oh, I have something to show you," I said, remembering the photo Mum had emailed. I pulled my phone out and scrolled to the photo, then handed him the phone.

He had a slight frown of concentration as he peered at the photo, then he smiled, shook his head and ran his hand through his hair. I should have given up one wish to do *that*. It looked so soft and shiny, perfect for running your fingers through.

"Oh, yes. I remember this. I am such ... a *boy*." He scrutinised the photo again and his bottom lip disappeared between his teeth.

"Well, yes, and I'm such a girl. It was a long time ago."

"You look the same, I think. Obviously, a woman, but still you. Me? So different. I am ..." He seemed at a loss for words and my mind filled in the blank with a number of options—gorgeous, super-hot, a manly-man, ridiculously handsome.

I settled on, "You've become a man."

"*Oui*," he sighed out. "Taller, broader, my nose fits me now." He laughed quietly at himself and handed back the phone.

I had another look at the photo I'd already committed to memory. "You were cute back then."

"You are just being kind."

There was a tiny glimpse of the teenager in his modesty, and I realised I needed to reassure him, this handsome, accomplished man. "No, I'm not, honestly. But you *have* changed.

That's why I didn't recognise you when Jaelee accosted you on the street. I mean, you seemed familiar, but I thought you must have been a French actor or something."

He laughed aloud and shook his head. "That is ... no, definitely not an actor."

"I mean, you looked familiar and you are like, super-hot, so I—" I cut myself off. I hadn't even had any wine yet and I'd already confessed my attraction to him. There was no way to retract it.

He regarded me with raised eyebrows and a smile tugging at the corner of his mouth. "Super-hot?" he said, dragging each word out as much as possible. It came out as "sooo-peh ot".

"Jean-Luc Caron, you do not need me, or anyone else, to tell you that you are a handsome man, so stop with the false modesty." I refrained from punctuating my rebuke with a tut.

He nodded his head, raising both hands. "*D'accord, d'accord.*" All right, all right.

A waiter flew past our booth, dropping a wine menu on the table, and mumbling something to us in Italian. I suspected it was something like, "Be with you in a moment." Like the French, the Italians seemed to have perfected the "officious efficiency" type of service.

"You should probably order for us. You chose well last time," I said, referring to the wine we'd had in Paris.

"I was thinking we should have some prosecco, yes, to celebrate our reunion."

"*Parfait,*" I replied. It *was* perfect. *He* was perfect. He lifted his hand to call the waiter over and ordered two glasses—in Italian.

"So, you speak Italian too?"

"A few words."

"Your accent was ... you sounded Italian." He shrugged. "What other languages do you speak, besides German?" I had my smattering of (bad) French, but other than being able to say "please" and "thank you" and "hello" in a handful of languages, I was like most native English speakers—embarrassingly inept at speaking anything other than my mother tongue.

He did the French thing of blowing out air through his lips while he thought. "Well, yes, the German, and I have Spanish, some Italian as you see, a little Portuguese, Dutch. But mostly when I am in the Netherlands, we speak English to each other. Actually, in Germany too—English. And, I also speak some Australian," he added deadpan.

"You dag," I teased, digging out one of my favourite Aussie slang words.

Smiling, he said, "You see? I even know what that means."

"Seriously, though, the languages thing. It's impressive."

He shrugged. "Thank you, but it is part of my work. And the more I travel, the more I learn—something new every time, especially in Germany. They seem to have a word for everything."

"Oh yes, they have all those nouns which are just a bunch of other nouns strung together."

"*Exactement.*" Exactly.

Two glasses of prosecco, filled nearly to the brim, appeared on the table. Impressively, the waiter managed not to spill a drop.

"*Grazie*," I called after him. I heard a distant "*Prego*" in reply.

"See? You are already perfecting your Italian." I gave him a "ha-ha, very funny" look, which he seemed to ignore. "A toast. To old friends getting reacquainted." There was nothing wrong with the toast—*friend* Cat loved it—but before I clinked my glass against his, I silently added to it.

To discovering what you look like under those clothes. The lusty part of me satisfied—for the moment at least—I smiled as our glasses came together.

"That cannot be true. I am trying to imagine it, but Ron is … he's a man's man. Is that how you would say it?"

"I would, yes. That's exactly why it was so funny. But that's not even the end."

Jean-Luc had asked after my family, something we hadn't got to in Paris, and I was telling him a story from my last visit home to Sydney.

I'd been out to lunch with some uni friends and was meeting my dad for a drink at a bar in Coogee, on the beach. My dad is notoriously early and while he was waiting, he started chatting to a guy at the bar. It was only when he said something funny and the guy laughed and put his hand on Dad's leg that he twigged the guy was hitting on him.

This all happened before I got there and to his credit, my dad's response was something like, "Good for you, mate, being yourself, but I'm not interested." The guy had left by the time I arrived.

"So, when I get there, I give Dad a kiss on the cheek and the bartender comes over and says, 'It's a good thing you got here when you did. Your husband's been chatted up by some gay bloke.'"

"Oh, my God."

"I *know*. I wasn't sure which part to respond to first—that he thought I was married to my *dad*, or that Dad had been chatted up by a guy, *or* that the bartender sounded horribly homophobic. Meanwhile, my mouth is hanging open and my dad's just sitting there laughing to himself. He says to me, 'Don't worry about it, love. But let's go somewhere else.' So we did."

"I always liked Ron. He was good to me. And your mother. I liked being with your family."

"They *loved* you, especially Sarah. Actually, I spoke to her yesterday—no, sorry, the day before. Anyway, she says hello. She says you were like a baby brother to her."

"Oh, that is very nice. And she is happy? She has a good life?"

"Yes, I think so. She does now, anyway. Earlier this year, she broke up with this awful guy she'd been dating. I never met him, which is probably a good thing, 'cause I would have slapped him—he cheated on her. She was in a bad way for quite a while, but *then* she went on this incredible trip to Greece—a sailing trip. A couple of months ago now."

"And you? Did you go as well?"

"No, I was teaching." He nodded. "But she stayed with me afterwards. You know, she met someone in Greece—actually, *two* someones." He looked surprised. "I *know*, right?" I laughed. "She basically came back from Greece with two boyfriends."

"So ...?"

"So, what happens next?"

"*Oui.*"

"Well, she's spending time with both of them and I guess, eventually, she'll have to decide."

"This is ... I have many questions ..."

"So, one is older than her—James—he lives in London— and the other is younger—Josh. He's American. And in December, she's going to Hawaii with Josh for New Year's, and James is going to Sydney to see her in January."

"This is like a film."

"Hah! That's what I said. Anyway, I suppose it will all play out over the next few months. But, for me, the most important thing is that she seems happy. And while she was with me in London, she talked about finding her 'bigger life'—you know, really embracing life, not just existing. Greece was good for her. I think she needed the shake-up."

"And what about you? Do you aim for a big life? Is also this your philosophy?"

Sarah had committed to shaking up her life, and though she'd only been back in Sydney a couple of months, it was thrilling to see her actively *live* her life. But I hadn't any impetus to make huge changes to mine. I loved my life. Well, I definitely *liked* it.

How many people could say that?

Even so, it was a hefty subject to dig into with Jean-Luc and I wasn't quite ready. He watched me with unblinking eyes, not letting me off the hook. "Oh look, our glasses are empty," I said, presenting him with a cheeky smile instead of an answer.

He raised his forefinger, "We will return to this." He flicked through the extensive wine list. Apparently, they had over a thousand different wines by the bottle. He turned to the "wines by the glass" section, which also looked impressive. "Do you like French wine?"

"Sure." He looked up, his eyes narrowing. "I mean, I've had French wine before—lots—but I'm not good at remembering varietals and labels, so ..." I trailed off. "Oh, gamay!" I exclaimed. "We had that at the *chateau* and I liked that."

A smile tugged at the corner of his mouth. "Perhaps a better question is, what characteristics do you enjoy in a wine?"

That was a better question—and an easier one. "I like crisp white wines—not heavy oaky ones—and for reds, I like it best when they taste like Christmas. Does that help?"

He responded with a smile and a slow nod of his head. "*Oui*, it does." He went back to studying the menu, then signalled for the waiter and ordered for us.

"You haven't told me about your work, your teaching," he said when the waiter retreated. "You enjoy it?"

"You know, I really do. My pupils, they're so *worldly* now. So much more so than I was—maybe even more than you were. They are bright and interested in the world. They have such great questions. I'm stumped by them constantly, almost daily."

"But this is a good thing, yes?"

"Oh, absolutely. You've tapped right into what I mean. I

love that they challenge me, that *I* learn from *them*. And when we come up on something which raises those more complex questions, we work it out together.

"Sometimes, they are more like young colleagues, you know. Honestly, with Brexit and Trump going for a second term and all the craziness in the world—even back in Australia, there's constant political upheaval—I have this overwhelming sense that everything will be all right, that this generation of children have it figured out and, somehow, they'll save us from ourselves."

"That's ... that's wonderful, Catherine. I think you must make a fine teacher."

"Thank you. I like to think so. Most days, in any case."

"And if they misbehave?"

I waved it off. "Oh, you know, they're young adults by the time they come to me. Sometimes, they don't do what they're supposed to, but if that happens, I just talk to them. I mean, I sit them down and we *talk*. There's usually some reason for them behaving like a little troll."

He chuckled. "You love them."

"I suppose I do. Collectively, at least. Some more than others. But I do love teaching."

"Your passion, it shows."

"Thank you." I took the compliment, somewhat proud of myself. Teaching was something I was good at.

"So, I remember this expression," he said, playing with the stem of his glass, "you are still 'on the hook', *non*?" Bollocks. I'd hoped he'd forgotten. He lifted his eyes from the glass. "You are happy with your life? It is big enough, like Sarah's?"

The weight of the question was stifling. Tempering my tone, I replied, "I think I am happy with my life, yes." Those Kelly-green eyes narrowed again, scrutinising me. I tried to focus on anything besides how sexy he was when he looked at me like that.

"You said you don't have someone in your life right now." Had I? I'd said I was single, which wasn't quite the same thing. I thought about my current fuckbuddy, one of the casual teachers from school. Casual teacher, casual lover—we typically saw each other once a month or so, maybe more. Although I was not going to divulge anything about Angus to Jean-Luc.

And, I knew what Jean-Luc had meant.

"No. I'm not in a relationship—not since Scott." I saw him wince ever so slightly at Scott's name, and I felt a pang of guilt. *Why did I say his name?*

"It is such a long time ago, Catherine. Really, no one since then?"

"Nope." I tried to sound confident, totally at ease with the state of my love life. He peered at me and I thought I detected a smidge of pity. I needed to steer this conversation in any other direction—*immédiatement*.

"I am sorry, but it is hard to believe. You are beautiful, you are intelligent, funny ... It is a little, how do you say? Baffling."

I went on the defensive—I couldn't help it. I'd been backed into a very tight corner and I wanted out. "What about you? Since your divorce?" The word sat fat and heavy in my mouth. "Have *you* been in love?" I was pulling out the big guns, my tone bordering on cynical.

"Of course." *Of course?* "It is like breathing, *non?*" *Non, Jean-Luc, being in love is not like breathing. Because if it was, I'd have been dead a long time ago.*

In a moment of imperfect timing, our wine showed up. I snatched mine off the table and gulped a mouthful. *Damn him, it's delicious.*

"Catherine." I looked up to see him studying me, concern etched onto his handsome features. He reached across the table and took one of my hands. "I have upset you." It was a statement, not a question, and stupid frigging tears prickled in my eyes. I willed them to bugger right off, but they slid down my face as I gulped in breaths of air. "I have. I am so sorry. Please, tell me what I can say."

I shook my head. The truth was, I didn't know why I'd reacted like that. What the hell was wrong with me? I *was* happy in my life. I had a good job and a nice flat and a wardrobe full of designer clothes I'd bought for a bargain. I went on mini-breaks and had good sex from time to time. I had friends and I was close to my family. Yes, I'd messed up with Alex, but he was moving out soon, and Jane and I would find the perfect flatmate. Maybe, we'd even get a pet, like a fish or something.

Seriously, what was wrong with me?

If I was going to spend the rest of the evening with Jean-Luc—if we had any chance of salvaging it—I needed to get a grip. I imagined all my rogue emotions swirling inside me, gathered them up and tucked them into a box and closed it. The visualisation helped. I took some slow breaths and, eventually, I was able to meet Jean-Luc's eyes. His expression nearly busted open that box, but I held it together. I squeezed his hand, then took mine back.

"I'm sorry. Just touched a nerve, I think. It's all good. This wine is delicious, by the way." *Deflection is the best defence*.

I could see the thoughts flash across his face and remembered he'd been like that as a teenager—an open book. It was one of the things I'd loved about him. *Oh dear*. I didn't mean *love* exactly.

His face settled into the perfect picture of kindness and he smiled warmly at me. I was free and clear. "So, tell me about your family," I said, abruptly changing the subject. "What's Cecile up to now?" I sipped more wine.

He leant back in his seat. "Well, I think the biggest news is that I am an uncle."

"Oh, my God, you are? That's wonderful. Nieces? Nephews?"

"Two nieces. They have two and four years." He said their ages the French way—"I have this many years." "Here." He took his phone from his pocket and scrolled through his photos. The one he settled on was the three of them together, both girls sitting on his lap and giggling. He was looking at the older one and grinning. My heart skipped a beat. There was so much love in that photo.

He leant over the table and pointed to the screen. "Abigail—Abby—and Alice." "Ah-leese", he'd said—also the French way.

"They're so sweet," I said, handing the phone back. "They obviously love their Uncle Jean-Luc."

He laughed, his affection for them dancing in his eyes. "It is mutual. They are fun. Lots of energy. I am like a playground.

They always want to climb all over me." *I wanted to climb all over him.*

"Do they live in Paris?"

"No, Lyon. One of the reasons I try to go back at least once every month."

Seriously, is there anything wrong with this man? I thought. *Oh right, he equates love with air.*

At that thought, I could feel the chance of ever seeing him naked slipping away.

Chapter 11

Jean-Luc caught me up on the rest of his family as we finished our wine. I had never met them, but he'd written about them so often, I'd been fond of them from afar. He was obviously still close to his family, something we shared. Although he got to see his family a lot more than I saw mine.

And seeing how Jean-Luc's face lit up as he talked about them made me feel a rush of affection for mine. Maybe I would look at flights to Australia when I got back to London.

"Are you hungry?" he asked as we left the wine bar.

"Starving."

"Excellent. I am taking you to one of my favourite places here in Roma."

"You have a favourite place? How often do you come here?"

"To Roma? Ahh, five or six times a year."

"Wow. No wonder your Italian is so good."

"My Italian is *okay*."

"I thought we talked about false modesty. It's a very unattractive trait," I teased. "Uh, do you mind if we slow down a bit?" I was having to speed walk to keep up with him—one of the disadvantages of being under five-two. There are others—*many* others—that I won't bore you with.

"Oh, yes. I am sorry. I just *love* Roma. I am excited like a little boy, but no need for jogging," he said mischievously. We slowed down. "I should say, it is not an extravagant place, but the *food*! It is *incredible*." "On-kwoy-ab-le", he'd said. It was quite sexy how he peppered his English with French words. "I always try to go when I am here."

"So, they must know you by now."

"Ah, *oui*, you will see." He grinned down at me with that gorgeous smile of his. It was impossible not to reciprocate.

It was about a ten-minute walk from the wine bar to the restaurant and Jean-Luc spent most of the time talking about some of the dishes he'd had on previous visits to this mystery restaurant.

"They must have a high rating on Google."

"I don't know. *Peut-être*. It is very small. A family place. *And* we are here." He stepped to the side of a doorway, so I could go on ahead of him, but it wasn't clear where to go. There was only a plain door.

"In here?"

"*Oui*." I tentatively opened the door, and a waft of delicious smells and a burst of Italian chatter greeted us. With his hand on my back, Jean-Luc guided me into the tiny restaurant.

I counted eight tables along one side of the narrow room. A glass-fronted display case ran nearly the length of the other wall. It was in sections and looked like the counter at a particularly nice deli—cheeses, cured meats, fresh beef, two types of fish, and bowls of chopped veggies and herbs.

It was only when I saw the woman behind the counter take handfuls and scoops from various bowls and trays and combine them in a large silver bowl, that I realised the display case was her fridge. She tossed the silver bowl a few times, then threw the ingredients into a hot pan where they sizzled. It was mesmerising.

Jean-Luc led the way to a small round table towards the back of the room, which took a little manoeuvring as we weaved between the tables. As we passed by, I snuck a peek at what other people were eating. Every dish looked amazing. When we got to our table, one of only two empty ones, I sat down with a breathless, "Wow."

He tilted his head as if to say, "I told you."

"Jean-Luc! *Benvenuto, amico mio!*" Jean-Luc stood and hugged the young man in the back-slappy way men have, then turned to me to make introductions.

"Carlo, this is Catherine."

Carlo took my hand and looked into my eyes warmly. "Welcome, Caterina. Thank you for bringing Jean-Luc back to us," he said, seamlessly switching to English. I loved how he called me "Caterina". My name in other languages and accents was far better than the Aussie "Caaaath-rin".

"Oh, I cannot take any credit. He insisted we come to the best restaurant in Roma and I simply agreed." I can be quite charming, too, sometimes.

Carlo threw Jean-Luc a look which was difficult to read. I hoped it said, "You are a very lucky man." "Well, Mamma will be very happy to see you—both." He turned towards the woman in the kitchen, who seemed to be making several dishes all at once. "*Mamma, indovina chi è qui,*" he called. A few heads from other tables lifted—one of a very attractive woman in her forties, who didn't bother hiding her appreciation of Jean-Luc, from me *or* her husband.

Mamma let out a cry of joy from behind the counter and called Carlo back to the kitchen. He was left in charge while she came around the front of the glass case, both arms outstretched and exclaiming loudly in Italian. You would have thought Jean-Luc had been lost at sea for years. A quick glance at Carlo and it was clear he was just as much in his element in the kitchen as his mamma.

The woman, who must have been in her late fifties or early sixties, was tiny—way tinier than me—*Gabriella* tiny, only she wore her salt-and-pepper hair very short. She was unlike the glamorous Roman women I'd been crushing on that afternoon, but with her face alight at seeing Jean-Luc, she was beautiful.

She pulled him down to her for her two cheek kisses and as big a hug as a tiny woman could manage. As soon as the hug was over, she hit him with a barrage of words, which, if the finger pointing was anything to go by, was her giving him a good telling off.

He took it well, nodding and saying, "*Mi dispiace,*" over and over again, which I knew was him apologising. Maybe he hadn't been in the last time he was in Rome and she'd found out. She probably had connections. Maybe she was telling him he was too thin—he wasn't, he was perfect—but didn't Italian mothers always want to feed everyone up?

When there was a break in her rant, he turned her around

to face me. I stood; it seemed like the right thing to do. "*Buonasera*." I pointed to myself, "Caterina," I said, adopting the Italian way.

"*Mi chiamo Anna*," she said, pointing to herself and smiling. I smiled back, and she pulled me in for cheek kisses. I guessed she approved of me. She looked a couple of times between Jean-Luc and me, then nodded decisively and winked at Jean-Luc. Yes, I'd definitely passed the test.

She waved her hands over her head in a universal "I have so much to do" gesture and returned to the kitchen, shooing Carlo out of the way, the whole time talking to herself. I was in love.

We sat back down. "Well, no wonder you love coming here. You're very popular." He smiled one of his eye-crinkling smiles. "By the way, I *love* Anna. I think I may want her to adopt me," I added.

"Wait until you taste her food," he replied.

"Is there a menu?" I said, looking around. I couldn't see one.

"Not really. In a moment, Carlo will come and ask how hungry we are, and if we want fish or meat for secondi. Then she will cook for us." He shrugged as if to say, "Simple."

Carlo's ears must have been burning. He arrived holding a tray and on the table he placed a basket of bread, a small carrier which held olive oil and vinegar, a carafe of wine—white—and two glasses. "*Acqua frizzante o naturale?*" he asked Jean-Luc. Even I knew what *that* meant, so I answered, "*Naturale*," with the best Italian accent I could muster. I was rewarded with a wink. Then, as Jean-Luc had predicted, he asked how hungry we were—*very*—and what we wanted for our second course. We both opted for the beef and Carlo disappeared to give Anna our order.

Without tasting a bite, it was already my favourite meal in months.

Carlo returned shortly with our water. I picked up a piece of bread, pulled off a chunk, and dunked it in the olive oil. I popped the bite into my mouth and groaned.

"I told you, even the bread is good here. She makes it fresh every morning. But it's a trap, because everything else is even better and you will not want to fill up on the bread."

I nodded as I stuffed another bite into my mouth. I swallowed. "Noted. Please put *that*," I said, pointing to the scrumptious bread, "as far from me as possible."

"No self-control?" he teased. I wiped around my mouth with my fingertips. Was that a loaded question?

"When it comes to bread, no. Other things, I am better at controlling myself." He poured the wine.

"What 'other things' do you mean?" He threw me a look, held up his wine in a half-toast, then took a sip. Oh, yes, he was definitely flirting. Game on, Monsieur Caron.

"Well, when it comes to resisting the charms of ridiculously handsome men who speak several languages and travel the world for work, which is incredibly interesting and important, men who are close with their families and have adorable nieces, I can control myself."

He nodded and stroked his chin, mock seriousness playing across his face. "I see. But bread?"

"Oh no. Bread is my kryptonite. I can't even have it in the house." It was a lie, but he didn't know that.

"Mmm, I understand. And it is quite specific, this type of man you are so practised in resisting."

"Well, they're everywhere. It's simply a matter of survival."

"Ah, yes, I have heard of this epidemic of such men."

"I have many, *many* friends who have fallen prey to this type of man."

"Oh, that's terrible."

"It is. They've started a support group." I wasn't sure if it translated, but I was on a roll.

"Mmm, and what are the symptoms of this affliction?"

I had no intention of holding back.

"Typically, sparkling conversation, lots of flirting, smiling, laughing, some handholding, which unavoidably leads to kissing, and then the inevitable ..." I let the thought trail off as I took a sip—all right, it was a slug—of wine.

"And the inevitable? That would be?" His tongue flicked out and licked his bottom lip—the same bottom lip with its name etched on a coin at the bottom of the Trevi Fountain. It almost distracted me, but I'd had enough wine by then to forge ahead.

"Oh," I said, looking him square in the eye. "Making love, of course."

I thought I saw him gulp. His eyes widened—just for a second, but I'd definitely scored with the "making love" part. I'd also managed to surreptitiously drop in there that handholding, something we'd already done a lot of, led to kissing. And I really wanted to kiss him—badly. And other things, naked things, but I'd be happy to start with the kissing.

Food arrived, and Jean-Luc seemed to appreciate the reprieve from my flirtatious onslaught.

"*Pasta primavera*," announced Carlo as he placed two plates on the table. It smelled incredible and looked like a garden was having a party on the plate. "Mamma, she cheats a little—not spring vegetables, but a different way." He seemed to struggle for the word, and realising we were well into autumn, I gave him the word. "*Sì*, yes, autumn. Is like in Italian. *Pasta autunno*. Enjoy!"

Having restrained myself with the bread, I had moved from hungry to bloody starving. Still, I knew there was at least one other course to come, and there was more food on the plate in front of me than I usually had for dinner, so I needed to pace myself. I swirled some pasta onto my fork and took a bite. Jean-Luc did the same. "Oh, my God," I said, my hand covering my mouth. "That's amazing."

Carlo swung by the table with a fresh carafe of white wine. Had we already finished the first one? I watched as he moved with grace among the tables. It was a practised ease as he chatted with customers, brought food to the tables, took plates away, and made everyone feel at home. I never wanted to leave.

I took another bite and glanced at the clock above the kitchen. We still had two hours before I had to meet the coach. Even so, the Rome campsite was even further from the city than the Paris one was, and I didn't want to have to pay for a cab. It would cost a mint.

It took almost as much willpower to leave some pasta on the plate as it did to stop my hand from reaching across the table and pulling the breadbasket towards me. When Carlo cleared my plate, he was concerned I hadn't liked it. I hoped I did a good enough job of conveying A) It was delicious and B) I'm a tiny person, and even when I'm hungry, I can't eat as much as, say, someone Jean-Luc's size. "I will hide this from Mamma," he said, throwing another wink my way.

I was grateful. I wanted Anna to adore me. I like being adored. Especially by tall, handsome Frenchmen. Hmm—I'd probably had enough wine.

Secondi came to the table. "*Braciole*," said Carlo with a verbal flourish.

Jean-Luc groaned, and I looked across at him, amused. "It's my favourite," he replied without me having to ask.

"*Si, si*," said Carlo, laughing. "You are Mamma's favourite—right after me." He made himself laugh again and left us to our *braciole*, thin slices of beef stuffed and rolled and baked into a red sauce. I already knew I was going to love it. It smelled like a corner of heaven.

I barely needed a knife, the meat was so tender. Jean-Luc seemed absorbed in his eating, so I left him to it. I had loved the pasta, but this dish was beyond. It may have been the best thing I'd ever eaten—it was certainly the best thing I could *remember* eating. We cleaned our plates with only a few utterances between us.

I sat back and took in the empty plate in front of me. It was a good thing there wasn't going to be any "wanna come back to my place?" that night. I was stuffed. If sex *had* been on the table, I would have eaten two strands of tagliatelle and called it good. I would even have risked upsetting Mamma Anna, my new favourite person.

There's *nothing* worse than having sex when you have a food baby—except maybe having food-baby sex with your flatmate who's been secretly in love with you forever. That's probably worse.

"Please tell me she's not going to insist we have dessert."

His look said, "What do *you* think?" I thought I was going to burst open like that man in *The Meaning of Life*. I pictured Anna trying to shovel a *cannoli* into my mouth while telling me, "It's only wafer thin," in Italian.

"Could I get away with just an Amaretto instead?" I asked.

"Let's try." This time, it was Jean-Luc who winked at me.

Anna pardoned us from dessert, and I could have kissed her. I probably wouldn't need to eat again until dinner the next night. Carlo brought two glasses of Amaretto to the table and before leaving, leant down to say in my ear, "Mamma still likes you." He left before I could react.

I smiled to myself. It really had been an incredible meal—an incredible night, actually—if I forgot about nearly bursting into tears at the wine bar.

"*Dis-moi, tu es heureuse?*" I didn't quite catch what he was asking me. "Happy?" he added, helpfully.

I watched those intense green eyes watching me. "Yes. Very. It's been a lovely date." He smiled, licked that bottom lip again, and my lady parts lit up like a frigging pinball machine.

An important question leapt to mind: How was I going to ever see him naked if I didn't know when I would see him again?

"So ..." we both started at the same time.

"You, please," he said, deferring.

"I ... how do I say this?" The wine, the Amaretto—my mind wasn't clear. I couldn't just come out and say, "Hey, I really want to shag you senseless—you coming to mine, or should I pop 'round to yours?" Especially because "mine" and "yours" were in two different countries.

I chickened out. "Can you go first, instead?"

"But, of course. I was going to say, it has been wonderful seeing you, hearing about your life, meeting Catherine the woman."

I smiled and nodded. "Yes. Likewise, meeting Jean-Luc the *man*." A little smile played on his lips. He obviously had more to say, so I shut up.

"Our last time together, in Paris, I said something about the Eurostar. London is not so far, you know." I did know and felt my head nod without me telling it to. "I just think I would like to spend more time with you ... to see ..."

To see? To see what? My naked body? Because if that's what he meant, I was definitely on board. I mentally booked into some Pilates classes and I didn't even do Pilates.

He continued. "Because, twenty years, it is a long time. Well, less, really, because of the letters, but still ..." Still? I really wasn't following his train of thought. I willed my alcohol-fuzzed brain to focus. "I mean, yes, we are adults now, but I believe there are some things, our true selves, which stay the same our whole lives. *Oui?*"

Sure, I guess.

As if he knew he needed to spell it out for me, he finally got to his point. "And, I admit I'm a little embarrassed for my teenaged self. It must have been so obvious, even if he never had the courage to say so, that he was in love with you."

Oh, I see.

Wait, what???

Chapter 12

His words hung in the air and I told myself to close my mouth.

Jean-Luc looked at his lap, closed his eyes and shook his head, seeming to chastise himself. I didn't want him to feel bad about what he'd said, but I'd been caught off-guard.

I reached for one of his hands across the table right as he said, "I am sorry." And there he was, the boy I knew so many years ago. He was there in the hang of Jean-Luc's head and the whisper of his voice. My heart broke a little. I had missed him so much. I had to make this right.

"No, *I'm* sorry. I ... I had no idea. I was only a *kid*—and *so* stupid. Please, look at me." He did, reluctantly. "There's so much ..." My own thoughts were a jumble and the alcohol wasn't helping. I shook my head hoping to clear the fuzziness from my thoughts, then looked him in the eye.

"First, I need to make you understand, I deeply regret ending our friendship." He started to speak and I cut him off. "No, I know you said in Paris that it was all right, but it wasn't. It isn't. I was immature and stupid and you didn't deserve that. If I could go back and tell my ex to bugger right

247

off I would. He had no right to insist I stop writing to you and I shouldn't have. I was a coward, and I'm sorry."

He nodded, and I hoped he truly understood my regret—that he would accept my apology for what it was—heartfelt and honest.

"And, I didn't know how you felt back then." I couldn't say the words, "that you were in love with me." They were too real, and if I accepted those words, I would have far more to mourn than the loss of a friend. At some point I would have to unpack the "sliding doors" possibilities of what could have been, but not right then.

"How could you not?" He didn't seem cross or defensive, just perplexed.

I smiled, laughing at myself. "Did you hear the part about me being stupid?" He smiled, sort of, pulling his mouth into a taut line—a sad, fraught smile. I kept holding his hand and I tightened my grip. "I'm sorry, all right? Please tell me you forgive me—for everything, for all of it?"

His face softened and he nodded, squeezing my hand in return. "Of course, I forgive you."

A sheen of tears slicked my eyes. "Thank you," I said quietly. "And I do think we should make plans to see each other again. I've loved tonight, and I loved spending time with you in Paris."

This time his smile had joy in it. "We will rediscover our friendship, *non?*"

"Yes. You know the thing you said about us being inherently the same people our whole lives—I think that's true. I think it's why it's been so easy between us tonight."

"And because I am super hot, as you say." He had a knack for breaking the tension when it all got too intense and I rolled my eyes, playfully.

"I know I told you that false modesty is unattractive, but so is conceit," I teased.

"I will keep this in mind," he replied with a twitch of his mouth. God, I wanted to kiss that mouth. But with what he'd revealed and everything we'd just said, I knew it would muddy things. *Bollocks to hell and back again.*

Jean-Luc glanced at his watch. I knew we needed to leave the restaurant soon and the thought of saying goodbye made me feel a little sick. I still didn't know when we would see each other again. All we'd agreed was that we lived close enough for it to happen.

"We should—" he said.

"Yes, we should." I lifted my head and caught Carlo's eye, then signalled for the bill with the universal "drawing on my hand" gesture. He nodded and held up a finger.

"I am buying dinner," said Jean-Luc.

"I'm going to have to say no to that. You bought the drinks—you *insisted* on buying the drinks—and besides, this has been one of the best meals I've ever had. You already did your part—you brought me here." I aborted another attempted protest with, "Please." He acquiesced with a slight tilt of his head.

I made short work of paying the bill—a ridiculously small amount for the incredible meal we'd had—and we soon stood outside, the cooling night air giving me goosebumps. I slipped on my jacket, but still felt the chill.

He must have noticed. "Here." He put his arm around me and pulled me close. The warmth of his body was welcome but also massively distracting. My lady parts had no way of knowing this was chivalry and not seduction.

I tried to send a signal to them, but they ignored me. "So, we meet the bus near Castel Sant'Angelo, *non*?" he asked. He was so good at remembering details—probably why he was so successful as a journalist.

"*Oui*," I replied.

"This way." We walked slowly, our heights making the whole "arm wrapped around me" thing a little awkward, but I didn't want him to let me go.

When we arrived at the pick-up point, there were a few people from the tour group already there, but none that I knew very well, so I just smiled my hellos. We were ten minutes early, and part of me wanted Jean-Luc to leave right away, so we could say goodbye without a huge audience. Another part wanted him to stay as long as possible.

I looked across the nearest bridge spanning the Tiber and saw Georgina leading a large group of people towards us. *Bollocks*. They'd be at the pick-up point in moments.

"Hey, you guys!" called a cheery voice behind us. Lou. We turned around to greet her, Dani, Jaelee, Craig and Jason. Lou made introductions between the men, who all shooks hands, then gave Jean-Luc a hug he clearly didn't expect. He returned it good-naturedly.

"How was your night?" she asked looking back and forth between us.

"Lovely. We, uh, explored a little. There are definitely some places we need to go back to tomorrow. Oh, and we had the most amazing dinner." I had a thought and turned to Jean-Luc. "Do you think Anna would mind if I took the girls there for dinner tomorrow night?"

I heard, "Hey!" from Craig. Oops, I'd forgotten Craig.

"And Craig."

"And me."

"And Jason."

Jean-Luc laughed. "I think she would be very happy to see you again and to cook for everyone."

"She will miss you, though."

"Yes, but I think you are, how do you say, a good substitute."

"High praise." I smiled up at him, forgetting we had an audience of five. When I realised, I was met with a collection of amused faces. I bit my bottom lip. "Uh," I said to Jean-Luc, "come with me." I grabbed him by the hand and pulled him away from the group. I was fairly certain I heard a disappointed, "Aww," from Dani.

When we were far enough away from my friends, I stopped and faced him. "Hi."

"Hi."

I was hit with a rush of sadness and regret.

How had I ever cut ties with this person, the boy who had become this wonderful, funny, beautiful man? I was such an idiot. And now I had to say goodbye to him not knowing when I would see him again—*if* I would see him again. Would we end up like those acquaintances you run into at the shops? *Oh, we must catch up soon. Oh, I'd love that. Give me a call.*

Regret was fast turning into panic. "I really do want to make sure we see each other again."

"Good," he replied. "So do I."

"Are you ... do you ... are you coming to London any time soon, for work?"

"Nothing planned at the moment, but I can let you know."

"Right." I bit the lip again. "So ..."

"This is terrible, yes?"

"It's the worst."

Jean-Luc threw a look over his shoulder at my friends. When I looked, I saw that Georgina and the large group had arrived, but Tom and the coach hadn't—another moment or two to drag out this excruciating goodbye.

"This may surprise you," he said, turning back to me. "But I was hoping to kiss you."

It did surprise me, but it was also thrilling. I'd wanted to kiss him—badly—since the moment we saw him on the street in Paris, before I even knew who he was. And standing there in Rome, after the night we'd had together, I didn't care that it was probably a terrible idea.

"You should." I peered up at him. "You should definitely kiss me."

His eyes lit up and a soft smile alighted on his face. His hands—his large, strong, warm hands—found my waist and snaked around to the small of my back, pulling me closer to him. I stretched onto my tiptoes and lifted my face to meet his.

He tilted his head and his hair fell across one eye as our lips met. His were firm and warm as they moved against mine, tentatively at first, then with an ardour I knew I would remember all my days. I felt a flick of his tongue against mine, and his arms tightened as he held me close against him. My feet lifted off the ground for an instant—just long enough for me to feel like a beloved little being.

The sophomoric chorus of "Ooh"s receded into the background, and when my feet were back on the ground and we slowly pulled apart, I was a little breathless. I looked up into those incredible green eyes.

So was he—breathless.

"I have waited twenty years to do that."

I stared at him wide-eyed.

"It was worth it, the wait," he concluded. I broke into a huge grin and he did the same. "I will call you. We will make plans." All doubts that we'd see each other again dissipated into the cool Roman air.

"Sounds good."

I heard the coach pull up and people started to file on, the bright lights from inside spilling onto the footpath.

Jean-Luc grasped both my hands and I turned back towards him. He leant down and kissed one cheek, then the other, then softly pressed his lips to my forehead. "Goodbye, *ma chérie*."

Oh! So *that's* what forehead kisses meant!

"Bye!" I stood on tiptoes again and planted a big smack on his lips, then skipped off to the coach. I was the last to board and as I passed a scowling Georgina I said, "*Buona notte*, Georgina." I saw confusion register on her face as I stepped onto the coach.

But I didn't give a flying fig about Georg-bloody-ina. I'd got my first wish.

Early the next morning, the whole tour group was up, dressed, breakfasted, and on the coach by 6:00am—because when you're going to the Vatican in a large group, you need to be in line by 6:45am to meet your guide and get your tickets.

When Tom pulled the coach to a stop, close to the Vatican's entrance, we hustled out and lined up on the footpath like schoolchildren. Georgina seemed pleased with how well we executed this manoeuvre, but really, she'd explained it in such excruciating detail on the ride into the city, we were hardly going to mess it up.

Gabriella, our guide from the day before, approached us, seemingly unhurried but bustling with efficiency. "*Buongiorno!*" she said cheerily. It was a vast contrast to how she'd greeted us the day before. Perhaps she was a morning person. Only half of us replied; the others were probably still half-asleep.

I was usually a morning person, but the late nights of the tour were taking their toll. I hadn't once woken up without the help of an alarm, something I rarely used in the real world. I stifled a yawn so I didn't insult her.

I saw Gabriella hand a thick packet to Georgina, who handed back an envelope stuffed with the euros we'd given her on the ride into the city. Georgina walked the line and handed us our tickets.

"Everyone, this is a very busy time here at the Vatican and you are a large group," said Gabriella. "I will need you to be close to me and to each other. Unfortunately, there is not a lot of time to explore yourselfs."

I noticed the incorrect word, but really, English is so stupid sometimes. "Yourselfs" *should* be grammatically correct. "Now, the Sistine Chapel. It is small and crowded, so please stay as a group, *sì*?" I nodded, even though she probably couldn't see me. Being a teacher meant that certain behaviours were indoctrinated. When someone gave you a set of instructions, you affirmed you had heard and understood them—at least that's what I tried to drum into my pupils.

We entered the Vatican at 7:45am and by 10:00am, we were wandering around Saint Peter's Cathedral with a free pass to do as we liked for the rest of the day. Lou and I had decided on a day of sightseeing, which Jaelee allowed on the proviso that we'd meet her and Dani mid-afternoon for shopping, then prosecco.

I wasn't sure if I was up for the shopping part, but we were halfway through the tour and I thought it would be nice to spend some time together, just the four of us. I'd given Jason and Craig the restaurant's address, so they could meet us there at seven.

It was going to be a huge day.

I loved the Sistine Chapel, by the way. We only got to spend about ten minutes there, and it was a lot smaller than I'd imagined, but that *ceiling*. Unlike the *Mona Lisa*, it was not over-hyped; it was breathtaking.

And the whole time we were there, as I drank in as much detail as I could, I couldn't get it out of my head that it had been painted without the ability to step back and make sure the perspective was right. He'd painted it on his back. He'd just *known* how to make it seem like the figures were three-dimensional, reaching for us mere mortals on the floor. Incredible.

Vatican ✓
Sistine Chapel ✓
Saint Peter's ✓

"I have wanted to do this *forever*!" Lou was so excited about the Trevi Fountain, it was infectious. She had her three coins at the ready—all one-euro coins—she refused to scrimp. She turned away from the fountain and, like I'd done the day before, closed her eyes and tossed them one at a time into the fountain. Three coins, three wishes.

She opened her eyes and grinned at me, her shoulders rising in excitement. "We need a selfie. Come stand here." She pulled me into position and swivelled her phone's camera to take the shot. "Awesome," she said, then pocketed her phone.

I had a sudden realisation. "Oh no, Lou. I didn't get a photo with Jean-Luc last night! Oh, how stupid." I tapped on my forehead with my palm.

"Is now a good time to tell you I have *two* photos of you together?"

"You what?" I was getting jostled by the swelling crowd of people. Lunchtime at the Trevi Fountain was obviously a popular time.

"Let's get out of here and I'll show you."

I trailed Lou through the hordes into a side street where

it was more subdued. She leant on a wall and scrolled on her phone. "Here."

She handed it to me and there was a grainy photo of Jean-Luc and me from the night before, kissing. "Huh. Well, that's not pervy at all." I gave her a "please explain yourself" look.

"Okay, it's weird, I know. But that's your first kiss. And when I send it to you, you'll have a photo of your *first kiss!*"

It may have been misguided, but she was right. "Well, that's true. Uh, thank you, I guess. And there's another one?"

"Yes." She took her phone and scrolled some more, then turned back it towards me. "This one." It was Jean-Luc and me in the Irish pub. We were seated at the table alone, so it was after I'd had my swooning episode, and we were smiling at each other. It was lovely.

"Oh, Lou." I blinked back tears that came from nowhere. "Oh, thank you. I—wow. Thank you."

She took her phone back, tapped on it a few times, and my phone beeped. "I've sent it to you. I would have given it to you before, but I didn't want you to think I'd been all stalkerish and I thought you'd probably get some photos last night. It was just back-up."

I hugged her, tight and quick. "You are the best. Right, now. I want to show you the Pantheon—you're going to love it—*and* this incredible fountain—a different one. Then we can look at what else is on our list, all right?" I got my bearings. "The Pantheon's this way," I said, taking the lead.

Lou loved the Pantheon and I loved seeing it again. We stayed longer than Jean-Luc and I had, reverently talking in low voices as we stood in front of every statue and pointed out details to each other. She also loved Piazza Navona and we decided to stop there for lunch before we made our way to the Spanish Steps.

With so many choices for lunch, we chose the closest restaurant and sat side by side, looking out over the busy piazza. We knew we'd overpay for lunch, simply because of the location, but we didn't care. It was noon on a bright sunny day in one of the world's most beautiful cities. We could spring for a pricey plate of pasta.

A waiter approached and brought us two menus in English. Was it that obvious? I've sometimes been told I look Italian—also Greek, even Lebanese—but, clearly, to the practised eye of Giancarlo, not so much.

"Only a couple of days left in Italy. I'm having pasta," said Lou.

"Mmm. I know what's in store for dinner. I'm going with the Caprese salad."

"Oh, should I have something light? Breakfast was, like, ages ago. I'm kinda starving."

"True." Breakfast had been at 5:30am *and* it was only sweet rolls. My stomach gurgled and I looked at the time. We wouldn't be eating dinner for nearly seven hours. *To hell with it.* I was having pasta too. When Giancarlo came back, I ordered the Napolitana and Lou ordered the Carbonara. I added still water and a carafe of white wine to the order—in Italian. Bad Italian, but Giancarlo didn't laugh at me or even wince, so I did all right.

"I want to know everything," said Lou. We'd been on the

258

go for hours and this was our first chance to properly talk. I waited as our waiter put bread and oil on the table, then poured our water and wine before he disappeared. Italian waiters were so efficient.

"I'm not sure where to start."

"Start with what you wished for," she said, a cheeky grin on her face. "Was it to marry Jean-Luc and have his beautiful babies?"

"What's with everyone asking about the damned wishes? And no, I didn't wish for that. What did *you* wish for?" I retorted.

"Nope. You first. I didn't spend last night with a hot French guy."

It wasn't like telling Lou my wishes would make them *not* come true. But still, there were more interesting things to tell. I started with us meeting up and pointed to where Jean-Luc had been standing when I'd first seen him. She nodded as though she could visualise it. I also told her about how I'd nearly cried at the wine bar—and why—then about the meal at Anna's, and finally Jean-Luc's confession.

"I can't believe we get to go there tonight. It sounds amazing."

Somehow, she'd managed to ignore the massive reveal about Jean-Luc being in love with me twenty years ago. I tried to temper my annoyance. "It is. I'm sure you'll love it, but what about what he said? About *love?*"

"Mmm. Yeah, that's huge."

I stared at her. "Yes, I know, Lou."

"I'm not being very helpful."

"No."

Our pasta arrived. Giancarlo held up a wedge of parmesan with a questioning look on his face. I nodded and so did Lou. He grated a smattering over my plate and I wished I knew the Italian for, "just leave the wedge." There was never enough parmesan. Like all other cheese, I love the stuff.

"So, you really had no idea? About the love part?" Lou loaded up a fork with Carbonara.

"Nope. I keep replaying memories in my head, but in each one we're just besties, like you and me. You're not secretly in love with me, are you?"

She swallowed and shook her head. After a sip of wine, she said, "Hey, that's good." I tried a sip. She was right. "Nope, not in love with you. But be assured, if I was going to fall in love with a woman, I'd consider you a catch."

"Aww, Lou, thanks."

"You are! Anyway, memories ..." she prompted.

"Oh yes. Well, he left Australia when we were fifteen and I can't wrap my brain around how a boy that age knows he's in love. I didn't know *anything* back then—*anything*. Sometimes I still feel like I don't."

"And has your mum sent the letter yet?"

"*No.* I guess scanning a letter is more challenging than Mum's usual foray into technology. She can't even figure out how to watch Netflix without my dad's help. I should have called him instead."

Lou laughed. "My dad's the same. He's always calling to ask me why his TV screen's gone blank. But my eighty-year-old *grandmother*, she's on Twitter."

"Hah! You'll have to show me so I can follow her. What does she tweet about?"

"Mostly she tweets photos of her daily martini and selfies from when she goes to the Y."

"The gym?"

"Yep?"

"Your eighty-year-old grandma goes to the gym?"

"Three times a week."

"Oh, my God. I want to be like that when I'm eighty. Oh, speaking of fabulous older women, I forgot to tell you, Jean-Luc and I saw Isabella Rossellini yesterday. On the street. She even smiled at me." I couldn't believe it, but Lou clearly had no idea who Isabella Rossellini was. "You don't know who she is, do you?"

She grimaced apologetically. "Should I?"

"Um, yes. You should. She's uber famous, and she's in her sixties and she's still breathtakingly beautiful." Nothing I was saying was ringing a bell for Lou. "At least tell me you don't know the names of all the Kardashians."

"Oh goodness, no. They're heinous."

"We can still be friends then. Oh, and she was one of my wishes. Well, not her, but I wished that when I'm in my sixties, I'll look as good as she does."

"Oh, good wish! And you probably will. You've got great skin."

"Thank you, and maybe if I adopt your grandma's life-style—daily cocktails and trips to the Y—it will come true. I think she may be my guru."

"Isabelle Rossa-whatsit?"

"It's not—never mind. I meant your grandma."

"Oh, yeah. Nana's great."

"When I said that to Jean-Luc, about looking good in my sixties, he said he was sure I would."

"I just said that."

"Yes, but you're not some super-hot French guy who used to be in love with me."

"True."

I twirled some spaghetti onto my fork. My appetite had abandoned me, but if we were going to traverse Rome for the next few hours, I needed to eat something.

"Have you at least made plans to see each other again?" she asked.

"No. And it makes me feel a little bit sick." So *that's* why I wasn't hungry anymore. I put the fork down.

"I totally get it. *I'd* want to have something on the calendar if I were you, something to look forward to."

"Especially now, since he's kissed me. That was another wish, by the way."

She had a mouthful of pasta, but I could tell her close-lipped smile was a grin in disguise. "So, what was your third wish?" she said after she swallowed.

I'd told her numbers one and two—I figured I might as well tell her everything. "I wished for Jean-Luc to forgive me for breaking off our friendship."

"Ohhh, that's sweet," said Lou. She dragged out "sweet" and I hoped it wasn't pity I saw on her face.

"Actually, I apologised again last night." I twirled the stem of my wine glass between my fingers and nearly spilled it.

262

I took a sip as Lou replied, "Oh, good! And?"

"He said I was forgiven." As I mulled over the thought, I realised I felt a lightness, as though a long-held burden, something I'd been used to lugging around, had gone.

"So, *two* wishes have come true," said Lou.

"Oh, my God, you're right. How did I not realise? I'm such an idiot."

"Or love-struck."

"I'm not 'love-struck', Lou. I may be a little *lust*-struck, however. Scratch that, I am definitely lust-struck."

"Well, yeah. Hello? He looks like he stepped off the cover of a romance novel."

"What, like Fabio or something?" I laughed.

"Nooo. Not one of those. Like chick lit, you know. I bet he's got a great body."

"I bet he does too. I've felt some of it. It's ... he's ..." I struggled to find words and Lou laughed at me.

"Yeah, *it's* definitely and *he's* definitely."

"But it's not love, Lou."

"Sure." She looked dubious.

"It's lust," I said, my left hand marking one end of a spectrum, "*and* it's a rekindled friendship." My right hand marked the opposite end of the spectrum. "Those two things are totally different. I'm hoping to get a little more action down this end of the spectrum without making a huge mess of this end." I couldn't ignore Lou's scrutinising look. "What?"

"You know what true friendship plus lust equals?"

"What? What do you mean?"

"Like if you were to put those two things together in a

relationship equation, what do you think those two things—the ones you put on opposite ends of the spectrum—would add up to?"

"I don't follow."

"I'm going to take your word for it that you're not being deliberately obtuse." Counsellor Lou had arrived at lunch. "Cat, friendship plus lust is *love*." She wafted her hand over the table. "This part, this part in the middle that you seem so afraid of, that's where love is."

"But I don't want to be in love."

"Sometimes, love doesn't give a crap whether you want it or not." Lou punctuated her love speech with a giant bite of pasta, which I watched her chew while a frown settled onto my face.

I had two thoughts stewing. One: I really didn't want to fall in love—with Jean-Luc or anyone. And, two: Lou had said "crap", which in her world was a swear word. She must have really meant the whole "love doesn't care" thing.

To quote my friend Lou, *crap!*

Chapter 13

The rest of our time in Rome was wonderful—harried and action-packed, but I loved it. I definitely wanted to return and I wondered if there was some brass somewhere that I was supposed to be rubbing. Then I realised how superstitious that was, and I am not the superstitious type.

I made a vow to stop wishing on coins and throwing them into fountains and to stop rubbing brass all over Europe. If I saw a black cat, I would pet it and I'd happily walk under any ladders propped up against buildings.

Although I really did want that Isabella Rossellini wish to come true. I still couldn't believe I'd seen her in person.

Lou and I had a funny moment as we were walking to the Spanish Steps—they were just steps, by the way. *Nice* steps, sure—people seemed very happy to sit on them and while away the time—but really, they were *steps*. I digress. As we passed a department store, there she was, Isabella Rossellini, her face twelve feet tall. I stopped and pointed. "That, Lou, is *her*."

She looked at the exquisite photograph. "Sorry, it's who?"

"My second wish."

265

"Ohhh. Yeah, I think I've seen her before." I rolled my eyes. How could she not have?

Spanish Steps ✓

From the Spanish Steps, we walked north to Piazza del Popolo and climbed the hill to the massive park which overlooks the city. "I'm beat," said Lou as she took refuge on a park bench.

I joined her. "Yes. Lots of walking the past couple of days."

"Well, at least it burns off the pasta."

We hung out there for a little while, resisting the urge to buy gelato from a nearby cart. How good can cart gelato be, anyway, even in Rome?

"Where are we meeting Jaelee and Dani again?"

"Not far. Via del Corso. It's down there somewhere." I pointed in its general direction.

"I don't know if I can handle shopping today. It's just walking that costs money."

"Hah! Hilarious. I could text them and tell them to meet us at a wine bar or something. Jaelee did say shopping then prosecco."

"Text them. Say, 'prosecco, no shopping.' Then we can find somewhere to go."

"Jean-Luc took me to this great wine bar yesterday, but it's a bit of a walk from here."

"Don't say the 'W' word."

"Sorry."

"Honestly, I'll go anywhere—close. There must be some place down there." She pointed to the Piazza del Popolo below us.

"I'll look."

And that's how we ended up tipsy at four in the afternoon. Dani and Jaelee met us laden with bags—seriously, how were they cramming this stuff into their luggage?—and caught up to us soon afterwards. "Another bottle, *por favor*," Jaelee called out, speaking Spanish to the Italians. The calling out part was unnecessary. It was a very small place.

By the time we got to Anna's restaurant to meet the guys, we were completely sloshed. Thank goodness for the pin I'd dropped on Google Maps the night before, or it would have been a minor miracle if I'd found it.

Carlo and Anna greeted me like a long-lost friend and though I wasn't usually the sort of person who liked to clock up social karma, I was well chuffed.

Carlo squeezed together two tables and the six of us clambered around. Knees pressed against knees, but I knew they'd think the meal was worth it. As the veteran, I told them how it all worked.

Surprisingly, my meal was completely different from the previous night, though, not surprisingly, every bite of it was delicious.

As we were leaving, Anna herself came around the counter to kiss me goodbye. I made a mental note to invite her and Carlo to the wedding, which made it official. I was off my trolley and just plain drunk.

Craig took charge and got us to the pick-up point ahead of schedule. Lou was cognisant enough to clap her hand over my mouth as I started spouting not very nice things about Georgina when the coach pulled up.

I was put to bed and shaken awake with enough time to down some headache tablets, grab a very quick shower in the hideous concrete ablution block, and get on the coach with all my belongings by 8:00am.

"Have I mentioned how much I love you, Lou?" I said as we took our seats.

Her tight lips told me that the feeling wasn't mutual at that particular moment. This was confirmed by what she said next. "I've had a lot of experience putting a drunk person to bed." Oh dear. I was really going to have to make it up to her.

The drive to Venice was *five hours*. Sorry. You can't drive to Venice. The drive to *Fusina*, where we were staying, was five hours. Then we'd catch a water taxi to Venice.

After enduring the day song, which Georgina played every morning right before she got on the microphone to tell us the day's itinerary, I fell into a deep sleep, my face pressed against the window. I should say that it wasn't a bad song, but after the tour, it was going to be a long time before I could listen to Pharrell Williams's "Happy" without cringing.

I slept until the mid-morning rest stop.

"Lou, seriously, I do love you."

"Uh huh."

"Can I buy you a tea? How about a pastry? What can I get you? Morning tea is on me."

I could tell she was trying to stay miffed, but Lou was one of those people who got cross and almost instantly forgave, so she was doing a poor job of it. And, I can do pretty amazing

268

puppy-dog eyes, especially when I want my bus bestie to forgive me for being drunk.

She pointed to a pastry in the glass cabinet and muttered, "*And* tea." I ordered. Sipping my tea as we settled back on the coach, I started to feel more like myself.

"I had fun in Rome," I said, feeling the waters.

"Mmm."

"Did you?" I was half-turned in my seat watching her and she honoured me with a sideways glance and half a smile that told me she was giving in to my charm.

"*Yes*. I had a good time in Rome."

"I'm really sorry I got so drunk."

"It's okay."

"I forget sometimes that I'm only five-foot-one-and-three-quarters. In my head, I'm six-foot-two, so I tend to drink like a man—a big one." She snort-laughed and I think a little tea came out of her nose. I handed her the napkin from my pastry. "I really am sorry. And thank you for looking after me."

"No problem. By the way, I really needed this." She held up the tea. "I have a huge hangover."

"Oh, my God, Lou!" I started digging around in my bag. "You should have said! Here." I found my stash of ibuprofen and paracetamol and popped two of each into my hand. "Take these." She eyed them dubiously. "I know. It seems like a lot, but they work together, and it's totally safe. Trust me." She must have, because she tipped them into her mouth and took a sip of tea.

She started snoozing not long after—Lou, who couldn't sleep sitting up. She must have been shattered, the poor woman. I gently took her empty takeaway cup from her. Our Mama Lou—so busy looking after everyone else.

The campsite at Fusina, where we would be sleeping in tiny caravans for two, was dreadful. As soon as we stepped off the coach we were swarmed by mosquitoes, our caravan smelled like stale urine, and it was a good five-minute walk to the ablution block.

And we had exactly fifteen minutes before we were due at the dock to take the water taxi into Venice. *Merde, merde, merde*.

I prioritised the following: changing clothes and brushing my teeth—hangover teeth are furry and disgusting and must take precedence when you are about to spend six hours exploring a fifteen-hundred-year-old city.

The first priority was easy. When we got to our caravan, I flung the contents of my case about until I found a dress I hadn't worn yet and changed into it, slipping my jacket on over the top.

To brush my teeth in the ablution block would have taken far too long, so I did a camper's brush, which included swishing from a water bottle and spitting into the bushes next to our steps. Lou made a face to indicate I *might* have slipped out of her good books once again. With these two tasks completed and three minutes left until we were due at the dock, I took a moment to zhuzh my hair with some leave-in conditioner, slather on some SPF30 tinted moisturiser, and swipe on some lip gloss.

We sprinted to the dock and made it onto the water taxi

with thirty seconds to spare. And even though we weren't late, we were the last ones on board and, once again, I'd put us in Georgina's firing line. If glares were bullets, I'd have been dead about a hundred times over.

You know what, Georgina? The schedule is too frigging tight! Fifteen minutes to get our bags, get our caravan assignment, find our caravan, then get ready for an evening out in Venice? Im-bloody-possible. Grrr.

It didn't take long for me to forget all about Georg-bloody-ina, because Venice materialised ahead—and gawking in awe became involuntary. *Ah, Venice.* The first thing to hit me was the smell. We were inside a water taxi, yet the heady brininess of the water and air permeated. It wasn't unpleasant, just distinctive, just *Venice.*

As we docked, which took an incredibly long time, I succumbed to apprehension. With regards to sightseeing, I had no idea where to start and I didn't want to miss anything important. Plus, I was still mildly hungover, and the boat ride had unsettled my stomach.

Lou eyed my bouncing knee. "Everything okay?"

"Yes," I replied. "I'm just excited—and a little daunted. I mean, *look*, Lou. How are we going to see all that?"

Dani leant across the aisle. "You should come hang out with Jaelee and me today. She's been before."

My head spun towards Dani and I got a little dizzy. *Am I still drunk?* "Really, Jae?"

"Oh yeah, I came here after college with my boyfriend, Roger." Jaelee did not strike me as the type of woman who dated guys called Roger, but I let it go.

"I've already pre-booked for us to go up the campanile," said Dani. She must have read the blank look on my face. "That." She pointed to a giant tower and I peered up at it through the window.

"Oh. Wow. I want to go up that. Lou?"

"Oh yeah, for sure."

"You've already got tickets though. Do you think we could get some?" How had I not done any research on Venice? What was I, a *tourist*? Actually, a tourist would have done all the research, and what I quickly realised was that with only six hours, we *needed* to act like bloody tourists.

"Done!" Dani held up her phone triumphantly.

"Done, what's done?"

"I booked you and Louise tickets for the same time as us. Four-thirty."

"Dani! Thank you. We'll fix you up, of course."

"Yeah, no problem. Buy me lunch or something."

I grinned at Lou. "We're going up the camper-thingie."

She shook her head at me. "Uh huh."

We disembarked and, though she was hardly my favourite person, I listened carefully to Georgina as she told us the pick-up location. I peered down at my phone, which was a little blurry—*good grief, how much did I drink yesterday?*—and compared my map pin to Lou's, so if I got lost, I didn't *actually get lost*. "Yep," she confirmed.

The tour group dispersed in pairs and small groups and Lou and I walked over to Jaelee and Dani. "Right," I said, unable to contain my enthusiasm. "What's first?"

"I need to eat," said Jae. "I want a pizza."

272

I blinked twice, once for each thought. First, I was in *Venice*. Did I really want to waste time *eating*? And second, I knew that Jae *actually* ate sometimes—I'd seen her do it—but *pizza*? It seemed a little "off-brand" for Jaelee.

"Well, do you know a good place? Like, from when you were here before?" asked Lou.

Jae threw her a look to convey how stupid she thought the question was. "That was nearly ten years ago, and this is *Venice*. It's impossible to find *anything* again. I mean, the whole *point* of Venice is to get lost."

At that moment, I wanted Jaelee to get lost. How rude. I opened my mouth to say something, but Dani stepped up.

"No need to be a bitch about it, Jaelee."

Jae was *clearly* taken aback. I wondered if it was because she didn't know she'd been bitchy or because she was used to being bitchy without anyone calling her on it. I'd been on the receiving end of it a few times and I'm a big girl and all, but still, Lou was *Lou* and she *definitely* didn't deserve it.

"Oh, sorry." She shook her head, as though shaking the bitch away. "Sorry, Louise. Can I start over?" It was a rhetorical question and we stared at her, waiting. "Venice is ... well, the best thing to do is just to wander and soak it all in. If we find a place we want to stop, we will, but the walkways and bridges and streets—they're the real drawcard."

"Okay, sounds good." Lou, always so quick to forgive.

"So, if it's all about getting lost, how are we going to find our way back here?" Dani looked up at the camper-thingie.

"There are signs. I'll show you when we see one."

"All right, great," I said, hoping to get us moving. Pizza sounded good and I was getting hungry.

"Let's go have a quick look at Saint Mark's first, though," said Jae. "We won't have to line up for long and it's definitely worth seeing. It's, like, a thousand years old. Then I'll take you around to the Bridge of Sighs." *Oh! I've heard of that!* "*Then* pizza. Okay?"

We agreed and let Jaelee lead us from the waterfront, past a giant pink building with lots of arches (I later learnt it was the Doge's Palace) to San Marco's Basilica. When we arrived, I almost didn't want to go in. The outside was so ornate and interesting I could have stayed right there just soaking in all the details. Unexpectedly, I decided to do just that. "Hey, I'm not coming in. I'll wait for you here."

"You sure?" asked Lou.

"Yes, totally. This is ..." I looked up at the wondrous structure. "I'm happy here." How very *traveller* of me. While the others joined a short queue to get inside, I took out my phone and did a quick search on Wikipedia.

I know, it's a little cringe-worthy, but I learnt a lot, like how the cathedral—sorry, *basilica*—was an excellent example of Byzantine *and* European architecture. East meets west, with its onion shaped domes and mosaics from the east, and Gothic archways and stonework, which reminded me a little of Sainte-Chapelle.

It's embarrassing to say this, but I learnt more about Venetian history in those fifteen minutes than I'd bothered to learn in my thirty-five years—*and* I'd taught *The Merchant of Venice* the year before. I was such a fraud. Traveller indeed! I vowed to lift my head more often, especially when I was away from my safe little patch of London.

When they made their way back to me, Lou was bouncing like a little kid, her face flushed. "Oh, my goodness. All of these historical churches. It's just so unbelievable to think I've stood in places where people have worshipped for centuries!"

Jaelee looked at Lou with affection—also a little off-brand for her, but I understood. Lou was a darling.

San Marco's Basilica ✓

"Okay, let's head around this way and see the Bridge of Sighs and get the obligatory photos," said Jaelee the photo queen. "And then we can get off the main drag and get ourselves lost." The Jaelee who'd come out of the basilica was different from the one who'd stepped off the water taxi. I wondered if, like me, Venice was having a calming effect on her.

We jostled for position at the Bridge of Sighs along with dozens of others. In truth, I was less than impressed—maybe because I'd seen the Bridge of Sighs in Oxford *and* the one in Cambridge—*Bridges of Sighs?*—and they were all pretty much the same.

Also, I couldn't help but ruminate on what they each represented, that last glimpse of freedom as prisoners were marched to their deaths. When it was my turn for the photo, my grim thoughts left me confused about whether to smile or not. Was it appropriate to smile? Macabre? I ended up with a sort of grimace on my face—definitely not a photo for Facebook, just proof I'd been there.

I was relieved when we were done and I forced myself to

shelve all thoughts of death. There were other things to dwell on, such as this wonderful city, the warm afternoon sun, and the brilliant blue of the sky.

Bridge of Sighs ✓

We escaped into a side street away from the touristy crowds and walked along a canal, Jaelee slightly in the lead. I lagged behind because I couldn't stop gawking. The further we got from the main square, the more intrigued I became. All of Venice was like, well, like *Venice*. I'd thought there would be the parts that looked like the Venice I saw in films, but that most of it would be more like the suburbs of other towns and cities—generic, soulless and "could be anywhere".

Even the lines of washing strung between the buildings were charming.

We stopped at a little trattoria which, as Jae had promised, I would never have been able to find again, even if I was pressed. I was pretty sure Google had no idea where we were.

The trattoria was dark and when my eyes adjusted to the dimness, I saw fixtures which looked a millennium old and furniture from a previous century. We crowded around a small table and Dani pointed to a chalkboard resting against the small bar. "The pizzas are only six euros. Probably just for one person, don't ya think?"

I *did* think, yes, and I was starving by then, so I wholeheartedly agreed we would each get our own. Also, I don't like to share—well, food anyway. I detest those restaurants where you're expected to get an array of sharing plates then split the bill. I want to order what I want and eat it.

Sarah tells this embarrassing story about me from when we were teenagers. We'd gone to the cinema, and I'd got a bag of my favourite lollies, Jaffas, from the pick'n'mix. Right before the film started, she asked for one and I said, "No. I got exactly the amount of Jaffas I wanted. If you wanted some, you should have said so." I thought that was perfectly reasonable. She thought it was fodder for making fun of me for the next twenty years. I digress—again ...

Jaelee asked us what pizzas we wanted, and shamelessly ordered for us in Spanish. The lovely older man seemed to understand enough and when our pizzas arrived, we all had what we'd asked for. What we hadn't counted on, however, was that the six-euro pizzas were *enormous*. They couldn't even fit on the table. After laughing nervously at their arrival, we commandeered a second table to make enough room for four fifteen-centimetre pizzas.

Even more surprising was that after groaning at the sight of them—*how am I going to eat all that?*—we all ate all of our pizzas. Even Jaelee.

The crust was thin and crispy underneath and chewy around the edges. The tomato sauce zinged with tanginess and a bit of heat from chili and pepper. The basil was fragrant and tasted a little of aniseed, and the mozzarella was so creamy I practically had a food orgasm. It was, without question, the best pizza I'd ever had, and we mostly ate in silence, as though we were sharing some sort of spiritual experience. Perhaps, in a way, we were.

Eventually, we sat back from the tables and regarded each other and the empty platters in front of us. Our shared looks indicated a communal feeling of, "Oh my, what have we done?" and I couldn't help it. I smirked, which soon turned into a giggle, and then there were four of us sitting around two tables giggling like idiots while the lovely older man looked at us sideways—which, of course, made us laugh even more.

I got the bill for lunch—to thank Lou for looking after me the night before and Jaelee for the tour, and to pay back Dani for the camper-thingie ticket. Speaking of which, it was time to find our way back to the camper-thingie.

"It's *campanile*," said Dani. "Geez."

"Campanile," I said.

"Yes."

"What does that even mean?"

"I have no idea."

"It means belltower," said Jae helpfully.

"Ohhh."

At the campanile, we moved quickly through the queue and I was grateful to see an elevator. It was a very tall campanile and I hadn't fancied climbing what would have been a *lot* of stairs, especially as I was weighed down with half a kilo of scrummy pizza.

To say the view from the campanile was "epic" would be an understatement. With blue skies in every direction, we could see all of Venice, all of the surrounding islands, and the mainland. I was even sure I could make out our hideous campsite and those pokey little wee-ridden caravans.

The only thing marring the view was the wire mesh that enclosed all the openings. I could understand why it was there and why it was so robust, but the squares were teeny, and it was tricky getting a photo which wasn't spoiled by grey cross-hairs.

After twenty minutes of oohing and ahhing we collectively agreed it was time to leave.

Campanile ✓

"I want to ride on a gondola," drawled Dani in that half-whine she did sometimes.

I hadn't even thought of a gondola ride, but once she said it, it was the only thing in the world I wanted to do. How quintessentially Venetian! "We have to do that," I said with urgency. Jae looked like she could go either way and Lou's face scrunched up. "What? What's that face?"

"Nothing."

"No. Sorry, but *that*—" I circled my hand in front of her face to make sure it was clear that "that" meant her expression "—is not nothing."

She sighed. "It's just, well, I've always wanted to go on a gondola."

I was frowning at her, confused and a little annoyed. "Right, and ...?" I said in my best kindly-sarcastic-and-ever-so-slightly-passive-aggressive (a.k.a. English) tone of voice.

"And we always said we'd do that for our tenth wedding anniversary. It was supposed to be Paris, Florence, then Venice."

Well, I was a total cow. I'd forgotten.

"Oh Lou! I'm so sorry."

"It's okay." She brushed off her feelings and I tried my best not to be annoyed, because her feelings were *important*. I looked at Jaelee and Dani for support. Nope. Nothing. Jaelee seemed extremely uncomfortable and Dani, perplexed. It was all on me.

"Lou, seriously. If it's too much, we can skip the gondola." She was avoiding eye contact, but I tugged on her hand and she looked at me. "Really. It's fine." It wasn't *really* fine, but sometimes being a good friend takes priority.

A frown scuttered across her face for a second. Then she shook her head, tucked her hair behind her ears, straightened herself to her full five-foot-ten and said, "No. We're going. I was supposed to go up the Eiffel Tower with Jackson, and I did that by myself. The Louvre, the Arc de Triomphe, the Duomo, all of it—all supposed to be with him on our second honeymoon, but he messed it up. *He* did this to us. I know, I know in my heart of hearts, it's an illness, that he's *sick*, but isn't there something inside him that's supposed to take responsibility? Do I have to be the grown-up the whole darned time?"

She had worked herself up and I felt for her so much, my heart was breaking. Lou. Our Mama Lou. Lou, who was always generous and sweet and kind. All she wanted was for someone to be there for *her*, for her to have someone to lean on. And she deserved that. After being so strong for Jackson. After being so good to us—strangers only a week before—she deserved something just for her. I reached up and hugged her tight as the tears started streaming down her face.

"Oh, Lou," I said, my voice muffled by her shoulder. "We're taking you on a gondola!"

And we did.

Apparently, gondola rides are something else you should book ahead in Venice. But most people didn't have Dani. Dani had mad skills when it came to online searches and figuring out how to get to or into places. She found us a gondola ride for four on Viator. It left twenty minutes after she booked it, and we had to speed walk to the dock, but we made it.

We stood between two lines of red velvet ropes as though we were queuing to get into a nightclub, and I noticed Jaelee keeping a sharp eye on the gondoliers. "What are you doing?" I whispered.

"I want a hot one."

"What?"

"I want us to get a hot gondolier," she said pointedly.

I looked at the tightly packed gondolas and the group of men who leapt between them, some pushing back from the dock and some docking their gondolas, all working with grace and ease. They each wore the traditional uniform: black pants, striped shirt and red kerchief. All of them were young(ish), all had jet black hair and olive skin, and there wasn't one among them who wasn't at least attractive.

They were like a boyband—something for everyone.

"Well, does it matter? They're a nice-looking bunch."

She looked at me as though I'd said, "They all bathe in rubbish and have citrus reamers for penises."

We moved to the front of the line and a gondola manoeuvred into place. Our gondolier smiled at us, and the ticket taker helped us on one at a time. We got seated and settled, which was when I learnt two things. One: Dani had sprung for a bottle of prosecco, which she held up with a smile. And two: Jaelee did not think we got a "hot one".

"*Buonasera*," said our gondolier. He said some other things in Italian, which could have been him reciting his shopping list for all I cared. He was lovely.

Then, as we rounded the corner of the nearest building and glided into a smaller canal, he started singing! And not just any singing, opera. And he was good! With the acoustics in the canal, his voice echoing off the walls and accompanied by the mesmerising sound of the gondola slipping through the water, it was simply beautiful.

"I wanted a *hot* one," hissed Jaelee.

Three pairs of eyes pinned her to her seat. "What? There were *way* hotter ones. I mean, come on." The eyes remained fixed on her. I gave her what I hoped was my best teacher glare. She rolled her eyes in reply, unapologetic.

"That's enough," said Lou in a low growl I hadn't heard from her before. "This ride is not about you wanting a hot one. This is about the four of us experiencing something special together. And, darn you, he sings like an angel!"

Jae put her hands up in surrender and the tension dissipated. Though it may have been because Dani chose that moment to crack open the bubbles. She poured it into four plastic cups and handed them around.

"I'd like to propose a toast," she said. "To *quattro bella*." Jaelee started to correct her syntax, but she closed her mouth when I flashed her a look. I didn't know enough Italian—or Spanish—to know what Dani was *supposed* to say, but I understood the toast. I tapped my plastic cup against the other three and drank to that. Four beauties. My friends. My bus besties.

My phone beeped in my bag and on reflex I pulled it out and looked at it.

Mum had finally scanned Jean-Luc's letter!

Chapter 14

Ma très chère Catherine,

I have exciting news. I received an acceptance letter from the University of Lyon to study ethics and foreign relations. I think I said to you this was my first choice, so I am very happy. I was also accepted into the University of Reims and the Sorbonne, which is an honour, but of course I want to stay closer to my family, especially my mother.

She says she wants me to be close. She will miss me too much. This is okay. Lyon is the best choice for me.

My father does not understand. Who turns down the Sorbonne? Me! Maybe I am crazy, but Lyon has a very good ethics program. I will learn to solve all the problems of the world – so much work to do! Maybe Australia needs an ethicist? (a look-up word)

It is hard to believe that you have already been studying for a few months. I wish the European academic year was sooner. I want to start immediately, but you know that is me—impatient!

I will spend the summer in the south. My father has a

friend who is the manager of a resort in Nice. I will work there in the bar and they will give me a small room to share with someone else. Maybe it will be a cute girl. I am joking. Unless she is from Australia and called Catherine.

The wages is not a lot of money, but there are gratuities (another look-up word). I will save money and buy a car for university. My father says he will give me the same money I save to buy it—so I do not think he is very mad about the Sorbonne. It is possible I will make so much gratuities, I will buy the Venturi Atlantique. If I do, maybe I will let you drive it when you visit. Ha ha.

PLEASE come for Christmas!!! My family wants to meet you. Also I miss you. Three years is a long time. My friends here are not the same as you. You know this, but I can tell you things that I cannot tell them. It's hard to talk to them about things that matter—like pressure from my parents to take different paths. I wonder if they talk to each other at all (my parents).

I miss you, but letters have to be enough for now I think. If you do come, you can stay as long as you want. How much time do you have at Christmas?

Cecile says hello and thank you for sending the Vegemite. She is the only one in the family who eats it. I still do not like it – I still do not forgive you for making me try it in Sydney. My father was brave and he tried it. He says it tastes like bouillon. My mother would not try it. Her face! She made the funnest face when she smelled it. And she eats anchovies from the tin!

I kept all the Tim Tams for myself. Most of them were

*broken—lots of small pieces, but I invented a new way to
have them. I put the small pieces in a glass of milk.
Delicious. You can try it. If you like it, call it the Jean-Luc
after me. Ha ha again.*

*Please say hello to Karen and Ron and Sarah for me—
my Aussie family. I know I will see you all again one day.
Maybe they can come for Christmas too.*

Gros bisous!

J-L

"That was nice," said Lou. *Nice?* It was confusing more
than anything.

The whole time I was reading aloud, my mind vacillated
between Jean-Luc the boy from the photo and Jean-Luc the
man I'd kissed in Rome. But the Jean-Luc who'd written the
letter, the one who was apparently in love with me, had been
somewhere in between. A young man, a man-child.

I scanned back over the letter looking for the clues. "And
he told you the other night he was in love with you when he
wrote it?" Jae asked.

I nodded. "Mmm, yes."

"Huh."

It was exactly what I was thinking. I looked up from my
phone. "Am I missing something? I'm not seeing 'I'm in love
with you.'"

"Well, he does sign off '*gros bisous*'—that's just for loved
ones," said Dani.

"And there's the part about the cute girl from Australia,"
added Lou.

287

"I guess." I scanned back over the letter. Since the night with him in Rome, I'd been anxious for Mum to send the letter, thinking there'd be some glaring reveal, something I'd missed all those years ago. But at most, there was some mild flirting. Had he always flirted with me? And if he had, how did I not remember that?

"Give it," said Jaelee. I handed her the phone and watched her face as she reread the letter. A couple of times her eyes narrowed as though she was scrutinising a particular line. When she was done, she handed back the phone. "He may have *thought* he was hinting in that letter, but if he was, he did a bad job of it."

"What about in other letters? You said you guys wrote all the time," said Dani.

"I don't know. I don't remember anything like, 'Hey, I love you,' so I don't think he ever declared it or anything."

"The most important thing is what he said the other night," said Jaelee.

"You think so?"

"Yes."

I considered it. "So, he sees me fifteen years later and—"

"And tells you he's in love with you," cut in Dani.

"Well, that he *was*. Once." Jaelee was being pedantic and I did not find it particularly helpful.

"What about your last letter to him? Do you remember what you wrote?" asked Lou.

"More or less."

"And?" asked Jae, impatience in her tone.

"It was horrible. Especially knowing what I know now. I said it had been fun being his pen pal."

"Ouch," Jae said with a grimace. Dani raised her eyebrows and hid behind her cup of bubbles, and Lou's lips disappeared into a thin line. There was a moment of silence while we all considered how much I had screwed up—well, how much younger Cat—Catey—had.

I wanted to defend her, to say that she hadn't known how Jean-Luc felt about her, but I knew it was rubbish, because our friendship was *far* more than "pen pals". It was awful that I'd assigned such an insipid label to it, as though we were strangers who exchanged polite letters from time to time.

"Is that how you really saw him?" asked Lou, reading my mind.

No.

My stomach churning, I stared at the passing walls of the crumbling buildings and conjured up memories of young Jean-Luc—us lying on my bed, head to toe, reading for hours, us riding our bikes to the beach so we could beachcomb, returning hours later with a haul of shells and smooth rocks, us staying up most of the night watching DVDs and eating an impressive array of junk food. Jean-Luc was the one who'd added Coco Pops to our popcorn, transforming it into CocoCorn, our signature dish.

Hours and hours we'd spent together, sometimes talking, sometimes reading or watching something, but always together. And our letters had been an extension of that. I could tell him things I couldn't tell anyone else, except maybe Sarah. Things I couldn't even tell Scott.

When Jean-Luc left, I missed him terribly—even years later when I was in a relationship with Scott.

Scott and I never had long conversations, or went beach-combing, walking side by side and talking about anything and everything. And we certainly didn't read for hours, content to just *be* together, because Scott didn't read—ever.

When I'd cut Jean-Luc out of my life, I'd lost something I'd never really replaced. I met Lou's eyes. "No. He wasn't just a pen pal. I loved him."

"Like, in love?" asked Dani.

"I don't know," I whined, hating the sound of my own voice. "Maybe. I did love Scott, but we never had the same kind of connection I had with Jean-Luc.

"Looking back, I think I loved the *idea* of Scott more than I loved him. He fit the picture of what I thought I was supposed to want—get married, house in the suburbs, two-point-four kids, barbecues at the weekend ..." I trailed off. "Does that make sense? I mean, doesn't everyone think they want those things when they're young and stupid?"

"Well, I wanted those things," said Lou. "I still do ... someday." Oh, God, I'd stuck my foot in it—again.

"Oh, Lou. I'm so sorry." She shrugged, but that made me feel worse. There I was whinging about a relationship that had ended a decade before, and her wounds were so fresh.

"But it turned out you didn't want that?" prompted Jaelee.

"No. I didn't," I replied, tempering my tone. "Scott wasn't a bad guy." Well, he *was* a cheater and a liar, but I left that part out. "But we should never have been together. We wanted different things."

"And Jean-Luc?"

"I guess we wanted similar things—back *then* anyway. You know, usual teenage stuff—make a difference, see the world, get all those stamps in our passports."

"That sounds like you now," said Lou, being kinder than I deserved. I gave her a grateful smile.

"So, more compatible than you and Scott?" cut in Jaelee. She kept pressing me to go deeper, clearly wanting to get to the bottom of my mess.

"Definitely. *Way* more, but I obviously didn't think like that at the time."

"If you could go back, what would you do?" asked Dani.

"But I can't, Dan."

"But if you could?" Lou the dreamer.

I knew the answer. I also knew I needed to say it aloud, make it real. "I'd dump Scott when he asked me—sorry, when he *told* me—to break it off with Jean-Luc. I'd save myself five years of being with the wrong person."

"And *maybe* you would have ended up with Jean-Luc." Apparently, Dani was also a dreamer.

"Maybe. But right now, thinking about the young man who wrote this letter, I feel awful for what I did to him."

"Hey, he did okay," said Jaelee. "He's successful, well-travelled. He even got married, you said." I winced at the thought of the beautiful Vanessa, but Jae's point rang true. It wasn't like I'd ruined Jean-Luc for love.

The only person I'd ruined for love was me.

"Okay, so now what?" asked Dani. It was a good question, but I didn't know what was next. I'd already apologised to him, but a thought niggled at me, like a canker sore inside my head.

"I ... what if I *had* dumped Scott? What if Jean-Luc and I had ended up together?" Hearing myself say it made me feel sick. Had I really wasted fifteen years of my life?

"Is that helpful?" asked Jaelee pointedly. I saw Lou shoot her a look, but I probably needed a dose of Jaelee's pragmatism.

I shook my head. "You know what? You're right, Jae, it's not helpful. I spent five years with Scott and it wasn't all bad. And whatever it was—good or bad—it led me to my life in London, which I love." Was I trying to convince my friends or myself? "So, let's enjoy the rest of the gondola ride and finish those bubbles."

"But are you going to see him again?" Clearly, Dani was unwilling to let the "Jean-Luc and Cat" sub-plot go.

"I don't know. I guess it's up to him. I mean, I definitely want to stay friends and we're connected on Facebook now." She made a face. It said, "That's not what I was talking about." I ignored it. "And, he's ridiculously hot, so if there's a chance of sleeping with him, I'll jump at it." I was making light, but none of my friends even cracked a smile.

"But he *told* you about being in love with you. If he didn't wonder about you two having a future, he wouldn't have said anything about love."

"That's a good point, Dani," said Lou. Great, they were ganging up on me.

I looked to Jaelee for support, but it wasn't forthcoming. "Dani's right. It all comes back to that. I think you need to be open to whatever happens."

"You mean sleeping with him?" That's what she meant, right?

She shrugged. "Sure, maybe, but probably more than that. I mean it, *be open to whatever happens.*" I could tell she was losing patience with me, but the thought sat heavily in my mind. If seeing him meant risking him falling for me—*again*—maybe I shouldn't see him. I didn't want to hurt him—*again*.

At least we're Facebook friends.

It was my last thought before I put an end to the Jean-Luc conversation by asking Dani about her and Jason.

She waved her hand, "Oh, it's just a bit of fun—kissing and stuff. We're not sleeping together. I mean, where would we even *do* that?" It was a good question. I hadn't even thought about it. I guessed if they wanted to, there could be some Tetris-like rooming changes, but it would be a little obvious on a coach tour.

"So, you don't think you'll see him again after the trip?" Lou asked Dani. I breathed a slow sigh of relief that the conversation was no longer about me and Jean-Luc. As much as I needed their counsel after I'd read the letter, my friends had given me more than enough to chew over for the time being.

"Nah," said Dani, laughing. "I mean, he lives in New Zealand! It's, like, literally on the other side of the planet."

Whereas Jean-Luc and I lived a three-hour train ride from each other.

Our gondolier with the golden voice held out his hand to steady us as we stepped off the gondola, one by one. I was the last off and as my feet hit terra firma, he said in perfect

293

English, "I hope you enjoyed the journey. Have a lovely evening."

Lou and I looked at each other, horrified. He spoke English!

I could only hope he hadn't heard Jaelee whining about not having a hot one. I dug into my bag and pulled out a twenty-euro note and showed it to Lou who nodded. When I gave him the tip, he smiled warmly, "Thank you. *Grazie.*" I smiled back. If he *had* heard Jaelee, the tip was as much an apology as thanks for a lovely ride.

"And thank you for the singing," said Lou. "It was beautiful." He bowed his head.

"That was a big tip," said Jaelee as we walked away. Lou grabbed my hand, which I read as, "Say nothing, she knows not what she does." I kept quiet, which was very hard for me. Our gondolier had been lovely and Jae had been so rude, simply because of his looks. I can't abide that kind of rudeness.

Gondola ride ✓

We spent the rest of our time in Venice wandering and Jae was right, it was sublime. I asked the girls about stopping at a mask shop, so I could buy one of those elaborate Venetian masks made of *papier-mâché*. I ended up buying two. I couldn't help myself—they were just so beautiful, and I knew Sarah would love the one I chose for her. Although I'd be carting the damned things around for another week and, enveloped in bubble wrap, they were nearly twice their actual size. I thought about asking Jaelee to stuff them into her Tardis luggage.

We made it to the pick-up point with twelve minutes to spare, even beating Georgina. I was relieved, because being in her firing line was becoming exhausting.

Ah, Venice, I thought again as we left the floating city in our wake. Six hours was not long enough; I would have to go back. I longed to wander her streets and canals, to get lost in her for days on end, a certain Frenchman by my side.

A man who had loved me once.

Venice ✓

We arrived at the campsite around 9:00pm and, taking advantage of an early night, disappeared to our respective caravans. Apparently, there was a bar at the campsite, but our escapades the previous night had left me craving an early bedtime.

Lou and I said goodnight to Jaelee and Dani—hugs all around—and after a quick trip to the ablution block, were in our wee-ridden cabin and ensconced in our sleeping bags by 9:30pm.

"That was an incredible day," said Lou.

I turned my head so I could see her in the dim light seeping in through the skylight. "I am so glad, Lou. Those plans you had with Jackson ... well, it must have been hard for you."

"I've been doing so well up 'til now."

"You have. You're amazing."

"But then the whole thing with the gondola ... it just brought it all back, you know, the hundreds of times I'd tried to work it into conversations—every time we talked about how to spend one of his work bonuses, or where we wanted to go for our vacation. All those times I *hoped*—that he would get better, that we'd actually *go* somewhere." I could hear the anger in her voice, then she was quiet for a moment.

"All the times I hoped I hadn't married the wrong person." The fight had left her voice, resignation in its place. I wanted to comfort her, but I didn't know what to say. Lou would know, if our situations were reversed.

"You girls, you were awesome today," she added, giving us far more credit than we deserved. "I loved Venice."

"Even the Jaelee-and-the-gondolier incident?"

She giggled. "Oh, that girl. She can be quite the little witch, huh?" Understatement of our tour.

"There's a lot more going on there than she lets on, I think."

"Oh, I know there is. That's why I give her a pass so often." Mama Lou was back.

I smiled into the darkness. "It's been a good tour so far."

"It has."

"You know, I always swore I'd never do one of these."

"A bus trip?"

I didn't correct her. "Yes. The way Sarah described them, they never had any appeal."

"So, if you hadn't slept with your roommate, uh ..."

"Alex."

"Right, Alex—then you wouldn't be here."

"Huh. I guess that's true."

"And we wouldn't have met."

"Hmm. Also true."

"You should thank him."

I chuckled quietly. "I guess I should. Although he is moving out now. I'm not sure I'll even see him when I get back."

"He must be really upset."

How had I not thought of that? Here I was feeling all sorts of guilt about Jean-Luc and I hadn't given Alex a second thought. He'd said he was in love with me. And even if it was misguided and unreciprocated, that didn't make his feelings any less real. And I'd *literally* run away from him without even the courtesy of a proper conversation.

I was a complete and utter cow.

"Did you send it?" asked Lou. We'd been on the road for several hours, having already stopped for morning tea, and the whole time I'd been agonising over the Alex palaver. I'd decided to text him an apology.

"Yep. Longest text message ever," I replied.

"What did you say?"

"That I'm sorry I didn't know how he felt about me, and I didn't want to hurt him, but I know I probably did, and I'm sorry he thought he had to move out, and that I hope we can still be friends."

"Yeah, that is long."

"That's the abridged version."

"Right. Did you mean the last part?"

"About staying friends?"

"Yup."

"No. I mean, we weren't really friends to begin with. We were just flatmates, but it's what you say, isn't it? To be polite?" My inner Englishwoman speaking.

"I guess. It's not exactly honest, though."

"Geez, Louise. I think the most important thing is that I

apologised. He probably doesn't want to 'stay friends'—" I used air quotes "—Sheesh!" She raised her hands in surrender and I immediately back-pedalled. "Sorry, Lou."

"No problem." It seemed so easy for her, forgiving people. I wanted to be like Lou.

And I wasn't sure why I was so tetchy; I had no reason to be. I'd had a whopping nine hours of sleep—a new tour record—and we'd had a decent breakfast of bacon, eggs and toast. And even though we were going to be on the coach a long time that day—more than six hours—Northern Italy had epic scenery. I mean, *epic*.

So, no reason to be grumpy other than my inner voice chastising me for being, as I'd realised, an utter cow. I got out my phone and sent a series of messages to my people.

To Jane:

Hi. Any ideas about a new flatmate? I'll ask around at school next week. Hope you're having a good week. Leaving Italy today for Switzerland. Amazing scenery. Ciao! Cat x

To Mum:

Thanks for the letter! Tour is very good. Will call when I get home for a proper catch up. Love to Dad. Catherine xx

To Sarah:

May try to FaceTime you later. I saw J-L. He kissed me!
And he said he was in love with me years ago. OMG!
Anyway now I'm all confused. ARGH! Going to
Lauterbrunnen today. Loved Rome and Venice. Love you.
Cx

I sent the last message, then sat back and looked out the window again. We were on a highway wending through a mountain pass somewhere north of Verona when I saw signs for Lake Como and immediately thought of George Clooney. *Maybe we could take a little detour and pop in.* Surely, he would *love* having a busload of strangers show up for some Nespresso. "*Buongiorno*, George, Amal!"

My mind is a weird place sometimes.

I thought Northern Italy was stunning and then we got to Switzerland. It was like seeing the Duchess of Cambridge and thinking, "Wow, she's beautiful," and then Gal Gadot walks by.

The valleys were so incredibly *green*. I couldn't think of any time I'd seen that vibrant a colour in nature—it was like the grass was made of parakeets. The slopes of the valleys rose to rocky peaks dusted in snow and dotted with chalets, dark wood structures with apex roofs and green shutters. If I hadn't seen it myself, I would have thought the entire scene was CGI.

We stopped for a late lunch and a quick visit in Lucerne, which looked like a film set. Yes, Italy was nice, but Tom could have taken me straight to Switzerland and left me there for two weeks and I would have been happy. We only had an hour to go, see, and eat, and I was far more interested in going and seeing than eating, so I talked Lou into buying takeaway so we could wander around while we ate.

Confession: in Lucerne, takeaway meant McDonald's. We would have had *anything else*, if anything else had been available, but fast food was scarce. It was a minor indiscretion never to be repeated on the tour. And, let's be honest, McDonald's fries are amazing.

Burgers and fries in hand, we headed across the nearly seven-hundred-year-old wooden bridge that traversed the Reuss River, Chapel Bridge. It was magnificent and as we crossed from south to north, we got an incredible view of Mount Pilatus in the distance.

The greenish-blue water was like glass and on both banks the town was reflected in perfect twins. The single apex roofs we'd seen on chalets all the way to Lucerne were mirrored in the architecture of the town's buildings—offices, hotels, residences—but were more formal than the chalets, more austere. The air *smelled* clean and I took in great gulps of it as I downed my yearly quota of saturated fat.

"This is unbelievable," said Lou, echoing my thoughts.

"I know. I had no idea that somewhere so pristine even existed. It's as though every single detail has been chosen with care. Even *Monaco* isn't like this."

"It's like we're on a movie set."

"I was thinking that too."

"I wish we were staying here instead."

"Stop reading my mind," I teased.

She smiled at me, then checked her watch. "We should make our way back."

I nodded and stuffed the rest of the fries into my mouth as we walked back across the bridge.

On the coach, I doused my hands in hand sanitiser to rid them of the smell of grease. Lou held her hand out and I squeezed out another dollop.

"We hope you had a good lunch," said Georgina. Lou raised her eyebrows at me. My stomach lurched and I was already regretting the burger. "We're going to make a quick stop before we head to Lauterbrunnen—"

There were groans—*loud* groans—from some people on the coach. I knew that sound. It was the sound of thirty teenagers being assigned homework over the weekend. To be fair to the groaners, and you may be surprised to learn that I wasn't one of them, it *was* a long travel day. But still, Georgina looked like she was going to cry.

"Ahem." She cleared her throat into the microphone—not passive-aggressively, but clearly trying to keep it together. She threw Tom a quick look. "Uh, so, we have a quick—really quick—stop planned. It's, uh, something pretty special, so, yeah." She sat down quickly.

It was the first time I'd seen her flustered and I felt a modicum of pity for her.

Tom drove us north for about ten minutes, past a gun shop, a post office and a hair salon, and turned off into a side street and parked. As soon as we stopped, he opened the door and Georgina practically leapt off the coach. Then, for the first time during the whole tour, Tom picked up the microphone.

"Okay, guys. There's a path just over there," he said, pointing to his left, "and you'll want to follow signs to the Lion of Lucerne. It's a monument and it's pretty amazing. Be back here in fifteen minutes. Don't be late."

There was loud silence as fifty-three people realised we had upset Mum and now Dad was in charge. When the moment ended, we shuffled off the coach, chastised and contrite, and walked en masse to the monument.

Wow.

It was a giant, intricate lion carved into the rockface. He'd been impaled and was dying, his face in anguish. The monument commemorated the Swiss Guards who had defended the French royal family and were massacred during the French Revolution in 1792. It was an incredible sculpture and very moving, leaving me a little breathless.

As Tom had directed us, we went, we saw, and we took photos. Less than fifteen minutes later, we were all back on the coach—even Georgina, who looked a little paler than usual—and Tom drove us up into the mountains to our next overnight destination, Lauterbrunnen.

Views of Lake Lucerne emerged and disappeared as we rounded bend after bend of the steep road. It was a magnificent sight, with teal water surrounded by what I will forever call "Swiss green" hills, and steep steel-grey mountains rising on all sides.

Each minute we drove further into the heart of Switzerland revealed more incredible beauty. It was emotionally exhausting gasping for breath that much, and at that altitude I was in grave danger of hyperventilating.

Lauterbrunnen pretty much put me over the edge.

"Oh, my fucking God," I said as we drove along the valley floor between two sheer cliff faces. Lou gave a quiet "Ahem" next to me. She didn't swear and she certainly didn't blaspheme, so I figured the combination of "fucking" and "God" was too much for her. I apologised—although it *was* an OMFG moment.

The Swiss-green valley floor, with its pockets of leafy trees, undulated in a sequence of low hills. Giant mountains loomed either side, one casting half the valley into afternoon shadow. The narrow road wound among homes and shops, all textbook Swiss chalets in varying colours—chocolate brown, rusty brown and brilliant white. Window boxes spilled cascading flowers in vibrant splashes of red, yellow and pink, contrasting with wooden shutters in dusty green, white and natural wood. We passed a small paddock with the prettiest cows I'd ever seen, big brown eyes blinking placidly at us.

"Scratch what I said before about Lucerne," I said to Lou over my shoulder.

"No kidding. This is ... I don't have the right words."

"I know, right. Sublime? Epic? Paradise?"

"Those will do."

My phone beeped with a message notification. Alex:

Okay. Thanks.

My mouth flattened into a line and I showed the phone to Lou.

"Oh, well, at least he got your apology."

"I guess so." I was certain there was nothing more I could say to Alex, so I closed the message and put my phone in my bag. Besides, there were more pressing matters—like the view.

Georgina looked a little brighter as she took up the microphone and I noticed that, like me, everyone sat up and shut up, giving her their full attention. "Okay," she smiled brightly, and I wondered if she was doing the "fake it 'til you make it" thing. I'd done it myself *many* times, particularly when I was having a hard time and didn't want to let on to my pupils. Teaching could be a soul-crushing job sometimes, and I knew from Sarah that managing a tour could be just as gruelling and thankless.

"As you can see, Lauterbrunnen is quite spectacular." "Spectacular" was a good word. I filed it away. "You will have noticed on the rooming sheet that there are more people in each room than we've had before, but the rooms are quite unique. I also managed to get us into top-floor rooms, which have these great skylights. The stargazing is quite something here." *Good on you, Georgina! Way to make a comeback*, I thought, suddenly her biggest fan.

"So, when you get off the coach, the reps will lead the way into the chalet and show you to your rooms. Dinner tonight is in the dining hall and tomorrow is a coach-free day, so if you're not doing any of the excursions, have a great day exploring. The reps can give you some tips if you're not sure what to do. Okay, so, I'll see you later."

We didn't know it then, but we wouldn't see her again until it was time to leave Lauterbrunnen the day after next.

"I feel awful about before. Poor Georgina," said Lou as we gathered our things and waited to get off the coach.

"Yes, me too." I decided to seek her out and see if she was all right, teacher to tour manager. I figured, at the very least, we had "controlling a wayward mob" in common.

When I stepped off the coach, I slung my bag onto my shoulder and stretched my arms up above my head. It had been a long day. Right as I indulged myself in a wide and very loud yawn, I heard a voice say, "Hello, Catherine."

My mouth shut as though my puppeteer had closed her hand, and I spun in the direction of the voice.

Oh. My. Fucking. God.

"Jean-Luc!" It came out as a squeak.

Chapter 15

My mouth dropped open again and hung in a loose variation of an O. I must have looked fabulous.

He moved closer, as people from the tour group parted around us like I was Moses. He took my hands in his and looked down at me with the kind of look film heroines dream of. "Hi," he said, his mouth stretching into a *spectacular* grin.

"Hi," I coughed out, quickly taking in the lived-in jeans and grey T-shirt draped perfectly from his perfect body. Jean-Luc. In Switzerland. I could not have been more surprised if Alex was standing there—or Scott. And how had it happened? I had so many questions.

Before I could ask any of them, Dani poked her head between us. "Hello, lovebirds." *Lovebirds? Mental note: kill Dani.* "Cat, I hope you'll forgive us for interfering, but ..." She shrugged. It was hardly an apology and it was a monumental interference. *Mental note: Really, kill Dani.*

"So, how did you ...?" I was baffled.

Jean-Luc took over explaining. I was glad, because Dani's coy looks and ambiguous gesturing weren't doing the trick.

"I contacted Dani to ask where your next stop was after Venice. I wanted to see you again."

All right, that makes sense. Did it, though? I had about half a second before I was expected to say something, and I spent all of it trying to remember how we'd left things in Rome. I certainly hadn't said, "Hey, come to Switzerland and surprise me." Maybe that was why they were called surprises.

The thing was, I was elated, thrilled, over the moon to see him, but at the same time my stomach was twisting into knots. I did the only thing I could do with all those expectant eyes on me. I threw my arms around his neck and hugged him. I swore I heard another "Aww" from Dani. My life was turning into an episode of *Ellen*.

When I stepped back from the hug, Dani and Jaelee were edging away, and Lou ran over and gave me a quick squeeze. "Have a wonderful time!" she whispered in my ear. *Wait, what? Where are they going? What's happening?* I was bewildered, having no idea what had been planned without me.

Tom did me the favour of bringing my case over and placed it on the ground next to me with a smile. "Thank you, Tom," I heard myself say.

"This must be ..." said Jean-Luc. I faced him, a frown nestled between my brows.

"Confusing," I said, finishing the thought.

"Yes. *Je suis désolé.* I asked Dani to keep this a secret. I wanted to surprise you." His smile had vanished and he looked like he might be regretting the whole "surprise Cat in Switzerland" thing. My head was trying to make sense of everything, but my heart just wanted to scrub that look off his face—*tout de suite*!

"No, *I'm* sorry. It's a wonderful surprise. The other night, saying goodbye ... it was all so rushed. This? This is good ... it's *wonderful* that you're here."

"Really? I know it is ..." he squeezed his eyes shut for a moment and I could *see* him searching for the word in English. It was *presumptuous*, that's what it was, but I doubted he was going to come up with that word in English and *I* certainly wasn't going to supply it. "... presumptuous," he said, eventually. So he didn't need the English teacher's help after all.

"A little, but it's all right. It's good." I grabbed his hand to doubly—*triply*—reassure him. "Really."

"So, let me get your luggage. We are staying just a little way down, closer to town."

Wait, what?

"Sorry, you got *us* a *room*?" Now *that* was presumptuous, and I didn't know how I felt about it. Actually, yes, I did. I was quite cross.

"No, well, yes, but not a room. I rented an apartment. There are two rooms." Those beautiful green eyes with their flecks of gold and brown looked down at me. What could I say but yes? We had separate rooms. And if I could keep my libido in check and not crawl into his bed in the middle of the night, it would all be fine and dandy.

"Here we are," he said, leading us into an incredible apartment. I made a beeline for a giant picture window which had a view of the valley.

"Oh, my God, this *view*!"

He laughed and disappeared with my case—probably to put it in my room. "It's the sole reason I chose this place," he called.

"Airbnb?"

"Yes." He came back into the room. "Actually, there was one other thing. Come with me." He took my hand and my heart leapt to my throat. Was he taking me to *his* bedroom? Was I about to be seduced? Because if so, it wasn't going to take much. "Here, look at this."

Right, I was officially seduced.

It was a giant, free-standing, white porcelain bathtub, and it stood by another picture window. I nearly burst into tears. "Do you know how long it's been since I've bathed without standing in someone else's shower water?" I asked rhetorically. I made my way over to it and stroked it lovingly.

He chuckled from where he leant against the doorframe. "I thought you might like that."

I turned to face him and perched on the edge. "Is that so?"

"*Oui.*"

"You don't *really* get extra points for thinking a *woman*—one who's been travelling on a *bus* and staying in *campsites*—would swoon over a bath, especially one like this." I deliberately said "bus" for effect.

He raised one eyebrow. *Could he always do that?* It was becoming a fun little game I was playing with myself—Jean-Luc then vs Jean-Luc now.

"So, you have some choices."

"Oh, *now* I get choices?" I teased.

He pretended to scowl at me. "You have *some* choices," he repeated. I sat up straight and nodded along, taking it all very seriously. In truth, I was content just to stare at him, learning the features that belonged to the man.

"You can take a bath and relax. I can bring you some wine. Or we can drink the wine together on the balcony—"

"There's a balcony?"

"But of course." How could I have doubted there was a balcony?

"Or, if you're hungry, I bought some food I will cook for dinner."

I looked at my watch. "A very early dinner." It was 4:00pm.

"Yes. But we could pretend we are eighty years old."

"Hah! That was pretty funny." He smiled. "So, I'm not going to lie, the bathtub is calling me, but you've come all this way, and there's that." I turned my head to indicate the view. "So, I think I would like to start with option number two, please."

"*Parfait.*" That crinkly-eyed smile made my lady parts stand to attention. *Down, girls.*

"I do want to freshen up a bit, though. I've been on the coach all day. I might change, actually."

"Of course. I put your luggage in the main bedroom."

"Oh, thank you." He was giving *me* the master bedroom?

"I will get the wine and meet you outside." He left.

I patted the edge of the tub and whispered to it, "I will see you very soon, my lovely." As I passed through the living area, Jean-Luc was busy in the sleek but tiny kitchen, putting together a platter of nibbles. I gave him a smile, which he returned.

Seeing him there like that was a tiny glimpse into a "what if" that was both jarring and appealing. *If we lived together, we could have drinks on the balcony every day.* If we had a balcony, that is.

I turned down a short hallway and came to two side-by-side bedrooms. The master bedroom had a California king bed—wider than it was long—and the other bedroom had two single beds pushed against opposite walls. A small overnight bag sat on one bed. I tried to imagine Jean-Luc, who was at least six-foot-one, lying on the bed with his feet dangling over the edge. *I should have this room*, I thought. I'd talk to him about it later.

I unzipped my case and pulled out my toiletries bag, my makeup case, a clean pair of knickers and a fresh top. When I got back to the living area, Jean-Luc was no longer in the kitchen and I could see the back of his head on the balcony through one of the windows. I'd be quick, but I really did feel a little stale after such a long journey.

In the beautiful bathroom, I brushed my teeth and splashed water on my face, then dabbed on some moisturiser and reapplied my makeup. I'm not one of those women who likes full coverage, so it was just a bit of concealer under my eyes—I may have had nine hours' sleep the night before, but the bags from all the other late nights were stubbornly still in place—some cream blush, and some sheer raspberry-red lip gloss. I finished by tidying up my brows with a little brush.

I spritzed some leave-in conditioner into my hair and smoothed down the fly-aways, and before I changed into my clean knickers and top, I wet one of the fluffy washcloths and performed a quick spruce up of the important bits—you know what I mean. When I was presentable, I returned to my room to put everything away. My phone beeped on my way out and I went back for it.

Sarah:

He kissed you! That's amazing. I want to know everything. Call me soon. S x

She had *no* idea. I would call her later.
There was also a message from Dani:

I hope you're not mad. Have a great time. Dani, Jaelee and Louise xxx

And one from Lou:

The Love Bus!!! :D

I smiled to myself. I loved my girls.

I put my phone on silent and left the room. When I stepped onto the balcony, I didn't know which was more spectacular, the view or the man. All right, I did. It was Jean-Luc.

He sat in one of two canvas deckchairs, his legs stretched out casually in front of him. He held a glass of white wine, condensation forming on the outside. It was still quite warm out, low twenties, I guessed. I sat down in the other chair and it nearly swallowed me up.

313

"Are you okay?" he asked, telling me I hadn't quite pulled off the incredibly tricky act of *sitting down*.

"Yes." I wriggled into a more comfortable position, deciding that *our* balcony would have better chairs.

"Here," he said, handing me a glass of wine. "I brought this from home." He clinked the rim of his glass gently against mine and we each took sips, our eyes meeting over the top of our glasses. We'd done that in Paris, I recalled.

God, his eyes. I am a goner.

I liked the wine; it was almost floral. "It's delicious." I took another sip and let it roll around on my tongue.

"Oh, you like it? I hoped you would. My brother-in-law, he makes it."

"Cecile's husband?"

"Well, *his* brother, Victor. He has a little winery just outside of Lyon. Actually, if I can, I go there for harvest."

"You pick the grapes?"

"We all do. Cecile, Louis, me—even my father will come sometimes. Victor has friends who come too. We pick the grapes in the day—it breaks my back, this work, but it is good, you know, to *work* like that, on the land with my *bare hands*." I smiled, enjoying his exaggerated description of grape picking.

"Then after dark, we gather around a big table in the house, and we eat simple food—bread, cheese, olives, some meat, like this." He indicated the tray of antipasti sitting on the low table between us. "Only much more, because we are very hungry after working all day."

"Of course." He was describing a scene remarkably close to the one I'd imagined—the one where I met his family.

"Then we sleep—wherever we can—on the sofa, on the floor, in the loft. Some people bring tents. And after we wake up, we have a large breakfast and do it all again."

"It sounds amazing." It did—I wasn't just being polite.

"*And* we do the stomping."

"You stomp the grapes?" The thought was delightful.

"Yes, it is very messy work and it feels strange, but I like it. And because the picking is done, it is a little celebration. Like a dance in the grapes." He grinned. I grinned back.

"I've always wanted to do that, the stomping."

"You should come. You missed harvest this year. It was last month, but perhaps next year, yes?"

"I'd love it."

"Good, we have a date." He raised his glass to me and took a sip.

Perhaps he was teasing me, I wasn't sure. And I wasn't one to make plans for the following month, let alone the following year, but right then I wanted nothing more than to go to a little winery somewhere in the middle of France and stomp grapes with Jean-Luc.

Maybe I am falling for him. Or, I'm madly in lust and just need to get him out of my system.

I let my two minds bicker in the background while I cut off a slice of cheese, laid it on a cracker, then popped it in my mouth. I washed it down with some wine and leant back to take in the view. I could *feel* my heartbeat slowing down.

I breathed in the mountain air, the scent of grass and sunshine and maybe a hint of bovine animal, making me feel a little heady. I suppose it could have been the wine, *or* the man next to me.

I glanced over at his hand, which held his glass by the stem and slowly swirled the wine.

Oh, what a beautiful hand. I want that hand on my bare body. My libido was winning. I needed to distract it.

"So, tell me, how did all this happen?"

His mouth twitched, nearly a smile. "You mean *this*? You and me here?"

"You know I do. Don't be coy."

"Coy?"

"You're fluent enough to know that one."

He nodded and the smile broke across his face. "True." His eyes locked on mine. "Well, I got on the train on Friday morning—only two days ago, *non*?"

He was right—it *had* only been two days since he'd left Rome. The tour was doing odd things to my perception of time. It was as if each day lasted several days, but at the same time it was all going by extremely fast.

"And on the train, I realised it was too soon to say goodbye. I only just found you and I didn't know when we would see each other again. When I got home, I could not pull myself away from thoughts of you." My eyes were riveted to his. "I could not write up my notes from the interview. I was," he sighed, "distracted. The whole day, the whole next day—yesterday.

"So, last night I sent a message to Dani, because I have her

316

number, and we exchanged several messages. And I decided to come here, to see you." I found myself gently nodding. "And this morning, I got in my car—very early, before the sun came up—and I drove here."

"Oh, wait, you *drove* here?"

"*Oui.*"

"How long did it take?"

"It was about seven hours." He said it as though he'd just popped down to the shop a mile away.

"I can't believe you did that."

"I wanted to see you."

I let the words permeate, and my warring minds hushed. I was left with one definite thought. I wanted to kiss him. I *needed* to kiss him, but we were in those stupid deckchairs. I stood up as elegantly as I could and reached out my hand. "Come here."

He stood, effortlessly, and looked down at me, his features ill at ease and questioning.

"It is okay? That I came."

I had no words. Here was this man whom I barely knew—really, it was true, I didn't know the *man*—not yet—and he'd driven across half of Western Europe to see me. No man had ever done anything like that for me before. Instead of speaking, I wrapped a hand behind his neck, stood on my tiptoes and pulled his lips to meet mine.

It was as though we'd both been holding our breath and the kiss was letting it go.

His hands found the small of my back and our bodies pressed together. His lips were soft and warm, his kiss was ardent, confident. I never wanted it to end, and my lady parts were doing a jig in my freshly changed knickers. Maybe we wouldn't need the second bedroom after all. My libido, clearly in the lead, was smug.

But if that was true, and I really wanted to believe it was, why did I have tears in my eyes?

The kiss did eventually end, as all kisses do. He stroked the side of my face. I couldn't remember any man ever doing that before either. How was it possible to be so turned on and nearing emotional wreckage at the same time?

"Wait here," he said, leaving me perplexed and wanting more of him. He disappeared inside and after a few moments, came back out to collect the wine bottle and the platter of food. "Will you bring the glasses?" he asked.

"Of course." I followed him back inside. He had moved the sofa so it faced the window. He placed the platter and the wine on a small table in front of the sofa, then opened the window so the fresh breeze wafted into the room.

"Those chairs," he said. "Too far apart. Now we have the view and we can sit together."

"Perfect." I placed the glasses on the table and sat down— *much* more comfortable than the stupid deckchairs.

Jean-Luc sat beside me, reached for both glasses and handed me mine. "It is better, *oui?*"

"*Oui.*" I twisted my body so I faced him and put a throw pillow behind my back. I didn't know how much longer I could just sit there and make polite conversation. "You know what?"

"No."

318

"Look, I'm just going to come out and say this, because you came all this way and we've known each other a long time ..." My voice trailed off as I watched a frown settle on his face. "It's not something bad. I—I only want to be honest."

"Okay." The frown was still there.

"Here goes. I am madly, I mean *madly* attracted to you." As if I had flicked a switch, the frown changed into a grin, and he ran a hand through his hair. "See? That, right there. Every time you do that, *I* want to do it."

"Go ahead." He lifted his chin and raised that single eyebrow, challenging me. It was such a stupid thing to want to do—like out of a romance novel or something—but I lifted my hand and trailed a fingertip over his hairline, then ran my fingers through his hair, resting at the nape of his neck and stroking it softly. He closed his eyes and the softest moan escaped his lips.

My lady parts were on high alert. How could something so simple cause so much of a reaction—in both of us? I pulled my hand away and his eyes opened.

"See what I mean?" I asked quietly. He nodded almost imperceptibly. "And kissing you? I mean, that's just ... next level."

"Is that not a good thing?" Ah, there it was, the million-pound question. I was at the point where I needed to decide: put a halt to the physical stuff in case it led to unwelcome *feelings*, or ride it out, so to speak.

My libido won, a victory for the lady parts.

"It is a very good thing," I answered.

He placed his glass on the table, then leant close and kissed my cheek—not one of those quick taps, the French way of greeting someone, but a sensuous kiss where his lips lingered, and I felt his breath on my ear. *Oh, good lord.* "I agree," he whispered.

The kiss trailed under my jaw and I lifted my chin, gently leaning into to him. "So, if the kissing is 'next level', just think of what the lovemaking will be like." I had, Jean-Luc. I had spent many hours thinking about the lovemaking. Those were long coach rides.

The kissing moved to my throat and I reclined as Jean-Luc's body moved over mine. I had the presence of mind to keep my wine glass upright—just. He saw it and with amusement in his eyes, took it from me and placed it on the floor. He shifted, his body stretching the length of me, the weight of it held by one of his taut, muscular arms.

"Cat-er-ine," he almost whispered. "Look at me." I did. He dipped his face to mine and captured my lips with his. This kiss was possessive, hungry, and my arms went around his back, feeling the muscles rigid underneath his T-shirt. His erection pressed against my inner thighs and I lifted a hand to his neck and entwined my fingers in his hair.

I had never been so turned on in my life.

He broke the kiss and I nearly cried out in protest. He pressed his forehead to mine, our heavy breaths mingling in the space between us. "I have something, in my room."

"I'm on the pill," I said, understanding instantly.

"Do you want to go to the bedroom?"

"Not this time." This time? I obviously thought there would be at least one repeat performance, maybe more.

We both reached between us, undoing our own jeans. I shimmied mine down, along with my knickers, and he did the same. When he entered me, his eyes locked with mine and the pleasure was acute.

We fell into a harmonised rhythm, all the while watching each other intensely. I felt the orgasm building inside me, surprising me, and closed my eyes to give myself over to the wondrous cascade as I came. Jean-Luc was still moving inside me and when I opened my eyes a slight smile played on his lips. I gripped him with my legs, pulling him into me and he came with his face buried against my neck.

He lay on me, the full weight of him nearly crushing me, but I didn't want to let him go. Our breathing slowed, and he must have realised he was resting on me. He pressed himself up with one hand, hovering over me. "*Désolé, ma chérie.*" I shook my head. He kissed me, lightly, his tongue playing across my lips, and I closed my eyes and allowed myself to be licked and nibbled.

How utterly delightful.

Although we had shared something incredibly intimate, there were nervous chuckles as we reinstated our various pieces of clothing and tidied ourselves up. I excused myself to go to the bathroom.

Closing the door, I leant my head against it. "Holy cow," I said to myself quietly. I had never had an orgasm just from sex before. Ever. I thought they were a myth perpetuated by Hollywood scripts written by men. I may have just had the best sex of my life.

Whatever it was, my libido was doing a victory lap.

Of my two minds, I was fervently ignoring the one telling me to be kind with Jean-Luc's heart. If I really didn't want him falling in love with me again, I was doing a poor job of it. A niggling thought keep popping to the surface. *This is* not *how old friends reconnect.*

I walked over to the sink and turned on the cold tap. I splashed some water on my cheeks, careful to avoid my mascara. I looked at myself in the mirror above the sink. My cheeks were still flushed, and I had that post-orgasm glow cosmetics companies the world over have tried to bottle. I met my own eyes. "Do not break his heart. Again." I said it aloud—in a soft voice, yes—but *aloud* so I knew I was serious.

I had no intention of falling in love with Jean-Luc—or anyone—and I would have to figure out a way to let him know, *before* we parted ways again.

I had a quick wee, freshened up my lady parts again and went back out to the living room. Jean-Luc was standing with his back to the room, looking out the window. "Uh, I've finished in the bathroom." Men liked to freshen up after sex, too, right?

He turned, smiling, suddenly a little shy. "Thank you. *Oui,* just give me a moment." He almost jogged past me. *I guess they do.*

I hated this part—the after-sex part. It was why I rarely stayed the night, and I never let him—whoever he was—stay the night. It went: sex, goodnight, blissful sleep all by myself. But it was only 5:00pm. We were hardly going to bed at five o'clock!

Jean-Luc came back into the room and we stood looking

at each other like adolescents across a dance floor. "I think if we are to finish the wine and the cheese, we should move back out to the balcony, yes? Otherwise, we will just end up making love again, and although that is a nice way to spend the evening, the wine will get warm."

A burst of laughter broke free. *Thank God for a man with a sense of humour.*

"Agreed!" We carried the rest of the wine and the platter back to the view, making do with uncomfortable chairs while I told him about our adventures in Venice.

"And *then*, in *perfect* English—I mean, it sounded like he'd learnt English in *England*, he wishes us a good evening and says, 'I hope you enjoyed the gondola ride.'" Jean-Luc threw his head back and laughed, and it echoed out across the valley before us. *What a lovely sound.*

"Jaelee, she is, ah, how would you say?" He rolled his wine glass between his hands as he mulled over his choice of words.

"In French or in English?"

A finger pointed at me as if to say, "Good point." "Perhaps it is more flattering to her in French." He raised his eyebrows at me.

"Perhaps it is more flattering if we don't finish the sentence." He replied with a wry smile. "Anyway, Lou and I tipped him—heavily—and gave him a gushing thank you, which, I *hope*, made up for it."

"She was very bold, that night in Paris."

"When she approached you on the street?"

"*Oui.*"

"She was. I get the feeling she is quite forthright in general." His look told me I needed to explain "forthright". "She is clear about what she wants."

"Ah, *oui*. That seems true."

"Her being *forthright* worked out for us, though," I said.

"It did."

"But I can't help thinking, maybe her path in life would be smoother if she was more ..."

"Empathetic?" he supplied.

"Yes, sort of. Maybe, more *kind*. No, hold on, that sounds wrong. She is kind, in her own way. She's generous and she can be very thoughtful. Only I think her manner ... sometimes she could be less abrasive."

I could tell from his face it was another "look-up word". "Harsh," I added, to clarify.

"I understand."

"Do you get to converse in English much?" I hoped my non sequitur made sense.

He smiled and tilted his head. "Is it obvious?"

"What do you mean?"

"That I don't."

"No. I just had a thought that it might be a little exhausting for you, translating everything I'm saying."

"It is not conscious, or it is a little for the first few minutes of speaking, yes, but soon I start to think in English and it is fine."

"Good. *Parce que mon français est très mauvais*."

"She says in perfect French."

I shrugged. "That's my problem. I can say I don't know

how to speak a language in such a way that I sound fluent in the language. It can be very confusing for people."

"I am sure."

We finished the bottle and Jean-Luc went back inside for another of the same. He opened it while standing in the doorway, and he lightly scolded us for quaffing too quickly. "I only have one more bottle after this one."

"No problem. I think we can pace ourselves for the rest of the night."

"But there is tomorrow night too, *n'est-ce pas?*"

I hadn't thought of that. "Tomorrow night?"

"*Oui*, you are here until Tuesday morning, yes? I have booked for two nights."

It was both a lovely and a terrifying thought. Most of me *wanted* to spend the night, have the whole of the next day with him, then spend another night with him before saying goodbye—*so* much of me—maybe ninety per cent. But the cautious me, the part that knew I wasn't going to start a relationship with him, hesitated. For a second.

I let the ninety per cent win. "That sounds wonderful. What do you think we should do while we're here?"

Besides have lots and lots of sex. Oh, and take a bath.

Chapter 16

After a hot-pink sunset so beautiful I'd rushed inside for my phone so I could take photos, Jean-Luc cooked us a quick and simple dinner of pan-fried trout, baked potatoes topped with farm-fresh butter, and steamed asparagus—my favourite.

I love most meals I don't have to cook myself, but Jean-Luc clearly knew what he was doing in the kitchen and everything was delicious. I also loved watching him gracefully move around the compact kitchen, as though he'd lived in the apartment for years, instead of a few hours. I let my mind linger on the fantasy again, the one where we lived together and it was the end of a normal workday. It was naughty of me, indulging those thoughts. Perhaps I could blame the wine.

I loved the food, but Jean-Luc had served me as much as he'd served himself and being "just little", I was nearly full when I placed my knife and fork next to each other on the plate.

"That was delicious," I said, hoping to reassure him.

"You are finished?" He eyed the half-a-potato and small piece of trout I'd left on the plate.

327

"Yes. I loved it, but I think you're like Anna, wanting to feed me up." He smiled, seemingly satisfied with my answer.

"So, you do not have room for dessert?" he asked as he stood and cleared away the plates.

My mind leapt to something extremely adult and a little crass, so I left the thought unsaid. "Uh, not right this minute, but I do love most desserts. What's on offer?" *Is it you?*

"Just this." He held up a block of dark chocolate Lindt.

"Hah! Brilliant. I love dark chocolate. A lucky guess."

"No," he shook his head, "I, of course, knew this about you." We both knew there was no way he could have known. I'd been mad for milk chocolate as a teen.

"Right, I see." We smiled at each other across the kitchen island.

"Or, I could run a bath for you?"

"Oh, yes, please." Once he'd said it, all I could think about was luxuriating in that bath. And once I'd followed Jean-Luc into the bathroom, where he turned on the taps and poured in a generous dollop of bubble bath, all I could think about was sharing the bath with him.

He lit the three candles that sat on the windowsill and flicked off the bright bathroom lights, and the room filled with a warm yellow glow. "There," he said, turning to me at last. "Oh, let me get your wine."

"Bring yours too." He looked at me, his head tilted to the side and a slow smile spread across his face.

"I'll be right back."

***

"This may be the best bath I've ever had."

"Really?"

"Actually, I'd like to go on the record to say that this *is* the best bath I've ever had. There's that," I said, pointing to the view, "there's this tub—amazing—and the bubble bath smells divine. I mean, honestly, I am being spoiled for every other bath for the rest of my life."

"Anything else?" he teased.

"Hmm. Oh, and the wine!"

"I see."

We were head to toe in the giant bath and the bubbles were high under my chin. They only came up to Jean-Luc's chest, which was muscular with fine dark hair in a triangle that I knew trailed down his stomach in a thin line. He had a terrific body—not too bulky like some guys—just deliciously fit and masculine. I stared at this chest and arms shamelessly while he held one of my feet captive between his hands.

"Oh, and you," I added nonchalantly. I placed my wine glass on the windowsill.

"I wondered if you noticed I was here." I looked into his eyes and pulled my foot from his hands. Carefully, so we didn't lose any bathwater, I crawled up his body until I was lying on top of him.

"Oh, I've noticed." I kissed him, my tongue teasing his. "Ready for round two, Monsieur Caron?" His right hand trailed down my back, lingered on the curve of my bum, then cupped it firmly.

"*Mais oui, ma chérie.*" His mouth took mine hungrily, and

neither of us cared that the water sloshed over the sides of the bath.

Some time later, I didn't want to leave the bath, to break contact with Jean-Luc, but the water was getting cold. He must have been thinking the same thing, because he pulled me closer, then pushed the hot water tap into action with his toe.

I nestled into the crook of his arm, my fingers tracing a path over the features of his face. His thick black lashes resting on his cheeks, that proud French nose, the wide cheekbones, those full, soft lips, his brows, the line of his chin.

He is without a doubt the most beautiful man I've ever seen. And *the best lover I've ever had*, I thought. *I wonder how he feels about friends with benefits.*

He murmured softly with pleasure at my delicate caresses, and his eyes opened to stare into mine. He landed a soft kiss on my lips. "We should get out of this bath, *chérie.*" He held up his wrinkly fingertips. "We are like the prune, *non?*"

I sighed, resigned to leave our watery love nest, then climbed out and reached for a towel, wrapping it tautly around me. I shivered a little in the cool air, then turned to watch the magnificent man emerge from the water, his long limbs swathed in that smooth olive skin, slick with water. Before reaching for a towel, he self-consciously fixed his hair, which was such a sweet gesture, my heart leapt a little.

He briskly dried himself, then wrapped a towel around his waist, while I stood, transfixed, dripping onto the sodden bathmat. His hand ran through his damp hair again, and he fixed his eyes on mine. Without speaking, he knelt before me, and prised the towel from its loose knot above my breasts. He took two corners in his hands then ran the towel down the length of my left leg, drying me.

His face was a picture of concentration as he dried each leg in turn, then the crevice between them, my stomach, my back, the fabric soft against my skin as he slowly stood, following the curves and lines of my body with the towel, drying every part of me.

My face tipped to his and he finally met my eyes as he wrapped the towel around my shoulders and pulled me close to him.

"Catherine, *tu es si belle*," he said quietly. There was something in his voice, the way it caught slightly, that tugged at my heart and I felt the sting of tears in my eyes. *No. Stop it. This is sex, amazing sex—that's all.*

I wanted to believe that. I *had* to believe that. I was *not* going to fall in love with Jean-Luc.

But whatever I believed in that moment, I wanted him. My arms reached up and fastened behind his neck and I pulled him into a kiss. I didn't even feel the towel drop to the floor as he scooped me up and carried me out of the bathroom.

It's probably not surprising that we didn't use the second bedroom.

There are times in your life when you're so awestruck you run out of words and your heart leaps about in your chest with glee. I got to experience that with Jean-Luc the following day on our journey up—and down—the mountain.

Our plan was reasonably simple: catch a train to Kleine Scheidegg and hike back down to Lauterbrunnen. What I didn't know, as I booked our train tickets online, was how incredible the excursion would be. Had I known beforehand, it would have zipped straight to the top of my bucket list.

The train that went to Kleine Scheidegg was possibly the cutest train in the world—boxy, red with yellow stripes, and giant picture windows. If she was in the cast of *Thomas the Tank Engine*, she (I was sure she was a she) would have been called "Inge".

Jean-Luc gave me the window seat, chalking up another point for how good a friend he was. *Just friends, just friends, just friends with benefits.*

The slate-grey mountains surrounding us were craggy and pointed and, in many places, we could see the striations of the earth's crust. They wore patchy blankets of white—in some places the snow seemed dense and deep, and in others the rock asserted itself, the snow just a dusting.

The mountains seemed to have been placed just so, a design to their haphazardness, as though they were modelled on the Toblerone and not the other way around. Quite honestly, I wouldn't have put it past the Swiss. They are master engineers, and I knew that in some of those mountains were bunkers, stocked and ready for whatever apocalyptic antics the world's politicians came up with.

In our foreground, was Swiss-green grass so vibrant it didn't look real as it swathed the rolling foothills. Their roundness contrasted starkly with the mountains, as though someone had painted a giant incongruous backdrop behind them.

There were dense pockets and loose smatterings of wild-flowers, throw-rugs of white, with dots of blue, yellow and pink.

Not quite Richard Attenborough, but this English teacher does have a few descriptive words up her sleeve.

A little way into our journey, the couple in front of us opened their window, sliding the bottom half up, and the wash of fresh air was invigorating. It smelled like sunshine and grass and had a slightly sweet smell, perhaps the wild-flowers.

"Well, this is lovely," I said.

"It's incredible."

"You haven't been here before, right? I didn't ask you."

"Here? No. I've been to Bern and to Zurich—for work. But, when you are interviewing and writing, there are not many opportunities to sightsee."

"So, the travelling journalist's glamorous life is not always so glamorous."

He chuckled. "It is almost never glamorous. It is hotel rooms—often cheap ones, because half the time I pay for them myself—and trains and airports and me alone in my apartment."

"What's your apartment like?"

"It is ... an apartment. Nice, I think."

"'Nice'? Really? From the writer?"

He shrugged. "It was once the, uh, attic (nearly a 'look-up word', I noted) and the floor below, and the building is old—nineteenth century—so there have been some adaptations (knowing he meant 'renovations', I didn't correct him). I spent the first few months hitting my head on the rafters. The edges of the bedroom are quite low. But it has good light and large windows and I like it."

I pictured him in his attic flat, typing away at a small desk under a gable window, and I longed to see it.

"And, you know, it is mine, so ..."

"You own it?"

"Well, me and the bank, *non?*"

"Wow. I rent. With two other people." I wasn't sure why I'd volunteered information about my flatmates as it was very close to dangerous territory and I didn't want to discuss Alex with him. *So, my lover before you is the guy who lives in my flat.*

I steered the conversation away from Jane and Alex. "I don't think I'll ever be able to buy in London—a schoolteacher's salary and all that."

"Well, Paris is probably similar. I was fortunate. Well, unfortunate. My grandmother, when she died, she left a substantial amount to Cecile and me. Of course, I would rather have my grandmother with us. She was quite a formidable woman. She would have liked you, I think."

I smiled at him. "Really?"

"Yes, she was *forthright*," he said, using the word I'd taught him the night before, "and very funny. I think she would have seen those things in you."

So, I was forthright and funny. I didn't mind the description, especially "forthright"—because that was not how most people characterised my propensity to speak my mind.

"I'm sorry I didn't get to meet her."

334

"Yes, well, if you had ever come to visit ..." He was teasing, but the words stung a little. Yes, I had been young and it would have been hard to save up the money to go to France—especially in the late 90s when airfares from Australia to anywhere in the world were ridiculously expensive—but I could have. Maybe if I hadn't met Scott, I would have gone to France and seen Jean-Luc and met his whole family, including his grandmother.

"What was her name?"

"Eleanor. We called her *Grand-mère* Ellie."

"Ellie," I said quietly to myself. "I'm sorry I never came." Another thing to regret.

"You do not need to apologise—again."

"I wanted to come." I glanced at him and he was nodding, a small frown on his face. "You know, I asked my mum to send me one of your letters." I didn't mention it was the final one, and I'm not sure why I thought it was a good idea to bring it up at all.

"Oh, yes?" He seemed curious, maybe even amused.

"Yes. I have it here. She scanned it." I unlocked my phone and scrolled to the PDF attached to Mum's email. He held out his hand to read it. "Before you do, I want you to tell me which parts were supposed to be my clues for the whole ... you know ..."

"For the childhood love?" His depiction of his younger self's feelings surprised me. It seemed like he was playing them down.

"Uh, yes, exactly." I handed him the phone and watched his face as he read. His eyes crinkled in a smile and his lips pursed a few times, clearly from amusement at what he'd written. He scrolled to the top and I watched his eyes scan back over the letter.

"Here," he said, pointing to the part about the cute Australian girl. "Here." He showed me the invitation to come to France. "And here." He pointed to how he'd signed off with many kisses. "And, I think all of it."

"Oh, really? The whole thing was pretty much a love letter?"

"*Oui*," he said, definitively. He handed me the phone.

"Uh, so we *did* say the part about the Australian girl and the kisses, but the whole thing?" I teased.

"We?" he countered. *Oops.*

"Fine, I'm sprung, but after what you said in Rome, I needed help, so I asked the girls. I thought maybe I'd missed something."

Amusement danced in his eyes. "You did miss something. You missed all the clues. And that is only *one* letter."

I bit my bottom lip. "Will you at least concede that it's a little, um, unclear?" The word seemed to translate.

He lifted his hand, his thumb and forefinger close together. "*Oui*, a little."

I rolled my eyes and nudged him with my right side. "Right, sure."

"I think the young Jean-Luc thought he was very clever and a great wooer of women."

"Hah!" We shared a smile at his expense.

"And I think the young Catherine was a little self-absorbed and clueless," I added.

"*Oui, c'est vrai.*" That's true.

"Hey!" I backhanded his shoulder.

"*Désolé, désolé!*" Sorry, sorry.

"I'll *désolé* you."

He reached for my hand and I let him hold it, our fingers laced together. I leant into him and watched out the window as the most beautiful landscape I'd ever seen unfolded.

"I have something for you, too, when we go back," he said quietly. "One of your letters." My stomach clenched. I didn't want to read that wretched letter, but all I could say was, "Oh." I had to put it out of my mind, or it could ruin the rest of the day, possibly the rest of my time with him. I'd face the music—I owed him that—but not right then.

The train arrived in Kleine Scheidegg less than an hour after departing from Lauterbrunnen and we disembarked into a sunny morning in the low twenties. We both donned sunglasses and stood on the platform looking around. I supposed it could be called a town, but really it was just a small collection of buildings—nice buildings, but not much more.

Its main purpose was to serve as the junction between the train line we'd ridden and the line which went to the top of the mountain, Jungfrau. I'd thought about going to the top. It was an optional excursion some people on the tour were doing, but it cost more than a hundred pounds and that was two designer handbags if I got them at TK Maxx.

"Shall we look around before we hike down?" asked Jean Luc.

"Definitely, and I want morning tea first." Jean-Luc's idea of breakfast leant towards "Parisian"—sans the cigarette, but essentially just a cappuccino. Our apartment, as I was dangerously calling it in my head, was stocked with the bare essentials of coffee pods and milk, but no teabags and nothing much else by way of breakfast. In short, I was starving and desperate for some tea.

We homed in on the aptly named Chalet Restaurant Lounge, where I resisted the urge to order *Glühwein*, the spiced mulled wine which I associated with Christmas markets, and settled instead for tea and a slice of *apfelstrudel*. I was fairly certain I could never move to Switzerland as I would soon run out of money. Tea and a pastry came to the equivalent of £8.50, or a decent meal at Nando's.

I savoured my breakfast and stared out the window as I ate and drank, pinching myself that I was halfway up a Swiss mountain. Jean-Luc had another coffee and stole little pieces of my strudel. As I've mentioned, I don't like to share, so after the third time I slapped his hand.

"Go and get your own or leave mine alone." He smiled at me cheekily. I took the moment to appreciate that he was just as beautiful as the scenery, maybe more. *How could Vanessa divorce him?* It was a perilous thought, one that hinted at a future and falling in love. I pushed it aside.

"Excuse me for a moment," I said, as I crumpled up my napkin and stood up.

"I need the toilet also," he said. I felt a little foolish for being shy about needing a wee. When we were teenagers, we spent so much time together that I'd boldly announce it, then leave the room before he had a chance to reply.

We both headed to our respective bathrooms and recon-

vened on the deck of the restaurant. Jean-Luc was waiting for
me when I came out.

"Ready?" he asked, looking up from his phone.

"Yes." I looked around for what I hoped would be obvious
trail signage.

"It's this way," he said, pointing. He held up his phone
briefly. "I looked it up."

"You mean, you cheated?"

"I mean, I looked it up so we don't get lost on a mountain."
He raised that eyebrow at me.

"Good point," I conceded.

I'd dressed for hiking as best I could from the clothes I'd
packed. I was wearing jeans, a white T-shirt and my sneakers.
I wore my messenger bag across my body, in it a bottle of
water, a cardigan in case it got chilly, and my usual bag
stuff—minus my Kindle, as I didn't think there would be
many opportunities to stop and read.

On the trail, heading in both directions, were some seriously kitted-out hikers—proper hiking boots, walking poles,
which looked a lot like ski poles, Camelbacks, windbreakers
and hiking trousers made from that expensive quick-dry
fabric. In comparison, Jean-Luc and I looked like we were
heading out for a picnic, not hiking down a mountain. I hoped
we weren't going to hit any rough terrain.

I needn't have worried, because the Swiss do many things
well and, as I soon discovered, hiking trails are one of them.
The path was firmly packed and clearly marked. There were
no tripping hazards and a gentle slope took us all the way
down the mountain. Not long into the walk, I realised that

it was everyone else, in their hundreds of pounds' worth of gear, who was overdressed.

Jean-Luc was kind enough to let me set the pace. His legs were much longer than mine, and I really didn't want to have to half-jog down the mountain just to keep up with him. Still, it was a good opportunity to work off some of the gelato, pizza, bread, and cheese which made up ninety per cent of what I was eating, so it was a brisk pace.

We were in the midst of a conversation about our respective jobs, when Jean-Luc asked, "So, do you think you will ever go back to Australia?"

"You mean to live?"

"*Oui.*"

"Oh. I don't know. Why do you ask?"

"I wondered if you could still teach there."

"I suppose. I mean, my qualifications are from there, but I'd have to register with the state education board and get certified. I could, but I'm not sure why you asked."

"I think about it sometimes, going back to Australia."

"Oh, you do?"

"Yes. I mean, I had a home there—only for a year, but still … I think it would be interesting to live there again. Practise my English."

"Your English is great."

"It is rusty."

"Hardly."

Wait, is he thinking about us going back to Australia together?

That was the thing about hiking and breathing boundless gulps of fresh mountain air—great for thinking, which was either terrific or troubling. For me, at that moment, thinking too much was probably inadvisable. Because of the great gaping rabbit hole on the edge of which I was balancing precariously.

"Have you thought of living anywhere else in the world?" I asked, steering the conversation away from Australia.

"I have thought about going back to Central America."

"Wait, you've been there, or you've lived there?"

"We lived there—a short while, only six months."

"And 'we' is …?"

"Vanessa and me."

"Oh."

"She was doing research there. She is an anthropologist." *Of course she is*. Beautiful *and* brilliant. An image of the stunning Vanessa—the one from his Facebook friends—imposed itself on my mind. She dressed like Lara Croft and made incredible discoveries in the jungles of Peru. Peru was in Central America, right?

Well, since he brought her up …

"And you said you're still friends?"

"Yes." No further explanation or additional information. Men were so obtuse sometimes. Didn't he know I was fishing?

"So, what does that mean? Do you see each other often?"

Not content to balance on the edge of the rabbit hole, I was now pirouetting around it—wearing rollerblades. Conversationally speaking, it was perilous ground, but I couldn't help myself.

His reply seemed to take forever and I imagined that the

writer Jean-Luc was forming a faultless response. "Not so much. Perhaps two or three times a year." Well, that was *nothing*—amiable, but not excessive. I could live with that.

But why would I need to live with any arrangement at all? He was my current lover and an old friend whom I hoped to stay in touch with. I had no proprietorship. Was I just testing my own waters? If Jean-Luc and I did become romantically involved, would I be all right with him seeing his ex-wife a few times a year? I supposed I'd have to be.

It was moot anyway, as I didn't want a relationship.

We came to a part of the trail which gave us a two-hundred-and-seventy-degree panorama of the valley below, including the town of Lauterbrunnen—or at least, what I presumed was Lauterbrunnen. I hardly wanted to break out Google Maps and spoil the adventure. We stopped for a water break and I took a few photos. Avoiding a digital map was one thing, but I wanted photos of that vista!

"Well, this is not terrible," I said after I'd taken a series of shots my phone would stitch together into a panorama.

He smiled. "No, it is not terrible."

"Can we take a selfie?" I asked, suddenly shy.

"Of course."

"Here, you have longer arms." I handed him my phone. He came and stood behind me, one arm around my waist as we looked up into the phone's camera. He took the photo. "Oh, and one without sunglasses." I didn't know if we'd see each other again after Switzerland, and I wanted proper proof of how gorgeous he was, especially those green eyes. I lifted my sunglasses onto my head and he palmed his.

"Ready?"

"Yep." We both grinned at the camera. *That's going to be a great shot.*

Before he let me go, he pulled me close to him and nuzzled my neck. "You will send those to me, yes?"

"Absolutely." I turned around inside the frame of his arms and put mine around his neck. "Kiss me."

He did. I liked it—a lot.

A couple in their fifties were approaching us on the trail on their way up the mountain. I was self-conscious about snogging in front of strangers and pulled away from Jean-Luc. He handed me my phone and I sent him the selfies. As he responded to the ping of his phone, I turned back to the view and realised what it reminded me of. "I feel like Julie Andrews up here."

"Like ...?" He cocked his head a little.

"You know, from *The Sound of Music.*"

"Ahh, yes, but that was in Austria."

"Yes, but it still reminds me of the opening scene." I threw my arms out wide and started singing, "The hills are alive with the sound of music ... ahhhh-ahhh-ahh-ahhhhhh," to the valley below.

Kissing in front of strangers, not so much. Singing? Why not?

He laughed. "You actually have a good voice."

He was being nice. My voice is *all right*—mediocre at best. Instead of replying, I started walking and kept singing. "With songs they have sung for a thousand yeeeeeaaaaarrrs." The last note was quite a high one and I almost hit it.

"So, you know all the words?"

To show that, yes, I *did* know all the words, I kept singing. He shook his head, smiling, and I knew there were eye crinkles behind those sunglasses. I sang the entire song at full voice, nodding to the few people we passed, who seemed rather amused, perhaps even entertained. When I got to, "And I'll sing once mooooooorrre," I stopped still and directed the last line of the song back out over the valley.

I couldn't say if my bow or Jean-Luc's whistle came first, but I was quite pleased with myself and grinned at him as I headed off down the trail. He jogged to catch up to me.

"You are quite the talent," he said. I took it as a straight-up compliment.

"Thank you. I know." He laughed, and we fell into step together.

As we approached the valley floor some time later, we came to a paddock of cows—those extremely beautiful Swiss dairy cows. One of them had her head between the wires of the fence, eating some tall grass on the other side. I stopped and approached her slowly. Those big brown eyes looked at me, but she didn't stop chewing. I pulled up some grass and held it out to her. She took it gently from my hand and chewed slowly, all the while watching me. I reached out and stroked her nose and she let me.

"Look at her eyes," I said over my shoulder.

Jean-Luc stood a little way away watching me with a smile. "They are very beautiful."

"Hello, girl," I said as I pulled her some more grass. Other cows started to make their way over. Very friendly, Swiss cows.

I got a few more pats in and left them to eat their Swiss-green grass and the occasional wildflower.

"I might have to become a vegetarian," I said as we got back on the trail. We could see the town not too far ahead.

"Those are dairy cows," he said.

"I know, but still … I mean, I try not to think about it, where meat comes from. I go to the shop and buy it on a tray. If I spend any time thinking about the actual animal, I don't want … ugh, maybe I'm a closet vegetarian. Maybe it's right there below the surface. You've never been a vegetarian, have you?"

"*Mon dieu, non.*"

"As you know, Dad raised us as total carnivores. I still eat everything, beef, *lamb*—oh, God, I love lamb."

"I remember the barbecues at your house."

"Oh, I miss those. And *right* before I moved to London, Dad learnt how to make his own sausages. They were unbelievable."

"You could learn."

"Probably not. I am rather hopeless in the kitchen—and, besides, meat is far more expensive in the UK than Australia. Mostly, I stick to single-girl dinners. I make a great cup of tea though—and toast. I'm good at toast."

"Toast?" he sounded amused.

"Yes. Most people don't know this, but it's easy to mess up toast. *I* do it correctly."

"I see. So, it is your kryptonite, but toasted, it is okay …?" At first, I wondered what the heck he was talking about. Then I remembered Anna's restaurant in Rome and the breadbasket.

"Good catch. I *do* occasionally buy bread, but only proper artisanal bread. And when I *do* buy it, I make excellent toast."

"I see," he replied, a mock-serious tone to his voice. "And what is a 'single-girl dinner'?"

"Oh, uh ..." I was suddenly self-conscious.

"I am curious, because most of the time I am by myself in the evening. I wonder if it is the same as a 'single-man dinner'."

He was teasing me, and I could feel my cheeks getting hot. I'd been able to talk to him about anything when we were teenagers—big picture, life-changing stuff, right down to the minutiae, so why was something so trivial getting a rise out of me? I was annoyed—at him for teasing me, but mostly at myself. He was getting under my skin.

I forged ahead regardless.

"A single-girl dinner is usually something like frozen peas or asparagus cooked in the microwave, a handful of cherry tomatoes, maybe some olives, and a tin of salmon—for protein. Or, I eat a Lean Cuisine, or some ready-made soup from Marks & Spencer. I certainly can't cook fish like you did last night and even if I could, I probably wouldn't bother just for me."

How on earth had I ended up defending eating salmon from a tin as though it was my basic human right? I stole a glance at him. Still amused, the bastard.

He reached down and took my hand. "So, we should buy some bread when we get into town—for dinner. I think it is your turn to cook, yes?"

There was a beat before I burst out laughing. "All right, very funny. How about we go out for dinner instead?"

"A *very* good idea." Still teasing me.

"Hey!"

"We could perhaps meet your friends, ask them to join us?"

"Oh, fun! Yes, let's do that."

"*Bien.* And, Catherine, it is okay that you do not cook."

"I *know*." *Touchy much? Lighten up, Cat.*

He pulled my hand up to his lips and kissed it. "I am happy to be the chef."

What? I suddenly realised why I'd been so apprehensive about the whole cooking conversation. It was about real-life—domesticity—and it had led exactly where my unconscious mind was worried it would—to Jean-Luc thinking about us in a relationship, sharing a home, divvying up domestic duties.

I'd stepped into the rabbit hole.

Chapter 17

We met the others, Craig and the girls, at a family-style restaurant close to where Jean-Luc and I were staying.

"Hey," I said, giving Craig a big hug. "How are you?"

"Great. I went up Jungfrau today."

"Oh, wow, I want to hear all about that." He and Jean-Luc shook hands and started chatting, and I took the opportunity to hug my girls.

"You look *happy*," said Dani, a grin on her face.

"I am. *Very*."

She giggled with approval, then walked around to the other side of our table and sat down. Craig took the seat next to her, still chatting with Jean-Luc, who sat opposite him.

"You're sitting with me tomorrow," said Jaelee. "I'm living vicariously through you. I want details." It wasn't the time to remind her that she'd had her own adventures at the *château*. She took the chair next to Dani.

"I've missed you, Lou." I reached up for a hug. Only a day had gone by since I'd seen her, but when you go cold turkey on your bus bestie, it stings a little.

"Me too."

"Sit next to me?" I asked. I ended up in the middle of Jean-Luc and Lou. I could hardly talk about him with him sitting *right there*, but she and I would catch up when we left Lauterbrunnen. At the thought, my stomach lurched. Leaving Lauterbrunnen meant saying goodbye to Jean-Luc until the next time—if there would be one.

As the table filled with plates of wursts and varieties of potatoes *and* as we ordered a second round of Appenzeller, a beer, the conversation whizzed between us as we filled each other in on our days.

Craig, Dani, and Jaelee had all gone up Jungfrau and I was a little jealous as they described the view from the mountain top, though not so much of Craig's depiction of the ice caves— far too closed in. I got a little breathless at the thought of them.

Lou had gone on a valley hike with some of the others from the tour group. "Oh, I totally agree, Swiss cows are the prettiest cows I've ever seen," she said.

"See?" I asked Jean-Luc.

He raised his hands in surrender. "You are right. They are the most beautiful cows in the world." Teasing me again. "Actually, I got a good photograph of Catherine feeding a cow."

He did? "You did?"

"Oh, I want to see!" Dani was like a kid sometimes.

Jean-Luc took his phone out of his pocket and scrolled to the photo, then handed it to Craig. It went all the way around the table before I got to see it. It was actually a nice photo of me. I looked at Jean-Luc over the top of the phone. "You like it?" he asked.

"I do, yes."

"I will put it on Facebook?" I'd seen his Facebook feed. He hardly ever went on Facebook and now he was going to post a photo of me to it.

"Uh, sure." He smiled.

"And, there is one more thing," he said to the table, taking the phone from me. "Catherine, she is quite the singer." He was scrolling on his phone again and I frowned at him.

"You didn't."

"But, yes, I did." He tapped the phone, then laid it in the middle of the table. My terrible singing erupted from the phone and everyone leant in to watch the video. My frown was met with a grin, and when I looked around the table the expressions ranged from amused—Jaelee and Craig—to outright delighted—Dani and Lou. When I took a bow on the screen— how had I missed that he was filming me?—Lou clapped.

Jean-Luc took his phone off the table and pocketed it. He reached around my shoulders and pulled me towards him so he could kiss the top of my head.

Like a boyfriend would.

Just friends. Madly in lust. Do not let him fall in love with you.

At my next thought, however, the wurst hardened into a knot in my stomach.

Whatever this is, I want it. Want, want, want.

"So, are you coming?" Lou pressed. She and the others had invited us to the chalet for a party—a "what were you doing when the cops knocked on the door?" party.

"But what does that even mean?" I asked.

Jaelee butted in. "Exactly what it says. That's how you dress. Say the cops are knocking on your door—what are you doing at that exact moment? And you wear *that*."

"I think it's clever," added Dani.

"Yeah, it's so we can dress up from whatever we have in our suitcases," said Lou. The three of them were fully drinking the Kool-Aid.

I looked at Jean-Luc. "Do you want to go?"

He shrugged, smiling. "Sure. We have drink, some dancing, *oui*? Sounds fun."

What sounded fun to me was going back to our apartment, cracking open the third bottle of wine and giving the bathtub another go. I looked at the expectant pairs of eyes. Even Craig was ganging up on me.

"Sure," I said, resigned.

"Geez, don't go out of your way to hang out with us or anything," said Jaelee. It was a little snarky, but maybe I was being selfish wanting to spend the rest of the evening with Jean-Luc, just the two of us.

He and I returned to our apartment, promising to meet Lou in the chalet's lobby before going to the party. It was being held in the basement and I wondered if that was a Ventureseek thing, the subterranean dance parties.

Jean-Luc and I couldn't walk through town in just our costumes. We donned enough clothing to be appropriate and when we got to the chalet, Lou took us up to the room she was sharing with Jaelee, Dani, and three others, so could we put the finishing touches on our costumes.

And by "finishing touches" I mean we took off some of what we'd worn to traverse the town.

What *we* were doing when the cops knocked on the door was making love. I was wearing one of Jean-Luc's dress shirts and nothing else and he was wearing jeans and nothing else. Undressed in our costumes, we needed to make a couple of tweaks before we were ready—I mussed up my hair, planted some lipstick kisses all over Jean-Luc's face, then smeared my own lipstick.

"Wow. You guys look *hot!*" said Lou.

"Thanks, Lou. You too." She was half-dressed, and she'd taken it literally. One half of her was dressed, and the other half was in a bra and undies. It was an impressive feat of engineering, and at least I wasn't the only woman showing some flesh.

We met the others in the lobby. Dani was dressed all in black—black leggings, black turtleneck T-shirt and black ballet flats. "I'm a cat burglar," she said. *Cop out*, I thought. Jaelee, in a shocking lack of vanity, had rollers in her hair—*she brought rollers?*—and some sort of goopy green mask on her face, and she was wearing pyjamas. I applauded her creativity *and* her willingness to look so ordinary—definitely off-brand for her.

Craig was in drag. "Oh, my God, you look amazing!" I laughed.

"Dani and Jaelee helped with the makeup, and Louise with the outfit."

"Amazing," I said again, genuinely in shock. At eighteen, I would have been far too self-conscious to wear something

353

that outrageous. I just adored our baby bro. When we got to the bar downstairs, the Kiwi boys were also in drag. I gave Jason a hug. "You look great," I said over the music. "You're a very pretty guy!"

He shook his head. "Stop it."

"No, really!"

"Really?" He genuinely seemed to care.

"Yes! You look great!" He beamed. I waved to the other guys and gave them the thumbs up. Lachie looked me up and down and gave me one in return. I was fine with that; I knew I looked good.

"Drink?" asked Jean-Luc in my ear.

"Yes, please!" He kissed my neck and I nuzzled against his lips. When I watched him walk to the bar, I saw many sets of eyes following him. The tour's ratio of women-to-men was not in our favour, and Jean-Luc wearing only jeans was a sight to behold. I was looking forward to beholding him all over our apartment later.

"So, things are going well with Jean-Luc?" asked Lou.

"Yes. It's been lovely."

She looked at me, dubious. "Lovely?"

"Fine. It's screaming bloody hot. Oh, my God, Lou, it's the best sex I've ever had!"

She held up a hand, wanting a high-five. I gave her one. "I'm living vicariously through you, you know."

"That's what Jaelee said at dinner," I replied, laughing. "No pressure."

She smiled at me. "I'm gonna go dance, okay?"

"I'll see you out there in a little bit."

I looked out over the venue. It was dimly lit, but much bigger than the converted wine cellar under the *château*. There was a mirror ball—of course there was—and a DJ, who was playing a decent mix of noughties dance music.

With the energy in the room—the music, the costumes, my friends—I was already glad we were there. I saw Jean-Luc heading back to me from the bar, two tumblers in hand.

"Vodka tonic," he said into my ear.

"Great, thank you." We clinked our glasses against each other and I took a sip.

"You look *magnifique*, Catherine," he said, his breath warm on my ear. I wondered if we were going to last long at the party. "Very sexy."

I threw him a coy look and shook my mussed-up hair. "Even with my bed hair?"

"I think especially with your bed hair."

"You look pretty damned hot yourself, Monsieur Caron." I lifted my chin to him and pursed my lips. He rewarded me with a kiss.

"We could finish these and go back to the apartment," I said.

"Uh, well, I know you can sing, but before we leave, I want to see if you can dance."

"Is that so?"

"*Oui.*"

I was actually a pretty good dancer—far better than I was a singer, in any case. "Well," I said, putting my barely touched drink on the nearest table. "Let's dance then."

Not waiting to see if he followed me, I made a beeline for

the dance floor and when I found a spot, started dancing. I felt him come up from behind and press against me, wrapping one arm around my waist as we moved in time with Justin Timberlake.

Stand aside, Justin. We're bringing sexy back all by ourselves.

At first, I was aware of being watched, but soon it felt like we were alone on the dance floor. My God, he was sexy— definitely the hottest man I'd ever laid hands on. I was so completely in lust, I thought of asking Lou to "borrow" her room.

"Low" by Flo Rida started and Jean-Luc surprised the hell out of me by singing along. I couldn't hear him above the music, but he knew all the words. "Them apple bottom jeans ..." he mouthed. I danced apart from him, watching as he got "... low, low, low, low ..." I grinned and he waggled his eyebrows at me. At the end of the song, I clapped and he pulled me into a hug. "You are not the only one who sings," he said in my ear. I leant back so I could kiss him.

"Can we please leave now? I want you all to myself." "Get Lucky" by Daft Punk started and I jumped up and down.

"After this one?" he asked. I nodded as I started to move to my favourite 70s throw-back song. Lou came over. "Bus stop!" she called out over the music.

"Oh yes! But I don't know if I remember it."

"Follow me!" She started the moves and after the first round, I was fluent again. Jean-Luc had joined in and soon we were a group of about fifteen. We wouldn't have won any dance competitions, but I was giggling with glee by the time the song ended. There was a round of hugs and high-fives from the impromptu dance troupe, and when I flapped a hand in front of my sweaty face, Lou led the way off the dance floor. "I need a drink," she said. "Want one?"

"We've got drinks over here." I pointed to the table where our vodka tonics sat, the ice well and truly melted. She nodded and went to the bar. At our table, I took a sip of my vodka. I should probably have been drinking water after all that dancing but watered-down vodka would have to do.

I searched the dance floor for Jean-Luc. He'd accumulated quite the fan club since I'd left him. Six women danced around him, all laughing or smiling. He was too. I didn't mind. I knew he was coming home with me.

Lou came back with her drink. "You guys are really cute together."

My eyes flew to her face, but she was watching the dancing. "What do you mean?" She looked at me and I knew from her expression I'd spoken too harshly. "Sorry."

"It's okay. You're not ...?" She let the question trail off as she shook her head, questioningly.

"I don't know, Lou. I mean, look at him. He's so hot, it's ridiculous. And I wasn't kidding about the sex. It's definitely the best I've ever had."

"*And* he adores you. That's obvious."

"But, I—"

"Cat, come on. He came all this way for you, and you guys get along so well."

"He ... he's amazing. But I'm really scared I'm going to break his heart again."

"Why?" She was clearly baffled.

"Because I don't want anything beyond *this*." I caught myself. My voice had shot up about three octaves. I was getting defensive and Lou didn't deserve that. *I* was the one I was annoyed with. I took a breath. "I've loved—sorry, *really enjoyed*—my time with him, but for me it's just sex and catching up with an old friend."

She was frowning at me. She searched my eyes as if she was looking for clues, and I felt like I'd disappointed her. Finally, she said, "Really? The man drives halfway across the continent. *That* man there, who is charming to your friends, and gives you forehead kisses, and looks at you like you're the most precious thing on this planet. *That* guy, that super-hot guy, and you're 'just friends'?"

She punctuated her point with, "I don't buy it." Her eyes locked onto mine. She wasn't backing down.

"Well," I said, with as much conviction as I could muster. "It's the truth. I'm not interested. I don't do relationships," I added matter-of-factly.

"Well, what I've found is, sometimes things happen that you don't plan for."

I knew she was talking as much about her and Jackson as she was about me and Jean-Luc. I also knew that everything she was saying was coming from a place of love. A rush of affection for Lou—my dear, sweet, recently appointed bestie—engulfed me. I reached up and gave her a hug.

"I love you, Lou," I said.

She returned the hug, but when I stepped back, she was frowning again. "I love you, too. So, *don't* screw this up."

"Hah!" I laughed. She tried to keep a straight face, but

caved, giving me a reluctant smile. The man himself arrived right afterwards.

"Hello, ladies," he said, grabbing me in a big sweaty hug. I didn't even mind. "Louise, I am going to steal her away now."

She handed me the key to her room, so we could retrieve the rest of our clothes. "Here. Just leave it at the front desk when you're done."

I gave her a kiss on the cheek. "Coach leaves at eight?" I confirmed.

"Yup."

Jean-Luc gave her two kisses, one on each cheek, and I saw her tight mouth soften. "*Au revoir*, Louise. Please say goodbye to the others for me. And thank you." He said the last part a little quieter and I wondered exactly what he was thanking her for. She smiled and gave one of his hands a squeeze.

It was a little chilly on the walk back to our apartment, and I was happy for Jean-Luc's arm around me, like that night in Rome. At the apartment, we opted for a quick shower to wash the dance floor off us. That was when we discovered that standing sex is a little tricky when your height difference is nearly a foot.

It was a good thing Jean-Luc was strong enough to lift me up, which he did before having me against the shower wall, my legs around his waist and my arms wrapped tightly around his neck.

Dry and naked we retired to the California king and took our time, savouring each other, giving each other pleasure. Making love.

I double-checked that the alarm on my phone was set for

6:30am, then we fell into a welcome sleep around midnight. But as easy as it was to fall asleep, I was wide-awake at 4:00am, my stomach in knots and I knew it had nothing to do with the wurst.

I don't want to say goodbye.

I finally fell back into a restless sleep around 5pm The alarm—aptly named—startled me awake. Jean-Luc moaned sleepily, and I leapt out of bed to get in the shower. I knew if I hit "snooze", I would miss the coach's departure.

"You are very quiet," he said.

We were seated next to each other at the kitchen counter and I was sipping my Parisian breakfast of a milky coffee. *I'd kill for a cup of tea.*

I knew I could no longer put off what I needed to say. The coach was leaving in forty-five minutes.

"Am I?" Stalling. *Coward*, I thought.

He trailed fingers up and down my back and I shrugged him off. A quick glance showed what I already knew. I'd hurt him—I *was* hurting him. "I'm sorry. I guess I ... I don't like goodbyes." *Liar.* Saying goodbye to a lover was easy. *This is easy. You know how to do this.*

"I want to see you again." There it was. Had he said, "Hey, when can we catch up again?" I would have known we were on the same page. What he *had* said was loaded with far more meaning.

"Sure. Yes. We should make plans." The acquaintance in the street. Non-committal. Casual.

"Catherine, look at me."

I did.

He tentatively took my hand and I let him. What else could I do? "By chance, fate, we found each other again. I ..." He looked down, as though searching for the words. I welcomed the reprieve from both his words and his eyes, which were wrenching my heart.

I was about to break his and I could barely stand it.

"I loved you once. I was a boy then, but I am a man now." He looked up. "I am wiser now. I know that this is not love—*yet*. But it could be. It is not usual, what is between us."

"There is a strong attraction, yes." A flicker of honesty.

"It is more. There is a pull, yes?" he looked at me intensely.

"Yes." *Madly in lust. Madly in lust.* "But—"

"You have been on my mind *constantly* since that night in Paris. In Naples, I am working and I am thinking about you. In Roma, waiting for you to arrive, you. After kissing you, all I could think about the next day and the entire drive here, was you. Making love to you. Holding you. Talking to you. All of it.

"The physical pull is very strong between us. I know this. Making love to you, it takes me out of myself. I know you feel that too. But it is *more*, Catherine. There are old feelings that have come again. I missed my dear friend, and now she—*you*—are here. And where my body and my heart meets, that's where *you* are." He clenched his jaw and his eyes seemed to will me to understand.

The thing was, I did understand. And it was the most beautiful thing anyone had ever said to me and it spun around inside me whipping up a frenzy of turmoil.

It was my turn to talk. "Yes. To everything you just said. The attraction, how it is physically between us, that is unde-niable." I smiled, hoping to break the tension and I saw his jaw unclench—a little.

"And once there was this boy I loved—and I did love you. You were my best friend and even though it was my doing, I really missed that boy when he wasn't a part of my life anymore. And when I'm with you, or thinking about you, I am trying to see the boy, to reconcile you—this gloriously handsome, grown, accomplished *man*—with the sweet, hopeful, precocious boy. Because part of me wants him back."

I saw relief in his eyes, which tore at me. I knew I needed to get the next part out before I lost my nerve.

"Wait. There's more." A look of concentration settled on his face. I took a slow breath. I had one chance not to mess this up. "We have this attraction, this physical intensity between us *here* ..." I indicated one end of the spectrum with my hand "... and over *here*, we have the friendship we both want to rekindle." He nodded, listening intently. "But here, in the middle, is a spectre. You said you were once in love with me, and I am very afraid that will happen again. I don't want to hurt you."

A thousand thoughts seemed to flutter across his eyes in an instant. It took a lot of courage not to break eye contact with him.

"You ..." He looked down. "You do not want to be in love." It was a statement, a realisation.

"No."

"So, you are afraid of love?"

"I wouldn't say I'm afraid." Defensive.

"What *would* you say?" There was an angry edge to his tone and I didn't blame him.

"I—" I tried to answer. He deserved an answer. "I ... this is what I want, to *not* be in love."

I sounded far less convincing to myself than I hoped I sounded to him. Tears filled his eyes but didn't fall. He drew a sharp intake of breath. "Are you sure?"

Was I? Why wouldn't I budge on this, even for Jean-Luc?

But I knew why. Like I'd told Lou, I became a shadow of myself after Scott and I parted ways in Paris. The whole excruciating thing—the cheating, the lies, the accusations that it was all my fault—it broke me. I had moved through life like a marionette, doing everything I was supposed to and feeling none of it. I smiled when it was expected and cried in private. Eventually, after aeons, I stopped crying and went numb. It took years to get back to myself.

I wasn't chancing that again. Not ever. Not even for Jean-Luc.

I nodded, steadfast. He made a sound, a slight groan. He said nothing more—just left the room and went to stand on the balcony.

As I watched him lean against the railing and his head drop to his chest, my heart breaking at what I'd done, I couldn't ignore the thought buzzing around my mind. *It wasn't Jean-Luc who broke my heart.*

Somehow, I got through those minutes—*we* got through them. I finished my unwanted coffee and washed the mugs in the sink, then brushed my teeth. I did a final check of the room for wayward clothing that might have been flung across it during our lovemaking. *Lovemaking.* The word sat like lead in my stomach.

Never again, Cat.

I zipped up my case and when it was time to walk to the chalet, Jean-Luc insisted on carrying it down the stairs to the street. I raised the handle so I could pull it behind me. He walked alongside me and I took a moment to enjoy the sunny morning and the crisply scented air. It was so beautiful there and I didn't want the memories of Lauterbrunnen to be marred by the last half an hour.

When the coach was in sight, with Tom and some of the women from the tour loading the group's baggage underneath, Jean-Luc stopped. I set my case upright and forced myself to look at him. I owed him that much.

"I, uh … I wanted you to have this," he said. He pulled out the letter he'd mentioned the day before, still in its envelope, from his back pocket. "I have read it perhaps a hundred times."

Oh God, the letter. I'd forgotten. I didn't want it, but how could I refuse it?

"Oh, right." I took it and tucked it into my messenger bag. "Thanks," I added weakly.

The silence between us seemed never-ending. "Jean-Luc—"

"Goodbye, Catherine." He reached down and enveloped me up in a hug. I wrapped my arms around his waist. He held me for some time, resting his head on mine. Then he kissed the top of my head, turned and walked away before I could say anything more.

What the frigging hell had I done?

Chapter 18

I was numb as I handed my case to Tom. He flashed me a smile, but it disappeared as soon as he saw my face.

Most of the group were milling about outside the coach, perhaps enjoying their last moments in Lauterbrunnen, but I just wanted to get on the coach and hide away from everyone. I chose a window seat at the back, facing away from the direction Jean-Luc had walked—away from "our apartment".

With my head pressed to the glass, I replayed the morning in my head at least a dozen times, and there wasn't one iteration where I came out as anything other than awful.

I was awful.

But I was also safe from heartbreak—or so I tried to convince myself.

I glanced at the clock at the front of the coach: 7:47. Where was Lou? I needed her.

People started to file on. By now, every face was familiar and I even knew a few more names, but I wasn't in the mood for polite niceties. I stared hard out the window until I felt someone sit down next to me.

"Hey," said Lou gently.

Her kind tone was my undoing. Silent sobs racked my body and I squeaked out, "Oh, Lou."

She wrapped her arms around me and patted my back and made shushing sounds. I let her. She eventually let me go and pulled a packet of tissues out of her bag. "Here."

"Thank you," I said through a nose full of snot. It sounded like "tonk oo". I blew my nose and wiped my face.

"So, tell me."

The coach pulled away. I hadn't even noticed the minutes tick away or the coach filling up, but I was grateful for the droning lull of the engine to mask my words from the people around us. "I tried not to, but I think I hurt him." I played with a soggy tissue in my lap.

She sighed. "You said the thing about the middle, didn't you?" I turned to meet her eyes and nodded. "And it's definitely what you want?"

"I think so. Yes. No, it *is* what I want." She gave me the look I'd given other people many times. I was usually the one who counselled, who delivered the doses of tough love, who told it like it was. I probably wasn't going to like what she had to say.

"You don't sound particularly sure."

"I am." I wasn't.

I could *see* the machinations of her thoughts playing across her face. "Okay, so obviously the sex was good." I nodded like a child. "And you seemed to have a lot of fun with him, there was an ease between you." It was a statement, not a question. Still, I continued to nod. "And how was the conversation?"

I considered the last two days and smiled involuntarily as

I recalled the quips, the banter, the teasing. There had also been more important conversations about where our lives had gone, where they might be heading.

"Good. We talked—a lot."

"So, the friendship is there, the attraction is there, but ..." She left the thought unfinished, but with her stating it so simply, I had a sickening realisation.

"I *am* afraid of the middle," I said to myself.

"Say again?"

"Jean-Luc said I was afraid of love, but I've been telling myself I'm not afraid. All I want is to protect myself from something that kicked the living daylights out of me. I thought I was being smart—brave even."

"You can only really be brave if you feel the fear and do it anyway. Brave people aren't *fearless* people. They're brave *because* they're scared and they don't let the fear stop them."

I digested what she'd said. I didn't like being wrong, but it made sense. "That ... it's really astute, Lou."

She laughed lightly. "Well, we can thank Susan Jeffers for the catchphrase, but yeah, the sentiment is well-founded."

"So, I'm not brave, I'm a big fat coward." Self-pity crept back in.

"Well, you're not big or fat." I looked at her, shocked she would be so harsh, but the kind smile on her face disarmed me. "How did you leave things?"

"Badly. It was a total palaver."

"And that means ...?"

"I told him I just want to be friends, even though he wants to see where things can go. And from what he's said over the past couple of days ... well, he's alluded to us being together, you know, *together* together."

"And you told him outright that you don't want that?"

"Yes."

There was no more supposing. I had definitely hurt him. Again.

"I don't even know if we're still friends." I was awash with shame and regret and confusion. Convinced I was doing the right thing, I had done the wrong thing and I'd probably lost my friend. *You stupid cow, Cat.*

"Oh," I said, suddenly remembering the letter. I took it out of my bag. "And he gave me this." I held up the offending item and frowned at it.

"Is that ...?" she said, taking it from me and reading the return address on the envelope.

"Yes."

"Oh."

"As if I didn't feel bad enough."

She nodded solemnly. "Oh, Cat. This is quite the dilemma." Coming from Lou, a professional counsellor, it was not soothing.

If anything, my inner turmoil was increasing tenfold every time I remembered the look on Jean-Luc's face that morning as I'd broken his heart, or how his arms felt around me when he said goodbye, or how wonderful it felt to snuggle up in the crook of his arm in our huge bed. *Our bed.*

"I've completely cocked this up," I declared, more to myself than to Lou. She was quiet, so I knew she agreed. People who don't agree with you when you're self-flagellating say so.

"Do you want a distraction? Some gossip?" Lou asked. Lou didn't strike me as the gossiping type, but perhaps she was delving into her stash of desperate measures.

"God, yes."

She ignored the "God" part. "Well, Georgina was essentially AWOL for the past two days."

"Oh, really? How do you know?"

"You know how she was upset about the lion monument?" I nodded. "Well, I overhead one of the reps saying she called head office and asked to be taken off the tour."

"What? What do you mean? We're not *that* bad." I recalled how snarky I'd been. Maybe I *had* been a little hard on her.

I half-stood in my seat and saw Georgina reflected in the giant mirror hanging above the dashboard. It was there so she could see the length of the coach without turning around, but it also meant we could see her no matter where we sat. "She's here, though. She's up the front."

"I *know*. They must have told her no."

"Actually, I didn't see her at the party last night."

"None of us saw her after we arrived on Saturday."

"What day is it?"

"Seriously? It's Monday," she replied.

"You haven't lost track of the days once—on this whole tour?"

"Nope."

"Well, good for you." She took the jibe with her usual good humour. The news about Georgina had done the trick, though. I had been pulled out of the maelstrom of emotions threatening to suck me under.

"Where are we going again?" I asked.

"Germany." *Oh, right.*

Georgina pressed play on the day song. "Because I'm happy … blahdeblahblahblah …" I was really starting to hate that song. When it ended, she stood up to tell us about the day. She looked terrible and that said a lot considering *my* wretched state. Even from the back of the coach I could see she hadn't bothered with makeup and had dark circles under her eyes. What on earth was going on with her?

She told us we were heading to St Goar on the Rhine where we would have time to explore or do an optional wine tasting. Then we'd drive to Koblenz, where we would stay overnight in a boutique hotel. At the word "hotel" my ears pricked up. "Lou. A *hotel*. Not a garden shed." Said *me*, who had spent two nights in a luxury apartment with epic views and giant bathtub. I quashed the thoughts of "our apartment". I didn't like what they did to my stomach.

"The accommodation's definitely improving. You saw our room in Lauterbrunnen."

"Oh, right, you had one giant bed." Their room was built entirely of wood—wooden floors, wooden beams running across the wooden ceiling, wooden walls, and flush against one wall was a giant wooden-framed bed. It was normal length and the width of about four queen-sized beds.

"Yeah, it was cool, though—huge. More than enough room and we each had our own sheets and comforters."

"I forgot to look out the skylight. Georgina said you could stargaze from bed."

"That was the awesome part. There was some cloud cover

last night, but the night before last, it was incredible. We still shared bathrooms, though—dorm-style ones, but yeah, much better than Paris, or Antibes."

"Or even Rome."

"It's definitely been a little more rustic than I thought it would be," she said.

"So, a new country today, and another one tomorrow."

"Mm-hm."

I couldn't believe how soon it was all coming to an end. After Koblenz, we'd drive to Amsterdam, stay two nights, then head back to London on Friday. I'd have the weekend to recover and to sleep in my own bed, before starting back at school the following Monday.

But I'd be sleeping in my bed alone—completely my doing. I'd screwed things up with Jean-Luc and I certainly wasn't going to ask Angus to pop around. The thought of sleeping with anyone besides Jean-Luc made me nauseous.

I wished I had a stack of marking waiting for me, or *something* work-related to fill up my weekend, but other than washing my travel clothes and storing my case in the storage cage, my weekend loomed ahead of me wide open.

I looked at Lou, who had taken out her Kindle and was reading. Only a few more days with my bus bestie, too. I didn't want to think about that either. Sarah had been right about the friendships you made on these tours. I remembered it being a big part of her first day spiel: "Look around you. Even if you're travelling with someone else, you are bound to meet people who will become lifelong friends." Or something like that.

Lou would definitely be a lifelong friend. I'd always wanted to go to Vancouver. I could visit her. And maybe Jaelee and Dani would be lifelong friends too. And Craig.

New people, new friendships. And yet there was one person, whom for a long time I thought I would know my whole life, and I'd just said a final goodbye to him. *Bollocks. Bugger. Fuck. Bum. Crap.*

I stared gloomily out the window.

Switzerland ✓

At the morning tea rest stop, just outside Strasbourg, my posse convened. I had already given Jaelee and Dani the abridged version of the morning's events when Craig walked up and gave me a much-needed bear hug. "Lou said you needed a hug," he said as he lifted me up and smushed my face into his chest. I bit the insides of my cheeks so I didn't start crying again.

"Thanks," I said when he put me down. I smiled a big fat fake smile while Dani stroked my arm and looked at me with pity.

"I really liked Jean-Luc," Craig said, clearly thinking he was being helpful.

Jaelee cleared her throat and I saw her subtly shake her head at him. He looked horrified that he'd said something wrong, which he had.

"All right, everyone. Thank you for your support, but what will help is not talking about ..." I couldn't say his name "... uh, *that*. No pity, no sympathy. Just ... we should get some food, huh?" I turned and marched towards the services. I would squash my feelings down the way I was raised to, with food. Sarah often joked that "Food is love" is our family motto and at that moment, I needed lots of fattening, carb-filled love.

Inside, I opted for a giant pretzel coated in melted cheese, covering two of the major European food groups, and I ordered tea—only because it was too early in the day for several shots of vodka.

Back on the coach, I ate my giant pretzel in silence as I stared out the window. I could *feel* when the carbs hit my bloodstream, a flood of sugar making everything feel marginally better. I could never be one of those people who did a no-carb diet. I mean, what is the point of living if you are going to subject yourself to that?

"Hey." Craig was standing in the aisle.

"Hi."

"I wanted to apologise. I didn't know."

"You don't need to—"

Lou cut me off by offering her seat to Craig. "Here. Sit. I'll go up to your seat for a while." She smiled at us both and scooched past Craig. He sat down.

"Really, you don't need to apologise."

"It's just that Dani said you needed a hug and I thought you were sad because you had to say goodbye."

"I was—am—but ..."

"She filled me in. Again, I'm really sorry."

"Craig, have you been spending too much time with the Canadians? Seriously, stop apologising. It's fine."

"I'm s—" He cut himself off before he said it again, then sat there looking awkward.

"So, tell me about you," I asked. "How's the tour been so far?"

"Good, yeah. I mean, Switzerland was *beyond*, you know?"

"I do, yes."

"And I'm from *Oregon*." He'd said that a few times, as though Oregon was some benchmark I should have understood.

"And?" I prompted.

"Well, I mean, we *have* mountains, and lakes, and *incredible* scenery, but Lauterbrunnen was next level." I smiled. "It makes me want to travel more. Actually, this whole trip has. I'm thinking I'll come back next summer and backpack around, you know?"

"That would be amazing."

"Did you ever do that, you know, when ...?"

"You mean when I was young like you?"

He flushed. "Oh, God, I didn't mean—what is *wrong* with me today?"

I laughed and it felt good. "I'm *kidding*. Really. I teach kids your age—I mean, young adults—sorry. See? It's not just you who's putting your foot in it." He grinned. "And, no I never did the backpacking thing. Maybe I should have, but I like proper showers and I *hate* sharing a room—also, I don't really like *getting* somewhere. I prefer *being* somewhere, but the whole 'in transit' thing ... I've just described a Ventureseek tour, haven't I?"

"Uh, yeah. So, why did you come if you hate all that stuff?"

"It's a long story." *Warning, Will Robinson—deflect, deflect, deflect.*

Craig, who was more child than man, did not need to know the ins and outs of my sex life, so to speak. It was strange enough that he'd met my latest lover.

Jean-Luc.

His name sat like a tongue ulcer in my head. It hurt to touch it, but I couldn't leave it alone.

"So, any trysts since the *château*?" I asked, turning the spotlight back on Craig. He blushed again, so utterly adorable I wanted to pinch his cheeks. "So, that's a yes, then?"

"One of the reps. Isla. She's Scottish."

"From Lauterbrunnen?" He nodded. "Hmm. Well, good for you." He dropped his head and stared at his lap. "Want me to change the subject?"

"More than anything."

"Right. Oh, I meant to ask you—sorry—how's your mum?" The extent of my self-absorption was becoming more evident every day. I squirmed under my own scrutiny.

"Oh, yeah, actually, she's great. Well, hang on, she's kinda upset right now, but it's because she and her boyfriend broke up."

"You mean the horrid boyfriend?"

"That's the one."

"So, ultimately a good thing, but her heart is currently broken."

"Exactly." He ran a hand through his hair and the gesture nearly undid me. I hadn't seen him do that before and it was so *Jean-Luc*. "I'm mostly relieved, you know. And when I get home, I can be there to support her, but she's better off without him. He was *really* bad for her."

"So, good news then?"

"Yep."

"She's lucky to have you."

He smiled. "Thanks. I just want her to be happy, you know. It'll make it easier when I do go away to school. Hey, I'm gonna let Louise come back now, 'kay?"

"Sure. Thanks for the chat," I added lightly. He smiled again and he and Lou swapped places.

"He's such a sweetheart," she said as she sat down.

"He is."

"Hey, Sez," I said quietly. I wanted to talk to my sister and I'd decided to call from the coach instead of waiting for the next rest stop.

"Hi, Cat! How's it all going? How's Jean-Luc?" I winced at his name.

"Um, actually, that's why I'm calling."

"Oh, sounds ominous. What happened?"

"I think he has feelings for me, *major* ones."

"Oh, wow!" I was silent for a beat and she leapt back in with, "Hang on, what's wrong with that?"

"Well, you know. I don't want anything serious. That hasn't changed."

"But, isn't it different with Jean-Luc?"

"No."

"Oh."

I was quiet again, wishing I'd texted instead of called. "Look," she said, "I'm a little confused about what you want me to say."

"That makes two of us." It was her turn to go quiet. Maybe I'd lost the connection. "Sez?"

"I'm here."

"I—look, sorry, I probably shouldn't have called. It's just—I feel like an utter cow, Sez."

"I'm sorry, Cat. That sounds awful."

"Yes."

"Look, when you get home, FaceTime me and we'll have a proper chat, okay?"

"Yep. Will do. Bye."

"Hey. I love you."

"I love you too." I tapped the big red button on my phone. *Well, that went well.* I snuck a glance at Lou and she was clearly pretending she hadn't heard the whole exchange. "What?" I snapped, instantly regretting it. "Sorry, Lou."

"It's okay."

Why was I treating the people I cared about like rubbish? I gave myself a mental slap about the face.

"We should do the wine tasting," I said.

"In St Goar? I thought you wanted to avoid the excursions."

"Yes, I know, but I'd like to go. Basically, I want to get drunk." At that moment, getting drunk and not feeling anything was preferable to wallowing.

"At a wine tasting?"

"Yes. Don't judge me."

"No judgement. How much is it?"

"I think it's only ten euros. Doesn't matter, though. My treat."

"You don't need to do that."

"I'd like to."

"Sure, okay, thank you. Want me to check with the girls, see if they want to go?"

"I can."

"Eh, I'm on the aisle. I'll go."

She returned a few minutes later. "They were already going. I asked Georgina if it was too late to add us, but it's fine."

"Oh, good. Thanks for taking care of that."

"She looks terrible, like she hasn't had any sleep."

"Georgina? What's going on there, do you think?" She started to stand up. "Lou?" I grabbed her arm and she sat back down. "You can't go talk to her."

"She may need a friendly ear. The whole time we were talking, she looked like she was about to cry."

"It's nice you want to help, but you'd have an audience." A frown skimmed across her face.

"I feel bad I left her there like that."

"If it was me, I wouldn't want to have a heart-to-heart up there in front of the whole group."

"Yeah, okay, you're probably right. I'll see if I can get a moment with her later. The poor thing." Lou was right. I couldn't find a shred of the annoyance I'd felt when she'd been "Georg-bloody-ina". In its place was curiosity and a smidgeon of pity. Well, maybe more than a smidgeon.

I grew up in a family of wine lovers, and whenever I flew home to visit Australia, we'd invariably drive out to the Hunter Valley, the closest wine region to Sydney, and spend the day going from winery to winery doing tastings. My dad would drive, and if one of us said a particular wine was worth trying, he'd taste it and spit. He took his role as skipper—or designated driver—seriously.

The Hunter's tasting rooms typically had high ceilings and glass for days, many of them overlooking neat rows of vines that tumbled over gently rolling hills. Timber abounded, as did polished concrete floors and furniture made from old wine barrels. More often than not, the winery had a dog, usually friendly, often old, and always named something quintessentially Australian, like Mac, or Bluey, or Sally.

Our late-afternoon wine tasting in St Goar, a quaint and welcoming town nestled in the Rhine Valley, was quite different from my experiences in the Hunter Valley. It was held in a giant cellar, for a start—not a pane of glass in sight. The walls were made of brick and the low ceiling was raw wooden beams which had been smoothed by time. It was cool, as you'd expect from a cellar, but not dank or musty. We sat at long tables of polished blonde wood, and there were candles interspersed every few feet which, along with the soft electric lighting overhead, gave off a warm glow.

A handful of young women and men scurried about, pouring generous splashes of wine into the four glasses set before each of us—three white and one red—and placing large platters of soft cheese and pumpernickel-style bread along the table. It had been quite a good turn-out with about twenty people from the tour taking part.

Once everything was on the tables, our host called for our attention and told us his name was Gunther. He was long and lean, with angular cheekbones that would have made

Johnny Depp envious. His English was slightly accented but fluent, and when he smiled at us, I found myself smiling back.

I'd had a pretty crappy day. Yes, it was mostly my own doing, but after six hours on the coach—far too much time for someone in my predicament to think—I was ready to lose myself in a favourite pastime. I wasn't much of a connoisseur and I rarely retained what I learnt, but I enjoyed the wine-tasting experience.

The wines were a *gewürztraminer*, a *spätburgunder*, or what German winemakers call pinot noir, and two sweet rieslings, which we would taste last. For each wine, Gunther explained where it was grown and made, and the main characteristics to look out for. Only the rieslings were grown in the immediate region. I had some vague knowledge from a long-ago wine tasting that they were sweet in the Rhine because it was a colder region and something, something, something ... See? Wine knowledge is wasted on me.

I liked the crisp, almost floral taste of the *gewürztraminer*, which I'd never had before. I'd seen it in Sainsbury's and Tesco sometimes, but I'd figured it would be sweet like the rieslings, so I never bought it. I made a mental note to pick some up the next time I went shopping.

The *spätburgunder* was amazing, but that didn't surprise me—I *love* pinot noir. What did surprise me was learning that the Germans produce more of it than any other country. Until then, I'd thought New Zealand had the monopoly.

As we tasted each wine and as the cheese on the platter in front of us started disappearing, I could feel myself unwinding.

Tea was one thing, but was there anything nicer at the end of a long, awful day than some wine?

Lou loved the rieslings best. "Oh my gosh, this one's delicious!" she whispered as she tasted wine number four. "I mean this one is *good*, but *this* one. I'm going to have to buy a bottle of this." Was Lou getting tiddly? The thought made me smile, then examine myself. *I* was getting tiddly. Still, being tiddly was far better than being clear-headed and thinking too much.

When Gunther finished talking us through all the wines, he asked if anyone had questions. A few hands went up, including Lou's. He called on her first. "This last wine is yummy. Can we buy a bottle?"

He chuckled. "*Ja*, no problem. My colleagues upstairs will be able to help with that. I'm glad you enjoyed it."

She beamed. I leant into her. "You good, Lou?"

"Oh yeah. That was *awesome*. I don't usually do this kind of thing."

I was an idiot. Of course she didn't—she was married to a man with a drinking problem. She didn't do wine tastings or have nights out like the ones we'd had together. How had I not thought of that earlier? I gave myself another mental slap for the mounting evidence that I was a self-centred cow.

After Gunther answered the other questions, he signalled to the team of waiters. They did the rounds with the opened but unfinished bottles. That was how I ended up with a full glass of the *spätburgunder* and Lou got a glass of the "yummy one".

Dani came up behind us. "Hey, guys," she said. Jaelee followed closely, both holding glasses of white wine. Jae pulled a chair over from the table next to us, and Lou and I turned ours around to face her. Dani seemed happy to stand. "That was fun, yeah?" she asked.

"It was good value for ten euros, too," I added. "Which one did you choose?" I asked Jae.

"The *gewürztraminer*. I don't like sweet wine."

"Oh, I love it." Lou.

"I can see that," teased Jae before taking a sip.

"I went with the last one, the second riesling," said Dani. "The same as you, I think, Lou. If you're getting a bottle, I'll share with you."

"Definitely."

"Jae? Did you want to share a bottle? I'd have the *gewürztraminer*, or if you liked the red …"

"Sure. I'd rather the white though."

"No worries." My inner Aussie came out to play; perhaps it was the wine.

We ended up with three bottles of wine between the four of us. What could go wrong?

Many hours later, and long after we should have been asleep, we were two bottles down with the third about to be opened— the sweetest one. I was well past the stage where I cared about *what* I was drinking more than I cared *that* I was drinking.

Because we were talking about Jean-Luc.

Lou was sitting cross-legged on the end of her bed and Jae had commandeered her bedhead, propping herself against it. I was reclining on my bed and Dani, for some reason, had opted for the floor, where she sat on one of my pillows.

"Can I please read it?" she whined. Having exhaustively recounted the last two days—everything we'd said and most of what we did (I left out details about the sex)—we'd moved onto The Letter (note the capitals).

"*No*, for the umpteenth time." We all looked at the offending envelope, which was sitting on the bedside table between the two beds. If we'd been in a film, ominous music would have played.

"Let's put it this way," said Jaelee, sounding far more sober than she likely was, "it will probably drive you crazy if you don't. And it might not be that bad," she added.

"Lou. Do you need help?" I asked. She was struggling with the third bottle, and it was a good distraction from the letter. She made a face and handed it to Dani.

Dani also struggled. "It won't unscrew." She gritted her teeth and finally the cap loosened. She stood to pour each of us a glass, then sat back down. I wasn't off the hook, though. "I agree with Jaelee," Dani said. "You need to know what you wrote. And maybe it's not all that bad."

I looked at Lou. "What do you think?"

She tilted her head in that way I'd grown to love. It meant she was considering all aspects of the situation, weighing them up. "I know you probably don't want to hear this ..."—*uh oh*—"... but it would be good for closure."

Ugh. That awful word.

After Scott and I broke up, I'd gone to see a counsellor. I'd lasted exactly two sessions, because she kept going on and on about how I needed closure. Only, Scott lived across the world and we'd cut all ties. I was hardly going to ping him on

Facebook. "Hey, Scott, how's Helen? Can I have some closure please?" I'd cancelled the third appointment and never went back. My lack of closure went into a box inside my heart—one I never opened. Ever.

I sighed. "All *riiiiight*." I took as long to say that word as it's humanly possible to do.

Dani bobbed up and down on my pillow, clapped her hands and said, "Eeee," as though I'd told her we were going to Disneyland. I glared at her. "Sorry." She sat still, looking contrite.

I took the envelope in my hands and turned it over. Jean-Luc had clearly been impatient when he'd opened it, as the envelope's seam was torn and ragged. I took a slow breath and pulled the letter out. A small white card fluttered onto my lap.

"What's that?" asked Dani unnecessarily. I set the letter down and picked up the card.

I thought we could start writing again. Here's my address.
Talk soon.

   Love, Jean-Luc

Below that was his address in Paris. I gulped and gasped at the same time and ended up in a minor coughing fit. Lou stood and reached around to pat me on the back. "You okay?" she asked, her face concerned. "Here." She handed me the bottle of water I'd barely sipped from. I drank some and the coughs subsided.

Jae took the card gently from my other hand and read it,

then showed it to Lou and Dani. "Oh," said Lou. "Yikes," said Dani. I didn't bother throwing Dani another look. I put the water bottle down and stared at the letter laying in my lap.

"I don't think I can do it," I said to no one in particular.

"Here. Let me," said Lou in her "Mama Lou" voice. I looked up and nodded weakly. She held out her hand and I gave her the letter. "I'll read it and if you like, I'll just summarise it, okay?" I nodded again and gulped down the lump growing in my throat.

She unfolded the letter and seemed to skim-read to the bottom of the first page, then moved just as quickly through the second page. She turned both pages over, as if she was looking for more writing, then shuffled the pages and read back over the whole thing again. It was killing me, the waiting.

"Lou, *please*, what?"

"This isn't the last letter, Cat."

"What? What do you mean?" I was frozen in place.

"I mean, this is a sweet, newsy letter. There's nothing about ending your friendship, or just being pen pals, or any of that. It's just a normal letter."

What???

"Let me see," I said. She handed it over and Dani climbed on the bed and sat beside me to read over my shoulder.

Dear Jean-Luc,

I'm at uni at the moment, so this will be an unusually short letter, but you know me—I'll probably write again tomorrow anyway. I'm <u>supposed</u> to be listening to the world's most boring lecture. It's about semiotics. SNORE!

Actually, I think someone behind me is snoring. Anyway … If you don't know—and you probably do, because you're way smarter than I am—semiotics is about how signs signify stuff and words are signs or something. Ha ha! Maybe I should actually pay attention.

Anyway … I think it's so cool that you applied to the Sorbonne. If you get in and you move to Paris I will totally come and visit you. For real! At least I will try. Maybe at the end of the year. I could have my first white Christmas! Does it snow in Paris at Chrissie time? Actually, you probably go home for Christmas, right? What about Lyon? Does it snow there? Someone is definitely snoring now. Oh my God, will this lecture ever end???

Mostly I love uni. Not at this particular moment, obviously, but it's just SO COOL! The lecturers actually listen to our opinions and we have these interesting discussions in the tutes, like we're actual grown-ups. It's way better than high school where you got the best marks if you just regurgitated what the teacher said. You're so lucky you left before the HSC. I know I've told you before, but seriously I think my mum nearly asked me to move out. I was such a nightmare stresshead all the time.

Anyway … I have made some cool friends. My bestie is Alison. She's ridiculously pretty—the opposite of me, tall, thin, long blonde hair. She's smart and funny so I don't hate her, even though I probably should. You'd like her. You'd probably LIKE like her. No, scratch that. I wouldn't want you going out with my bestie. That would be weird.

Nothing on the romance front. The guys here are kind

of dumb and a bit too ocker for my taste. I don't know if you remember but ocker means super blokey and macho, only it's fake macho, just stupid really—like a bunch of ten-year-olds running around being dicks. It makes me miss you. A lot. If ANY of these guys were like you, I would have had a boyfriend ages ago.

Anyway … I have to go. He's FINALLY finished. Yayyyyyyy!

Catchya later.

Love, Cat xxxxxxxx

I stared numbly at my name followed by—I counted—eight kisses. I blinked a few times and eventually looked at Lou. "It's not the letter."

"No." Dani and Lou spoke in unison.

"I want to read it." Jae had been patient and I handed it to her.

"It's so sweet," cooed Dani.

"He said he read it a hundred times."

"Aww." Dani, the romantic.

We sat in silence while Jae finished reading it. Well, nearly silence. There was the sound of Dani topping up everyone's wine glasses.

I took a tentative sip from mine and watched Jae over the rim, her face set with concentration. She bit her top lip, then her bottom lip. She frowned, then made a little sound like, "Hunh." Finally, she looked at me.

"You realise what this means, right?"

"No." *Panic, panic, panic.* "What?"

"You were in love with him too."

"What? What do you mean? No, I wasn't." As I protested, Dani said, "Ohhh," and Lou said, "I did wonder about that."

Jae came and sat next to me. "Here." She pointed to the paragraph about the ocker guys. "No one measured up. You only wanted him. And there was the part about you not wanting him to be with Alison."

I read back over the last part of the letter. Then the very large penny dropped from an incredibly great height.

I had been in love with Jean-Luc.

And I might be again.

"Oh, bollocks." This time I said it out loud.

Chapter 19

"**C**an we please talk about something else? *Anything* else?" I glanced between them and they peered back at me. Lou's eyes narrowed a little, but I could handle Mama Lou. It was coming up on midnight and we were due on the coach at 8:00am. I needed to sleep, but I knew if I didn't get the whole "Jean-Luc" situation out of my head, I'd end up staring at the ceiling until the wee hours.

"Amsterdam!" I said a little too loudly for the small room.

Jaelee went back to her position on Lou's bed. "What about it?" she said, stifling a yawn.

"What are you looking forward to?" I donned an expression of fake enthusiasm, like a nursery teacher trying to get small children excited about something mundane.

Lou answered, "Well, I'm actually going to see my family."

"Oh, cool," drawled Dani.

The fake enthusiasm vanished. "I didn't know you had family in the Netherlands." Why hadn't she told me that? Or maybe she had but I'd been too busy obsessing about my trainwreck of a love life.

"Oh, I thought I'd mentioned it. Hang on, maybe I didn't.

389

Well, anyway, we're Dutch on my dad's side and his first cousin lives in Rotterdam. I'm staying with her and her husband. Oh, and her kids are our age, so that'll be cool."

"Wait, so you're staying with them?" asked Jaelee. "Are you leaving the tour early?"

Great questions, Jaelee. How had my bus bestie failed to reveal such important information?

"No, I'll finish out the trip, but when you go back to London on Friday, Dad's cousin, Mila, is picking me up from the hotel. I fly straight to Vancouver from Amsterdam on Monday."

"That's awesome," said Dani. Her excitement about Lou's plans was annoying me senseless.

"So, we have to say goodbye on Friday morning?" I asked, a slight edge in my voice. A whole day less with Lou. I was deflated. I almost wanted to go back to talking about Jean-Luc. *Almost.*

"Yeah, but we still have two more days together." She smiled brightly at me, which made me feel even worse. *She* had something to look forward to over the weekend. And then my thoughts flew to Jackson and the pending divorce and the heinous mess she had waiting for her back home in Vancouver. I was being a cow—*again*. To Lou, whom I loved.

On impulse, I got up and gave her a hug. It was a little awkward, because she was sitting and I was standing, but when you feel a wave of love for someone, you should act on it.

"Okay, that's our cue," said Jae.

"You don't have to go," I said. Yes, I needed sleep, but now

I had something else to fret over. I'd be staring at the ceiling for hours.

"I'm beat," Jae replied. She stood and stretched her clasped hands behind her, like someone who did yoga all the time, or a ballerina. "I'm taking this with me," she said picking up her glass.

"Right behind you," said Dani, even though she looked like she wasn't going anywhere.

Jae left our room and Dani sipped her wine. "Uh, Dan? Is everything all right?" I asked.

"Mm-hm." She drank some more wine and pulled at a thread hanging off the bottom of her cigarette pants.

I shared a look with Lou and she was clearly as baffled as I was. "Is it Jason?" Lou posed the question lightly, then took a sip of wine. I saw her close her eyes for a second as she savoured it.

"What? Oh, no. That's old news. He hooked up with that girl, Joanne. You know, the one from New Zealand?"

"How did I miss that?"

"You've been busy," said Lou. I wasn't sure if that was a dig or not.

"But when?" I asked.

"At the last stop," said Dani matter-of-factly. "Didn't you see them at the party last night?" I hadn't, no. My "good friend" karma was going into deficit, and fast.

"And you're okay with it?" Lou sounded dubious. *I* was dubious. They'd been so cute together, and how on earth did Jason have time for *two* romances on such a short tour?

Dani waved it away, as though shooing a fly. "No," she said

with a laugh. "I really don't care. He wanted to sleep with me and I was like, meh. I mean, he's cute, and I liked him enough to kiss him, but how would we even *do* that? It's not like we get private rooms." She'd mentioned that before and I had to agree. "Anyway, he was totally cool about it and then he moved onto Joanne."

"Huh." Lou and I said it at the same time. I caught her eye and we shared a smile.

Dani stared at the carpet. "Dani, spill," I said. "It's not Jason, so what is it?" Mama Lou was not the only one who could dish up tough love.

She sighed. "I don't want to bug you guys. It's nothing, really."

"You're literally sitting on our floor sighing. Out with it."

She looked up at me with those big grey eyes with the precisely drawn eyeliner flicks. Then she looked at Lou, who nodded encouragingly. "It's Nathalie, my best friend." I knew her best friend was Nathalie, because I surrogate-hated Nathalie for what she'd done to Dani.

"And?" Even Lou was getting impatient.

Dani's bottom lip starting quivering. She bit it and took a breath. "There are wedding photos on Facebook."

"Oh. Well, that sucks," I said, "Sorry, Dani."

She shook her head. "That's not why I'm upset. Well, yeah, I mean the photos are upsetting, but the worst part is that it wasn't only the two of them—at the wedding."

"Wait, but you said she was eloping? That still means the same thing, right? Going somewhere to get married, just the

392

two of you?" Lou and I telepathically communicated over Dani's head; I wasn't the only one who was confused.

"That's what she told me." Bitterness crept into her voice. "But *no*. Her mom and dad were there. Her brother and his *girlfriend* were there, and they only just started going out! *And* there were two other couples there. People I don't know, and I know all her friends and all her family, so I'm not sure why Nathalie was completely fine with strangers being at her wedding, but she didn't want *me* there."

Her lip had stopped quivering. She was no longer upset—she was furious—and I couldn't blame her.

"And the worst part is, I'm going to have to see her and say congratulations and all the other things you're supposed to say, like, 'Oh, how was it?' and *smile* and suck it up! It's fucking bullshit. I bet she doesn't even know the photos are on there, because *she* didn't even post them. Someone else did, then tagged her. So, not only do I have to be all nice about her eloping, which is a super shitty thing to do to your *best friend* since high school, I'm going to have to ask why there were random people at her fucking wedding when *I* wasn't allowed to go."

"Sorry, Dan," I said again, putting my hand on her shoulder in solidarity. There was no moral ambiguity in the situation. Bitchface Nathalie was lucky we'd never meet, because I would berate her until she cried.

"Dani, it totally sucks that she did this to you. You don't deserve that," said Mama Lou, channelling Counsellor Lou. "We love you. You have us, okay?" Dani chewed on the inside of her mouth.

"Dani?" She looked at Lou. "I know we don't live in the same cities or anything, but we're your friends now. And that's a promise. You need me—*us* ..." She looked at me for confirmation and I squeezed Dani's shoulder. "... We're here for you. Okay?"

"Okay." She'd lost a bit of her steam.

"And Jaelee too," added Lou.

"Oh." Dani seemed uncomfortable.

"Hey, are things all right between you and Jae?" I asked.

"Yeah, I guess. It's just, I felt kinda dumb telling her about all this. It's like, so minor and—"

"No way. This is not minor. I swear, if my sister pulled something like this, I would have her guts for garters."

Dani's eyed widened and she started laughing. "What expression is *that*?" she asked through her laugh.

"You haven't heard that one?"

"No." Still laughing.

"Well, I *think* it's Australian. Could be English. Anyway, it means—"

"Oh, no, I get what it means. I am totally stealing it." She started to get up. "Oh, crap, my foot's gone to sleep." She sat down heavily on the bed next to me, spilling some of her wine on the carpet. She handed the glass to me and started massaging her right foot. I put her glass on the bedside table.

"I'm going to have to go to bed too." She shook her foot and tested standing on it. She would have to limp, but she was only going next door. She leant down and gave me a hug. "Thank you." Then Lou. "You too. I'm glad I could talk about it."

"Sure," said Lou patting her on the back like she was a colicky baby.

"Okay." She straightened up and hobbled to the door. "See you in the morning."

"Night."

"Goodnight."

When the door closed and she was out of earshot, Lou turned to me and said, "I hope I never meet that Nathalie girl. I don't think I could stop myself from smacking her one." Mama Lou was one formidable chick.

I woke with a surprisingly clear head around seven, and the first thing I saw when I opened my eyes was Dani's unfinished wine. The second was the letter. Lou was still sleeping when I propped myself up against the bedhead and picked up the letter. Without waking her, I took it out and unfolded it. I took my time, reading between the lines like Jean-Luc, a boy with a crush, would have done.

Only it wasn't a crush. He had loved me.

And I had loved him. It was there on the page.

Cosy in my hotel bed, I was awash with fondness for nineteen-year-old Cat—Catey. She was funny and self-deprecating, hopeful and loving. She wasn't yet broken. I refolded the letter and put it back in the envelope, then got out of bed and tucked it safely into my messenger bag.

As we drove out of the charming German burg an hour later, I was a little regretful that my entire experience of Germany had boiled down to lots of wine and a decent bed. And yes, the landscape was nice, but after Switzerland, I wondered if any other scenery could ever elicit more than a shoulder shrug, perhaps another way I was ruined for life.

Germany ✓

It was a straight shot between Koblenz and Amsterdam, and a relatively short drive, compared to others we'd had. And at least Amsterdam gave me something to look forward to.

I'd seen enough photos to know it would be picturesque and I knew it had incredible galleries. I really wanted to go to the Van Gogh museum. My sister was obsessed with him, especially *Sunflowers*, and her obsession had rubbed off on me a bit. It would be nice to go, so I could tell her about it. Apparently, they had built a whole new wing since she'd last been.

And, of course, the further we travelled north-west, the more distance there was between me and Jean-Luc.

Hours later, after we'd crossed another border and the land-scape flattened, I poked around in my heart to see if I still felt anything for Scott, the ghost of boyfriend past.

After conjuring his face, or at least a blurry facsimile, after dipping into a catalogue of Kodak moments and epic fights, and dredging through the minutiae of our five-year relation-ship, I realised I felt nothing. Finally.

He'd been an insecure kid when we'd had that massive fight about Jean-Luc. How could I be angry at him? He was doing what he thought he should to show how much he loved me, that I belonged to him.

What we think love is when we're young, I mused.

It could be sweet and honest and real, or completely screwed up and possessive, like with Scott. Possession wasn't love. And making one person the centre of your entire world, forcing them to leave everyone else behind and be everything to you, that wasn't love either.

For years, I thought I had loved Scott and that he had loved me, but in that moment, I knew I'd been wrong. Scott and I had been two drowning people clinging to each other. It was not love.

Love lifted you up. Love made you hopeful of the future, and brave enough to face whatever life threw at you. It made you laugh and feel and want and *be*—be *yourself*. I had a lot of love in my life—Sarah, my parents, my new friends, Mich. I wasn't afraid of *those* relationships, of being vulnerable, of being myself. I'd jumped right in with the girls. In less than two weeks they'd seen me at my worst many times over. And it was fine. I loved them and they loved me.

So why was I walking away from something with Jean-Luc? What the hell was wrong with me? And then it hit me.

I was walking away because I was a stupid bloody idiot.

"Lou." She had nodded off and I shook her awake.

She woke with a start. "Mmm. What, sorry." She blinked a few times. "What's up?"

"I have to go to Paris."

"I'm not following, sorry."

"I ... I'm stupid and I need to go to Paris."

She shook her head, like someone in a cartoon would. "Okay. You are not stupid—"

"Don't counsel me right now. I have been inordinately stupid. I mean, Lou, seriously, *Jean-Luc*. Did you *see* him?"

She laughed. "Yeah, I saw him. He's, uh, very, uh ..."

"Exactly, and him being super hot is the worst thing about him. I mean, he's kind and he's thoughtful, and he's so smart, Lou—even when we were kids—and he's ..." Tears prickled my eyes.

"He's such a good man, and I am such a *stupid idiot*." The tears turned to sobs and Lou patted my knee, a concerned look on her face. "I need to go to Paris," I managed to say through the tears. "I have to tell him."

"Okay, okay, just shush." I sniffed loudly and fished in my bag for a tissue. Lou tapped on the seat in front of her and Dani poked her face between the two seats.

"Hey, what's up?" She took headphones out of her ears.

"Is Jaelee awake?" asked Lou.

"She's sleeping."

"Wake her, then come back here."

I was trying to get my sobs under control and failing miserably. I am not usually much of a crier—I was unpractised, which may have been why I'd gone from zero to sixty in three-point-two seconds.

It only took a couple of moments before Dani and Jaelee were crouched down in the aisle next to Lou. "Cat, are you okay?" Dani's concern set me off again. "Hey, what's going on?"

Lou adopted her calm, soothing tone. "Cat has realised that she needs to go to Paris."

"For Jean-Luc?" Even through my tears I thought it was a dumb question.

"Of *course* for him," said Jae, rolling her eyes.

Dani did her delighted little clap and grinned at me, then frowned when she saw my expression.

"So, why the tears?" asked Dani.

"Yeah, shouldn't you be happy?" added Jae.

I nodded. "Yes, but I am *so* stupid. How could I have been so stupid all these years?" I hiccupped a little and Lou tipped me gently forward and started rubbing my back, all while cooing that I wasn't stupid. It didn't help.

"Okay, so what?" said Jae. "We've all done it—*all* of us have done stupid things when it comes to love. I mean, look at me. At least you know he wants you. He's not with anyone else. He wants *you*. Okay?"

I nodded, then snuffled up some snot. Dani's nose crinkled in disgust. "Sorry." I wiped my nose roughly with a sodden wad of tissue.

Right as I was starting to calm down and breathe normally, a hideous thought popped in my head. I looked at my friends, stricken. "But what if I completely cocked it up? What if I hurt him too much—*again*—and he doesn't want me anymore?" The sobs started again.

Dani looked on helpless. Lou intensified the back rubbing and I had to shrug her off. Jaelee spoke, her firm voice cutting through my mini meltdown. "Stop that." I took a sharp intake of breath. "Stop with the wallowing. You do not want to show up in Paris all tear-stained and puffy."

Those were the magic words. The sobs stopped, and I stared at her wide-eyed, waiting for the next instruction. This must have been what it felt like for toddlers after the trance of a tantrum.

Jae stood up. "Can't crouch down anymore. Right, so it's Friday. You have to be back at work on Monday, I assume?" I nodded. Lou handed me some fresh tissues and I wiped tears and snot from my face, all while transfixed on Jaelee in "fix-it" mode. "Here's what we're going to do. Dani and I will look for flights to get you from Amsterdam to Paris. Give me your credit card."

I rummaged in my bag, then handed it to her. "When we get to the hotel in Amsterdam, you'll go tell Georgina that you're leaving the tour, then fix yourself up. You are a hot mess right now." I wasn't even offended. "Then we'll get you to the airport—Uber or a train or something. Okay?"

I nodded, numb, and gave the details over to my friends. All I had to focus on was getting a grip and working out what I wanted to say to Jean-Luc when I saw him. I figured that, "Hey, you know all the stuff I said about love? I was wrong. I think I love *you*. Let's get married and have lots of babies," wouldn't be quite right.

We were due to get into Amsterdam around noon and the flight Dani and Jaelee found on Air France flew out at four. It was going to be a tight turnaround, but by the time we arrived at the hotel, the plan was etched in exquisite detail and we were all systems go.

We got our room assignment—dormitory-style, one room for the four of us and a bathroom down the hall. As soon as we unlocked the door, I was sent to take a shower and conduct a quick but thorough upkeep of my lady parts. By the time I got back to the room, someone had been through my luggage

400

and had laid out one of my unworn dresses, and the only matching set of bra and knickers I'd packed. Thank goodness they were clean.

"Who—?"

"Who do you think?" Jaelee rolled her eyes at me. "Unless you want to borrow something of mine?"

I looked at the tastefully low-cut dress, blue with bell-shaped sleeves, a nipped-in waist, and embroidered flowers on the hem. It was one of my favourite dresses—I'd been saving it for the final night of the tour—and it was perfect. I smiled. "No, I love it." I felt a little like Cinderella getting ready for the ball when I stepped into the dress and Lou zipped it up.

Jaelee brought out her curling wand and gave me some structured curls rather than my usual beachy waves, and Dani offered to do her signature eyeliner on me with its precise little flicks. I added some blush, some mascara and cherry-red sheer lip gloss—even though it would be hours until I saw Jean-Luc and I'd have to reapply it about fifty times.

I stood in front of my girl posse and held out my arms, so they could admire me. "Well?"

Dani clapped and grinned, Lou looked like a proud mother, and Jae said, "Much better than you looked an hour ago." I took that as the highest compliment.

I looked at my watch. "What time did you book the Uber for, Dan?" She'd used the app on my phone. I didn't want anyone else to foot the bill for my grand romantic gesture.

"Two o'clock."

"All right, I need to go find Georgina. Oh, and pack all this up."

"I'll do that," said Lou, as she gathered up my things.

"Oh, Lou, thank you." *I will not cry. I will not cry. I will see Lou again.*

I was rooted to the spot, looking at my three friends. I would miss out on spending the next couple of days with them and it sucked.

"Go!" Jaelee shooed me out the door.

I climbed six flights of stairs to the fourth floor of the hotel where the Ventureseek crew had the penthouse apartment. When I knocked on the door, I waited for what felt like a long time. No answer. *Hmm.* I knocked again, louder this time, and when the door opened my mouth fell open.

Tom. With no shirt on.

"Oh, hey. Uh, can I do something for you?"

"Yes, actually, I just wanted a quick word with Georgina— if she's here."

He scratched his belly and I looked away. I wanted to think of Tom as the capable, clean-cut guy who drove us around Europe, not this sloppily attractive guy who was obviously having the rest of the day off.

"Uh, yeah. Hang tight, I'll get her." I waited in the doorway, not wanting to intrude on the crew's private space. I couldn't imagine having to be "on" twenty-four-seven, always polished and professional. It was hard enough having to do that as a teacher eight hours a day, five days a week.

Georgina emerged from what I assumed was a bedroom, and Tom gave me a salute. I lifted a hand in response.

"Hi, Catherine," she said, her voice as weary as she looked.

"Hi!" *Dial it down a bit, Cat.* "Um, I just wanted to let you know I've had a change of plans, and I'm actually flying to Paris this afternoon." She stared at me blankly, then blinked. "I'm leaving the tour."

She closed her eyes for a moment and, to my horror, started to cry. "I'm sorry," she said several times, and I got a glimpse of how I must have looked to my friends that morning. I cringed inwardly. Outwardly, I patted her on the arm and did what Lou would have done. I made shushing noises and said, "There, there." Eventually, she got a hold of herself.

"Georgina, what's going on?" I seriously doubted she'd miss me so much as to induce tears.

I could tell by the way she was looking at me that she was deciding whether to confide in me, but I was genuinely concerned. "Is there somewhere we can talk?" I asked. She nodded numbly, then turned and led the way through the penthouse. It was quite nice compared to the rest of the tour accommodation. She opened the door I'd seen her come out of and I followed her inside.

She sat down on the bed and I stayed standing. "What's going on?"

"This is my first tour."

"What? Really?" She nodded again. "But it's October. Doesn't your season start in April or something?"

"March, actually, but right after the training trip, my dad got really sick."

"Oh, God, I'm so sorry." A quick nod acknowledged my sympathy.

403

"Anyway, I flew back home to Perth so I could be with him, and I only just made it. He died a couple of days later. It was all so quick, you know?" I didn't, but I nodded. "And Mum was just *bereft*. I had to stay, at least for a little while, to help her get things sorted out, you know, with the house and all Dad's things. And it's just me. I'm an only child." *Oh, you poor woman.*

"Ventureseek was great about it. They said I could defer for a year, but I wanted to come back. Mum seemed a bit better and my auntie said she'd be around for her. So, I took this tour."

"And you've done a great job."

She looked up from her hands. Her look said, "Don't bullshit me."

"You *have*. If you hadn't told me this was your first tour, I would never have known. No one else knows." She still looked dubious. "Really. It's a small coach. News travels fast. I would have heard something." Her face softened a little.

"I feel like I keep screwing things up and that no one likes me."

"We like you," I lied. Blatantly. To her face.

"Really?"

"Yes. You and Tom have gone out of your way for us, and you know, my sister used to be a tour manager and she'd come back from tours *shattered*." Maybe it was better not to harp on that in a pep talk. I changed tack. "Anyway, what I mean is, it's a hard job, but you are doing great."

I hoped I'd convinced her. I'd given more than my share of pep talks in my eleven years as a teacher, but she wasn't a teenaged girl who didn't know what course to do at uni. A weak smile alighted on her face, and I was relieved.

"Thank you. It's just been so much *more* than I ever expected, you know?"

"For sure." Another lie, but I could imagine.

"And I *am* shattered. *And* this is one of the shortest tours. What's gonna happen when they give me a longer one? *If* they do?"

"What do you mean, 'if'?"

"Well, I need to get good feedback, or they'll make me defer until next season."

"Oh, right, of course. Look, I'm sure it will be fine. Should I be filling in a form or something?"

"Oh, yes, right, you're leaving today." She ferreted about in her day pack, pulled out a stack of printed sheets and handed me one.

"Great. I'll fill it in and give it to Lou to give to you. Is there anything else I need to do, officially, to leave the tour, I mean?"

"No. All good."

"Georgina, look, I'm sorry I made you feel like you weren't doing a good job."

"Oh, it wasn't you—"

"Well, we both know that's a lie. Maybe not just me, but I *am* sorry." I reached over and gave her a hug. "And I'm really sorry about your dad." I pulled away. "Bollocks," I said, thinking of the time. "I really need to go."

She smiled through her tears. "Is it the guy from Rome?"

"What? Oh. Yes, actually, it is."

"Good. Good for you." She added a nod to her smile.

I left her in her room and crossed back through the living room. "Bye, Tom," I called over my shoulder. I didn't check to see if he'd heard me. I needed to get downstairs, complete the form and fill in the girls.

"We like Georgina again," I said, a little out of breath from running down the stairs.

"Explain," said Jaelee from her bed, where she was filing a nail.

I did—and quickly, because my Uber was on its way. I scribbled my name onto the form and ticked "excellent" all the way down, then signed the back. I gave it to Lou for safe keeping. I'd been an utter cow to Georgina, and the poor girl had been through the worst thing imaginable. I hoped that excellent reviews from everyone on the coach would make up for it, and I left Dani in charge of making that happen.

Ten minutes later, I was saying a premature and heart-wrenching goodbye to my posse. I stood on my tiptoes to hug Craig. "Keep me posted about school." I'd keep an eye on him via Facebook and if—*when*—I visited Lou in Vancouver, I could pop down to Oregon. They weren't that far apart.

"Bye, Dani. Thanks for everything, especially for your help today."

"No problem. I'm totally living vicariously through you, I hope you know." She was the third person to tell me that in less than a week.

I smiled, then grabbed her hand. "Hey, pip me if you want to talk about the whole wedding thing."

She pressed her lips together. "Sure."

"Jae, you gorgeous woman." I hugged my height twin.

"Great meeting you," she said.

I pulled back and we regarded each other. "You too."

"Come to Miami anytime. Hey, you should come for New Year's." She raised her eyebrows and her eyes lit up.

"We're coming back to that—soon," I said. "I'll email you."

"Holding you to it."

I had saved Lou for last, because our goodbye was the hardest. She wrapped me up in the last Mama Lou hug I'd have in a while. "Love you," she said.

"Love you too, bus bestie."

She squeezed me tighter. When we stepped back from the hug, we both had tears in our eyes. "Don't you ruin that eyeliner," said Dani. Lou and I smiled.

"I'll call you next week. I want to know how everything goes with Jackson." She nodded.

"Fly safe," she said.

"I will."

My car pulled up and the driver got out. He pointed to my case and I nodded. When I turned back to my friends, Lou and Dani had their arms around each other, and I saw Jae wipe an uncharacteristic tear from her cheek.

Bollocks. Do not cry, your eyeliner is perfect.

Of course, the real reason I didn't want to cry was that it would be excruciatingly hard to stop. These were my friends, my dear friends, and I was going to miss having them with me twenty-four-seven.

I put my hand to my lips, blew them all a kiss, and got in the back seat of the car. I lowered the window as we drove away and called, "Bye. I love you!" then nestled against the leather seat.

"Water, miss?" asked my driver.

"Yes, please." I blinked away the tears, eyeliner still intact. The second hardest part of the day was done.

My time in Amsterdam amounted to only four hours, but what I'd seen made me want to go back someday—the bustling streets filled with bicycles, the tall, narrow terraced houses, the canals and bridges. It was beautiful, and I promised myself to return.

As we left the inner city, I took a sip of water, then sent couple of texts.

To Jane:

Slight change of plans. Won't be back til Sunday. See you then. Cat

To Sarah:

Sorry about the call yesterday. I'm a cow. On my way to Paris to see Jean-Luc! I'll FaceTime when I get back to London on Sunday—sooner if he sends me away. Love you. Cx
  ps I hope he doesn't send me away. :(

The flight from Schiphol to Charles de Gaulle was uneventful—from a travel perspective, anyway. Everything went smoothly at check-in and security, there were no delays, and I had an empty seat next to me for the flight—we didn't even have any turbulence.

Unless you count the turbulence in my stomach.

I have a nervous stomach, always have. It's often my canary in the coalmine, so to speak, and sometimes it asserts itself at the least opportune times. On my way to see Jean-Luc, it had gone into hyperdrive. In a one-hour-fifteen-minute flight, I used the toilet three times.

In the taxi from the airport, I fidgeted with the strap of my messenger bag, my nervous energy escaping my belly and moving into my extremities.

What was I going to say?

I had played the scene over and over again in my head. Jean-Luc's face splitting into a smile. Him slamming the door in my face. Him dropping to his knees and begging me to never leave him again (probably the least plausible). Him not being home (probably the most plausible). I realised I wouldn't know what to say until I saw him, until I saw his face, his reaction.

I hoped he liked surprises more than I did.

The taxi turned into a narrow, deeply shadowed street, then pulled to a stop a few doors along and double-parked. "*C'est l'adresse, madame. Ici.*" The driver pointed to a tall dark-green door.

"Merci." I handed him forty euros and waved away the change. He gave a curt nod and got out of the car to retrieve my case from the boot. I took a deep, steadying breath and stepped out. The driver put my case on the pavement and left me standing in front of the door.

409

Jean-Luc's door. *All right, Parsons. Do not cock this up—again.*

There were two buzzers and no security camera. The top buzzer said, "Caron" and I pressed it. A sharp, flat sound emitted. There was a long moment of silence, while my heart hammered away in my chest. "*Oui?*"

I gulped, then found my voice. "Jean-Luc. It's me. It's Cat. Uh, Catherine." I could barely catch my breath, and I waited for what seemed like a millennium for his reply.

"Catherine? Uh, come to the top of the stairs."

The staticky sound ceased, and I heard the click of the door. I pushed on it and lifted my case over the threshold into a small and chilly foyer. No elevator, just a steep set of stairs on the left wall. I eyed my case, then the stairs. It could stay down there for now. Jean-Luc could come and get it. Or, maybe I'd be loading it back into a taxi in a few minutes.

I started up the stairs and, at the first landing, passed the door to the other apartment. The second set of stairs was even steeper, and I had to hold the railing. As I was about to step onto the small landing, Jean-Luc's door opened.

He stood in the doorway, wearing a grey T-shirt and jeans, barefoot and with at least a two-day beard. He wasn't grinning, but he wasn't frowning. I, however, was rooted to the spot two steps from the top of the staircase. He stepped aside and tilted his head, an invitation to come in.

I tentatively walked into the apartment and took in as many details as I could. It was just as I had imagined it. It was so *Jean-Luc.*

Blonde-wood floors; floor-to-ceiling shelves along one wall, brimming with haphazardly stacked books and magazines; two linen couches, the kind that beckon you to sprawl on them, faced each other; a low coffee table sat between the couches, also covered with books and magazines; and a wooden staircase led to the second floor of the apartment, more books stacked along the edge of each step. At the back of the room was a long kitchen bench with two bar stools at one end, their backs to the room, and against the rear wall of the apartment were the fridge and stove, either side of a large window.

It was a beautiful space, welcoming. But was he?

I turned to Jean-Luc, who was watching me look around. "It's lovely. Your home."

A slight smile, no eye crinkle. "Thank you."

I was so nervous I audibly blew out a stream of breath. "Hi," I said, stupidly. None of the scenarios I'd played over in my head had me speechless and acting like a twit.

His face softened, just a touch, but noticeably. "Hi," he said back.

"I read the letter," I blurted.

He nodded. "And?"

"And it wasn't the one I thought it was—you know, the *last* one."

"The one where you told me not to write anymore."

"Yes. That one. I was afraid to read it, because I didn't want to read all those awful things I'd said, how I'd played down our friendship, our ..." I trailed off, not knowing quite what we'd been back then.

"It *was* quite bad, that letter."

411

Wait, was he teasing me?

Surely not. I forged ahead. "I know, that's why I apologised ..."

"And I, uh, I burned that letter."

He took me by surprise. "Sorry? You *burned* it?"

"Yes. In the backyard. Then I took the ashes and I buried them."

"Well, that's a little dramatic."

He shrugged. "I was nineteen."

"Mmm."

"But the one I gave you, I read that letter many times. I once thought ... well, in the letter, it seemed like you felt the same."

"I did."

That took *him* by surprise. "What do you mean?"

"I did feel the same. Back then. I only realised it when we were reading it—"

"We?"

My shoulders dropped in resignation. "Come on, you must know by now that women need a second opinion on these things. Besides, this one was *my* letter, and also besides ..." *also besides?* I inwardly rolled my eyes at how inarticulate I'd become. "And *also*, I didn't even see it until Jaelee pointed it out, especially the part about the blokey Australian guys."

"That was my favourite part." A smile with a slight eye crinkle.

"I was massively stupid."

"I agree." Definitely teasing me.

I realised we were moving towards each other. "And I have been massively stupid even more recently."

412

"Yes. I also agree with that." The corner of his mouth twitched.

We were only a few feet apart. "I was afraid." No more banter, only truth.

"I know. And now?"

"I'm still afraid, but I'm being brave."

His eyes searched mine. "You don't have to be afraid at all, Catherine, not of me."

"I'm not afraid of you. You're perfect."

A quick wry laugh. "I'm not. I am flawed, like you."

Truth, only truth. "All right, yes, true."

"So, what *are* you afraid of?"

It was here. The moment where I laid myself bare and he either wanted me or he didn't.

"That I completely cocked this up—and I'll lose you again." Tears sprang to my eyes, but I dared not touch them—Dani's eyeliner! I blinked them away.

"Oh, Catherine. *Ma chérie.*" He was close to me, his body almost touching mine as he took my hands in his. "You do not have to worry about that. I am right here."

I chewed on my lip.

"So, you don't hate me?"

He laughed and wiped away a tear that had escaped. "No. I definitely do not hate you. I adore you. I long for you. You are my Catherine, *non?*"

A gasp escaped me—overwhelming relief. I hadn't completely cocked it up. Jean-Luc and I had a real chance to be together, to fall in love—again. I experienced a lightness I'd never experienced before. A burst of laughter erupted from me, then I stopped and looked into the eyes that made my heart flutter.

"You are okay?" Amusement danced in those eyes.

"Yes." The understatement of the century.

"*Bien*. I'm going to kiss you now," he said.

I didn't speak. I just threw my arms around his neck as he pulled me close and pressed his mouth to mine. A zing of happiness pulsed through me, then I had a sudden thought.

I broke the kiss, "Oh, my case. I left it downstairs." Sometimes, I can be painfully practical.

"Later," he said, the low rumble of his voice awakening my lady parts. "You haven't seen the rest of my apartment yet." His smile held the promise of some delicious reacquainting. Then he took my hand and led me upstairs to his bedroom.

Fall in love ✓

Two and a half Months Later

I hear a car door slam and peek out between the blinds. "She's here!" I shout as I run out the door.

I leap down the three front steps, cross the lawn as fast as my jet-lagged little legs can carry me, and fling my arms around my sister's waist. "Merry Christmas!" I say, my voice muffled by her shoulder. She hugs me back tightly and when we pull apart, we are beaming at each other.

"Merry Christmas! You look amazing," she says, regarding my outfit—a bright-red summery dress, dangly silver earrings, and silver ballet flats.

"Thank you. I feel like utter crap, but you know, fake it 'til you make it, right?"

"Still jet-lagged?"

"It's only been a *day*, Sez."

"I can't believe you're actually here. This is ..." There are tears in her eyes as she squeezes my arm. I can't believe I'm here, either. It's been years since I was home for Christmas.

"Hello, Sarah," I hear behind me.

Sarah looks over my shoulder. "Jean-Luc! Oh, my God!"

He steps forward, then leans down and hugs her. I can hear her giggling, and when she steps back from him, her hands move to her cheeks. "I just—you really grew up. I mean ..." She blinks and grins, clearly awestruck by how gorgeous he is. I roll my eyes at her, the dork.

"You also, *tu es très belle*."

"All right, you two," I say, breaking up the meeting of the mutual admiration society. "What needs to come inside?" Sarah goes to her car and from the passenger side, takes out a giant pavlova covered in cream, raspberries and kiwi fruit. "Oh, my God. You made a *pav*?"

"Of course, I did. It's your fave." She gives it to me to carry inside. It's a dangerous move, because it looks so good, I could quite happily bury my face in it.

I restrain myself. "You're the best sister ever."

"Jean-Luc, would you mind?" She indicates two large carry bags on the back seat, both filled with gifts.

"*Pas de problème*." He retrieves them from the car with ease, as though Sarah has gift-wrapped boxes of air, and I watch with appreciation as he walks back to the house.

God, he's gorgeous. I still pinch myself sometimes.

"Okay, that's it." I turn at the sound of the car door closing, and Sarah has an overnight bag in one hand and a three-bottle wine carrier in the other. We grin at each other again. "I am so glad you're home."

"Me too."

"And Jean-Luc! I mean ... wow, Cat."

"Yes, he *is* very 'wow'." We share a giggle, conveying a world of sisterly understanding with a simple laugh.

"You girls need a hand?" our dad asks from the front door. We're in our thirties and he still calls us "girls". I love that about my dad.

"All good, Dad," Sarah replies as we start making our way across the lawn. To me, she says, "I'm going to need a friendly ear—not today, but maybe tomorrow?"

"Sure. Everything all right?"

"It is—I guess, it's just ..."

"Is it the whole 'two boyfriends' thing?"

"Yep." She stops walking, so I do too, although I'm worried for the pav if we stay out in this sunshine much longer. "I see Josh in less than a week—and I'm excited! But I'm really nervous too."

"Of course. I get that. The times Jean-Luc has come to London, or when I've gone to Paris, I always get a little nervous right before. And then, when we're together, all that goes away. It's just lovely—and normal."

"You're probably right. But, Cat, there's James too."

"Mmm, yes. How is that going?"

"Good, I mean, we're in contact, and he arrives late January." In the absence of having any sort of counsel to offer—because I am really out of my depth here—I simply nod. "I'm going to have to decide, aren't I?" she adds.

"Yes, you are, but not right now. Not until you've seen them both again and you know how you feel, all right?" It's her turn to nod. "Now, let's get this pav inside before the cream goes rancid."

I hope I've staved off one of her anxiety attacks; I'd hate for her to get upset on Christmas. Thankfully, her smile returns as we climb the steps. "I still can't believe you're here—*and* with Jean-Luc. Cat, I'm so happy for you."

"I'm happy for me too." I hold the pavlova precariously with one hand, while opening the screen door with the other.

"Here, darling, I'll take that." Dad reappears and relieves me of the pav.

"Thanks, Dad."

Sarah and I follow him down the hall, Sarah going first. "So, what wine did you bring?" I ask.

"Duh. Bubbles. Lots to celebrate."

"You're the best, sis, although I *may* have had a glass or two waiting for you to get here."

She barks out a laugh at my expense. "Shocker."

I enter my parents' great room—their combined kitchen, dining, lounge—and see my four favourite people milling about—Dad rearranging the contents of the fridge to fit the pavlova, Mum and Sarah hugging hello, and Jean-Luc unpacking Sarah's gifts under the tree.

I am overcome with love and I'm so exquisitely happy. This is already the best Christmas I've ever had.

THE END

If you enjoyed *That Night in Paris*, be sure to follow Sandy Barker on Twitter @sandybarker, on Facebook @sandybarkerauthor, and check out their website at www.sandybarker.com for all the updates on their latest work.

What's next for Sarah and Cat? Find out in *A Sunset in Sydney*, the next romantic comedy in the *Holiday Romance* series.

You can also find us at @0neMoreChapter_, where we'll be shouting about all our new releases.

Acknowledgements

A book is never written in a vacuum and this one is no exception.

I started this book perched on a trundle bed in my sister's guest room, while on sabbatical in 2018. I had a glimmer of an idea, knowing I wanted Cat from *One Summer in Santorini* to have her own story. As I wrote each chapter and the story unfolded, it was passed between my partner, Ben, my sister, Victoria (Vic), and my brother-in-law, Mark. They were my early readers, and their honesty, astute observations and suggestions are on the pages of this book. I'm so grateful to them.

Thank you, especially, to Victoria for inspiring the "just little" (but mighty), bright, funny and fiercely loyal Cat—although Vic is a far more of a hopeful romantic than Cat. She did, in real life, get the good hair, however, and I'm still green with envy. Thank you to Mark for editing my French, Italian, German and Spanish. Your knowledge and love of languages are awe-inspiring and came in very handy for this book! Thank you, as always, to Ben—my rock, my love, my sounding board and plotting partner, my biggest fan and my best friend.

I truly have the most supportive family and friends. They have embraced this new chapter in my life (pun intended) and are ferociously supporting me in my work as an author. A heartfelt and bottomless thanks to them, especially my parents, Lee, Ray and (step-mum) Gail.

Thank you, especially, to Michelle, Weyleen and Sophie, who inspired Mama Lou, Jaelee, and Danielle, respectively. They were once my very own bus besties as I toured around Europe nursing a shattered heart after a devastating break-up in Paris. And thank you to my cousin, Jaelee, who lent me her name for this book.

I am so fortunate to be under the wing of super-agent Lina Langlee. I have learned so much from her already, and I truly appreciate her guidance, counsel, feedback, and good humour. She champions, supports, and nudges me from the sidelines, and I wouldn't be writing these acknowledgements for my second novel if it weren't for her. It's no wonder that she was shortlisted for the Romance Novelists' Association's Agent of the Year Award for 2019—she's incredible.

I have another literary partner-in-crime in the formidable and fabulous Hannah Todd, my editor at One More Chapter. Hannah's forthright and insightful feedback has (already) made me a better writer, and she is so generous with her vast knowledge of the publishing industry.

Thank you to both Lina and Hannah for believing in me and for making my literary dreams come true. Thank you, also, to the incredible teams at Kate Nash Literary Agency and One More Chapter for all the work you do to support my literary journey.

The author community never ceases to amaze me with their generosity, support, guidance, and friendship, and I am grateful on a daily basis for my fellow authors. I learn from you, I admire you, I champion your successes, and I am grateful to you.

A special shout out to Julie Houston, Phillipa Ashley, Samantha Tonge, Emma Robinson, Ella Hayes, Dana L. Brown, Belinda Missen, Katie Ginger, Lynne Shelby, Lucy Coleman, and Sarah Louise Smith for being early readers and supporting my debut with your generous words.

Thank you to Eve Corso, Caroline Bertaud, Lucy Knott, Paige Toon, Lindsey Kelk, Kerry Fisher, Kate Field, Karen King, Kiley Dunbar, and many other wonderful authors for supporting me as an emerging author. Lucy Mitchell, thank you, thank you, thank you for being my beta reader for this book, and telling me to ditch chapter three—you were right! It has been wonderful watching your success—you are a fabulous writer.

Thank you to the (other) author friends I've met through UKRomChat (find them on Twitter), especially Jeanna Skinner, Lucy Keeling, Emily Royal, Eilidh Lawrence, Lucy Flatman, Rebecca Duval, and Anita Faulkner. You are fabulous, talented women who inspire me and I adore you. Huge thanks, as well, to my fellow #AusWrites authors. I love engaging with you daily—you brighten my early mornings and are there for me when I'm brooding in the dark, angst-ridden with doubt.

There are wonderful, supportive, and close-knit communities of authors at the Kate Nash Literary Agency and One More Chapter, and at the Romance Novelists' Association and the Romance Writers of Australia. Thank you for welcoming me, connecting with me, supporting me, teaching me and keeping me laughing and thinking with your hilarious and clever posts and tweets.

I truly appreciate the book blogging community, who are gracious and generous with their time and commitment to the love of a good story. I've been directly supported by many of you—thank you!

And, dear reader, thank *you*.

Thank you for making my dreams come true, for reading my books, and for diving into the world of the Parsons sisters and their friends, enemies, family, and lovers.

'Til next time ...